# The Battle Of The Strong
## A Romance Of Two Kingdoms—Complete

*by*

Gilbert Parker

# The Battle Of The Strong
## A Romance Of Two Kingdoms—Complete
### by Gilbert Parker

ISBN: 978-93-60461-03-4

**Published by**

# DOUBLE 9 BOOKS

2/13-B, Ansari Road
Daryaganj, New Delhi – 110002
info@double9books.com
www.double9books.com
Tel. 011-40042856

This book is under public domain

# ABOUT THE AUTHOR

Gilbert Parker was the pen name of Canadian author George Parker, 1st Baronet PC (23 November 1862 – 6 September 1932). He was born in Camden East, Addington, Ontario, and was the son of Captain Joseph Parker, R.A. In 1882, he became a teacher at the Ontario Institute for the Deaf and Dumb in Belleville, Ontario. Before that, he taught at the Marsh Hill and Bayside schools in Hastings County. His next stop was to teach at Trinity College. His trip to Australia in 1886 led him to work as a deputy editor for the Sydney Morning Herald for a while. He also did a lot of traveling in the Pacific, Europe, Asia, Egypt, the South Sea Islands, and later northern Canada. By the early 1990s, he was becoming better known in London as a romance fiction writer. The best of his books are the ones that were the first to focus on the past and daily lives of French Canadians. His lasting literary fame is built on the vivid and dramatic quality of his Canadian stories.

# CONTENTS

## IN FRANCE—NEAR FIVE MONTHS AFTER

## IN JERSEY FIVE YEARS LATER

## DURING ONE YEAR LATER

# INTRODUCTION

This book is a protest and a deliverance. For seven years I had written continuously of Canada, though some short stories of South Sea life, and the novel Mrs. Falchion, had, during that time, issued from my pen. It looked as though I should be writing of the Far North all my life. Editors had begun to take that view; but from the start it had never been my view. Even when writing Pierre and His People I was determined that I should not be cabined, cribbed, and confined in one field; that I should not, as some other men have done, wind in upon myself, until at last each succeeding book would be but a variation of some previous book, and I should end by imitating myself, become the sacrifice to the god of the pin-hole.

I was warned not to break away from Canada; but all my life I had been warned, and all my life I had followed my own convictions. I would rather not have written another word than be corralled, bitted, saddled, and ridden by that heartless broncho-buster, the public, which wants a man who has once pleased it, to do the same thing under the fret of whip and spur for ever. When I went to the Island of Jersey, in 1897, it was to shake myself free of what might become a mere obsession. I determined that, as wide as my experiences had been in life, so would my writing be, whether it pleased the public or not. I was determined to fulfil myself; and in doing so to take no instructions except those of my own conscience, impulse, and conviction. Even then I saw fields of work which would occupy my mind, and such skill as I had, for many a year to come. I saw the Channel Islands, Egypt, South Africa, and India. In all these fields save India, I have given my Pegasus its bridle-rein, and, so far, I have no reason to feel that my convictions were false. I write of Canada still, but I have written of the Channel Islands, I have written of Egypt, I have written of England and South Africa, and my public—that is, those who read my books—have accepted me in all these fields without demur. I believe I have justified myself in not accepting imprisonment in the field where I first essayed to turn my observation of life to account.

I went to Jersey, therefore, with my teeth set, in a way; yet happily and confidently. I had been dealing with French Canada for some years, and a step from Quebec, which was French, to Jersey, which was Norman French, was but short. It was a question of atmosphere solely. Whatever may be thought of The 'Battle of the Strong' I have not yet met a Jerseyman who denies to it the atmosphere of the place. It could hardly have lacked it, for there were twenty people, deeply intelligent, immensely interested in my design, and they were of Jersey families which had been there for centuries. They helped me, they fed me with dialect, with local details, with memories, with old letters, with diaries of their forebears, until, if I had gone wrong, it would have been through lack of skill in handling my material. I do not think I went wrong, though I believe that I could construct the book more effectively if I had to do it again. Yet there is something in looseness of construction which gives an air of naturalness; and it may be that this very looseness which I notice in 'The Battle of the Strong' has had something to do with giving it such a great circle of readers; though this may appear paradoxical. When it first appeared, it did not make the appeal which 'The Right of Way' or 'The Seats of the Mighty' made, but it justified itself, it forced its way, it assured me that I had done right in shaking myself free from the control of my own best work. The book has gone on increasing its readers year by year, and when it appeared in Nelson's delightful cheap edition in England it had an immediate success, and has sold by the hundred thousand in the last four years.

One of the first and most eager friends of 'The Battle of the Strong' was Mrs. Langtry, now Lady de Bathe, who, born in Jersey, and come of an old Jersey family, was well able to judge of the fidelity of the life and scene which it depicted. She greatly desired the novel to be turned into a play, and so it was. The adaptation, however, was lacking in much, and though Miss Marie Burroughs and Maurice Barrymore played in it, success did not attend its dramatic life.

'The Battle of the Strong' was called an historical novel by many critics, but the disclaimer which I made in the first edition I make again. 'The Seats of the Mighty' came nearer to what might properly be called an historical novel than any other book which I have written save, perhaps, 'A Ladder of Swords'. 'The Battle of the Strong' is not without faithful historical elements, but the book is essentially a romance, in which character was not meant to be submerged by incident; and I do not think that in this particular the book falls short of the design of its author. There was this enormous difference between life in the Island of Jersey and life in French Canada, that in Jersey, tradition is heaped upon tradition, custom upon custom, precept upon precept, until every citizen of the place is bound by innumerable cords of a code from which he cannot free himself. It is a little island, and that it is an island is evidence of a contracted life, though, in this case, a life which has real power and force. The life in French Canada was also traditional, and custom was also somewhat tyrannous, but it was part of a great continent in which the expansion of the man and of a people was inevitable. Tradition gets somewhat battered in a new land, and even where, as in French Canada, the priest and the Church have such supervision, and can bring such pressure to bear that every man must feel its influence; yet there is a happiness, a blitheness, and an exhilaration even in the most obscure quarter of French Canada which cannot be observed in the Island of Jersey. In Jersey the custom of five hundred years ago still reaches out and binds; and so small is the place that every square foot of it almost—even where the potato sprouts, and the potato is Jersey's greatest friend—is identified with some odd incident, some naive circumstance, some big, vivid, and striking historical fact. Behind its rugged coasts a little people proudly hold by their own and to their own, and even a Jersey criminal has more friends in his own environment than probably any other criminal anywhere save in Corsica; while friendship is a passion even with the pettiness by which it is perforated.

Reading this book again now after all these years, I feel convinced that the book is truly Jersiais, and I am grateful to it for having brought me out from the tyranny of the field in which I first sought for a hearing.

# NOTE

A list of Jersey words and phrases used herein, with their English or French equivalents, will be found at the end of the book. The Norman and patois words are printed as though they were English, some of them being quite Anglicised in Jersey. For the sake of brevity I have spoken of the Lieutenant-Bailly throughout as Bailly; and, in truth, he performed all the duties of Bailly in those days when this chief of the Jurats of the Island usually lived in England.

# PROEM

There is no man living to-day who could tell you how the morning broke and the sun rose on the first day of January 1800; who walked in the Mall, who sauntered in the Park with the Prince: none lives who heard and remembers the gossip of the moment, or can give you the exact flavour of the speech and accent of the time. Down the long aisle of years echoes the air but not the tone; the trick of form comes to us but never the inflection. The lilt of the sensations, the idiosyncrasy of voice, emotion, and mind of the first hour of our century must now pass from the printed page to us, imperfectly realised; we may not know them through actual retrospection. The more distant the scene, the more uncertain the reflection; and so it must needs be with this tale, which will take you back to even twenty years before the century began.

Then, as now, England was a great power outside these small islands. She had her foot firmly planted in Australia, in Asia, and in America—though, in bitterness, the American colonies had broken free, and only Canada was left to her in that northern hemisphere. She has had, in her day, to strike hard blows even for Scotland, Ireland, and Wales. But among her possessions is one which, from the hour its charter was granted it by King John, has been loyal, unwavering, and unpurchasable. Until the beginning of the century the language of this province was not our language, nor is English its official language to-day; and with a pretty pride oblivious of contrasts, and a simplicity unconscious of mirth, its people say: "We are the conquering race; we conquered England, England did not conquer us."

A little island lying in the wash of St. Michael's Basin off the coast of France, Norman in its foundations and in its racial growth, it has been as the keeper of the gate to England; though so near to France is it, that from its shores on a fine day may be seen the spires of Coutances, from which its spiritual welfare was ruled long after England lost Normandy. A province of British people, speaking still the Norman-French that the Conqueror spoke; such is the island of Jersey, which, with Guernsey, Alderney, Sark, Herm, and Jethou, form what we call the Channel Isles, and the French call the Iles de la Manche.

# CHAPTER I

In all the world there is no coast like the coast of Jersey; so treacherous, so snarling; serrated with rocks seen and unseen, tortured by currents maliciously whimsical, encircled by tides that sweep up from the Antarctic world with the devouring force of a monstrous serpent projecting itself towards its prey. The captain of these tides, travelling up through the Atlantic at a thousand miles an hour, enters the English Channel, and drives on to the Thames. Presently retreating, it meets another pursuing Antarctic wave, which, thus opposed in its straightforward course, recoils into St. Michael's Bay, then plunges, as it were, upon a terrible foe. They twine and strive in mystic conflict, and, in rage of equal power, neither vanquished nor conquering, circle, mad and desperate, round the Channel Isles. Impeded, impounded as they riot through the flumes of sea, they turn furiously, and smite the cliffs and rocks and walls of their prison-house. With the frenzied winds helping them, the island coasts and Norman shores are battered by their hopeless onset: and in that channel between Alderney and Cap de la Hague man or ship must well beware, for the Race of Alderney is one of the death-shoots of the tides. Before they find their way to the main again, these harridans of nature bring forth a brood of currents which ceaselessly fret the boundaries of the isles.

Always, always the white foam beats the rocks, and always must man go warily along these coasts. The swimmer plunges into a quiet pool, the snowy froth that masks the reefs seeming only the pretty fringe of sentient life to a sleeping sea; but presently an invisible hand reaches up and grasps him, an unseen power drags him exultingly out to the main—and he returns no more. Many a Jersey boatman, many a fisherman who has lived his whole life in sight of the Paternosters on the north, the Ecrehos on the east, the Dog's Nest on the south, or the Corbiere on the west, has in some helpless moment been caught by the unsleeping currents which harry his peaceful borders, or the rocks that have eluded the hunters of the sea, and has yielded up his life within sight of his own doorway, an involuntary sacrifice to the navigator's knowledge and to the calm perfection of an admiralty chart.

Yet within the circle of danger bounding this green isle the love of home and country is stubbornly, almost pathetically, strong. Isolation, pride of lineage, independence of government, antiquity of law and custom, and jealousy of imperial influence or action have combined to make a race self-reliant even to perverseness, proud and maybe vain, sincere almost to commonplaceness, unimaginative and reserved, with the melancholy born of monotony—for the life of the little country has coiled in upon itself, and the people have drooped to see but just their own selves reflected in all the dwellers of the land, whichever way they turn. A hundred years ago, however, there was a greater and more general lightness of heart and vivacity of spirit than now. Then the song of the harvester and the fisherman, the boat-builder and the stocking-knitter, was heard on a summer afternoon, or from the veille of a winter night when the dim crasset hung from the roof and the seaweed burned in the chimney. Then the gathering of the vraic was a fete, and the lads and lasses footed it on the green or on the hard sand, to the chance flageolets of sportive seamen home from the war. This simple gaiety was heartiest at Christmastide, when the yearly reunion of families took place; and because nearly everybody in Jersey was "couzain" to his neighbour these gatherings were as patriarchal as they were festive.

........................

The new year of seventeen hundred and eighty-one had been ushered in by the last impulse of such festivities. The English cruisers lately in port had vanished up the Channel; and at Elizabeth Castle, Mont Orgueil, the Blue Barracks and the Hospital, three British regiments had taken up the dull round of duty again; so that by the fourth day a general lethargy, akin to content, had settled on the whole island.

On the morning of the fifth day a little snow was lying upon the ground, but the sun rose strong and unclouded, the whiteness vanished, and there remained only a pleasant dampness which made sod and sand firm yet springy to the foot. As the day wore on, the air became more amiable still, and a delicate haze settled over the water and over the land, making softer to the eye house and hill and rock and sea.

There was little life in the town of St. Heliers, there were few people upon the beach; though now and then some one who had been praying beside a grave in the parish churchyard came to the railings and looked out upon the calm sea almost washing its foundations, and over the dark range of rocks, which, when the tide was out, showed like a vast gridiron blackened by fires. Near by, some loitering sailors watched the yawl-rigged fishing craft from Holland, and the codfish-smelling cul-de-poule schooners of the great fishing company which exploited the far-off fields of Gaspe in Canada.

St. Heliers lay in St. Aubin's Bay, which, shaped like a horseshoe, had Noirmont Point for one end of the segment and the lofty Town Hill for another. At the foot of this hill, hugging it close, straggled the town. From the bare green promontory above might be seen two-thirds of the south coast of the island—to the right St. Aubin's Bay, to the left Greve d'Azette, with its fields of volcanic-looking rocks, and St. Clement's Bay beyond. Than this no better place for a watchtower could be found; a perfect spot for the reflective idler and for the sailorman who, on land, must still be within smell and sound of the sea, and loves that place best which gives him widest prospect.

This day a solitary figure was pacing backwards and forwards upon the cliff edge, stopping now to turn a telescope upon the water and now upon the town. It was a lad of not more than sixteen years, erect, well-poised, having an air of self-reliance, even of command. Yet it was a boyish figure too, and the face was very young, save for the eyes; these were frank but still sophisticated.

The first time he looked towards the town he laughed outright, freely, spontaneously; threw his head back with merriment, and then glued his eye to the glass again. What he had seen was a girl of about five years of age with a man, in La Rue d'Egypte, near the old prison, even then called the Vier Prison. Stooping, the man had kissed the child, and she, indignant, snatching the cap from his head, had thrown it into the stream running through the street. Small wonder that the lad on the hill grinned, for the man who ran to rescue his hat from the stream was none other than the Bailly of the island, next in importance to the Lieutenant-Governor.

The lad could almost see the face of the child, its humorous anger, its wilful triumph, and also the enraged look of the Bailly as he raked the stream with his long stick, tied with a sort of tassel of office. Presently he saw the child turn at the call of a woman in the Place du Vier Prison, who appeared to apologise to the Bailly, busy now drying his recovered hat by whipping it through the air. The lad on the hill recognised the woman as the child's mother.

This little episode over, he turned once more towards the sea, watching the sun of late afternoon fall upon the towers of Elizabeth Castle and the great rock out of which St. Helier the hermit once chiselled his lofty home. He breathed deep and strong, and the carriage of his body was light, for he had a healthy enjoyment of all physical sensations and all the obvious drolleries of life. A broad sort of humour was written upon every feature; in the full, quizzical eye, in the width of cheek-bone, in the broad mouth, and in the depth of the laugh, which, however, often ended in a sort of chuckle not entirely pleasant. It suggested a selfish enjoyment of the odd or the melodramatic side of other people's difficulties.

At last the youth encased his telescope, and turned to descend the hill to the town. As he did so, a bell began to ring. From where he was he could look down into the Vier Marchi, or market-place, where stood the Cohue Royale and house of legislature. In the belfry of this court-house, the bell was ringing to call the Jurats together for a meeting of the States. A monstrous tin pan would have yielded as much assonance. Walking down towards the Vier Marchi the lad gleefully recalled the humour of a wag who, some days before, had imitated the sound of the bell with the words:

"Chicane—chicane! Chicane—chicane!"

The native had, as he thought, suffered somewhat at the hands of the twelve Jurats of the Royal Court, whom his vote had helped to elect, and this was his revenge—so successful that, for generations, when the bell called the States or the Royal Court together, it said in the ears of the Jersey people—thus insistent is apt metaphor:

"Chicane—chicane! Chicane—chicane!"

As the lad came down to the town, trades-people whom he met touched their hats to him, and sailors and soldiers saluted respectfully. In this regard the Bailly himself could not have fared better. It was not due to the fact that the youth came of an old Jersey family, nor by reason that he was genial and handsome, but because he was a midshipman of the King's navy home on leave; and these were the days when England's sailors were more popular than her soldiers.

He came out of the Vier Marchi into La Grande Rue, along the stream called the Fauxbie flowing through it, till he passed under the archway of the Vier Prison, making towards the place where the child had snatched the hat from the head of the Bailly.

Presently the door of a cottage opened, and the child came out, followed by her mother.

The young gentleman touched his cap politely, for though the woman was not fashionably dressed, she was distinguished in appearance, with an air of remoteness which gave her a kind of agreeable mystery.

"Madame Landresse—" said the young gentleman with deference.

"Monsieur d'Avranche—" responded the lady softly, pausing.

"Did the Bailly make a stir? I saw the affair from the hill, through my telescope," said young d'Avranche, smiling.

"My little daughter must have better manners," responded the lady, looking down at her child reprovingly yet lovingly.

"Or the Bailly must—eh, Madame?" replied d'Avranche, and, stooping, he offered his hand to the child. Glancing up inquiringly at her mother, she took it. He held hers in a clasp of good nature. The child was so demure, one could scarcely think her capable of tossing the Bailly's hat into the stream; yet looking closely, there might be seen in her eyes a slumberous sort of fire, a touch of mystery. They were neither blue nor grey, but a mingling of both, growing to the most tender, greyish sort of violet. Down through generations of Huguenot refugees had passed sorrow and fighting and piety and love and occasional joy, until in the eyes of this child they all met, delicately vague, and with the wistfulness of the early morning of life.

"What is your name, little lady?" asked d'Avranche of the child.

"Guida, sir," she answered simply.

"Mine is Philip. Won't you call me Philip?"

She flashed a look at her mother, regarded him again, and then answered:

"Yes, Philip—sir."

D'Avranche wanted to laugh, but the face of the child was sensitive and serious, and he only smiled. "Say 'Yes, Philip', won't you?" he asked.

"Yes, Philip," came the reply obediently.

After a moment of speech with Madame Landresse, Philip stooped to say good-bye to the child. "Good-bye, Guida."

A queer, mischievous little smile flitted over her face—a second, and it was gone.

"Good-bye, sir—Philip," she said, and they parted. Her last words kept ringing in his ears as he made his way homeward. "Good-bye, sir—Philip"—the child's arrangement of words was odd and amusing, and at the same time suggested something more. "Good-bye, Sir Philip," had a different meaning, though the words were the same.

"Sir Philip—eh?" he said to himself, with a jerk of the head—"I'll be more than that some day."

# CHAPTER II

The night came down with leisurely gloom. A dim starlight pervaded rather than shone in the sky; Nature seemed somnolent and gravely meditative. It brooded as broods a man who is seeking his way through a labyrinth of ideas to a conclusion still evading him. This sense of cogitation enveloped land and sea, and was as tangible to feeling as human presence.

At last the night seemed to wake from reverie. A movement, a thrill, ran through the spangled vault of dusk and sleep, and seemed to pass over the world, rousing the sea and the earth. There was no wind, apparently no breath of air, yet the leaves of the trees moved, the weather-vanes turned slightly, the animals in the byres roused themselves, and slumbering folk opening their eyes, turned over in their beds, and dropped into a troubled doze again.

Presently there came a long moaning sound from the tide, not loud but rather mysterious and distant—a plaint, a threatening, a warning, a prelude?

A dull labourer, returning from late toil, felt it, and raised his head in a perturbed way, as though some one had brought him news of a far-off disaster. A midwife, hurrying to a lowly birth-chamber, shivered and gathered her mantle more closely about her. She looked up at the sky, she looked out over the sea, then she bent her head and said to herself that this would not be a good night, that ill-luck was in the air. "The mother or the child will die," she said to herself. A 'longshoreman, reeling home from deep potations, was conscious of it, and, turning round to the sea, snarled at it and said yah! in swaggering defiance. A young lad, wandering along the deserted street, heard it, began to tremble, and sat down on a block of stone beside the doorway of a baker's shop. He dropped his head on his arms and his chin on his knees, shutting out the sound and sobbing quietly.

Yesterday his mother had been buried; to-night his father's door had been closed in his face. He scarcely knew whether his being locked out was an accident or whether it was intended. He thought of the time when his father had ill-treated his mother and himself. That, however, had stopped at last, for the woman had threatened the Royal Court, and the man, having no wish to face its summary convictions, thereafter conducted himself towards them both with a morose indifference.

The boy was called Ranulph, a name which had passed to him through several generations of Jersey forebears—Ranulph Delagarde. He was being taught the trade of ship-building in St. Aubin's Bay. He was not beyond fourteen years of age, though he looked more, so tall and straight and self-possessed was he.

His tears having ceased soon, he began to think of what he was to do in the future. He would never go back to his father's house, or be dependent on him for aught. Many plans came to his mind. He would learn his trade of ship-building, he would become a master-builder, then a shipowner, with fishing-vessels like the great company sending fleets to Gaspe.

At the moment when these ambitious plans had reached the highest point of imagination, the upper half of the door beside him opened suddenly, and he heard men's voices. He was about to rise and disappear, but the words of the men arrested him, and he cowered down beside the stone. One of the men was leaning on the half-door, speaking in French.

"I tell you it can't go wrong. The pilot knows every crack in the coast. I left Granville at three; Rulle cour left Chaussey at nine. If he lands safe, and the English troops ain't roused, he'll take the town and hold the island easy enough."

"But the pilot, is he certain safe?" asked another voice. Ranulph recognised it as that of the baker Carcaud, who owned the shop. "Olivier Delagarde isn't so sure of him."

Olivier Delagarde! The lad started. That was his father's name. He shrank as from a blow—his father was betraying Jersey to the French!

"Of course, the pilot, he's all right," the Frenchman answered the baker. "He was to have been hung here for murder. He got away, and now he's having his turn by fetching Rullecour's wolves to eat up your green-bellies. By to-morrow at seven Jersey 'll belong to King Louis."

"I've done my promise," rejoined Carcaud the baker; "I've been to three of the guard-houses on St. Clement's and Grouville. In two the men are drunk as donkeys; in another they sleep like squids. Rullecour he can march straight to the town and seize it—if he land safe. But will he stand by 's word to we? You know the saying: 'Cadet Roussel has two sons; one's a thief, t'other's a rogue.' There's two Rullecours—Rullecour before the catch and Rullecour after!"

"He'll be honest to us, man, or he'll be dead inside a week, that's all."

"I'm to be Connetable of St. Heliers, and you're to be harbour-master—eh?"

"Naught else: you don't catch flies with vinegar. Give us your hand—why, man, it's doggish cold."

"Cold hand, healthy heart. How many men will Rullecour bring?"

"Two thousand; mostly conscripts and devil's beauties from Granville and St. Malo gaols."

"Any signals yet?"

"Two—from Chaussey at five o'clock. Rullecour 'll try to land at Gorey. Come, let's be off. Delagarde's there now."

The boy stiffened with horror—his father was a traitor! The thought pierced his brain like a hot iron. He must prevent this crime, and warn the Governor. He prepared to steal away. Fortunately the back of the man's head was towards him.

Carcaud laughed a low, malicious laugh as he replied to the Frenchman.

"Trust the quiet Delagarde! There's nothing worse nor still waters. He'll do his trick, and he'll have his share if the rest suck their thumbs. He doesn't wait for roasted larks to drop into his mouth—what's that!" It was Ranulph stealing away.

In an instant the two men were on him, and a hand was clapped to his mouth. In another minute he was bound, thrown onto the stone floor of the bakehouse, his head striking, and he lost consciousness.

When he came to himself, there was absolute silence round him-deathly, oppressive silence. At first he was dazed, but at length all that had happened came back to him.

Where was he now? His feet were free; he began to move them about. He remembered that he had been flung on the stone floor of the bakeroom. This place sounded hollow underneath—it certainly was not the bakeroom. He rolled over and over. Presently he touched a wall—it was stone. He drew himself up to a sitting posture, but his head struck a curved stone ceiling. Then he swung round and moved his foot along the wall—it touched iron. He felt farther with his foot-something clicked. Now he understood; he was in the oven of the bakehouse, with his hands bound. He began to think of means of escape. The iron door had no inside latch. There was a small damper covering a barred hole, through which perhaps he might be able to get a hand, if only it were free. He turned round so that his fingers might feel the grated opening. The edge of the little bars was sharp. He placed the strap binding his wrists against these sharp edges, and drew his arms up and down, a difficult and painful business. The iron cut his hands and wrists at first, so awkward was the movement. But, steeling himself, he kept on steadily.

At last the straps fell apart, and his hands were free. With difficulty he thrust one through the bars. His fingers could just lift the latch. Now the door creaked on its hinges, and in a moment he was out on the stone flags of the bakeroom. Hurrying through an unlocked passage into the shop, he felt his way to the street door, but it was securely fastened. The windows? He tried them both, one on either side, but while he could free the stout wooden shutters on the inside, a heavy iron bar secured them without, and it was impossible to open them.

Feverish with anxiety, he sat down on the low counter, with his hands between his knees, and tried to think what to do. In the numb hopelessness of the moment he became very quiet. His mind was confused, but his senses were alert; he was in a kind of dream, yet he was acutely conscious of the smell of new-made bread. It pervaded the air of the place; it somehow crept into his brain and his being, so that, as long as he might live, the smell of new-made bread would fetch back upon him the nervous shiver and numbness of this hour of danger.

As he waited, he heard a noise outside, a clac-clac! clac-clac! which seemed to be echoed back from the wood and stone of the houses in the street, and then to be lifted up and carried away over the roofs and out to sea—-clac-clac! clac-clac! It was not the tap of a blind man's staff—at first he thought it might be; it was not a donkey's foot on the cobbles; it was not the broom-sticks of the witches of St. Clement's Bay, for the rattle was below in the street, and the broom-stick rattle is heard only on the roofs as the witches fly across country from Rocbert to Bonne Nuit Bay.

This clac-clac came from the sabots of some nightfarer. Should he make a noise and attract the attention of the passer-by? No, that would not do. It might be some one who would wish to know whys and wherefores. He must, of course, do his duty to his country, but he must save his father too. Bad as the man was, he must save him, though, no matter what happened, he must give the alarm. His reflections tortured him. Why had he not stopped the nightfarer?

Even as these thoughts passed through the lad's mind, the clac-clac had faded away into the murmur of the stream flowing by the Rue d'Egypte to the sea, and almost beneath his feet. There flashed on him at that instant what little Guida Landresse had said a few days before as she lay down beside this very stream, and watched the water wimpling by. Trailing her fingers through it dreamily, the child had said to him:

"Ro, won't it never come back?" She always called him "Ro," because when beginning to talk she could not say Ranulph.

Ro, won't it never come back? But while yet he recalled the words, another sound mingled again with the stream-clac-clac! clac-clac! Suddenly it came to him who was the wearer of the sabots making this peculiar clatter in the night. It was Dormy Jamais, the man who never slept. For two years the clac-clac of Dormy Jamais's sabots had not been heard in the streets of St. Heliers—he had been wandering in France, a daft pilgrim. Ranulph remembered how these sabots used to pass and repass the doorway of his own home. It was said that while Dormy Jamais paced the streets there was no need of guard or watchman. Many a time had Ranulph shared his supper with the poor beganne whose origin no one knew, whose real name had long since dropped into oblivion.

The rattle of the sabots came nearer, the footsteps were now in front of the window. Even as Ranulph was about to knock and call the poor vagrant's name, the clac-clac stopped, and then there came a sniffing at the shutters as a dog sniffs at the door of a larder. Following the sniffing came a guttural noise of emptiness and desire. Now there was no mistake; it was the half-witted fellow beyond all doubt, and he could help him—Dormy Jamais should help him: he should go and warn the Governor and the soldiers at the Hospital, while he himself would speed to Gorey in search of his father. He would alarm the regiment there at the same time.

He knocked and shouted. Dormy Jamais, frightened, jumped back into the street. Ranulph called again, and yet again, and now at last Dormy recognised the voice.

With a growl of mingled reassurance and hunger, he lifted down the iron bar from the shutters. In a moment Ranulph was outside with two loaves of bread, which he put into Dormy Jamais's arms. The daft one whinnied with delight.

"What's o'clock, bread-man?" he asked with a chuckle.

Ranulph gripped his shoulders. "See, Dormy Jamais, I want you to go to the Governor's house at La Motte, and tell them that the French are coming, that they're landing at Gorey now. Then to the Hospital and tell the sentry there. Go, Dormy—allez kedainne!"

Dormy Jamais tore at a loaf with his teeth, and crammed a huge crust into his mouth.

"Come, tell me, will you go, Dormy?" the lad asked impatiently.

Dormy Jamais nodded his head, grunted, and, turning on his heel with Ranulph, clattered up the street. The lad sprang ahead of him, and ran swiftly up the Rue d'Egypte, into the Vier Marchi, and on over the Town Hill along the road to Grouville.

# CHAPTER III

Since the days of Henry III of England the hawk of war that broods in France has hovered along that narrow strip of sea dividing the island of Jersey from the duchy of Normandy. Eight times has it descended, and eight times has it hurried back with broken pinion. Among these truculent invasions two stand out boldly: the spirited and gallant attack by Bertrand du Guesclin, Constable of France; and the freebooting adventure of Rullecour, with his motley following of gentlemen and criminals. Rullecour it was, soldier of fortune, gambler, ruffian, and embezzler, to whom the King of France had secretly given the mission to conquer the unconquerable little island.

From the Chaussey Isles the filibuster saw the signal light which the traitor Olivier Delagarde had set upon the heights of Le Couperon, where, ages ago, Caesar built fires to summon from Gaul his devouring legions.

All was propitious for the attack. There was no moon—only a meagre starlight when they set forth from Chaussey. The journey was made in little more than an hour, and Rullecour himself was among the first to see the shores of Jersey loom darkly in front. Beside him stood the murderous pilot who was leading in the expedition, the colleague of Olivier Delagarde.

Presently the pilot gave an exclamation of surprise and anxiety—the tides and currents were bearing them away from the intended landing-place. It was now almost low water, and instead of an immediate shore, there lay before them a vast field of scarred rocks, dimly seen. He gave the signal to lay-to, and himself took the bearings. The tide was going out rapidly, disclosing reefs on either hand. He drew in carefully to the right of the rock known as L'Echiquelez, up through a passage scarce wide enough for canoes, and to Roque Platte, the south-eastern projection of the island.

You may range the seas from the Yugon Strait to the Erebus volcano, and you will find no such landing-place for imps or men as that field of rocks on the southeast corner of Jersey called, with a malicious irony, the Bane des Violets. The great rocks La Coniere, La Longy, Le Gros Etac, Le Teton, and the Petite Sambiere, rise up like volcanic monuments from a floor of lava and trailing vraic, which at half-tide makes the sea a tender mauve and violet. The passages of safety between these ranges of reef are but narrow at high tide; at half-tide, when the currents are changing most, the violet field becomes the floor of a vast mortuary chapel for unknowing mariners.

A battery of four guns defended the post on the landward side of this bank of the heavenly name. Its guards were asleep or in their cups. They yielded, without resistance, to the foremost of the invaders. But here Rullecour and his pilot, looking back upon the way they had come, saw the currents driving the transport boats hither and thither in confusion. Jersey was not to be conquered without opposition—no army of defence was abroad, but the elements roused themselves and furiously attacked the fleet. Battalions unable to land drifted back with the tides to Granville, whence they had come. Boats containing the heavy ammunition and a regiment of conscripts were battered upon the rocks, and hundreds of the invaders found an unquiet grave upon the Banc des Violets.

Presently the traitor Delagarde arrived and was welcomed warmly by Rullecour. The night wore on, and at last the remaining legions were landed. A force was left behind to guard La Roque Platte, and then the journey across country to the sleeping town began.

With silent, drowsing batteries in front and on either side of them, the French troops advanced, the marshes of Samares and the sea on their left, churches and manor houses on their right, all silent. Not yet had a blow been struck for the honour of this land and of the Kingdom.

But a blind injustice was, in its own way, doing the work of justice. On the march, Delagarde, suspecting treachery to himself, not without reason, required of Rullecour guarantee for the fulfilment of his pledge to make him Vicomte of the Island when victory should be theirs. Rullecour, however, had also promised the post to a reckless young officer, the Comte de Tournay, of the House of Vaufontaine, who, under the assumed name of Yves Savary dit Detricand, marched with him. Rullecour answered Delagarde churlishly, and would say nothing till the town was taken—the ecrivain must wait. But Delagarde had been drinking, he was in a mood to be reckless; he would not wait, he demanded an immediate pledge.

"By and by, my doubting Thomas," said Rullecour. "No, now, by the blood of Peter!" answered Delagarde, laying a hand upon his sword.

The French leader called a sergeant to arrest him. Delagarde instantly drew his sword and attacked Rullecour, but was cut down from behind by the scimitar of a swaggering Turk, who had joined the expedition as aide-de-camp to the filibustering general, tempted thereto by promises of a harem of the choicest Jersey ladies, well worthy of this cousin of the Emperor of Morocco.

The invaders left Delagarde lying where he fell. What followed this oblique retribution could satisfy no ordinary logic, nor did it meet the demands of poetic justice. For, as a company of soldiers from Grouville, alarmed out of sleep by a distracted youth, hurried towards St. Heliers, they found Delagarde lying by the roadside, and they misunderstood what had happened. Stooping over him an officer said pityingly:

"See—he got this wound fighting the French!" With the soldiers was the youth who had warned them. He ran forward with a cry, and knelt beside the wounded man. He had no tears, he had no sorrow. He was only sick and dumb, and he trembled with misery as he lifted up his father's head. The eyes of Olivier Delagarde opened.

"Ranulph—they've killed—me," gasped the stricken man feebly, and his head fell back.

An officer touched the youth's arm. "He is gone," said he. "Don't fret, lad, he died fighting for his country."

The lad made no reply, and the soldiers hurried on towards the town.

He died fighting for his country! So that was to be the legend, Ranulph meditated: his father was to have a glorious memory, while he himself knew how vile the man was. One thing however: he was glad that Olivier Delagarde was dead. How strangely had things happened! He had come to stay a traitor in his crime, and here he found a martyr. But was not he himself likewise a traitor? Ought not he to have alarmed the town first before he tried to find his father? Had Dormy Jamais warned the Governor? Clearly not, or the town bells would be ringing and the islanders giving battle. What would the world think of him!

Well, what was the use of fretting here? He would go on to the town, help to fight the French, and die that would be the best thing. He knelt, and unclasped his father's fingers from the handle of the sword. The steel was cold, it made him shiver. He had no farewell to make. He looked out to sea. The tide would come and carry his father's body out, perhaps-far out, and sink it in the deepest depths. If not that, then the people would bury Olivier Delagarde as a patriot. He determined that he himself would not live to see such mockery.

As he sped along towards the town he asked himself why nobody suspected the traitor. One reason for it occurred to him: his father, as the whole island knew, had a fishing-hut at Gorey. They would imagine him on the way to it when he met the French, for he often spent the night there. He himself had told his tale to the soldiers: how he had heard the baker and the Frenchman talking at the shop in the Rue d'Egypte. Yes, but suppose the French were driven out, and the baker taken prisoner and should reveal his father's complicity! And suppose people asked why he himself did not go at once to the Hospital Barracks in the town and to the Governor, and afterwards to Gorey?

These were direful imaginings. He felt that it was no use; that the lie could not go on concerning his father. The world would know; the one thing left for him was to die. He was only a boy, but he could fight. Had not young Philip d'Avranche; the midshipman, been in deadly action many times? He was nearly as old as Philip d'Avranche—yes, he would fight, and, fighting, he would die. To live as the son of such a father was too pitiless a shame.

He ran forward, but a weakness was on him; he was very hungry and thirsty-and the sword was heavy. Presently, as he went, he saw a stone well near a cottage by the roadside. On a ledge of the well stood a bucket of water. He tilted the bucket and drank. He would have liked to ask for bread at the cottage-door, but he said to himself, Why should he eat, for was he not going to die? Yet why should he not eat, even if he were going to die? He turned his head wistfully, he was so faint with hunger. The force driving him on, however, was greater than hunger—he ran harder.... But undoubtedly the sword was heavy!

# CHAPTER IV

In the Vier Marchi the French flag was flying, French troops occupied it, French sentries guarded the five streets entering into it. Rullecour, the French adventurer, held the Lieutenant-Governor of the isle captive in the Cohue Royale; and by threats of fire and pillage thought to force capitulation. For his final argument he took the Governor to the doorway, and showed him two hundred soldiers with lighted torches ready to fire the town.

When the French soldiers first entered the Vier Marchi there was Dormy Jamais on the roof of the Cohue Royale, calmly munching his bread. When he saw Rullecour and the Governor appear, he chuckled to himself, and said, in Jersey patois: "I vaut mux alouonyi l'bras que l'co," which is to say: It is better to stretch the arm than the neck. The Governor would have done more wisely, he thought, to believe the poor beganne, and to have risen earlier. Dormy Jamais had a poor opinion of a governor who slept. He himself was not a governor, yet was he not always awake? He had gone before dawn to the Governor's house, had knocked, had given Ranulph Delagarde's message, had been called a dirty buzard, and been sent away by the crusty, incredulous servant. Then he had gone to the Hospital Barracks, was there iniquitously called a lousy toad, and had been driven off with his quartern loaf, muttering through the dough the island proverb "While the mariner swigs the tide rises."

Had the Governor remained as cool as the poor vagrant, he would not have shrunk at the sight of the incendiaries, yielded to threats, and signed the capitulation of the island. But that capitulation being signed, and notice of it sent to the British troops, with orders to surrender and bring their arms to the Cohue Royale, it was not cordially received by the officers in command.

"Je ne comprends pas le francais," said Captain Mulcaster, at Elizabeth Castle, as he put the letter into his pocket unread.

"The English Governor will be hanged, and the French will burn the town," responded the envoy. "Let them begin to hang and burn and be damned, for I'll not surrender the castle or the British flag so long as I've a man to defend it, to please anybody!" answered Mulcaster.

"We shall return in numbers," said the Frenchman, threateningly.

"I shall be delighted: we shall have the more to kill," Mulcaster replied.

Then the captive Lieutenant-Governor was sent to Major Peirson at the head of his troops on the Mont es Pendus, with counsel to surrender.

"Sir," said he, "this has been a very sudden surprise, for I was made prisoner before I was out of my bed this morning."

"Sir," replied Peirson, the young hero of twenty-four, who achieved death and glory between a sunrise and a noontide, "give me leave to tell you that the 78th Regiment has not yet been the least surprised."

From Elizabeth Castle came defiance and cannonade, driving back Rullecour and his filibusters to the Cohue Royale: from Mont Orgueil, from the Hospital, from St. Peter's came the English regiments; from the other parishes swarmed the militia, all eager to recover their beloved Vier Marchi. Two companies of light infantry, leaving the Mont es Pendus, stole round the town and placed themselves behind the invaders on the Town Hill; the rest marched direct upon the enemy. Part went by the Grande Rue, and part by the Rue d'Driere, converging to the point of attack; and as the light infantry came down from the hill by the Rue des Tres Pigeons, Peirson entered the Vier Marchi by the Route es Couochons. On one side of the square, where the Cohue Royale made a wall to fight against, were the French. Radiating from this were five streets and passages like the spokes of a wheel, and from these now poured the defenders of the isle.

A volley came from the Cohue Royale, then another, and another. The place was small: friend and foe were crowded upon each other. The fighting became at once a hand-to-hand encounter. Cannon were useless, gun-carriages overturned. Here a drummer fell wounded, but continued beating his drum to the last; there a Glasgow soldier struggled with a French officer for the flag of the invaders; yonder a handful of Malouins doggedly held the foot of La Pyramide, until every one was cut down by overpowering numbers of British and Jersiais. The British leader was conspicuous upon his horse. Shot after shot was fired at him. Suddenly he gave a cry, reeled in his saddle, and sank, mortally wounded, into the arms of a brother officer.

For a moment his men fell back.

In the midst of the deadly turmoil a youth ran forward from a group of combatants, caught the bridle of the horse from which Peirson had fallen, mounted, and, brandishing a short sword, called upon his dismayed and wavering followers to advance; which they instantly did with fury and courage. It was Midshipman Philip d'Avranche. Twenty muskets were discharged at him. One bullet cut the coat on his shoulder, another grazed the back of his hand, a third scarred the pommel of the saddle, and still another wounded his horse. Again and again the English called upon him to dismount, for he was made a target, but he refused, until at last the horse was shot under him. Then once more he joined in the hand-to-hand encounter.

Windows near the ground, such as were not shattered, were broken by bullets. Cannon-balls embedded themselves in the masonry and the heavy doorways. The upper windows were safe, however: the shots did not range so high. At one of these, over a watchmaker's shop, a little girl was to be seen, looking down with eager interest. Presently an old man came in view and led her away. A few minutes of fierce struggle passed, and then at another window on the floor below the child appeared again. She saw a youth with a sword hurrying towards the Cohue Royale from a tangled mass of combatants. As he ran, a British soldier fell in front of him. The youth dropped the sword and grasped the dead man's musket.

The child clapped her hands on the window.

"It's Ro—it's Ro!" she cried, and disappeared again.

"Ro," with white face, hatless, coatless, pushed on through the melee. Rullecour, the now disheartened French general, stood on the steps of the Cohue Royale. With a vulgar cruelty and cowardice he was holding the Governor by the arm, hoping thereby to protect his own person from the British fire.

Here was what the lad had been trying for—the sight of this man Rullecour. There was one small clear space between the English and the French, where stood a gun-carriage. He ran to it, leaned the musket on the gun, and, regardless of the shots fired at him, took aim steadily. A French bullet struck the wooden wheel of the carriage, and a splinter gashed his cheek. He did not move, but took sight again, and fired. Rullecour fell, shot through the jaw. A cry of fury and dismay went up from the French at the loss of their leader, a shout of triumph from the British.

The Frenchmen had had enough. They broke and ran. Some rushed for doorways and threw themselves within, many scurried into the Rue des Tres Pigeons, others madly fought their way into Morier Lane.

At this moment the door of the watchmaker's shop opened and the little girl who had been seen at the window ran into the square, calling out: "Ro! Ro!" It was Guida Landresse.

Among the French flying for refuge was the garish Turk, Rullecour's ally. Suddenly the now frightened, crying child got into his path and tripped him up. Wild with rage he made a stroke at her, but at that instant his scimitar was struck aside by a youth covered with the smoke and grime of battle. He caught up the child to his arms, and hurried with her through the melee to the watchmaker's doorway. There stood a terror-stricken woman—Madame Landresse, who had just made her way into the square. Placing the child, in her arms, Philip d'Avranche staggered inside the house, faint and bleeding from a wound in the shoulder. The battle of Jersey was over.

"Ah bah!" said Dormy Jamais from the roof of the Cohue Royale; "now I'll toll the bell for that achocre of a Frenchman. Then I'll finish my supper."

Poising a half-loaf of bread on the ledge of the roof, he began to slowly toll the cracked bell at his hand for Rullecour the filibuster.

The bell clanged out: Chicane-chicane! Chicane-chicane!

Another bell answered from the church by the square, a deep, mournful note. It was tolling for Peirson and his dead comrades.

Against the statue in the Vier Marchi leaned Ranulph Delagarde. An officer came up and held out a hand to him. "Your shot ended the business," said he. "You're a brave fellow. What is your name?"

"Ranulph Delagarde, sir."

"Delagarde—eh? Then well done, Delagardes! They say your father was the first man killed. We won't forget that, my lad."

Sinking down upon the base of the statue, Ranulph did not stir or reply, and the officer, thinking he was grieving for his father, left him alone.

# ELEVEN YEARS AFTER

## CHAPTER V

The King of France was no longer sending adventurers to capture the outposts of England. He was rather, in despair, beginning to wind in again the coil of disaster which had spun out through the helpless fingers of Neckar, Calonne, Brienne and the rest, and was in the end to bind his own hands for the guillotine.

The Isle of Jersey, like a scout upon the borders of a foeman's country, looked out over St. Michael's Basin to those provinces where the war of the Vendee was soon to strike France from within, while England, and presently all Europe, should strike her from without.

War, or the apprehension of war, was in the air. The people of the little isle, living always within the influence of natural wonder and the power of the elements, were deeply superstitious; and as news of dark deeds done in Paris crept across from Carteret or St. Malo, as men-of-war anchored in the tide-way, and English troops, against the hour of trouble, came, transport after transport, into the harbour of St. Heliers, they began to see visions and dream dreams. One peasant heard the witches singing a chorus of carnage at Rocbert; another saw, towards the Minquiers, a great army like a mirage upon the sea; others declared that certain French refugees in the island had the evil eye and bewitched their cattle; and a woman, wild with grief because her child had died of a sudden sickness, meeting a little Frenchman, the Chevalier du Champsavoys, in the Rue des Tres Pigeons, thrust at his face with her knitting-needle, and then, Protestant though she was, made the sacred sign, as though to defeat the evil eye.

This superstition and fanaticism so strong in the populace now and then burst forth in untamable fury and riot. So that when, on the sixteenth of December 1792, the gay morning was suddenly overcast, and a black curtain was drawn over the bright sun, the people of Jersey, working in the fields, vraicking among the rocks, or knitting in their doorways, stood aghast, and knew not what was upon them.

Some began to say the Lord's Prayer, some in superstitious terror ran to the secret hole in the wall, to the chimney, or to the bedstead, or dug up the earthen floor, to find the stocking full of notes and gold, which might, perchance, come with them safe through any cataclysm, or start them again in business in another world. Some began fearfully to sing hymns, and a few to swear freely. These latter were chiefly carters, whose salutations to each other were mainly oaths, because of the extreme narrowness of the island roads, and sailors to whom profanity was as daily bread.

In St. Heliers, after the first stupefaction, people poured into the streets. They gathered most where met the Rue d'Driere and the Rue d'Egypte. Here stood the old prison, and the spot was called the Place du Vier Prison.

Men and women with breakfast still in their mouths mumbled their terror to each other. A lobster-woman shrieking that the Day of Judgment was come, instinctively straightened her cap, smoothed out her dress of molleton, and put on her sabots. A carpenter, hearing her terrified exclamations, put on his sabots also, stooped whimpering to the stream running from the Rue d'Egypte, and began to wash his face. A dozen of his neighbours did the same. Some of the women, however, went on knitting hard, as they gabbled prayers and looked at the fast-blackening sun. Knitting was to Jersey women, like breathing or tale-bearing, life itself. With their eyes closing upon earth they would have gone on knitting and dropped no stitches.

A dusk came down like that over Pompeii and Herculaneum. The tragedy of fear went hand in hand with burlesque commonplace. The grey stone walls of the houses grew darker and darker, and seemed to close in on the dumfounded, hysterical crowd. Here some one was shouting command to imaginary militia; there an aged crone was offering, without price, simnels and black butter, as a sort of propitiation for an imperfect past; and from a window a notorious evil-liver was frenziedly crying that she had heard the devil and his Rocbert witches revelling in the prison dungeons the night before. Thereupon a long-haired fanatic, once a barber, with a gift for mad preaching, sprang upon the Pompe des Brigands, and declaring that the Last Day was come, shrieked:

*"The Spirit of the Lord is upon me! He hath sent me to proclaim liberty to the captives, and the opening of the prison to them that are bound!"*

Some one thrust into his hand a torch. He waved it to and fro in his wild harangue; he threw up his arms towards the ominous gloom, and with blatant fury ordered open the prison doors. Other torches and candles appeared, and the mob trembled to and fro in delirium.

"The prison! Open the Vier Prison! Break down the doors! Gatd'en'ale—drive out the devils! Free the prisoners—the poor vauriens!" the crowd shouted, rushing forward with sticks and weapons.

The prison arched the street as Temple Bar once spanned the Strand. They crowded under the archway, overpowered the terror-stricken jailer, and, battering open the door in frenzy, called the inmates forth.

They looked to see issue some sailor seized for whistling of a Sabbath, some profane peasant who had presumed to wear pattens in church, some profaner peasant who had not doffed his hat to the Connetable, or some slip-shod militiaman who had gone to parade in his sabots, thereby offending the red-robed dignity of the Royal Court.

Instead, there appeared a little Frenchman of the most refined and unusual appearance. The blue cloth of his coat set off the extreme paleness of a small but serene face and high round forehead. The hair, a beautiful silver grey which time only had powdered, was tied in a queue behind. The little gentleman's hand was as thin and fine as a lady's, his shoulders were narrow and slightly stooped, his eye was eloquent and benign. His dress was amazingly neat, but showed constant brushing and signs of the friendly repairing needle.

The whole impression was that of a man whom a whiff of wind would blow away; with the body of an ascetic and the simplicity of a child. The face had some particular sort of wisdom, difficult to define and impossible to imitate. He held in his hand a tiny cane of the sort carried at the court of Louis Quinze. Louis Capet himself had given it to him; and you might have had the life of the little gentleman, but not this cane with the tiny golden bust of his unhappy monarch.

He stood on the steps of the prison and looked serenely on the muttering, excited crowd.

"I fear there is a mistake," said he, coughing a little into his fingers. "You do not seek me. I—I have no claim upon your kindness; I am only the Chevalier Orvilliers du Champsavoys de Beaumanoir."

For a moment the mob had been stayed in amazement by this small, rare creature stepping from the doorway, like a porcelain coloured figure from some dusky wood in a painting by Claude. In the instant's pause the Chevalier Orvilliers du Champsavoys de Beaumanoir took from his pocket a timepiece and glanced at it, then looked over the heads of the crowd towards the hooded sun, which now, a little, was showing its face again.

"It was due at eight, less seven minutes," said he; "clear sun again was set for ten minutes past. It is now upon the stroke of the hour."

He seemed in no way concerned with the swaying crowd before him—undoubtedly they wanted naught of him, and therefore he did not take their presence seriously; but, of an inquiring mind, he was absorbed in the eclipse.

"He's a French sorcerer! He has the evil eye! Away with him to the sea!" shouted the fanatical preacher from the Pompe des Brigands.

"It's a witch turned into a man!" cried a drunken woman from her window. "Give him the wheel of fire at the blacksmith's forge."

"That's it! Gad'rabotin—the wheel of fire'll turn him back to a hag again!"

The little gentleman protested, but they seized him and dragged him from the steps. Tossed like a ball, so light was he, he grasped the gold-headed cane as one might cling to life, and declared that he was no witch, but a poor French exile, arrested the night before for being abroad after nine o'clock, against the orders of the Royal Court.

Many of the crowd knew him well enough by sight, but they were too delirious to act with intelligence now. The dark cloud was lifting a little from the sun, and dread of the Judgment Day was declining; but as the pendulum swung back towards normal life again, it carried with it the one virulent and common prejudice of the country—radical hatred of the French—which often slumbered but never died.

The wife of an oyster-fisher from Rozel Bay, who lived in hourly enmity with the oyster-fishers of Carteret, gashed his cheek with the shell of an ormer. A potato-digger from Grouville parish struck at his head with a hoe, for the Granvillais had crossed the strait to the island the year before, to work in the harvest fields for a lesser wage than the Jersiais, and this little French gentleman must be held responsible for that. The weapon missed the Chevalier, but laid low a centenier, who, though a municipal officer, had in the excitement lost his head like his neighbours. This but increased the rage against the foreigner, and was another crime to lay to his charge. A smuggler thereupon kicked him in the side.

At that moment there came a cry of indignation from a girl at an upper window of the Place. The Chevalier evidently knew her, for even in his hard case he smiled; and then he heard another voice ring out over the heads of the crowd, strong, angry, determined.

From the Rue d'Driere a tall athletic man was hurrying. He had on his shoulders a workman's hand basket, from which peeped a ship-builder's tools. Seeing the Chevalier's danger, he dropped his tool-basket through the open window of a house and forced his way through the crowd, roughly knocking from under them the feet of two or three ruffians who opposed him. He reproached the crowd, he berated them, he handled them fiercely.

By a dexterous strength he caught the little gentleman up in his arms, and, driving straight on to the open door of the smithy, placed him inside, then blocked the passage with his own body.

It was a strange picture: the preacher in an ecstasy haranguing the foolish rabble, who now realised, with an unbecoming joy, that the Last Day was yet to face; the gaping, empty prison; the open windows crowded with excited faces; the church bell from the Vier Marchi ringing an alarm; Norman lethargy roused to froth and fury: one strong man holding two hundred back!

Above them all, at a hus in the gable of a thatched cottage, stood the girl whom the Chevalier had recognised, anxiously watching the affray. She was leaning across the lower closed half of the door, her hands in apprehensive excitement clasping her cheeks. The eyes were bewildered, and, though alive with pain, watched the scene below with unwavering intensity.

Like all mobs this one had no reason, no sense. They were baulked in their malign intentions, and this man, Maitre Ranulph Delagarde, was the cause of it—that was all they knew. A stone was thrown at Delagarde as he stood in the doorway, but it missed him.

"Oh-oh-oh!" the girl exclaimed, shrinking. "O shame! O you cowards!" she added, her hands now indignantly beating on the hus. Three or four men rushed forward on Ranulph. He hurled them back. Others came on with weapons. The girl fled for an instant, then reappeared with a musket, as the people were crowding in on Delagarde with threats and execrations.

"Stop! stop!" cried the girl from above, as Ranulph seized a blacksmith's hammer to meet the onset. "Stop, or I'll fire!" she called again, and she aimed her musket at the foremost assailants.

Every face turned in her direction, for her voice had rung out clear as music. For an instant there was silence—the levelled musket had a deadly look, and the girl seemed determined. Her fingers, her whole body, trembled; but there was no mistaking the strong will, the indignant purpose.

All at once in the pause another sound was heard. It was a quick tramp, tramp, tramp! and suddenly under the prison archway came running an officer of the King's navy with a company of sailors. The officer, with drawn sword, his men following with cutlasses, drove a way through the mob, who scattered before them like sheep.

Delagarde threw aside his hammer, and saluted the officer. The little Chevalier made a formal bow, and hastened to say that he was not at all hurt. With a droll composure he offered snuff to the officer, who declined politely. Turning to the window where the girl stood, the new-comer saluted with confident gallantry.

"Why, it's little Guida Landresse!" he said under his breath—"I'd know her anywhere. Death and Beauty, what a face!" Then he turned to Ranulph in recognition.

"Ranulph Delagarde, eh?" said he good-humouredly. "You've forgotten me, I see. I'm Philip d'Avranche, of the Narcissus."

Ranulph had forgotten. The slight lad Philip had grown bronzed, and stouter of frame. In the eleven years since they had been together at the Battle of Jersey, events, travel, and responsibility had altered him vastly. Ranulph had changed only in growing very tall and athletic and strong; the look of him was still that of the Norman lad of the isle, though the power and intelligence of his face were unusual.

The girl in the cottage doorway had not forgotten at all. The words that d'Avranche had said to her years before, when she was a child, came to her mind: "My name is Philip; call me Philip."

The recollection of that day when she snatched off the Bailly's hat brought a smile to her lips now, so quickly were her feelings moved one way or another. Then she grew suddenly serious, for the memory of the hour when he saved her from the scimitar of the Turk came to her, and her heart throbbed hotly. But she smiled again, though more gently and a little wistfully now.

Philip d'Avranche looked up towards her once more, and returned her smile. Then he addressed the awed crowd. He did not spare his language; he unconsciously used an oath or two. He ordered them off to their homes. When they hesitated (for they were slow to acknowledge any authority save their own sacred Royal Court) the sailors advanced on them with drawn cutlasses, and a moment later the Place du Vier Prison was clear. Leaving a half-dozen sailors on guard till the town corps should arrive, d'Avranche prepared to march, and turned to Delagarde.

"You've done me a good turn, Monsieur d'Avranche," said Ranulph.

"There was a time you called me Philip," said d'Avranche, smiling. "We were lads together."

"It's different now," answered Delagarde.

"Nothing is different at all, of course," returned d'Avranche carelessly, yet with the slightest touch of condescension, as he held out his hand. Turning to the Chevalier, he said: "Monsieur, I congratulate you on having such a champion"—with a motion towards Ranulph. "And you, monsieur, on your brave protector"—he again saluted the girl at the window above.

"I am the obliged and humble servant of monsieur, and monsieur," responded the little gentleman, turning from one to the other with a courtly bow, the three-cornered hat under his arm, the right foot forward, the thin fingers making a graceful salutation. "But I—I think—I really think I must go back to prison. I was not formally set free. I was out last night beyond the hour set by the Court. I lost my way, and—"

"Not a bit of it," d'Avranche interrupted. "The centeniers are too free with their jailing here. I'll be guarantee for you, monsieur." He turned to go.

The little man shook his head dubiously. "But, as a point of honour, I really think—"

D'Avranche laughed. "As a point of honour, I think you ought to breakfast. A la bonne heure, monsieur le chevalier!"

He turned again to the cottage window. The girl was still there. The darkness over the sun was withdrawn, and now the clear light began to spread itself abroad. It was like a second dawn after a painful night. It tinged the face of the girl; it burnished the wonderful red-brown hair falling loosely and lightly over her forehead; it gave her beauty a touch of luxuriance. D'Avranche thrilled at the sight of her.

"It's a beautiful face," he said to himself as their eyes met and he saluted once more.

Ranulph had seen the glances passing between the two, and he winced. He remembered how, eleven years ago, Philip d'Avranche had saved the girl from death. It galled him that then and now this young gallant should step in and take the game out of his hands—he was sure that himself alone could have mastered this crowd.

"Monsieur—monsieur le chevalier!" the girl called down from the window, "grandpethe says you must breakfast with us. Oh, but come you must, or we shall be offended!" she added, as Champsavoys shook his head in hesitation and glanced towards the prison.

"As a point of honour—" the little man still persisted, lightly touching his breast with the Louis Quinze cane, and taking a step towards the sombre prison archway. But Ranulph interfered, drew him gently inside the cottage, and, standing in the doorway, said to some one within:

"May I come in also, Sieur de Mauprat?"

Above the pleasant welcome of a quavering voice came another, soft and clear, in pure French:

"Thou art always welcome, without asking, as thou knowest, Ro."

"Then I'll go and fetch my tool-basket first," Ranulph said cheerily, his heart beating more quickly, and, turning, he walked across the Place.

# CHAPTER VI

The cottage in which Guida lived at the Place du Vier Prison was in jocund contrast to the dungeon from which the Chevalier Orvilliers du Champsavoys de Beaumanoir had complacently issued. Even in the hot summer the prison walls dripped moisture, for the mortar had been made of wet sea-sand, which never dried, and beneath the gloomy tenement of crime a dark stream flowed to the sea. But the walls of the cottage were dry, for, many years before, Guida's mother had herself seen it built from cellar-rock to the linked initials over the doorway, stone by stone, and every corner of it was as free from damp as the mielles stretching in sandy desolation behind to the Mont es Pendus, where the law had its way with the necks of criminals.

In early childhood Madame Landresse had come with her father into exile from the sunniest valley in the hills of Chambery, where flowers and trees and sunshine had been her life. Here, in the midst of blank and grim stone houses, her heart travelled back to the chateau where she lived before the storm of persecution drove her forth; and she spent her heart and her days in making this cottage, upon the western border of St. Heliers, a delight to the quiet eye.

The people of the island had been good to her and her dead husband during the two short years of their married life, and had caused her to love the land which necessity made her home. Her child was brought up after the fashion of the better class of Jersey children, wore what they wore, ate what they ate, lived as they lived. She spoke the country patois in the daily life, teaching it to Guida at the same time that she taught her pure French and good English, which she herself had learned as a child, and cultivated later here. She had done all in her power to make Guida Jersiaise in instinct and habit, and to beget in her a contented disposition. There could be no future for her daughter outside this little green oasis of exile, she thought. Not that she lacked ambition, but in the circumstances she felt that ambition could yield but one harvest to her child, which was marriage. She herself had married a poor man, a master builder of ships, like Maitre Ranulph Delagarde, but she had been very happy while he lived. Her husband had come of an ancient Jersey family, who were in Normandy before the

Conqueror was born; a man of genius almost in his craft, but scarcely a gentleman according to the standard of her father, the distinguished exile and now retired watchmaker. If Guida should chance to be as fortunate as herself, she could ask no more.

She had watched the child anxiously, for the impulses of Guida's temperament now and then broke forth in indignation as wild as her tears and in tears as wild as her laughter. As the girl grew in health and stature, she tried, tenderly, strenuously, to discipline the sensitive nature, bursting her heart with grief at times because she knew that these high feelings and delicate powers came through a long line of ancestral tendencies, as indestructible as perilous and joyous.

Four things were always apparent in the girl's character: sympathy with suffering, kindness without partiality, a love of nature, and an intense candour.

Not a stray cat wandering into the Place du Vier Prison but found an asylum in the garden behind the cottage. Not a dog hungry for a bone, stopping at Guida's door, but was sure of one from a hiding-place in the hawthorn hedge of the garden. Every morning you might have seen the birds in fluttering, chirping groups upon the may-tree or the lilac-bushes, waiting for the tiny snow-storm of bread to fall from her hand. Was he good or bad, ragged or neat, honest or a thief, not a deserting sailor or a homeless lad, halting at the cottage, but was fed from the girl's private larder behind the straw beehives among the sweet lavender and the gooseberry-bushes. No matter how rough the vagrant, the sincerity and pure impulse of the child seemed to throw round him a sunshine of decency and respect.

The garden behind the house was the girl's Eden. She had planted upon the hawthorn hedge the crimson monthly rose, the fuchsia, and the jonquil, until at last the cottage was hemmed in by a wall of flowers; and here she was ever as busy as the bees which hung humming on the sweet scabious.

In this corner was a little hut for rabbits; in that, there was a hole dug in the bank for a hedgehog; in the middle a little flower-grown enclosure for cats in various stages of health or convalescence, and a small pond for frogs; and in the midst of all wandered her faithful dog, Biribi by name, as master of the ceremonies.

Madame Landresse's one ambition had been to live long enough to see her child's character formed. She knew that her own years were numbered, for month by month she felt her strength going. And yet a beautiful tenacity kept her where she would be until Guida was fifteen years of age. Her great desire had been to live till the girl was eighteen. Then—well, then might she not perhaps leave her to the care of a husband? At best, M. de

Mauprat could not live long. He had at last been forced to give up the little watchmaker's shop in the Vier Marchi, where for so many years, in simple independence, he had wrought, always putting by, from work done after hours, Jersey bank-notes and gold, to give Guida a dot, if not worthy of her, at least a guarantee against reproach when some great man should come seeking her in marriage. But at last his hands trembled among the tiny wheels, and his eyes failed. He had his dark hour by himself, then he sold the shop to a native, who thenceforward sat in the ancient exile's place; and the two brown eyes of the stooped, brown old man looked out no more from the window in the Vier Marchi: and then they all made their new home in the Place du Vier Prison.

Until she was fifteen Guida's life was unclouded. Once or twice her mother tried to tell her of a place that must soon be empty, but her heart failed her. So at last the end came like a sudden wind out of the north; and it was left to Guida Landresse de Landresse to fight the fight and finish the journey of womanhood alone.

This time was the turning-point in Guida's life. What her mother had been to the Sieur de Mauprat, she soon became. They had enough to live on simply. Every week her grandfather gave her a fixed sum for the household. Upon this she managed, that the tiny income left by her mother might not be touched. She shrank from using it yet, and besides, dark times might come when it would be needed. Death had once surprised her, but it should bring no more amazement. She knew that M. de Mauprat's days were numbered, and when he was gone she would be left without one near relative in the world. She realised how unprotected her position would be when death came knocking at the door again. What she would do she knew not. She thought long and hard. Fifty things occurred to her, and fifty were set aside. Her mother's immediate relatives in France were scattered or dead. There was no longer any interest at Chambery in the watchmaking exile, who had dropped like a cherry-stone from the beak of the blackbird of persecution upon one of the Iles de la Manche.

There remained the alternative more than once hinted by the Sieur de Mauprat as the months grew into years after the mother died—marriage; a husband, a notable and wealthy husband. That was the magic destiny de Mauprat figured for her. It did not elate her, it did not disturb her; she scarcely realised it. She loved animals, and she saw no reason to despise a stalwart youth. It had been her fortune to know two or three in the casual, unconventional manner of villages, and there were few in the land, great or humble, who did not turn twice to look at her as she passed through the Vier Marchi, so noble was her carriage, so graceful and buoyant her walk, so lacking in self-consciousness her beauty. More than one young gentleman of family had been known to ride through the Place du Vier Prison, hoping to get sight of her, and to offer the view of a suggestively empty pillion behind him.

She had, however, never listened to flatterers, and only one youth of Jersey had footing in the cottage. This was Ranulph Delagarde, who had gone in and out at his will, but that was casually and not too often, and he was discreet and spoke no word of love. Sometimes she talked to him of things concerning the daily life with which she did not care to trouble Sieur de Mauprat. In ways quite unknown to her he had made her life easier for her. She knew that her mother had thought of Ranulph for her husband, although she blushed whenever—but it was not often—the idea came to her. She remembered how her mother had said that Ranulph would be a great man in the island some day; that he had a mind above all the youths in St. Heliers; that she would rather see Ranulph a master ship-builder than a babbling ecrivain in the Rue des Tres Pigeons, a smirking leech, or a penniless seigneur with neither trade nor talent. Guida was attracted to Ranulph through his occupation, for she loved strength, she loved all clean and wholesome trades; that of the mason, of the carpenter, of the blacksmith, and most of the ship-builder. Her father, whom she did not remember, had been a ship-builder, and she knew that he had been a notable man; every one had told her that.

........................

"She has met her destiny," say the village gossips, when some man in the dusty procession of life sees a woman's face in the pleasant shadow of a home, and drops out of the ranks to enter at her doorway.

Was Ranulph to be Guida's destiny?

Handsome and stalwart though he looked as he entered the cottage in the Place du Vier Prison, on that September morning after the rescue of the chevalier, his tool-basket on his shoulder, and his brown face enlivened by one simple sentiment, she was far from sure that he was—far from sure.

# CHAPTER VII

The little hall-way into which Ranulph stepped from the street led through to the kitchen. Guida stood holding back the door for him to enter this real living-room of the house, which opened directly upon the garden behind. It was so cheerful and secluded, looking out from the garden over the wide space beyond to the changeful sea, that since Madame Landresse's death the Sieur de Mauprat had made it reception-room, dining-room, and kitchen all in one. He would willingly have slept there too, but noblesse oblige and the thought of what the Chevalier Orvilliers du Champsavoys de Beaumanoir might think prevented him. Moreover, there was something patriarchal in a kitchen as a reception-room; and both he and the chevalier loved to watch Guida busy with her household duties: at one moment her arms in the dough of the kneading trough; at another picking cherries for a jelly, or casting up her weekly accounts with a little smiling and a little sighing.

If, by chance, it had been proposed by the sieur to adjourn to the small sitting-room which looked out upon the Place du Vier Prison, a gloom would instantly have settled upon them both; though in this little front room there was an ancient arm-chair, over which hung the sword that the Comte Guilbert Mauprat de Chambery had used at Fontenoy against the English.

So it was that this spacious kitchen, with its huge chimney, and paved with square flagstones and sanded, became like one of those ancient corners of camaraderie in some exclusive inn where gentlemen of quality were wont to meet. At the left of the chimney was the great settle, or veille, covered with baize, "flourished" with satinettes, and spread with ferns and rushes, and above it a little shelf of old china worth the ransom of a prince at least. Opposite the doorway were two great armchairs, one for the sieur and the other for the Chevalier, who made his home in the house of one Elie Mattingley, a fisherman by trade and by practice a practical smuggler, with a daughter Carterette whom he loved passing well.

These, with a few constant visitors, formed a coterie: the huge, grizzly-bearded boatman, Jean Touzel, who wore spectacles, befriended smugglers, was approved of all men, and secretly worshipped by his wife; Amice Ingouville, the fat avocat with a stomach of gigantic proportions, the biggest heart and the tiniest brain in the world; Maitre Ranulph Delagarde, and lastly M. Yves Savary dit Detricand, that officer of Rullecour's who, being released from the prison hospital, when the hour came for him to leave the country was too drunk to find the shore. By some whim of negligence the Royal Court was afterwards too lethargic to remove him, and he stayed on, vainly making efforts to leave between one carousal and another. In sober hours, none too frequent, he was rather sorrowfully welcomed by the sieur and the chevalier.

When Ranulph entered the kitchen his greeting to the sieur and the chevalier was in French, but to Guida he said, rather stupidly in the patois—for late events had embarrassed him—"Ah bah! es-tu gentiment?"

"Gentiment," she answered, with a queer little smile. "You'll have breakfast?" she said in English.

"Et ben!" Ranulph repeated, still embarrassed, "a mouthful, that's all."

He laid aside his tool-basket, shook hands with the sieur, and seated himself at the table. Looking at du Champsavoys, he said:

"I've just met the connetable. He regrets the riot, chevalier, and says the Royal Court extends its mercy to you."

"I prefer to accept no favours," answered the chevalier. "As a point of honour, I had thought that, after breakfast, I should return to prison, and—"

"The connetable said it was cheaper to let the chevalier go free than to feed him in the Vier Prison," dryly explained Ranulph, helping himself to roasted conger eel and eyeing hungrily the freshly-made black butter Guida was taking from a wooden trencher. "The Royal Court is stingy," he added. "'It's nearer than Jean Noe, who got married in his red queminzolle,' as we say on Jersey—"

But he got no further at the moment, for shots rang out suddenly before the house. They all started to their feet, and Ranulph, running to the front door, threw it open. As he did so a young man, with blood flowing from a cut on the temple, stepped inside.

# CHAPTER VIII

**It was M. Savary dit Detricand.**

"Whew—what fools there are in the world! Pish, you silly apes!" the young man said, glancing through the open doorway again to where the connetable's men were dragging two vile-looking ruffians into the Vier Prison.

"What's happened, monsieur?" said Ranulph, closing the door and bolting it.

"What was it, monsieur?" asked Guida anxiously, for painful events had crowded too fast that morning. Detricand was stanching the blood at his temple with the scarf from his neck.

"Get him some cordial, Guida—he's wounded!" said de Mauprat.

Detricand waved a hand almost impatiently, and dropped upon the veille, swinging a leg backwards and forwards.

"It's nothing, I protest—nothing whatever, and I'll have no cordial, not a drop. A drink of water—a mouthful of that, if I must drink."

Guida caught up a hanap of water from the dresser, and passed it to him. Her fingers trembled a little. His were steady enough as he took the hanap and drank off the water at a gulp. Again she filled it and again he drank. The blood was running in a tiny little stream down his cheek. She caught her handkerchief from her girdle impulsively, and gently wiped it away.

"Let me bandage the wound," she said eagerly. Her eyes were alight with compassion, certainly not because it was the dissipated French invader, M. Savary dit Detricand,—no one knew that he was the young Comte de Tournay of the House of Vaufontaine, but because he was a wounded fellow-creature. She would have done the same for the poor beganne, Dormy Jamais, who still prowled the purlieus of St. Heliers.

It was clear, however, that Detricand felt differently. The moment she touched him he became suddenly still. He permitted her to wash the blood from his temple and forehead, to stanch it first with brandied jeru-leaves, then with cobwebs, and afterwards to bind it with her own kerchief.

Detricand thrilled at the touch of the warm, tremulous fingers. He had never been quite so near her before. His face was not far from hers. Now her breath fanned him. As he bent his head for the bandaging, he could see the soft pulsing of her bosom, and hear the beating of her heart. Her neck was so full and round and soft, and her voice—surely he had never heard a voice so sweet and strong, a tone so well poised, so resonantly pleasant.

When she had finished, he had an impulse to catch the hand as it dropped away from his forehead, and kiss it; not as he had kissed many a hand, hotly one hour and coldly the next, but with an unpurchasable kind of gratitude characteristic of this especial sort of sinner. He was just young enough, and there was still enough natural health in him, to know the healing touch of a perfect decency, a pure truth of spirit. Yet he had been drunk the night before, drunk with three noncommissioned officers—and he a gentleman, in spite of all, as could be plainly seen.

He turned his head away from the girl quickly, and looked straight into the eyes of her grandfather.

"I'll tell you how it was, Sieur de Mauprat," said he. "I was crossing the Place du Vier Prison when a rascal threw a cleaver at me from a window. If it had struck me on the head—well, the Royal Court would have buried me, and without a slab to my grave like Rullecour. I burst open the door of the house, ran up the stairs, gripped the ruffian, and threw him through the window into the street. As I did so a door opened behind, and another cut-throat came at me with a pistol. He fired—fired wide. I ran in on him, and before he had time to think he was out of the window too. Then the other brute below fired up at me. The bullet gashed my temple, as you see. After that, it was an affair of the connetable and his men. I had had enough fighting before breakfast. I saw your open door, and here I am—monsieur, monsieur, monsieur, mademoiselle!" He bowed to each of them and glanced towards the table hungrily.

Ranulph placed a seat for him. He viewed the conger eel and limpets with an avid eye, but waited for the chevalier and de Mauprat to sit. He had no sooner taken a mouthful, however, and thrown a piece of bread to Biribi the dog, than, starting again to his feet, he said:

"Your pardon, monsieur le chevalier, that brute in the Place has knocked all sense from my head! I've a letter for you, brought from Rouen by one of the refugees who came yesterday." He drew from his breast a packet and handed it over. "I went out to their ship last night."

The chevalier looked with surprise and satisfaction at the seal on the letter, and, breaking it, spread open the paper, fumbled for the eye-glass which he always carried in his waistcoat, and began reading diligently.

Meanwhile Ranulph turned to Guida. "To-morrow Jean Touzel and his wife and I go to the Ecrehos Rocks in Jean's boat," said he. "A vessel was driven ashore there three days ago, and my carpenters are at work on her. If you can go and the wind holds fair, you shall be brought back safe by sundown—Jean says so too."

Of all boatmen and fishermen on the coast, Jean Touzel was most to be trusted. No man had saved so many shipwrecked folk, none risked his life so often; and he had never had a serious accident. To go to sea with Jean Touzel, folk said, was safer than living on land. Guida loved the sea; and she could sail a boat, and knew the tides and currents of the south coast as well as most fishermen.

M. de Mauprat met her inquiring glance and nodded assent. She then said gaily to Ranulph: "I shall sail her, shall I not?"

"Every foot of the way," he answered.

She laughed and clapped her hands. Suddenly the little chevalier broke in. "By the head of John the Baptist!" said he.

Detricand put down his knife and fork in amazement, and Guida coloured, for the words sounded almost profane upon the chevalier's lips.

Du Champsavoys held up his eye-glass, and, turning from one to the other, looked at each of them imperatively yet abstractedly too. Then, pursing up his lower lip, and with a growing amazement which carried him to distant heights of reckless language, he said again:

"By the head of John the Baptist on a charger!" He looked at Detricand with a fierceness which was merely the tension of his thought. If he had looked at a wall it would have been the same. But Detricand, who had an almost whimsical sense of humour, felt his neck in affected concern as though to be quite sure of it. "Chevalier," said he, "you shock us—you shock us, dear chevalier."

"The most painful things, and the most wonderful too," said the chevalier, tapping the letter with his eye-glass; "the most terrible and yet the most romantic things are here. A drop of cider, if you please, mademoiselle, before I begin to read it to you, if I may—if I may—eh?"

They all nodded eagerly. Guida handed him a mogue of cider. The little grey thrush of a man sipped it, and in a voice no bigger than a bird's began:

"*From Lucillien du Champsavoys, Comte de Chanier, by the hand of a faithful friend, who goeth hence from among divers dangers, unto my cousin, the Chevalier du Champsavoys de Beaumanoir, late Gentleman*

*of the Bedchamber to the best of monarchs, Louis XV, this writing:*

"MY DEAR AND HONOURED Cousin" — *The chevalier paused, frowned a*

*trifle, and tapped his lips with his finger in a little lyrical emotion* — "My dear and honoured cousin, all is lost. The France we loved is no more. The twentieth of June saw the last vestige of Louis's power pass for ever. That day ten thousand of the sans-culottes forced their way into the palace to kill him. A faithful few surrounded him. In the mad turmoil, we were fearful, he was serene. 'Feel,' said Louis, placing his hand on his bosom, 'feel whether this is the beating of a heart shaken by fear.' Ah, my friend, your heart would have clamped in misery to hear the Queen cry: 'What have I to fear? Death? it is as well to-day as to-morrow; they can do no more!' Their lives were saved, the day passed, but worse came after.

"The tenth of August came. With it too, the end-the dark and bloody end-of the Swiss Guard. The Jacobins had their way at last. The Swiss Guard died in the Court of the Carrousel as they marched to the Assembly to save the King. Thus the last circle of defence round the throne was broken. The palace was given over to flame and the sword. Of twenty nobles of the court I alone escaped. France is become a slaughter-house. The people cried out for more liberty, and their liberators gave them the freedom of death. A fortnight ago, Danton, the incomparable fiend, let loose his assassins upon the priests of God. Now Paris is made a theatre where the people whom Louis and his nobles would have died to save have turned every street into a stable of carnage, every prison and hospital into a vast charnel-house. One last revolting thing alone remains to be done — the murder of the King; then this France that we have loved will have no name and no place in our generation. She will rise again, but we shall not see her, for our eyes have been blinded with blood, for ever darkened by disaster. Like a mistress upon whom we have lavished the days of our youth and the strength of our days, she has deceived us; she has stricken us while we slept. Behold a Caliban now for her paramour!

"Weep with me, for France despoils me. One by one my friends have fallen beneath the axe. Of my four sons but one remains. Henri was stabbed by Danton's ruffians at the Hotel de Ville; Gaston fought and died with the Swiss Guard, whose hacked and severed limbs were broiled and eaten in the streets by these monsters who mutilate the land. Isidore, the youngest, defied a hundred of Robespierre's cowards on the steps of the Assembly, and was torn to pieces by the mob. Etienne alone is left. But for him and for the honour of my house I too would find a place beside the King and die with him. Etienne is with de la Rochejaquelein in Brittany. I am here at Rouen.

"Brittany and Normandy still stand for the King. In these two provinces begins the regeneration of France: we call it the War of the Vendee. On that Isle of Jersey there you should almost hear the voice of de la Rochejaquelein and the marching cries of our loyal legions. If there be justice in God we shall conquer. But there will be joy no more for such as you or me, nor hope, nor any peace. We live only for those who come after. Our duty remains, all else is dead. You did well to go, and I do well to stay.

"By all these piteous relations you shall know the importance of the request I now set forth.

"My cousin by marriage of the House of Vaufontaine has lost all his sons. With the death of the Prince of Vaufontaine, there is in France no direct heir to the house, nor can it, by the law, revert to my house or my heirs. Now of late the Prince hath urged me to write to you—for he is here in seclusion with me—and to unfold to you what has hitherto been secret. Eleven years ago the only nephew of the Prince, after some naughty escapades, fled from the Court with Rullecour the adventurer, who invaded the Isle of Jersey. From that hour he has been lost to France. Some of his companions in arms returned after a number of years. All with one exception

*declared that he was killed in the battle at St. Heliers. One,*
*however, maintains that he was still living and in the prison*
*hospital when his comrades were set free.*

*"It is of him I write to you. He is—as you will perchance*
*remember—the Comte de Tournay. He was then not more than*
*seventeen*
*years of age, slight of build, with brownish hair, dark grey eyes,*
*and had over the right shoulder a scar from a sword thrust. It*
*seemeth little possible that, if living, he should still remain in*
*that Isle of Jersey. He may rather have returned to obscurity in*
*France or have gone to England to be lost to name and remembrance*
*—or even indeed beyond the seas.*

*"That you may perchance give me word of him is the object of my*
*letter, written in no more hope than I live; and you can well guess*
*how faint that is. One young nobleman preserved to France may yet*
*be the great unit that will save her.*

*"Greet my poor countrymen yonder in the name of one who still waits*
*at a desecrated altar; and for myself you must take me as I am, with*
*the remembrance of what I was, even*

*"Your faithful friend and loving kinsman,*

*"CHANIER."*
*"All this, though in the chances of war you read it not till*
*wintertide, was told you at Rouen this first day of September*
*1792."*

During the reading, broken by feeling and reflective pauses on the
chevalier's part, the listeners showed emotion after the nature of each. The
Sieur de Mauprat's fingers clasped and unclasped on the top of his cane, little
explosions of breath came from his compressed lips, his eyebrows beetled
over till the eyes themselves seemed like two glints of flame. Delagarde
dropped a fist heavily upon the table, and held it there clinched, while his

heel beat a tattoo of excitement upon the floor. Guida's breath came quick and fast—as Ranulph said afterwards, she was "blanc comme un linge." She shuddered painfully when the slaughter and burning of the Swiss Guards was read. Her brain was so swimming with the horrors of anarchy that the latter part of the letter dealing with the vanished Count of Tournay passed by almost unheeded.

But this particular matter greatly interested Ranulph and de Mauprat. They leaned forward eagerly, seizing every word, and both instinctively turned towards Detricand when the description of de Tournay was read.

As for Detricand himself, he listened to the first part of the letter like a man suddenly roused out of a dream. For the first time since the Revolution had begun, the horror of it and the meaning of it were brought home to him. He had been so long expatriated, had loitered so long in the primrose path of daily sleep and nightly revel, had fallen so far, that he little realised how the fiery wheels of Death were spinning in France, or how black was the torment of her people. His face turned scarlet as the thing came home to him now. He dropped his head in his hand as if to listen more attentively, but it was in truth to hide his emotion. When the names of Vaufontaine and de Tournay were mentioned, he gave a little start, then suddenly ruled himself to a strange stillness. His face seemed presently to clear; he even smiled a little. Conscious that de Mauprat and Delagarde were watching him, he appeared to listen with a keen but impersonal interest, not without its effect upon his scrutinisers. He nodded his head as though he understood the situation. He acted very well; he bewildered the onlookers. They might think he tallied with the description of the Comte de Tournay, yet he gave the impression that the matter was not vital to himself. But when the little Chevalier stopped and turned his eye-glass upon him with sudden startled inquiry, he found it harder to keep composure.

"Singular—singular!" said the old man, and returned to the reading of the letter.

When he ended there was absolute silence for a moment. Then the chevalier lifted his eye-glass again and looked at Detricand intently.

"Pardon me, monsieur," he said, "but you were with Rullecour—as I was saying."

Detricand nodded with a droll sort of helplessness, and answered: "In Jersey I never have chance to forget it, Chevalier."

Du Champsavoys, with a naive and obvious attempt at playing counsel, fixed him again with the glass, pursed his lips, and with the importance of a greffier at the ancient Cour d'Heritage, came one step nearer to his goal.

"Have you knowledge of the Comte de Tournay, monsieur?"

"I knew him—as you were saying, Chevalier," answered Detricand lightly.

Then the Chevalier struck home. He dropped his fingers upon the table, stood up, and, looking straight into Detricand's eyes, said:

"Monsieur, you are the Comte de Tournay!"

The Chevalier involuntarily held the silence for an instant. Nobody stirred. De Mauprat dropped his chin upon his hands, and his eyebrows drew down in excitement. Guida gave a little cry of astonishment. But Detricand answered the Chevalier with a look of blank surprise and a shrug of the shoulder, which had the effect desired.

"Thank you, Chevalier," said he with quizzical humour. "Now I know who I am, and if it isn't too soon to levy upon the kinship, I shall dine with you today, chevalier. I paid my debts yesterday, and sous are scarce, but since we are distant cousins I may claim grist at the family mill, eh?"

The Chevalier sat, or rather dropped into his chair again.

"Then you are not the Comte de Tournay, monsieur," said he hopelessly.

"Then I shall not dine with you to-day," retorted Detricand gaily.

"You fit the tale," said de Mauprat dubiously, touching the letter with his finger.

"Let me see," rejoined Detricand. "I've been a donkey farmer, a shipmaster's assistant, a tobacco pedlar, a quarryman, a wood merchant, an interpreter, a fisherman—that's very like the Comte de Tournay! On Monday night I supped with a smuggler; on Tuesday I breakfasted on soupe a la graisse with Manon Moignard the witch; on Wednesday I dined with Dormy Jamais and an avocat disbarred for writing lewd songs for a chocolate-house; on Thursday I went oyster-fishing with a native who has three wives, and a butcher who has been banished four times for not keeping holy the Sabbath Day; and I drank from eleven o'clock till sunrise this morning with three Scotch sergeants of the line—which is very like the Comte de Tournay, as you were saying, Chevalier! I am five feet eleven, and the Comte de Tournay was five feet ten—which is no lie," he added under his breath. "I have a scar, but it's over my left shoulder and not over my right—which is also no lie," he added under his breath. "De Tournay's hair was brown, and mine, you see, is almost a dead black—fever did that," he added under his breath. "De Tournay escaped the day after the Battle of Jersey from the prison hospital, I was left, and here I've been ever since— Yves Savary dit Detricand at your service, chevalier."

A pained expression crossed over the Chevalier's face. "I am most sorry; I am most sorry," he said hesitatingly. "I had no wish to wound your feelings."

"Ah, it is de Tournay to whom you must apologise," said Detricand musingly, with a droll look.

"It is a pity," continued the Chevalier, "for somehow all at once I recalled a resemblance. I saw de Tournay when he was fourteen—yes, I think it was fourteen—and when I looked at you, monsieur, his face came back to me. It would have made my cousin so happy if you had been the Comte de Tournay and I had found you here." The old man's voice trembled a little. "We are growing fewer every day, we Frenchmen of the ancient families. And it would have made my cousin so happy, as I was saying, monsieur."

Detricand's manner changed; he became serious. The devil-may-care, irresponsible shamelessness of his face dropped away like a mask. Something had touched him. His voice changed too.

"De Tournay was a much better fellow than I am, chevalier," said he—"and that's no lie," he added under his breath. "De Tournay was a fiery, ambitious, youngster with bad companions. De Tournay told me he repented of coming with Rullecour, and he felt he had spoilt his life—that he could never return to France again or to his people."

The old Chevalier shook his head sadly. "Is he dead?" he asked.

There was a slight pause, and then Detricand answered: "No, still living."

"Where is he?"

"I promised de Tournay that I would never reveal that."

"Might I not write to him?" asked the old man. "Assuredly, Chevalier."

"Could you—will you—despatch a letter to him from me, monsieur?"

"Upon my honour, yes."

"I thank you—I thank you, monsieur; I will write it to-day."

"As you will, Chevalier. I will ask you for the letter to-night," rejoined Detricand. "It may take time to reach de Tournay; but he shall receive it into his own hands."

De Mauprat trembled to his feet to put the question he knew the Chevalier dreaded to ask:

"Do you think that monsieur le comte will return to France?"

"I think he will," answered Detricand slowly.

"It will make my cousin so happy—so happy," quavered the little Chevalier. "Will you take snuff with me, monsieur?" He offered his silver snuff-box to his vagrant countryman. This was a mark of favour he showed to few.

Detricand bowed, accepted, and took a pinch. "I must be going," he said.

# CHAPTER IX

At eight o'clock the next morning, Guida and her fellow-voyagers, bound for the Ecrehos Rocks, had caught the first ebb of the tide, and with a fair wind from the sou'-west had skirted the coast, ridden lightly over the Banc des Violets, and shaped their course nor'-east. Guida kept the helm all the way, as she had been promised by Ranulph. It was still more than half tide when they approached the rocks, and with a fair wind there should be ease in landing.

No more desolate spot might be imagined. To the left, as you faced towards Jersey, was a long sand-bank. Between the rocks and the sand-bank shot up a tall, lonely shaft of granite with an evil history. It had been chosen as the last refuge of safety for the women and children of a shipwrecked vessel, in the belief that high tide would not reach them. But the wave rose up maliciously, foot by foot, till it drowned their cries for ever in the storm. The sand-bank was called "Ecriviere," and the rock was afterwards known as the "Pierre des Femmes."

Other rocks less prominent, but no less treacherous, flanked it—the Noir Sabloniere and the Grande Galere. To the right of the main island were a group of others, all reef and shingle, intersected by treacherous channels; in calm lapped by water with the colours of a prism of crystal, in storm by a leaden surf and flying foam. These were known as the Colombiere, the Grosse Tete, Tas de Pois, and the Marmotiers; each with its retinue of sunken reefs and needles of granitic gneiss lying low in menace. Happy the sailor caught in a storm and making for the shelter the little curves in the island afford, who escapes a twist of the current, a sweep of the tide, and the impaling fingers of the submarine palisades.

Beyond these rocks lay Maitre Ile, all gneiss and shingle, a desert in the sea. The holy men of the early Church, beholding it from the shore of Normandy, had marked it for a refuge from the storms of war and the follies of the world. So it came to pass, for the honour of God and the Virgin Mary, the Abbe of Val Richer built a priory there: and there now lie in peace the bones of the monks of Val Richer beside the skeletons of unfortunate gentlemen of the sea of later centuries—pirates from France, buccaneers from England, and smugglers from Jersey, who kept their trysts in the precincts of the ancient chapel.

The brisk air of early autumn made the blood tingle in Guida's cheeks. Her eyes were big with light and enjoyment. Her hair was caught close by a gay cap of her own knitting, but a little of it escaped, making a pretty setting to her face.

The boat rode under all her courses, until, as Jean said, they had put the last lace on her bonnet. Guida's hands were on the tiller firmly, doing Jean's bidding promptly. In all they were five. Besides Guida and Ranulph, Jean and Jean's wife, there was a young English clergyman of the parish of St. Michael's, who had come from England to fill the place of the rector for a few months. Word had been brought to him that a man was dying on the Ecrehos. He had heard that the boat was going, he had found Jean Touzel, and here he was with a biscuit in his hand and a black-jack of French wine within easy reach. Not always in secret the Reverend Lorenzo Dow loved the good things of this world.

The most notable characteristic of the young clergyman's appearance was his outer guilelessness and the oddness of his face. His head was rather big for his body; he had a large mouth which laughed easily, a noble forehead, and big, short-sighted eyes. He knew French well, but could speak almost no Jersey patois, so, in compliment to him, Jean Touzel, Ranulph, and Guida spoke in English. This ability to speak English—his own English—was the pride of Jean's life. He babbled it all the way, and chiefly about a mythical Uncle Elias, who was the text for many a sermon.

"Times past," said he, as they neared Maitre Ile, "mon onc' 'Lias he knows these Ecrehoses better as all the peoples of the world—respe d'la compagnie. Mon onc' 'Lias he was a fine man. Once when there is a fight between de Henglish and de hopping Johnnies," he pointed towards France, "dere is seven French ship, dere is two Henglish ship—gentlemen-of-war dey are call. Eh ben, one of de Henglish ships he is not a gentleman-of-war, he is what you call go-on-your-own-hook—privator. But it is all de same— tres-ba, all right! What you t'ink coum to pass? De big Henglish ship she is hit ver' bad, she is all break-up. Efin, dat leetle privator he stan' round on de fighting side of de gentleman-of-war and take de fire by her loneliness. Say, then, wherever dere is troub' mon onc' 'Lias he is there, he stan' outside de troub' an' look on—dat is his hobby. You call it hombog? Oh, nannin- gia! Suppose two peoples goes to fight, ah bah, somebody must pick up de pieces—dat is mon onc' 'Lias! He have his boat full of hoysters; so he sit dere all alone and watch dat great fight, an' heat de hoyster an' drink de cider vine.

"Ah, bah! mon onc' 'Lias he is standin' hin de door dat day. Dat is what we say on Jersey—when a man have some ver' great luck we say he stan' hin de door. I t'ink it is from de Bible or from de helmanac—sacre moi, I not know.... If I talk too much you give me dat black-jack."

They gave him the black-jack. After he had drunk and wiped his mouth on his sleeve, he went on:

"O my good-ma'm'selle, a leetle more to de wind. Ah, dat is right—trejous!... Dat fight it go like two bulls on a vergee—respe d'la compagnie. Mon onc' 'Lias he have been to Hengland, he have sing 'God save our greshus King'; so he t'ink a leetle—Ef he go to de French, likely dey will hang him. Mon onc' 'Lias, he is what you call patreeteesm. He say, 'Hengland, she is mine—trejous.' Efin, he sail straight for de Henglish ships. Dat is de greates' man, mon onc' 'Lias—respe d'la compagnie! he coum on de side which is not fighting. Ah bah, he tell dem dat he go to save de gentleman-of-war. He see a hofficier all bloodiness and he call hup: 'Es-tu gentiment?' he say. 'Gentiment,' say de hofficier; 'han' you?' 'Naicely, yank you!' mon onc' 'Lias he say. 'I will save you,' say mon onc' 'Lias—'I will save de ship of God save our greshus King.' De hofficier wipe de tears out of his face. 'De King will reward you, man alive,' he say. Mon onc' 'Lias he touch his breast and speak out. 'Mon hofficier, my reward is here—trejous. I will take you into de Ecrehoses.' 'Coum up and save de King's ships,' says de hofficier. 'I will take no reward,' say mon onc' 'Lias, 'but, for a leetle pourboire, you will give me de privator—eh?' 'Milles sacres'—say de hofficier, 'mines saeres—de privator!' he say, ver' surprise'. 'Man doux d'la vie—I am damned!' 'You are damned trulee, if you do not get into de Ecrehoses,' say mon onc' 'Lias—'A bi'tot, good-bye!' he say. De hofficier call down to him: 'Is dere nosing else you will take?' 'Nannin, do not tempt me,' say mon onc' 'Lias. 'I am not a gourman'. I will take de privator—dat is my hobby.' All de time de cannons grand—dey brow-brou! boum-boum!—what you call discomfortable. Time is de great t'ing, so de hofficier wipe de tears out of his face again. 'Coum up,' he say; 'de privator is yours.'

"Away dey go. You see dat spot where we coum to land, Ma'm'selle Landresse—where de shingle look white, de leetle green grass above? Dat is where mon onc' 'Lias he bring in de King's ship and de privator. Gatd'en'ale—it is a journee awful! He twist to de right, he shape to de left trough de teeth of de rocks—all safe—vera happee—to dis nice leetle bay of de Maitre Ile dey coum. De Frenchies dey grind dere teeth and spit de fire. But de Henglish laugh at demdey are safe. 'Frien' of my heart,' say de hofficier to mon onc' 'Lias, 'pilot of pilots,' he say, 'in de name of our greshus King I t'ank you—A bi'tot, good-bye!' he say. 'Tres-ba,' mon onc' 'Lias he say den, 'I will go to my privator.' 'You will go to de shore,' say de hofficier. 'You will wait on de shore till de captain and his men of de privator coum to you. When dey coum, de ship is yours—de privator is for you.' Mon onc' 'Lias he is like a child—he believe. He 'bout ship and go shore. Misery me, he sit on dat rocking-stone you see tipping on de wind. But if he wait until de men of de privator coum to him, he will wait till we see him sitting there now. Gache-a-penn, you say patriote? Mon onc' 'Lias he has de patreeteesm, and what happen? He save de ship of de greshus King God save—and dey eat up his hoysters! He get nosing. Gad'rabotin—respe d'la compagnie—if dere is a ship of de King coum to de Ecrehoses, and de hofficier say to me"—he tapped his breast—"'Jean Touzel, tak de ships of de King trough de rocks,'—ah bah, I would rememb' mon onc' 'Lias. I would say, 'A bi'tot-good-bye.'... Slowlee—slowlee! We are at de place. Bear wif de land, ma'm'selle! Steadee! As you go! V'la! hitch now, Maitre Ranulph."

The keel of the boat grated on the shingle.

The air of the morning, the sport of using the elements for one's pleasure, had given Guida an elfish sprightliness of spirits. Twenty times during Jean's recital she had laughed gaily, and never sat a laugh better on any one's countenance than on hers. Her teeth were strong, white, and regular; in themselves they gave off a sort of shining mirth.

At first the lugubrious wife of the happy Jean was inclined to resent Guida's gaiety as unseemly, for Jean's story sounded to her as serious statement of fact; which incapacity for humour probably accounted for Jean's occasional lapses from domestic grace. If Jean had said that he had met a periwinkle dancing a hornpipe with an oyster she would have muttered heavily "Think of that!" The most she could say to any one was: "I believe you, ma couzaine." Some time in her life her voice had dropped into that great well she called her body, and it came up only now and then like an echo. There never was anything quite so fat as she. She was found weeping one day on the veille because she was no longer able to get her shoulders out of the window to use the clothes-lines stretching to her neighbour's over the way. If she sat down in your presence, it was impossible to do aught but speculate as to whether she could get up alone. Yet she went abroad on the water a great deal with Jean. At first the neighbours gave out sinister suspicions as to Jean's intentions, for sea-going with your own wife was uncommon among the sailors of the coast. But at last these dark suggestions settled down into a belief that Jean took her chiefly for ballast; and thereafter she was familiarly called "Femme de Ballast."

Talking was no virtue in her eyes. What was going on in her mind no one ever knew. She was more phlegmatic than an Indian; but the tails of the sheep on the Town Hill did not better show the quarter of the wind than the changing colour of Aimable's face indicated Jean's coming or going. For

Mattresse Aimable had one eternal secret, an unwavering passion for Jean Touzel. If he patted her on the back on a day when the fishing was extra fine, her heart pumped so hard she had to sit down; if, passing her lonely bed of a morning, he shook her great toe to wake her, she blushed, and turned her face to the wall in placid happiness. She was so credulous and matter-of-fact that if Jean had told her she must die on the spot, she would have said "Think of that!" or "Je te crais," and died. If in the vague dusk of her brain the thought glimmered that she was ballast for Jean on sea and anchor on land, she still was content. For twenty years the massive, straight-limbed Jean had stood to her for all things since the heavens and the earth were created. Once, when she had burnt her hand in cooking supper for him, his arm made a trial of her girth, and he kissed her. The kiss was nearer her ear than her lips, but to her mind it was the most solemn proof of her connubial happiness and of Jean's devotion. She was a Catholic, unlike Jean and most people of her class in Jersey, and ever since that night he kissed her she had told an extra bead on her rosary and said another prayer.

These were the reasons why at first she was inclined to resent Guida's laughter. But when she saw that Maitre Ranulph and the curate and Jean himself laughed, she settled down to a grave content until they landed.

They had scarce reached the deserted chapel where their dinner was to be cooked by Maitresse Aimable, when Ranulph called them to note a vessel bearing in their direction.

"She's not a coasting craft," said Jean.

"She doesn't look like a merchant vessel," said Ranulph, eyeing her through his telescope. "Why, she's a warship!" he added.

Jean thought she was not, but Maitre Ranulph said "Pardi, I ought to know, Jean. Ship-building is my trade, to say nothing of guns—I wasn't two years in the artillery for nothing. See the low bowsprit and the high poop. She's bearing this way. She'll be Narcissus!" he said slowly.

That was Philip d'Avranche's ship.

Guida's face lighted, her heart beat faster. Ranulph turned on his heel.

"Where are you going, Ro?" Guida said, taking a step after him.

"On the other side, to my men and the wreck," he said, pointing.

Guida glanced once more towards the man-o'-war: and then, with mischief in her eye, turned towards Jean. "Suppose," she said to him archly, "suppose the ship should want to come in, of course you'd remember your onc' 'Lias, and say, 'A bi'tot, good-bye!'"

An evasive "Ah bah!" was the only reply Jean vouchsafed.

Ranulph joined his men at the wreck, and the Reverend Lorenzo Dow went about the Lord's business in the little lean-to of sail-cloth and ship's lumber which had been set up near to the toil of the carpenters. When the curate entered the but the sick man was in a doze. He turned his head from side to side restlessly and mumbled to himself. The curate, sitting on the ground beside the man, took from his pocket a book, and began writing in a strange, cramped hand. This book was his journal. When a youth he had been a stutterer, and had taken refuge from talk in writing, and the habit stayed even as his affliction grew less. The important events of the day or the week, the weather, the wind, the tides, were recorded, together with sundry meditations of the Reverend Lorenzo Dow. The pages were not large, and brevity was Mr. Dow's journalistic virtue. Beyond the diligent keeping of this record, he had no habits, certainly no precision, no remembrance, no system: the business of his life ended there. He had quietly vacated two curacies because there had been bitter complaints that the records of certain baptisms, marriages, and burials might only be found in the chequered journal of his life, sandwiched between fantastic reflections and remarks upon the rubric. The records had been exact enough, but the system was not canonical, and it rested too largely upon the personal ubiquity of the itinerary priest, and the safety of his journal—and of his life.

Guida, after the instincts of her nature, had at once sought the highest point on the rocky islet, and there she drank in the joy of sight and sound and feeling. She could see—so perfect was the day—the line marking the Minquiers far on the southern horizon, the dark and perfect green of the Jersey slopes, and the white flags of foam which beat against the Dirouilles and the far-off Paternosters, dissolving as they flew, their place taken by others, succeeding and succeeding, as a soldier steps into a gap in the line of battle. Something in these rocks, something in the Paternosters—perhaps their distance, perhaps their remoteness from all other rocks—fascinated her. As she looked at them, she suddenly felt a chill, a premonition, a half-spiritual, half-material telegraphy of the inanimate to the animate: not from off cold stone to sentient life; but from that atmosphere about the inanimate thing, where the life of man has spent itself and been dissolved, leaving— who can tell what? Something which speaks but yet has no sound.

The feeling which possessed Guida as she looked at the Paternosters was almost like blank fear. Yet physical fear she had never felt, not since that day when the battle raged in the Vier Marchi, and Philip d'Avranche had saved her from the destroying scimitar of the Turk. Now that scene all came back to her in a flash, as it were; and she saw again the dark snarling face of the Mussulman, the blue-and-white silk of his turban, the black and white of his waistcoat, the red of the long robe, and the glint of his uplifted sword.

Then in contrast, the warmth, brightness, and bravery on the face of the lad in blue and gold who struck aside the descending blade and caught her up in his arms; and she had nestled there—in those arms of Philip d'Avranche. She remembered how he had kissed her, and how she had kissed him—he a lad and she a little child—as he left her with her mother in the watchmaker's shop in the Vier Marchi that day.... And she had never seen him again until yesterday.

She looked from the rocks to the approaching frigate. Was it the Narcissus coming—coming to this very island? She recalled Philip—how gallant he was yesterday, how cool, with what an air of command! How light he had made of the riot! Ranulph's strength and courage she accepted as a matter of course, and was glad that he was brave, generous, and good; but the glamour of distance and mystery were around d'Avranche. Remembrance, like a comet, went circling through the firmament of eleven years, from the Vier Marchi to the Place du Vier Prison.

She watched the ship slowly bearing with the land. The Jack was flying from the mizzen. They were now taking in her topsails. She was so near that Guida could see the anchor a-cockbell, and the poop lanthorns. She could count the guns like long black horns shooting out from a rhinoceros hide: she could discern the figurehead lion snarling into the spritsail. Presently the ship came up to the wind and lay to. Then she signalled for a pilot, and Guida ran towards the ruined chapel, calling for Jean Touzel.

In spite of Jean's late protests as to piloting a "gentleman-of-war," this was one of the joyful moments of his life. He could not loosen his rowboat quick enough; he was away almost before you could have spoken his name. Excited as Guida was, she could not resist calling after him:

"'God save our greshus King! A bi'tot—goodbye!'"

# CHAPTER X

As Ranulph had surmised, the ship was the Narcissus, and its first lieutenant was Philip d'Avranche. The night before, orders had reached the vessel from the Admiralty that soundings were to be taken at the Ecrehos. The captain had at once made inquiries for a pilot, and Jean Touzel was commended to him. A messenger sent to Jean found that he had already gone to the Ecrehos. The captain had then set sail, and now, under Jean's skilful pilotage, the Narcissus twisted and crept through the teeth of the rocks at the entrance, and slowly into the cove, reefs on either side gaping and girding at her, her keel all but scraping the serrated granite beneath. She anchored, and boats put off to take soundings and explore the shores. Philip was rowed in by Jean Touzel.

Stepping out upon the beach of Mattre 'Ile, Philip slowly made his way over the shingle to the ruined chapel, in no good humour with himself or with the world, for exploring these barren rocks seemed a useless whim of the Admiralty, and he could not conceive of any incident rising from the monotony of duty to lighten the darkness of this very brilliant day. His was not the nature to enjoy the stony detail of his profession. Excitement and adventure were as the breath of life to him, and since he had played his little part at the Jersey battle in a bandbox eleven years before, he had touched hands with accidents of flood and field in many countries.

He had been wrecked on the island of Trinidad in a tornado, losing his captain and his ship; had seen active service in America and in India; won distinction off the coast of Arabia in an engagement with Spanish cruisers; and was now waiting for his papers as commander of a ship of his own, and fretted because the road of fame and promotion was so toilsome. Rumours of war with France had set his blood dancing a little, but for him most things were robbed of half their pleasure because they did not come at once.

This was a moody day with him, for he had looked to spend it differently. As he walked up the shingle his thoughts were hanging about a cottage in the Place du Vier Prison. He had hoped to loiter in a doorway there, and to empty his sailor's heart in well-practised admiration before the altar of village beauty. The sight of Guida's face the day before had given a poignant pulse to his emotions, unlike the broken rhythm of past comedies of sentiment and melodramas of passion. According to all logic of custom, the acuteness of yesterday's impression should have been followed up by today's attack; yet here he was, like another Robinson Crusoe, "kicking up the shingle of a cursed Patmos" —so he grumbled aloud. Patmos was not so wild a shot after all, for no sooner had he spoken the word than, looking up, he saw in the doorway of the ruined chapel the gracious figure of a girl: and a book of revelations was opened and begun.

At first he did not recognise Guida. There was only a picture before him which, by some fantastic transmission, merged into his reveries. What he saw was an ancient building—just such a humble pile of stone and rough mortar as one might see on some lone cliff of the AEgean or on abandoned isles of the equatorial sea. The gloom of a windowless vault was behind the girl, but the filtered sunshine of late September fell on her head. It brightened the white kerchief, and the bodice and skirt of a faint pink, throwing the face into a pleasing shadow where the hand curved over the forehead. She stood like some Diana of a ruined temple looking out into the staring day.

At once his pulses beat faster, for to him a woman was ever the fountain of adventure, and an unmanageable heart sent him headlong to the oasis where he might loiter at the spring of feminine vanity, or truth, or impenitent gaiety, as the case might be. In proportion as his spirits had sunk into sour reflection, they now shot up rocket-high at the sight of a girl's joyous pose of body and the colour and form of the picture she made. In him the shrewdness of a strong intelligence was mingled with wild impulse. In most, rashness would be the outcome of such a marriage of characteristics; but clear-sightedness, decision, and a little unscrupulousness had carried into success many daring actions of his life. This very quality of resolute daring saved him from disaster.

Impulse quickened his footsteps now. It quickened them to a run when the hand was dropped from the girl's forehead, and he saw again the face whose image and influence had banished sleep from his eyes the night before.

"Guida!" broke from his lips.

The man was transfigured. Brightness leaped into his look, and the greyness of his moody eye became as blue as the sea. The professional straightness of his figure relaxed into the elastic grace of an athlete. He was a pipe to be played on: an actor with the ambitious brain of a diplomatist; as weak as water, and as strong as steel; soft-hearted to foolishness or unyielding at will.

Now, if the devil had sent a wise imp to have watch and ward of this man and this maid, and report to him upon the meeting of their ways, the moment Philip took Guida's hand, and her eyes met his, monsieur the reporter of Hades might have clapped-to his book and gone back to his dark master with the message and the record: "The hour of Destiny is struck."

When the tide of life beats high in two mortals, and they meet in the moment of its apogee, when all the nature is sweeping on without command, guilelessly, yet thoughtlessly, the mere lilt of existence lulling to sleep wisdom and tried experience—speculation points all one way. Many indeed have been caught away by such a conjunction of tides, and they mostly pay the price.

But paying is part of the game of life: it is the joy of buying that we crave. Go down into the dark markets of the town. See the long, narrow, sordid streets lined with the cheap commodities of the poor. Mark how there is a sort of spangled gaiety, a reckless swing, a grinning exultation in the grimy, sordid caravanserai. The cheap colours of the shoddy open-air clothing-house, the blank faded green of the coster's cart; the dark bluish-red of the butcher's stall—they all take on a value not their own in the garish lights flaring down the markets of the dusk. Pause to the shrill music of the street musician, hear the tuneless voice of the grimy troubadour of the alley-ways; and then hark to the one note that commands them all—the call which lightens up faces sodden with base vices, eyes bleared with long looking into the dark caverns of crime:

"Buy—buy—buy—buy—buy!"

That is the tune the piper pipes. We would buy, and behold, we must pay. Then the lights go out, the voices stop, and only the dark tumultuous streets surround us, and the grime of life is ours again. Whereupon we go heavily to hard beds of despair, having eaten the cake we bought, and now must pay for unto Penalty, the dark inordinate creditor. And anon the morning comes, and then, at last, the evening when the triste bazaars open again, and the strong of heart and nerve move not from their doorways, but sit still in the dusk to watch the grim world go by. But mostly they hurry out to the bazaars once more, answering to the fevered call:

"Buy—buy—buy—buy—buy!"

And again they pay the price: and so on to the last foreclosure and the immitigable end.

One of the two standing in the door of the ruined chapel on the Ecrehos had the nature of those who buy but once and pay the price but once; the other was of those who keep open accounts in the markets of life. The one was the woman and the other was the man.

There was nothing conventional in their greeting. "You remembered me!" he said eagerly, in English, thinking of yesterday.

"I shouldn't deserve to be here if I had forgotten," she answered meaningly. "Perhaps you forget the sword of the Turk?" she added.

He laughed a little, his cheek flushed with pleasure. "I shouldn't deserve to be here if I remembered—in the way you mean," he answered.

Her face was full of pleasure. "The worst of it is," she said, "I never can pay my debt. I have owed it for eleven years, and if I should live to be ninety I should still owe it."

His heart was beating hard and he became daring. "So, thou shalt save my life," he said, speaking in French. "We shall be quits then, thou and I."

The familiar French thou startled her. To hide the instant's confusion she turned her head away, using a hand to gather in her hair, which the wind was lifting lightly.

"That wouldn't quite make us quits," she rejoined; "your life is important, mine isn't. You"—she nodded towards the Narcissus—"you command men."

"So dost thou," he answered, persisting in the endearing pronoun.

He meant it to be endearing. As he had sailed up and down the world, a hundred ports had offered him a hundred adventures, all light in the scales of purpose, but not all bad. He had gossiped and idled and coquetted with beauty before; but this was different, because the nature of the girl was different from all others he had met. It had mostly been lightly come and lightly go with himself, as with the women it had been easily won and easily loosed. Conscience had not smitten him hard, because beauty, as he had known it, though often fair and of good report, had bloomed for others before he came. But here was a nature fresh and unspoiled from the hand of the potter Life.

As her head slightly turned from him again, he involuntarily noticed the pulse beating in her neck, the rise and fall of her bosom. Life—here was life unpoisoned by one drop of ill thought or light experience.

"Thou dost command men too," he repeated.

She stepped forward a little from the doorway and beyond him, answering back at him:

"Oh, no, I only knit, and keep a garden, and command a little home, that's all.... Won't you let me show you the island?" she added quickly, pointing to a hillock beyond, and moving towards it. He followed, speaking over her shoulder:

"That's what you seem to do," he answered, "not what you do." Then he added rhetorically: "I've seen a man polishing the buckle of his shoe, and he was planning to take a city or manoeuvre a fleet."

She noticed that he had dropped the thou, and, much as its use had embarrassed her, the gap left when the boldness was withdrawn became filled with regret, for, though no one had dared to say it to her before, somehow it seemed not rude on Philip's lips. Philip? Yes, Philip she had called him in her childhood, and the name had been carried on into her girlhood—he had always been Philip to her.

"No, girls don't think like that, and they don't do big things," she replied. "When I polish the pans"—she laughed—"and when I scour my buckles, I just think of pans and buckles." She tossed up her fingers lightly, with a perfect charm of archness.

He was very close to her now. "But girls have dreams, they have memories."

"If women hadn't memory," she answered, "they wouldn't have much, would they? We can't take cities and manoeuvre fleets." She laughed a little ironically. "I wonder that we think at all or have anything to think about, except the kitchen and the garden, and baking and scouring and spinning"—she paused slightly, her voice lowered a little—"and the sea, and the work that men do round us.... Do you ever go into a market?" she added suddenly.

Somehow she could talk easily and naturally to him. There had been no leading up to confidence. She felt a sudden impulse to tell him all her thoughts. To know things, to understand, was a passion with her. It seemed to obliterate in her all that was conventional, it removed her far from sensitive egotism. Already she had begun "to take notice" in the world, and that is like being born again. As it grows, life ceases to be cliche; and when the taking notice is supreme we call it genius; and genius is simple and believing: it has no pride, it is naive, it is childlike.

Philip seemed to wear no mark of convention, and Guida spoke her thoughts freely to him. "To go into a market seems to me so wonderful," she continued. "There are the cattle, the fruits, the vegetables, the flowers, the fish, the wood; the linen from the loom, the clothes that women's fingers have knitted. But it isn't just those things that you see, it's all that's behind them—the houses, the fields, and the boats at sea, and the men and women working and working, and sleeping and eating, and breaking their hearts with misery, and wondering what is to be the end of it all; yet praying a little, it may be, and dreaming a little—perhaps a very little." She sighed, and continued: "That's as far as I get with thinking. What else can one do in this little island? Why, on the globe Maitre Damian has at St. Aubin's, Jersey is no bigger than the head of a pin. And what should one think of here?"

Her eyes were on the sea. Its mystery was in them, the distance, the ebb and flow, the light of wonder and of adventure too. "You—you've been everywhere," she went on. "Do you remember you sent me once from Malta a tiny silver cross? That was years ago, soon after the Battle of Jersey, when I was a little bit of a girl. Well, after I got big enough I used to find Malta and other places on Maitre Damian's globe. I've lived always there, on that spot"—she pointed towards Jersey—"on that spot one could walk round in a day. What do I know! You've been everywhere—everywhere. When you look back you've got a thousand pictures in your mind. You've seen great cities, temples, palaces, great armies, fleets; you've done things: you've fought and you've commanded, though you're so young, and you've learned about men and about many countries. Look at what you know, and then, if you only think, you'll laugh at what I know."

For a moment he was puzzled what to answer. The revelation of the girl's nature had come so quickly upon him. He had looked for freshness, sweetness, intelligence, and warmth of temperament, but it seemed to him that here were flashes of power. Yet she was only seventeen. She had been taught to see things with her own eyes and not another's, and she spoke of them as she saw them; that was all. Yet never but to her mother had Guida said so much to any human being as within these past few moments to Philip d'Avranche.

The conditions were almost maliciously favourable, and d'Avranche was simple and easy as a boy, with his sailor's bonhomie and his naturally facile spirit. A fateful adaptability was his greatest weapon in life, and his greatest danger. He saw that Guida herself was unconscious of the revelation she was making, and he showed no surprise, but he caught the note of her simplicity, and responded in kind. He flattered her deftly—not that she was pressed unduly, he was too wise for that. He took her seriously; and this was not all dissimulation, for her every word had glamour, and he now exalted her intellect unduly. He had never met girl or woman who talked just as she did; and straightway, with the wild eloquence of his nature, he thought he had discovered a new heaven and a new earth. A spell was upon him. He knew what he wanted when he saw it. He had always made up his mind suddenly, always acted on the intelligent impulse of the moment. He felt things, he did not study them—it was almost a woman's instinct. He came by a leap to the goal of purpose, not by the toilsome steps of reason. On the instant his headlong spirit declared his purpose: this was the one being for him in all the world: at this altar he would light a lamp of devotion, and keep it burning forever.

"This is my day," he said to himself. "I always knew that love would come down on me like a storm." Then, aloud, he said to her: "I wish I knew what you know; but I can't, because my mind is different, my life has been different. When you go into the world and see a great deal, and loosen a little the strings of your principles, and watch how sins and virtues contradict themselves, you see things after a while in a kind of mist. But you, Guida, you see them clearly because your heart is clear. You never make a mistake, you are always right because your mind is right."

She interrupted him, a little troubled and a good deal amazed: "Oh, you mustn't, mustn't speak like that. It's not so. How can one see and learn unless one sees and knows the world? Surely one can't think wisely if one doesn't see widely?"

He changed his tactics instantly. The world—that was the thing? Well, then, she should see the world, through him, with him.

"Yes, yes, you're right," he answered. "You can't know things unless you see widely. You must see the world. This island, what is it? I was born here, don't I know! It's a foothold in the world, but it's no more; it's not afield to walk in, why, it's not even a garden. No, it's the little patch of green we play in in front of a house, behind the railings, before we go out into the world and learn how to live."

They had now reached the highest point on the island, where a flagstaff stood. Guida was looking far beyond Jersey to the horizon line. There was little haze, the sky was inviolably blue. Far off against the horizon lay the low black rocks of the Minquiers. They seemed to her, on the instant, like stepping-stones. Beyond would be other stepping-stones, and others and others still again, and they would all mark the way and lead to what Philip called the world. The world! She felt a sudden little twist of regret at her heart. Here she was like a cow grazing within the circle of its tether—like a lax caterpillar on its blade of grass. Yet it had all seemed so good to her in the past; broken only by little bursts of wonder and wish concerning that outside world.

"Do we ever learn how to live?" she asked. "Don't we just go on from one thing to another, picking our way, but never knowing quite what to do, because we don't know what's ahead? I believe we never do learn how to live," she added, half-smiling, yet a little pensive too; "but I am so very ignorant, and—"

She stopped, for suddenly it flashed upon her: here she was baring her childish heart—he would think it childish, she was sure he would— everything she thought, to a man she had never known till to-day. No, no, she was wrong; she had known him, but it was only as Philip, the boy who had saved her life. And the Philip of her memory was only a picture, not a being; something to think about, not something to speak with, to whom she might show her heart. She flushed hotly and turned her shoulder on him. Her eyes followed a lizard creeping up the stones. As long as she lived she remembered that lizard, its colour changing in the sun. She remembered the hot stones, and how warm the flag-staff was when she stretched out her hand to it mechanically. But the swift, noiseless lizard running in and out of the stones, it was ever afterwards like a coat-of-arms upon the shield of her life.

Philip came close to her. At first he spoke over her shoulder, then he faced her. His words forced her eyes up to his, and he held them.

"Yes, yes, we learn how to live," he said. "It's only when we travel alone that we don't see before us. I will teach you how to live—we will learn the way together! Guida! Guida!"—he reached out his hands towards her—"don't start so! Listen to me. I feel for you what I have felt for no other being in all my life. It came upon me yesterday when I saw you in the window at the Vier Prison. I didn't understand it. All night I walked the deck thinking of you. To-day as soon as I saw your face, as soon as I touched your hand, I knew what it was, and—"

He attempted to take her hand now. "Oh, no, no!" she exclaimed, and drew back as if terrified.

"You need not fear me," he burst out. "For now I know that I have but two things to live for: for my work"—he pointed to the Narcissus—"and for you. You are frightened of me? Why, I want to have the right to protect you, to drive away all fear from your life. You shall be the garden and I shall be the wall; you the nest and I the rock; you the breath of life and I the body that breathes it. Guida, my Guida, I love you!"

She drew back, leaning against the stones, her eyes riveted upon his, and she spoke scarcely above a whisper.

"It is not true—it is not true. You've known me only for one day—only for one hour. How can you say it!" There was a tumult in her breast; her eyes shone and glistened; wonder, embarrassed yet happy wonder, looked at him from her face, which was touched with an appealing, as of the heart that dares not believe and yet must believe or suffer.

"It is madness," she added. "It is not true—how can it be true!"

Yet it all had the look of reality—the voice had the right ring, the face had truth, the bearing was gallant; the force and power of the man overwhelmed her.

She reached out her hand tremblingly as though to push him back. "It cannot be true," she said. "To think—in one day!"

"It is true," he answered, "true as that I stand here. One day—it is not one day. I knew you years ago. The seed was sown then, the flower springs up to-day, that is all. You think I can't know that it is love I feel for you? It is admiration; it is faith; it is desire too; but it is love. When you see a flower in a garden, do you not know at once if you like it or no? Don't you know the moment you look on a landscape, on a splendid building, whether it is beautiful to you? If, then, with these things one knows—these that haven't any speech, no life like yours or mine—how much more when it is a girl with a face like yours, when it is a mind noble like yours, when it is a touch that thrills, and a voice that drowns the heart in music! Guida, believe that I speak the truth. I know, I swear, that you are the one passion, the one love of my life. All others would be as nothing, so long as you live, and I live to look upon you, to be beside you."

"Beside me!" she broke in, with an incredulous irony fain to be contradicted, "a girl in a village, poor, knowing nothing, seeing no farther"— she looked out towards Jersey—"seeing no farther than the little cottage in the little country where I was born."

"But you shall see more," he said, "you shall see all, feel all, if you will but listen to me. Don't deny me what is life and breathing and hope to me. I'll show you the world; I'll take you where you may see and know. We will learn it all together. I shall succeed in life. I shall go far. I've needed one thing to make me do my best for some one's sake beside my own; you will make me do it for your sake. Your ancestors were great people in France; and you know that mine, centuries ago, were great also—that the d'Avranches were a noble family in France. You and I will win our place as high as the best of them. In this war that's coming between England and France is my chance. Nelson said to me the other day—you have heard of him, of young Captain Nelson, the man they're pointing to in the fleet as the one man of them all?—he said to me: 'We shall have our chance now, d'Avranche.' And we shall. I have wanted it till to-day for my own selfish ambition—now I want it for you. When I landed on this islet a half-hour ago, I hated it, I hated my ship, I hated my duty, I hated everything, because I wanted to go where you were, to be with you. It was Destiny that brought us both to this place at one moment. You can't escape Destiny. It was to be that I should love you, Guida."

He reached out to take her hands, but she put them behind her against the stones, and drew back. The lizard suddenly shot out from a hole and crossed over her fingers. She started, shivered at the cold touch, and caught the hand away. A sense of foreboding awaked in her, and her eyes followed the lizard's swift travel with a strange fascination. But she lifted them to Philip's, and the fear and premonition passed.

"Oh, my brain is in a whirl!" she said. "I do not understand. I know so little. No one has ever spoken to me as you have done. You would not dare"—she leaned forward a little, looking into his face with that unwavering gaze which was the best sign of her straight-forward mind—"you would not dare to deceive—you would not dare. I have—no mother," she added with simple pathos.

The moisture came into his eyes. He must have been stone not to be touched by the appealing, by the tender inquisition, of that look.

"Guida," he said impetuously, "if I deceive you, may every fruit of life turn to dust and ashes in my mouth! If ever I deceive you, may I die a black, dishonourable death, abandoned and alone! I should deserve that if I deceived you, Guida."

For the first time since he had spoken she smiled, yet her eyes filled with tears too.

"You will let me tell you that I love you, Guida—it is all I ask now: that you will listen to me?"

She sighed, but did not answer. She kept looking at him, looking as though she would read his inmost soul. Her face was very young, though the eyes were so wise in their simplicity.

"You will give me my chance—you will listen to me, Guida, and try to understand—and be glad?" he asked, leaning closer to her and holding out his hands.

She drew herself up slightly as with an air of relief and resolve. She put a hand in his.

"I will try to understand—and be glad," she answered.

"Won't you call me Philip?" he said.

The same slight, mischievous smile crossed her lips now as eleven years ago in the Rue d'Egypte, and recalling that moment, she replied:

"Yes, sir—Philip!"

At that instant the figure of a man appeared on the shingle beneath, looking up towards them. They did not see him. Guida's hand was still in Philip's.

The man looked at them for a moment, then started and turned away. It was Ranulph Delagarde.

They heard his feet upon the shingle now. They turned and looked; and Guida withdrew her hand.

# CHAPTER XI

There are moments when a kind of curtain seems dropped over the brain, covering it, smothering it, while yet the body and its nerves are tingling with sensation. It is like the fire-curtain of a theatre let down between the stage and the audience, a merciful intervention between the mind and the disaster which would consume it.

As the years had gone on Maitre Ranulph's nature had grown more powerful, and his outdoor occupation had enlarged and steadied his physical forces. His trouble now was in proportion to the force of his character. The sight of Guida and Philip hand in hand, the tender attitude, the light in their faces, was overwhelming and unaccountable. Yesterday these two were strangers—to-day it was plain to be seen they were lovers, and lovers who had reached a point of confidence and revelation. Nothing in the situation tallied with Ranulph's ideas of Guida and his knowledge of life. He had, as one might say, been eye to eye with this girl for fifteen years: he had told his love for her in a thousand little ways, as the ant builds its heap to a pyramid that becomes a thousand times greater than itself. He had followed her footsteps, he had fetched and carried, he had served afar off, he had ministered within the gates. He had, unknown to her, watched like the keeper of the house over all who came and went, neither envious nor over-zealous, neither intrusive nor neglectful; leaving here a word and there an act to prove himself, above all, the friend whom she could trust, and, in all, the lover whom she might wake to know and reward. He had waited with patience, hoping stubbornly that she might come to put her hand in his one day.

Long ago he would have left the island to widen his knowledge, earn experience in his craft, or follow a career in the army—he had been an expert gunner when he served in the artillery four years ago—and hammer out fame upon the anvils of fortune in England or in France; but he had stayed here that he might be near her. His love had been simple, it had been direct, and wise in its consistent reserve. He had been self-obliterating. His love desired only to make her happy: most lovers desire that they themselves shall be made happy. Because of the crime his father committed years ago—because of the shame of that hidden crime—he had tried the more to make himself a good citizen, and had formed the modest ambition of making one human being happy. Always keeping this near him in past years, a supreme cheerfulness of heart had welled up out of his early sufferings and his innate honesty. Hope had beckoned him on from year to year, until it seemed at last that the time had almost come when he might speak, might tell her all—his father's crime and the manner of his father's death; of his own devoted purpose in trying to expiate that crime by his own uprightness; and of his love for her.

Now, all in a minute, his horizon was blackened. This adventurous gallant, this squire of dames, had done in a day what he had worked, step by step, to do through all these years. This skipping seafarer, with his powder and lace, his cocked hat and gold-handled sword, had whistled at the gates which he had guarded and by which he had prayed, and all in a minute every defence had been thrown down, and Guida—his own Guida—had welcomed the invader with shameless eagerness.

He crossed the islet slowly. It seemed to him—and for a moment it was the only thing of which he was conscious—that the heels of his boots shrieked in the shingle, and with every step he was raising an immense weight. He paused behind the chapel. After a little the smother lifted slowly from his brain.

"I'll believe in her still," he said aloud. "It's all his cursed tongue. As a boy he could make every other boy do what he wanted because his tongue knows how to twist words. She's been used to honest people; he's talked a new language to her—tricks caught in his travels. But she shall know the truth. She shall find out what sort of a man he is. I'll make her see under his pretty foolings."

He turned, and leaned against the wall of the chapel. "Guida, Guida," he said, speaking as if she were there before him, "you won't—you won't go to him, and spoil your life, and mine too. Guida, ma couzaine, you'll stay here, in the land of your birth. You'll make your home here—here with me, ma chere couzaine. Ah, but then you shall be my wife in spite of him, in spite of a thousand Philip d'Avranches!"

He drew himself up firmly, for a great resolve was made. His path was clear. It was a fair fight, he thought; the odds were not so much against him after all, for his birth was as good as Philip d'Avranche's, his energy was greater, and he was as capable and as clever in his own way.

He walked quickly down the shingle towards the wreck on the other side of the islet. As he passed the hut where the sick man lay, he heard a querulous voice. It was not that of the Reverend Lorenzo Dow.

Where had he heard that voice before? A shiver of fear ran through him. Every sense and emotion in him was arrested. His life seemed to reel backward. Curtain after curtain of the past unfolded.

He hurried to the door of the hut and looked in.

A man with long white hair and straggling grey beard turned to him a haggard face, on which were written suffering, outlawry, and evil.

"Great God—my father!" Ranulph said.

He drew back slowly like a man who gazes upon some horrible fascinating thing, and then turned heavily towards the sea, his face set, his senses paralysed.

"My father not dead! My father—the traitor!" he groaned.

# · CHAPTER XII

Philip d'Avranche sauntered slowly through the Vier Marchi, nodding right and left to people who greeted him. It was Saturday and market day in Jersey. The square was crowded with people. All was a cheerful babel; there was movement, colour everywhere. Here were the high and the humble, hardi vlon and hardi biaou—the ugly and the beautiful, the dwarfed and the tall, the dandy and the dowdy, the miser and the spendthrift; young ladies gay in silks, laces, and scarfs from Spain, and gentlemen with powdered wigs from Paris; sailors with red tunics from the Mediterranean, and fishermen with blue and purple blouses from Brazil; man-o'-war's-men with Greek petticoats, Turkish fezzes, and Portuguese espadras. Jersey housewives, in bedgones and white caps, with molleton dresses rolled up to the knees, pushed their way through the crowd, jars of black butter, or jugs of cinnamon brandy on their heads. From La Pyramide—the hospitable base of the statue of King George II—fishwives called the merits of their conger-eels and ormers; and the clatter of a thousand sabots made the Vier Marchi sound like a ship-builder's yard.

In this square Philip had loitered and played as a child. Down there, leaning against a pillar of the Corn Market piazza was Elie Mattingley, the grizzly-haired seller of foreign silks and droll odds and ends, who had given him a silver flageolet when he was a little lad. There were the same swaggering manners, the big gold rings in his ears; there was the same red sash about the waist, the loose unbuttoned shirt, the truculent knifebelt; there were the same keen brown eyes looking you through and through, and the mouth with a middle tooth in both jaws gone. Elie Mattingley, pirate, smuggler, and sometime master of a privateer, had had dealings with people high and low in the island, and they had not always, nor often, been conducted in the open Vier Marchi.

Fifteen years ago he used to have his little daughter Carterette always beside him when he sold his wares. Philip wondered what had become of her. He glanced round.... Ah, there she was, not far from her father, over in front of the guard-house, selling, at a little counter with a canopy of yellow silk (brought by her father from that distant land called Piracy), mogues of hot soupe a la graisse, simnels, curds, coffee, and Jersey wonders, which last she made on the spot by dipping the little rings of dough in a bashin of lard on a charcoal fire at her side.

Carterette was short and spare, with soft yet snapping eyes as black as night—or her hair; with a warm, dusky skin, a tongue which clattered pleasantly, and very often wisely. She had a hand as small and plump as a baby's, and a pretty foot which, to the disgust of some mothers and maidens of greater degree, was encased in a red French slipper, instead of the wooden sabot stuffed with straw, while her ankles were nicely dressed in soft black stockings, in place of the woolen native hose, as became her station.

Philip watched Carterette now for a moment, a dozen laughing memories coming back to him; for he had teased her and played with her when she was a child, had even called her his little sweetheart. Looking at her he wondered what her fate would be: To marry one of these fishermen or carters? No, she would look beyond that. Perhaps it would be one of those adventurers in bearskin cap and buckskin vest, home from Gaspe, where they had toiled in the great fisheries, some as common fishermen, some as mates and maybe one or two as masters. No, she would look beyond that. Perhaps she would be carried off by one of those well-to-do, black-bearded young farmers in the red knitted queminzolle, blue breeches, and black cocked hat, with his kegs of cider and bunches of parsley.

That was more likely, for among the people there was every prejudice in her favour. She was Jersey born, her father was reputed to have laid by a goodly sum of money—not all got in this Vier Marchi; and that he was a smuggler and pirate roused a sentiment in their bosoms nearer to envy than aught else. Go away naked and come back clothed, empty and come back filled, simple and come back with a wink of knowledge, penniless and come back with the price of numerous vergees of land, and you might answer the island catechism without fear. Be lambs in Jersey, but harry the rest of the world with a lion's tooth, was the eleventh commandment in the Vier Marchi.

Yes, thought Philip idly now, as he left the square, the girl would probably marry a rich farmer, and when he came again he should find her stout of body, and maybe shrewish of face, crying up the virtues of her black butter and her knitted stockings, having made the yellow silk canopy above her there into a gorgeous quilt for the nuptial bed.

Yet the young farmers who hovered near her now, buying a glass of cider or a mogue of soup, received but scant notice. She laughed with them, treated them lightly, and went about her business again with a toss of the head. Not once did she show a moment's real interest, not until a fine upstanding fellow came round the corner from the Rue des Vignes, and passed her booth.

She was dipping a doughnut into the boiling lard, but she paused with it suspended. The little dark face took on a warm glow, the eyes glistened.

"Maitre Ranulph!" called the girl softly. Then as the tall fellow turned to her and lifted his cap she added briskly: "Where away so fast with face hard as hatchet?"

"Garcon Cart'rette!" he said abstractedly—he had always called her that.

He was about to move on. She frowned in vexation, yet she saw that he was pale and heavy-eyed, and she beckoned him to come to her.

"What's gone wrong, big wood-worm?" she said, eyeing him closely, and striving anxiously to read his face. He looked at her sharply, but the softness in her black eyes somehow reassured him, and he said quite kindly:

"Nannin, 'tite garcon, nothing's matter."

"I thought you'd be blithe as a sparrow with your father back from the grave!" Then as Ranulph's face seemed to darken, she added: "He's not worse—he's not worse?"

"No, no, he's well enough now," he said, forcing a smile.

She was not satisfied, but she went on talking, intent to find the cause of his abstraction. "Only to think," she said—"only to think that he wasn't killed at all at the Battle of Jersey, and was a prisoner in France, and comes back here—and we all thought him dead, didn't we?"

"I left him for dead that morning on the Grouville road," he answered. Then, as if with a great effort, and after the manner of one who has learned a part, he went on: "As the French ran away mad, paw of one on tail of other, they found him trying to drag himself along. They nabbed him, and carried him aboard their boats to pilot them out from the Rocque Platte, and over to France. Then because they hadn't gobbled us up here, what did the French Gover'ment do? They clapped a lot of 'em in irons and sent 'em away to South America, and my father with 'em. That's why we heard neither click nor clack of him all this time. He broke free a year ago. Then he fell sick. When he got well he set sail for Jersey, was wrecked off the Ecrehos, and everybody knows the rest. Diantre, he's had a hard time!"

The girl had listened intently. She had heard all these things in flying rumours, and she had believed the rumours; but now that Maitre Ranulph told her—Ranulph, whose word she would have taken quicker than the oath of a Jurat—she doubted. With the doubt her face flushed as though she herself had been caught in a lie, had done a mean thing. Somehow her heart was aching for him, she knew not why.

All this time she had held the doughnut poised; she seemed to have forgotten her work. Suddenly the wooden fork holding the cake was taken from her fingers by the daft Dormy Jamais who had crept near.

"Des monz a fou," said he, "to spoil good eating so! What says fishing-man: When sails flap, owner may whistle for cargo. Tut, tut, goose Carterette!"

Carterette took no note, but said to Ranulph:

"Of course he had to pilot the Frenchmen back, or they'd have killed him, and it'd done no good to refuse. He was the first man that fought the French on the day of the battle, wasn't he? I've always heard that." Unconsciously she was building up a defence for Olivier Delagarde. She was, as it were, anticipating insinuation from other quarters. She was playing Ranulph's game, because she instinctively felt that behind this story there was gloom in his mind and mystery in the tale itself. She noticed too that he shrank from her words. She was not very quick of intellect, so she had to feel her way fumblingly. She must have time to think, but she said tentatively:

"I suppose it's no secret? I can tell any one at all what happened to your father?" she asked.

"Oh so—sure so!" he said rather eagerly. "Tell every one about it. He doesn't mind."

Maitre Ranulph deceived but badly. Bold and convincing in all honest things, he was, as yet, unconvincing in this grave deception. All these years he had kept silence, enduring what he thought a buried shame; but that shame had risen from the dead, a living agony. His father had betrayed the island to the French: if the truth were known to-day they would hang him for a traitor on the Mont es Pendus. No mercy and scant shrift would be shown him.

Whatever came, he must drink this bitter cup to the dregs. He could never betray his own father. He must consume with inward disgust while Olivier Delagarde shamelessly babbled his monstrous lies to all who would listen. And he must tell these lies too, conceal, deceive, and live in hourly fear of discovery. He must sit opposite his father day by day at table, talk with him, care for him, shrinking inwardly at every knock at the door lest it should be an officer come to carry the pitiful traitor off to prison.

And, more than all, he must give up for ever the thought of Guida. Here was the acid that ate home, the black hopelessness, the machine of fate clamping his heart. Never again could he rise in the morning with a song on his lips; never again his happy meditations go lilting with the clanging blows of the adze and the singing of the saws.

All these things had vanished when he looked into a tent-door on the Ecrehos. Now, in spite of himself, whenever he thought upon Guida's face, this other fateful figure, this Medusan head of a traitor, shot in between.

Since his return his father had not been strong enough to go abroad; but to-day he meant to walk to the Vier Marchi. At first Ranulph had decided to go as usual to his ship-yard at St. Aubin's, but at last in anxious fear he too had come to the Vier Marchi. There was a horrible fascination in being where his father was, in listening to his falsehoods, in watching the turns and twists of his gross hypocrisies.

But yet at times he was moved by a strange pity, for Olivier Delagarde was, in truth, far older than his years: a thin, shuffling, pallid invalid, with a face of mingled sanctity and viciousness. If the old man lied, and had not been in prison all these years, he must have had misery far worse, for neither vice nor poverty alone could so shatter a human being. The son's pity seemed to look down from a great height upon the contemptible figure with the beautiful white hair and the abominable mouth. This compassion kept him from becoming hard, but it would also preserve him to hourly sacrifice—Prometheus chained to his rock. In the short fortnight that had gone since the day upon the Ecrehos, he had changed as much as do most people in ten years. Since then he had seen neither Philip nor Guida.

To Carterette he seemed not the man she had known. With her woman's instinct she knew that he loved Guida, but she also knew that nothing which might have happened between them could have brought this look of shame and shrinking into his face. As these thoughts flashed through her mind her heart grew warmer. Suppose Ranulph was in some trouble—well, now might be her great chance. She might show him that he could not live without her friendship, and then perhaps, by-and-bye, that he could not live without her love.

Ranulph was about to move on. She stopped him. "When you need me, Maitre Ranulph, you know where to find me," she said scarce above a whisper. He looked at her sharply, almost fiercely, but again the tenderness of her eyes, the directness of her gaze, convinced him. She might be, as she was, variable with other people; with himself she was invincibly straightforward.

"P'raps you don't trust me?" she added, for she read his changing expression.

"I'd trust you quick enough," he said.

"Then do it now—you're having some bad trouble," she rejoined.

He leaned over her stall and said to her steadily and with a little moroseness:

"See you, ma garche, if I was in trouble I'd bear it by myself. I'd ask no one to help me. I'm a man, and I can stand alone. Don't go telling folks I look as if I was in trouble. I'm going to launch to-morrow the biggest ship ever sent from a Jersey building yard—that doesn't look like trouble, does it? Turn about is fair play, garcon Cart'rette: so when you're in trouble come to me. You're not a man, and it's a man's place to help a woman, all the more when she's a fine and good little stand-by like you."

He forced a smile, turned upon his heel, and threaded his way through the square, keeping a look-out for his father. This he could do easily, for he was the tallest man in the Vier Marchi by at least three inches.

Carterette, oblivious of all else, stood gazing after him. She was only recalled to herself by Dormy Jamais. He was diligently cooking her Jersey wonders, now and then turning his eyes up at her—eyes which were like spots of greyish, yellowish light in a face of putty and flour; without eyelashes, without eyebrows, a little like a fish's, something like a monkey's. They were never still. They were set in the face like little round glow worms in a mould of clay. They burned on night and day—no man had ever seen Dormy Jamais asleep.

Carterette did not resent his officiousness. He had a kind of kennel in her father's boat-house, and he was devoted to her. More than all else, Dormy Jamaas was clean. His clothes were mostly rags, but they were comely, compact rags. When he washed them no one seemed to know, but no languid young gentleman lounging where the sun was warmest in the Vier Marchi was better laundered.

As Carterette turned round to him he was twirling a cake on the wooden fork, and trolling:

"*Caderoussel he has a coat,*
*All lined with paper brown;*
*And only when it freezes hard*
*He wears it in the town.*
*What do you think of Caderoussel?*
*Ah, then, but list to me:*
*Caderoussel is a bon e'fant—* "

"Come, come, dirty-fingers," she said. "Leave my work alone, and stop your chatter."

The daft one held up his fingers, but to do so had to thrust a cake into his mouth.

"They're as clean as a ha'pendy," he said, mumbling through the cake. Then he emptied his mouth of it, and was about to place it with the others.

"Black beganne," she cried; "how dare you! V'la—into your pocket with it!"

He did as he was bid, humming to himself again:

"M'sieu' de la Palisse is dead,

Dead of a maladie;

Quart' of an hour before his death

He could breathe like you and me!

Ah bah, the poor M'sieu'

De la Palisse is dead!"

"Shut up! Man doux d'la vie, you chatter like a monkey!"

"That poor Maitre Ranulph," said Dormy, "once he was lively as a basket of mice; but now—"

"Well, now, achocre?" she said irritably, stamping her foot.

"Now the cat's out of the bag—oui-gia!"

"You're as cunning as a Norman—you've got things in your noddee!" she cried with angry impatience.

He nodded, grinning. "As thick as haws," he answered.

She heard behind her a laugh of foolish good-nature, which made her angry too, for it seemed to be making fun of her. She wheeled to see M. Savary dit Detricand leaning with both elbows on the little counter, his chin in his hand, grinning provokingly,

"Oh, it's you!" she said snappishly; "I hope you're pleased."

"Don't be cross," he answered, his head swinging unsteadily. "I wasn't laughing at you, heaven-born Jersienne. I wasn't, 'pon honour! I was laughing at a thing I saw five minutes ago." He nodded in gurgling enjoyment now. "You mustn't mind me, seraphine," he added, "I'd a hot night, and I'm warm as a thrush now. But I saw a thing five minutes ago!" — he rolled on the stall. "'Sh!" he added in a loud mock whisper, "here he comes now. Milles diables, but here's a tongue for you, and here's a royal gentleman speaking truth like a travelling dentist!"

Carterette followed his gesture and saw coming out of the Route es Couochons, where the brave Peirson issued to his death eleven years before, Maitre Ranulph's father.

He walked with the air of a man courting observation. He imagined himself a hero; he had told his lie so many times now that he almost believed it himself.

He was soon surrounded. Disliked when he lived in Jersey before the invasion years ago, that seemed forgotten now; for word had gone abroad that he was a patriot raised from the dead, an honour to his country. Many pressed forward to shake hands with him.

"Help of heaven, is that you, m'sieu'?" asked one. "You owed me five chelins, but I wiped it out, O my good!" cried another generously.

"Shaken," cried a tall tarter holding out his hand. He had lived in England, and now easily made English verbs into French.

One after another called on him to tell his story; some tried to hurry him to La Pyramide, but others placed a cider-keg near, and almost lifted him on to it.

"Go on, go on, tell us the story," they cried. "To the devil with the Frenchies!"

"Here—here's a dish of Adam's ale," cried an old woman, handing him a bowl of water.

They cheered him lustily. The pallor of his face changed to a warmth. He had the fatuousness of those who deceive with impunity. With confidence he unreeled the dark line out to the end. When he had told his story, still hungry for applause, he repeated the account of how the tatterdemalion brigade of Frenchmen came down upon him out of the night, and how he should have killed Rullecour himself had it not been for an officer who struck him down from behind.

During the recital Ranulph had drawn near. He watched the enthusiasm with which the crowd received every little detail of the egregious history. Everybody believed the old man, who was safe, no matter what happened to himself, Ranulph Delagarde, ex-artilleryman, ship-builder—and son of a criminal. At any rate the worst was over now, the first public statement of the lifelong lie. He drew a sigh of relief and misery in one. At that instant he caught sight of the flushed face of Detricand, who broke into a laugh of tipsy mirth when Olivier Delagarde told how the French officer had stricken him down as he was about finishing off Rullecour.

All at once the whole thing rushed upon Ranulph. What a fool he had been! He had met this officer of Rullecour's these ten years past, and never once had the Frenchman, by so much as a hint, suggested that he knew the truth about his father. Here and now the contemptuous mirth upon the Frenchman's face told the whole story. The danger and horror of the situation descended on him. Instantly he started towards Detricand.

At that moment his father caught sight of Detricand also, saw the laugh, the sneer, and recognised him. Halting short in his speech he turned pale and trembled, staring as at a ghost. He had never counted on this. His breath almost stopped as he saw Ranulph approach Detricand.

Now the end was come. His fabric of lies would be torn down; he would be tried and hanged on the Mont es Pendus, or even be torn to pieces by this crowd. Yet he could not have moved a foot from where he was if he had been given a million pounds.

The sight of Ranulph's face revealed to Detricand the true meaning of this farce and how easily it might become a tragedy. He read the story of the son's torture, of his sacrifice; and his decision was instantly made: he would befriend him. Looking straight into his eyes, his own said he had resolved to know nothing whatever about this criminal on the cider-cask. The two men telegraphed to each other a perfect understanding, and then Detricand turned on his heel, and walked away into the crowd.

The sudden change in the old man's appearance had not been lost on the spectators, but they set it down to weakness or a sudden sickness. One ran for a glass of brandy, another for cider, and an old woman handed up to him a mogue of cinnamon drops.

The old man tremblingly drank the brandy. When he looked again Detricand had disappeared. A dark, sinister expression crossed his face, an evil thought pulled down the corners of his mouth as he stepped from the cask. His son went to him and taking his arm, said: "Come, you've done enough for to-day."

The old man made no reply, but submissively walked away into the Coin & Anes. Once however he turned and looked the way Detricand had gone, muttering.

The peasants cheered him as he passed. Presently, free of the crowd and entering the Rue d'Egypte, he said to Ranulph:

"I'm going alone; I don't need you."

"Where are you going?" asked Ranulph.

"Home," answered the old man gloomily.

Ranulph stopped. "All right; better not come out again to-day."

"You're not going to let that Frenchman hurt me?" suddenly asked Delagarde with morose anxiety. "You're going to stop that? They'd put me in prison."

Ranulph stooped over his father, his eyes alive with anger, his face blurred with disgust.

"Go home," said he, "and never mention this again while you live, or I'll take you to prison myself." Ranulph watched his father disappear down the Rue d'Egypte, then he retraced his steps to the Vier Marchi. With a new-formed determination he quickened his walk, ruling his face to a sort of forced gaiety, lest any one should think his moodiness strange. One person after another accosted him. He listened eagerly, to see if anything were said which might show suspicion of his father. But the gossip was all in old Delagarde's favour. From group to group he went, answering greetings cheerily and steeling himself to the whole disgusting business.

Presently he saw the Chevalier du Champsavoys with the Sieur de Mauprat. This was the first public appearance of the chevalier since the sad business at the Vier Prison a fortnight before. The simple folk had forgotten their insane treatment of him then, and they saluted him now with a chirping: "Es-tu biaou, chevalier?" and "Es-tu gentiment, m'sieu'?" to which he responded with amiable forgiveness. To his idea they were only naughty children, their minds reasoning no more clearly than they saw the streets through the tiny little squares of bottle-glass in the windows of their homes.

All at once they came face to face with Detricand. The chevalier stopped short with pleased yet wistful surprise. His brow knitted when he saw that his compatriot had been drinking again, and his eyes had a pained look as he said eagerly:

"Have you heard from the Comte de Tournay, monsieur? I have not seen you these days past. You said you would not disappoint me."

Detricand drew from his pocket a letter and handed it over, saying: "This comes from the comte."

The old gentleman took the letter, nervously opened it, and read it slowly, saying each sentence over twice as though to get the full meaning.

"Ah," he exclaimed, "he is going back to France to fight for the King!"

Then he looked at Detricand sadly, benevolently. "Mon cher," said he, "if I could but persuade you to abjure the wine-cup and follow his example!"

Detricand drew himself up with a jerk. "You can persuade me, chevalier," said he. "This is my last bout. I had sworn to have it with—with a soldier I knew, and I've kept my word. But it's the last, the very last in my life, on the honour of—the Detricands. And I am going with the Comte de Tournay to fight for the King."

The little chevalier's lips trembled, and taking the young man by the collar of his coat, he stood tiptoed, and kissed him on both cheeks.

"Will you accept something from me?" asked M. de Mauprat, joining in his friend's enthusiasm. He took from his pocket a timepiece he had worn for fifty years. "It is a little gift to my France, which I shall see no more," he added. "May no time be ill spent that it records for you, monsieur."

Detricand laughed in his careless way, but the face, seamed with dissipation, took on a new and better look, as with a hand-grasp of gratitude he put the timepiece in his pocket.

"I'll do my best," he said simply. "I'll be with de la Rochejaquelein and the army of the Vendee to-morrow night."

Then he shook hands with both little gentlemen and moved away towards the Rue des Tres Pigeons. Presently some one touched his arm. He looked round. It was Ranulph.

"I stood near," said Ranulph; "I chanced to hear what you said to them. You've been a friend to me today—and these eleven years past. You knew about my father, all the time."

Before replying Detricand glanced round to see that no one was listening.

"Look you, monsieur, a man must keep some decencies in his life, or cut his own throat. What a ruffian I'd be to do you or your father harm! I'm silent, of course. Let your mind rest about me. But there's the baker Carcaud—"

"The baker?" asked Ranulph dumfounded. "I thought he was tied to a rock and left to drown, by Rullecour's orders."

"I had him set free after Rullecour had gone on to the town. He got away to France."

Ranulph's anxiety deepened. "He might come back, and then if anything happened to him—"

"He'd try and make things happen to others, eh? But there's little danger of his coming back. They know he's a traitor, and he knows he'd be hung. If he's alive he'll stay where he is. Cheer up! Take my word, Olivier Delagarde has only himself to fear." He put out his hand. "Good-bye. If ever I can do anything for you, if you ever want to find me, come or send to—no, I'll write it," he suddenly added, and scribbling something on a piece of paper he handed it over.

They parted with another handshake, Detricand making his way into the Rue d'Egypte, and towards the Place du Vier Prison.

Ranulph stood looking dazedly at the crowd before him, misery, revolt, and bitterness in his heart. This French adventurer, Detricand, after years of riotous living, could pick up the threads of life again with a laugh and no shame, while he felt himself going down, down, down, with no hope of ever rising again.

As he stood buried in his reflections the town crier entered the Vier Marchi, and, going to La Pyramide, took his place upon the steps, and in a loud voice began reading a proclamation.

It was to the effect that the great Fishing Company trading to Gaspe needed twenty Jersiais to go out and replace a number of the company's officers and men who had been drowned in a gale off the rock called Perch. To these twenty, if they went at once, good pay would be given. But they must be men of intelligence and vigour, of well-known character.

The critical moment in Maitre Ranulph's life came now. Here he was penned up in a little island, chained to a criminal having the fame of a martyr. It was not to be borne. Why not leave it all behind? Why not let his father shift for himself, abide his own fate? Why not leave him the home, what money he had laid by, and go-go-go where he could forget, go where he could breathe. Surely self-preservation, that was the first law; surely no known code of human practice called upon him to share the daily crimes of any living soul—it was a daily repetition of his crime for this traitor to carry on the atrocious lie of patriotism.

He would go. It was his right.

Taking a few steps towards the officer of the company standing by the crier, he was about to speak. Some one touched him.

He turned and saw Carterette. She had divined his intention, and though she was in the dark as to the motive, she saw that he meant to go to Gaspe. Her heart seemed to contract till the pain of it hurt her; then, as a new thought flashed into her mind, it was freed again and began pounding hard against her breast. She must prevent him from leaving Jersey, from leaving her. What she might feel personally would have no effect upon him; she would appeal to him from a different stand-point.

"You must not go," she said. "You must not leave your father alone, Maitre Ranulph."

For a minute he did not reply. Through his dark wretchedness one thought pierced its way: this girl was his good friend.

"Then I'll take him with me," he said.

"He would die in the awful cold," she answered. "Nannin-gia, you must stay."

"Eh ben, I will think!" he said presently, with an air of heavy resignation, and, turning, walked away. Her eyes followed him. As she went back to her booth she smiled: he had come one step her way. He would not go.

# CHAPTER XIII

When Detricand left the Vier Marchi he made his way along the Rue d'Egypte to the house of M. de Mauprat. The front door was open, and a nice savour of boiling fruit came from within. He knocked, and instantly Guida appeared, her sleeves rolled back to her elbows, her fingers stained with the rich red of the blackberries on the fire.

A curious shade of disappointment came into her face when she saw who it was. It was clear to Detricand that she expected some one else; it was also clear that his coming gave no especial pleasure to her, though she looked at him with interest. She had thought of him more than once since that day when the famous letter from France to the chevalier was read. She had instinctively compared him, this roystering, notorious fellow, with Philip d'Avranche, Philip the brave, the ambitious, the conquering. She was sure that Philip had never over-drunk himself in his life; and now, looking into the face of Detricand, she could tell that he had been drinking again. One thing was apparent, however: he was better dressed than she ever remembered seeing him, better pulled together, and bearing himself with an air of purpose.

"I've fetched back your handkerchief—you tied up my head with it, you know," he said, taking it from his pocket. "I'm going away, and I wanted to thank you."

"Will you not come in, monsieur?" she said.

He readily entered the kitchen, still holding the handkerchief in his hand, but he did not give it to her. "Where will you sit?" she said, looking round. "I'm very busy. You mustn't mind my working," she added, going to the brass bashin at the fire. "This preserve will spoil if I don't watch it."

He seated himself on the veille, and nodded his head. "I like this," he said. "I'm fond of kitchens. I always was. When I was fifteen I was sent away from home because I liked the stables and the kitchen too well. Also I fell in love with the cook."

Guida flushed, frowned, her lips tightened, then presently a look of amusement broke over her face, and she burst out laughing.

"Why do you tell me these things?" she said. "Excuse me, monsieur, but why do you always tell unpleasant things about yourself? People think ill of you, and otherwise they might think—better."

"I don't want them to think better till I am better," he answered. "The only way I can prevent myself becoming a sneak is by blabbing my faults. Now, I was drunk last night—very, very drunk."

A look of disgust came into her face.

"Why do you relate this sort of thing to me, monsieur? Do—do I remind you of the cook at home, or of an oyster-girl in Jersey?"

She was flushing, but her voice was clear and vibrant, the look of the eyes direct and fearless. How dared he hold her handkerchief like that!

"I tell you them," he answered slowly, looking at the handkerchief in his hand, then raising his eyes to hers with whimsical gravity, "because I want you to ask me never to drink again."

She looked at him scarce comprehending, yet feeling a deep compliment somewhere, for this man was a gentleman by birth, and his manner was respectful, and had always been respectful to her.

"Why do you want me to ask you that?" she said. "Because I'm going to France to join the war of the Vendee, and—"

"With the Comte de Tournay?" she interrupted. He nodded his head. "And if I thought I was keeping a promise to—to you, I'd not break it. Will you ask me to promise?" he persisted, watching her intently.

"Why, of course," she answered kindly, almost gently; the compliment was so real, he could not be all bad.

"Then say my name, and ask me," he said.

"Monsieur—"

"Leave out the monsieur," he interrupted.

"Yves Savary dit Detricand, will you promise me, Guida Landresse—"

"De Landresse," he interposed courteously.

"—Guida Landresse de Landresse, that you will never again drink wine to excess, and that you will never do anything that"—she paused confused. "That you would not wish me to do," he said in a low voice.

"That I should not wish you to do," she repeated in a half-embarrassed way.

"On my honour I promise," he said slowly.

A strange feeling came over her. She had suddenly, in some indirect, allusive way, become interested in a man's life. Yet she had done nothing, and in truth she cared nothing. They stood looking at each other, she slightly embarrassed, he hopeful and eager, when suddenly a step sounded without, a voice called "Guida!" and as Guida coloured and Detricand turned towards the door, Philip d'Avranche entered impetuously.

He stopped short on seeing Detricand. They knew each other slightly, and they bowed. Philip frowned. He saw that something had occurred between the two. Detricand on his part realised the significance of that familiar "Guida!" called from outside. He took up his cap.

"It is greeting and good-bye, I am just off for France," he said.

Philip eyed him coldly, and not a little maliciously, for he knew Detricand's reputation well, the signs of a hard life were thick on him, and he did not like to think of Guida being alone with him.

"France should offer a wide field for your talents just now," he answered drily; "they seem wasted here." Detricand's eye flashed, but he answered coolly: "It wasn't talent that brought me here, but a boy's folly; it's not talent that's kept me from starving here, I'm afraid, but the ingenuity of the desperate."

"Why stay here? The world was wide, and France but a step away. You would not have needed talents there. You would no doubt have been rewarded by the Court which sent you and Rullecour to ravage Jersey—"

"The proper order is Rullecour and me, monsieur." Detricand seemed suddenly to have got back a manner to which he had been long a stranger. His temper became imperturbable, and this was not lost on Philip; his manner had a balanced serenity, while Philip himself had no such perfect control; which made him the more impatient. Presently Detricand added in a composed and nonchalant tone:

"I've no doubt there were those at Court who'd have clothed me in purple and fine linen, and given me wine and milk, but it was my whim to work in the galleys here, as it were."

"Then I trust you've enjoyed your Botany Bay," answered Philip mockingly. "You've been your own jailer, you could lay the strokes on heavy or light." He moved to the veille, and sat down. Guida busied herself at the fireplace, but listened intently.

"I've certainly been my own enemy, whether the strokes were heavy or light," replied Detricand, lifting a shoulder ironically.

"And a friend to Jersey at the same time, eh?" was the sneering reply.

Detricand was in the humour to tell the truth even to this man who hated him. He was giving himself the luxury of auricular confession. But Philip did not see that when once such a man has stood in his own pillory, sat in his own stocks, voluntarily paid the piper, he will take no after insult.

Detricand still would not be tempted out of his composure. "No," he answered, "I've been an enemy to Jersey too, both by act and example; but people here have been kind enough to forget the act, and the example I set is not unique."

"You've never thought that you've outstayed your welcome, eh?"

"As to that, every country is free to whoever wills, if one cares to pay the entrance fee and can endure the entertainment. One hasn't to apologise for living in a country. You probably get no better treatment than you deserve, and no worse. One thing balances another."

The man's cool impeachment and defence of himself irritated Philip, the more so because Guida was present, and this gentlemanly vagrant had him at advantage.

"You paid no entrance fee here; you stole in through a hole in the wall. You should have been hanged."

"Monsieur d'Avranche!" said Guida reproachfully, turning round from the fire.

Detricand's answer came biting and dry. "You are an officer of your King, as was I. You should know that hanging the invaders of Jersey would have been butchery. We were soldiers of France; we had the distinction of being prisoners of war, monsieur."

This shot went home. Philip had been touched in that nerve called military honour. He got to his feet. "You are right," he answered with reluctant frankness. "Our grudge is not individual, it is against France, and we'll pay it soon with good interest, monsieur."

"The individual grudge will not be lost sight of in the general, I hope?" rejoined Detricand with cool suggestion, his clear, persistent grey eye looking straight into Philip's.

"I shall do you that honour," said Philip with mistaken disdain.

Detricand bowed low. "You will always find me in the suite of the Prince of Vaufontaine, monsieur, and ready to be so distinguished by you." Turning to Guida, he added: "Mademoiselle will perhaps do me the honour to notice me again one day?" then, with a mocking nod to Philip, he left the house.

Guida and Philip stood looking after him in silence for a minute. Suddenly Guida said to herself: "My handkerchief—why did he take my handkerchief? He put it in his pocket again."

Philip turned on her impatiently.

"What was that adventurer saying to you, Guida? In the suite of the Prince of Vaufontaine, my faith! What did he come here for?"

Guida looked at him in surprise. She scarcely grasped the significance of the question. Before she had time to consider, he pressed it again, and without hesitation she told him all that had happened—it was so very little, of course—between Detricand and herself. She omitted nothing save that Detricand had carried off the handkerchief, and she could not have told, if she had been asked, why she did not speak of it.

Philip raged inwardly. He saw the meaning of the whole situation from Detricand's stand-point, but he was wise enough from his own stand-point to keep it to himself; and so both of them reserved something, she from no motive that she knew, he from an ulterior one. He was angry too: angry at Detricand, angry at Guida for her very innocence, and because she had caught and held even the slight line of association Detricand had thrown.

In any case, Detricand was going to-morrow, and to-day-to-day should decide all between Guida and himself. Used to bold moves, in this affair of love he was living up to his custom; and the encounter with Detricand here added the last touch to his resolution, nerved him to follow his strong impulse to set all upon one hazard. A month ago he had told Guida that he loved her; to-day there should be a still more daring venture. A thing not captured by a forlorn hope seemed not worth having. The girl had seized his emotions from the first moment, and had held them. To him she was the most original creature he had ever met, the most natural, the most humorous of temper, the most sincere. She had no duplicity, no guile, no arts.

He said to himself that he knew his own mind always. He believed in inspirations, and he would back his knowledge, his inspiration, by an irretrievable move. Yesterday had come an important message from his commander. That had decided him. To-day Guida should hear a message beyond all others in importance.

"Won't you come into the garden?" he said presently.

"A moment—a moment," she answered him lightly, for the frown had passed from his face, and he was his old buoyant self again. "I'm to make an end to this bashin of berries first," she added. So saying, she waved him away with a little air of tyranny; and he perched himself boyishly on the big chair in the corner, and with idle impatience began playing with the flax on the spinning-wheel near by. Then he took to humming a ditty the Jersey housewife used to sing as she spun, while Guida disposed of the sweet-smelling fruit. Suddenly she stopped and stamped her foot.

"No, no, that's not right, stupid sailor-man," she said, and she sang a verse at him over the last details of her work:

"Spin, spin, belle Mergaton!
The moon wheels full, and the tide flows high,
And your wedding-gown you must put it on
Ere the night hath no moon in the sky —
Gigoton Mergaton, spin!"

She paused. He was entranced. He had never heard her sing, and the full, beautiful notes of her contralto voice thrilled him like organ music. His look devoured her, her song captured him.

"Please go on," he said, "I never heard it that way." She was embarrassed yet delighted by his praise, and she threw into the next verse a deep weirdness:

"Spin, spin, belle Mergaton!
Your gown shall be stitched ere the old moon fade:
The age of a moon shall your hands spin on,
Or a wife in her shroud shall be laid —
Gigoton Mergaton, spin!"

"Yes, yes, that's it!" he exclaimed with gay ardour. "That's it. Sing on. There are two more verses."

"I'll only sing one," she answered, with a little air of wilfulness.

"Spin, spin, belle Mergaton!
The Little Good Folk the spell they have cast;
By your work well done while the moon hath shone,
Ye shall cleave unto joy at last —
Gigoton Mergaton, spin!"

As she sang the last verse she seemed in a dream, and her rich voice, rising with the spirit of the concluding lines, poured out the notes like a bird drunk with the air of spring.

"Guida," he cried, springing to his feet, "when you sing like that it seems to me I live in a world that has nothing to do with the sordid business of life, with my dull trade—with getting the weather-gauge or sailing in triple line. You're a planet all by yourself, Mistress Guida! Are you ready to come into the garden?"

"Yes, yes, in a minute," she answered. "You go out to the big apple-tree, and I'll come in a minute." The apple-tree was in the farthest corner of the large garden. Near it was the summer-house where Guida and her mother used to sit and read, Guida on the three-legged stool, her mother on the low, wide seat covered with ferns. This spot Guida used to "flourish" with flowers. The vines, too, crept through the rough latticework, and all together made the place a bower, secluded and serene. The water of the little stream outside the hedge made music too.

Philip placed himself on the bench beneath the appletree. What a change was all this, he thought to himself, from the staring hot stones of Malta, the squalor of Constantinople, the frigid cliffs of Spitzbergen, the noisome tropical forests of the Indies! This was Arcady. It was peace, it was content. His life was sure to be varied and perhaps stormy—here would be the true change, the spirit of all this. Of course he would have two sides to his life like most men: that lived before the world, and that of the home. He would have the fight for fame. He would have to use, not duplicity, but diplomacy, to play a kind of game; but this other side to his life, the side of love and home, should be simple, direct—all genuine and strong and true. In this way he would have a wonderful career.

He heard Guida's footstep now, and standing up he parted the apple boughs for her entrance. She was dressed all in white, without a touch of colour save in the wild rose at her throat and the pretty red shoes with the broad buckles which the Chevalier had given her. Her face, too, had colour—the soft, warm tint of the peach-blossom—and her auburn hair was like an aureole.

Philip's eyes gleamed. He stretched out both his hands in greeting and tenderness. "Guida—sweetheart!" he said.

She laughed up at him mischievously, and put her hands behind her back.

"Ma fe, you are so very forward," she said, seating herself on the bench. "And you must not call me Guida, and you've no right to call me sweetheart."

"I know I've no right to call you anything, but to myself I always call you Guida, and sweetheart too, and I've liked to think that you would care to know my thoughts," he answered.

"Yes, I wish I knew your thoughts," she responded, looking up at him intently; "I should like to know every thought in your mind.... Do you know—you don't mind my saying just what I think?—I find myself feeling that there's something in you that I never touch; I mean, that a friend ought to touch, if it's a real friendship. You appear to be so frank, and I know you are frank and good and true, and yet I seem always to be hunting for something in your mind, and it slips away from me always—always. I suppose it's because we're two different beings, and no two beings can ever know each other in this world, not altogether. We're what the Chevalier calls 'separate entities.' I seem to understand his odd, wise talk better lately. He said the other day: 'Lonely we come into the world, and lonely we go out of it.' That's what I mean. It makes me shudder sometimes, that part of us which lives alone for ever. We go running on as happy as can be, like Biribi there in the garden, and all at once we stop short at a hedge, just as he does there—a hedge just too tall to look over and with no foothold for climbing. That's what I want so much; I want to look over the Hedge."

When she spoke like this to Philip, as she sometimes did, she seemed quite unconscious that he was a listener, it was rather as if he were part of her and thinking the same thoughts. To Philip she seemed wonderful. He had never bothered his head in that way about abstract things when he was her age, and he could not understand it in her. What was more, he could not have thought as she did if he had tried. She had that sort of mind which accepts no stereotyped reflection or idea; she worked things out for herself. Her words were her own, and not another's. She was not imitative, nor yet was she bizarre; she was individual, simple, inquiring.

"That's the thing that hurts most in life," she added presently; "that trying to find and not being able to—voila, what a child I am to babble so!" she broke off with a little laugh, which had, however, a plaintive note. There was a touch of undeveloped pathos in her character, for she had been left alone too young, been given responsibility too soon.

He felt he must say something, and in a sympathetic tone he replied:

"Yes, Guida, but after a while we stop trying to follow and see and find, and we walk in the old paths and take things as they are."

"Have you stopped?" she said to him wistfully. "Oh, no, not altogether," he replied, dropping his tones to tenderness, "for I've been trying to peep over a hedge this afternoon, and I haven't done it yet." "Have you?" she rejoined, then paused, for the look in his eyes embarrassed her.... "Why do you look at me like that?" she added tremulously.

"Guida," he said earnestly, leaning towards her, "a month ago I asked you if you would listen to me when I told you of my love, and you said you would. Well, sometimes when we have met since, I have told you the same story, and you've kept your promise and listened. Guida, I want to go on telling you the same story for a long time—even till you or I die."

"Do you—ah, then, do you?" she asked simply. "Do you really wish that?"

"It is the greatest wish of my life, and always will be," he added, taking her unresisting hands.

"I like to hear you say it," she answered simply, "and it cannot be wrong, can it? Is there any wrong in my listening to you? Yet why do I feel that it is not quite right?—sometimes I do feel that."

"One thing will make all right," he said eagerly; "one thing. I love you, Guida, love you devotedly. Do you—tell me if you love me? Do not fear to tell me, dearest, for then will come the thing that makes all right."

"I do not know," she responded, her heart beating fast, her eyes drooping before him; "but when you go from me, I am not happy till I see you again. When you are gone, I want to be alone that I may remember all you have said, and say it over to myself again. When I hear you speak I want to shut my eyes, I am so happy; and every word of mine seems clumsy when you talk to me; and I feel of how little account I am beside you. Is that love, Philip—Philip, do you think that is love?"

They were standing now. The fruit that hung above Guida's head was not fairer and sweeter than she. Philip drew her to him, and her eyes lifted to his.

"Is that love, Philip?" she repeated. "Tell me, for I do not know—it has all come so soon. You are wiser; do not deceive me; you understand, and I do not. Philip, do not let me deceive myself."

"As the Judgment of Life is before us, I believe you love me, Guida—though I don't deserve it," he answered with tender seriousness.

"And it is right that you should love me; that we should love each other, Philip?"

"It will be right soon," he said, "right for ever. Guida mine, I want you to marry me."

His arm tightened round her waist, as though he half feared she would fly from him. He was right; she made a motion backward, but he held her firmly, tenderly. "Marry—marry you, Philip!" she exclaimed in trembling dismay.

"Marry—yes, marry me, Guida. That will make all right; that will bind us together for ever. Have you never thought of that?"

"Oh, never, never!" she answered. It was true, she had never thought of that; there had not been time. Too much had come all at once. "Why should I? I cannot—cannot. Oh, it could not be—not at least for a long, long time, not for years and years, Philip."

"Guida," he answered gravely and persistently, "I want you to marry me—to-morrow."

She was overwhelmed. She could scarcely speak. "To-morrow—to-morrow, Philip? You are laughing at me. I could not—how could I marry you to-morrow?"

"Guida, dearest,"—he took her hands more tightly now—"you must indeed. The day after to-morrow my ship is going to Portsmouth for two months. Then we return again here, but I will not go now unless I go as your husband!"

"Oh, no, I could not—it is impossible, Philip! It is madness—it is wrong. My grandfather—"

"Your grandfather need not know, sweetheart."

"How can you say such wicked things, Philip?"

"My dearest, it is not necessary for him to know. I don't want any one to know until I come back from Portsmouth. Then I shall have a ship of my own—commander of the Araminta I shall be then. I have word from the Admiralty to that effect. But I dare not let them know that I am married until I get commissioned to my ship. The Admiralty has set its face against lieutenants marrying."

"Then do not marry, Philip. You ought not, you see."

Her pleading was like the beating of helpless wings against the bars of a golden cage.

"But I must marry you, Guida. A sailor's life is uncertain, and what I want I want now. When I come back from Portsmouth every one shall know, but if you love me—and I know you do—you must marry me to-morrow. Until I come back no one shall know about it except the clergyman, Mr. Dow of St. Michael's—I have seen him—and Shoreham, a brother officer of mine. Ah, you must, Guida, you must! Whatever is worth doing is better worth doing in the time one's own heart says. I want it more, a thousand times more, than I ever wanted anything in my life."

She looked at him in a troubled sort of way. Somehow she felt wiser than he at that moment, wiser and stronger, though she scarcely defined the feeling to herself, though she knew that in the end her brain would yield to her heart in this.

"Would it make you so much happier, Philip?" she said more kindly than joyfully, more in grave acquiescence than delighted belief.

"Yes, on my honour—supremely happy."

"You are afraid that otherwise, by some chance, you might lose me?" she said it tenderly, yet with a little pain.

"Yes, yes, that is it, Guida dearest," he replied. "I suppose women are different altogether from men," she answered. "I could have waited ever so long, believing that you would come again, and that I should never lose you. But men are different; I see, yes, I see that, Philip."

"We are more impetuous. We know, we sailors, that now-to-day-is our time; that to-morrow may be Fate's, and Fate is a fickle jade: she beckons you up with one hand to-day, and waves you down with the other to-morrow."

"Philip," she said, scarcely above a whisper, and putting her hands on his arms, as her head sank towards him, "I must be honest with you—I must be that or nothing at all. I do not feel as you do about it; I can't. I would much—much—rather everybody knew. And I feel it almost wrong that they do not." She paused a minute, her brow clouded slightly, then cleared again, and she went on bravely: "Philip, if—if I should, you must promise me that you will leave me as soon as ever we are married, and that you will not try to see me until you come again from Portsmouth. I am sure that is right, for the deception will not be so great. I should be better able then to tell the poor grandpethe. Will you promise me, Philip-dear? It—it is so hard for me. Ah, can't you understand?"

This hopeless everlasting cry of a woman's soul!

He clasped her close. "Yes, Guida, my beloved, I understand, and I promise you—I do promise you." Her head dropped on his breast, her arms ran round his neck. He raised her face; her eyes were closed; they were dropping tears. He tenderly kissed the tears away.

# CHAPTER XIV

*"Oh, give to me my gui-l'annee,*
*I pray you, Monseigneur;*
*The king's princess doth ride to-day,*
*And I ride forth with her.*
*Oh! I will ride the maid beside*
*Till we come to the sea,*
*Till my good ship receive my bride,*
*And she sail far with me.*
*Oh, donnez-moi ma gui-l'annee,*
*Monseigneur, je vous prie!"*

The singer was perched on a huge broad stone, which, lying athwart other tall perpendicular stones, made a kind of hut, approached by a pathway of upright narrow pillars, irregular and crude. Vast must have been the labour of man's hands to lift the massive table of rock upon the supporting shafts—relics of an age when they were the only architecture, the only national monuments; when savage ancestors in lion skins, with stone weapons, led by white-robed Druid priests, came solemnly here and left the mistletoe wreath upon these Houses of Death for their adored warriors.

Even the words sung by Shoreham on the rock carried on the ancient story, the sacred legend that he who wore in his breast this mistletoe got from the Druids' altar, bearing his bride forth by sea or land, should suffer no mischance; and for the bride herself, the morgen-gifn should fail not, but should attest richly the perfect bliss of the nuptial hours.

The light was almost gone from the day, though the last crimson petals had scarce dropped from the rose of sunset. Upon the sea beneath there was not a ripple; it was a lake of molten silver, shading into a leaden silence far away. The tide was high, and the ragged rocks of the Banc des Violets in the south and the Corbiore in the west were all but hidden.

Below the mound where the tuneful youth loitered was a path, leading down through the fields and into the highway. In this path walked lingeringly a man and a maid. Despite the peaceful, almost dormant life about them, the great event of their lives had just occurred, that which is at once a vast adventure and a simple testament of nature: they had been joined in marriage privately in the parish church of St. Michael's near by. As Shoreham's voice came down the cotil, the two looked up, then passed on out of view.

But still the voice followed them, and the man looked down at the maid, repeating the refrain of the song:

*"Oh, give to me my gui-l'annee,*

*Monseigneur, je vous prie!"*

The maid looked up at the man tenderly, almost devoutly.

"I have no Druid's mistletoe from the Chapel of St. George, but I will give you—stoop down, Philip," she added softly, "I will give you the first kiss I have ever given to any man."

He stooped. She kissed him on the forehead, then upon the lips.

"Guida, my wife," Philip said, and drew her to his breast.

"My Philip," she answered softly. "Won't you say, 'Philip, my husband'?"

She shyly did as he asked in a voice no louder than a bee's. She was only seventeen.

Presently she looked up at him with a look a little abashed, a little anxious, yet tender withal.

"Philip," she said, "I wonder what we will think of this day a year from now—no, don't frown, Philip," she added. "You look at things so differently from me. To-day is everything to you; to-morrow is very much to me. It isn't that I am afraid, it is that thoughts of possibilities will come whether or no. If I couldn't tell you everything I feel I should be most unhappy. You see, I want to be able to do that, to tell you everything."

"Of course, of course," he said, not quite comprehending her, for his thoughts were always more material. He was revelling in the beauty of the girl before him, in her perfect outward self, in her unique personality. The more subtle, the deeper part of her, the searching soul never to be content with superficial reasons and the obvious cause, these he did not know—was he ever to know? It was the law of her nature that she was never to deceive herself, to pretend anything, nor to forgive pretence. To see things, to look beyond the Hedge, that was to be a passion with her; already it was nearly that.

"Of course," Philip continued, "you must tell me everything, and I'll understand. And as for what we'll think of this in another year, why, doesn't it hold to reason that we'll think it the best day of our lives—as it is, Guida?" He smiled at her, and touched her shining hair. "Evil can't come out of good, can it? And this is good, as good as anything in the world can be.... There, look into my eyes that way—just that way."

"Are you happy—very, very happy, Philip?" she asked, lingering on the words.

"Perfectly happy, Guida," he answered; and in truth he seemed so, his eyes were so bright, his face so eloquent, his bearing so buoyant.

"And you think we have done quite right, Philip?" she urged.

"Of course, of course we have. We are honourably disposing of our own fates. We love each other, we are married as surely as others are married. Where is the wrong? We have told no one, simply because for a couple of months it is best not to do so. The parson wouldn't have married us if there'd been anything wrong."

"Oh, it isn't what the clergyman might think that I mean; it's what we ourselves think down, down deep in our hearts. If you, Philip—if you say it is all right, I will believe that it is right, for you would never want your wife to have one single wrong thing like a dark spot on her life with you—would you? If it is all right to you, it must be all right for me, don't you see?"

He did see that, and it made him grave for an instant, it made him not quite so sure.

"If your mother were alive," he answered, "of course she should have known; but it isn't necessary for your grandfather to know. He talks; he couldn't keep it to himself even for a month. But we have been regularly married, we have a witness—Shoreham over there," he pointed towards the Druid's cromlech where the young man was perched—"and it only concerns us now—only you and me."

"Yet if anything happened to you during the next two months, Philip, and you did not come back!"

"My dearest, dearest Guida," he answered, taking her hands in his, and laughing boyishly, "in that case you will announce the marriage. Shoreham and the clergyman are witnesses; besides, there's the certificate which Mr. Dow will give you to-morrow; and, above all, there's the formal record on the parish register. There, sweetest interrogation mark in the world, there is the law and the gospel! Come, come, let us be gay, let this be the happiest hour we've yet had in all our lives."

"How can I be altogether gay, Philip, when we part now, and I shall not see you for two whole long months?"

"Mayn't I come to you for just a minute to-morrow morning, before I go?"

"No, no, no, you must not, indeed you must not. Remember your promise, remember that you are not to see me again until you come back from Portsmouth. Even this is not quite what we agreed, for you are still with me, and we've been married nearly half an hour!"

"Perhaps we were married a thousand years ago—I don't know," he answered, drawing her to him. "It's all a magnificent dream so far."

"You must go, you must keep your word. Don't break the first promise you ever made me, Philip."

She did not say it very reproachfully, for his look was ardent and worshipful, and she could not be even a little austere in her new joy.

"I am going," he answered. "We will go back to the town, I by the road, you by the shore, so no one will see us, and—"

"Philip," said Guida suddenly, "is it quite the same being married without banns?"

His laugh had again a youthful ring of delight. "Of course, just the same, my doubting fay," said he. "Don't be frightened about anything. Now promise me that—will you promise me?"

She looked at him a moment steadily, her eyes lingering on his face with great tenderness, and then she said:

"Yes, Philip, I will not trouble or question any longer. I will only believe that everything is all right. Say good-bye to me, Philip. I am happy now, but if—if you stay any longer—ah, please, please go, Philip!"

A moment afterwards Philip and Shoreham were entering the high road, waving their handkerchiefs to her as they went.

She had gone back to the Druid's cromlech where Philip's friend had sat, and with smiling lips and swimming eyes she watched the young men until they were lost to view.

Her eyes wandered over the sea. How immense it was, how mysterious, how it begot in one feelings both of love and of awe! At this moment she was not in sympathy with its wonderful calm. There had been times when she seemed of it, part of it, absorbed by it, till it flowed over her soul and wrapped her in a deep content. Now all was different. Mystery and the million happenings of life lay hidden in that far silver haze. On the brink of such a sea her mind seemed to be hovering now. Nothing was defined, nothing was clear. She was too agitated to think; life, being, was one wide, vague sensation, partly delight, partly trepidation. Everything had a bright tremulousness. This mystery was no dark cloud, it was a shaking, glittering mist, and yet there rose from it an air which made her pulse beat hard, her breath come with joyous lightness. She was growing to a new consciousness; a new glass, through which to see life, was quickly being adjusted to her inner sight.

Many a time, with her mother, she had sat upon the shore at St. Aubin's Bay, and looked out where white sails fluttered like the wings of restless doves. Nearer, maybe just beneath her, there had risen the keen singing of the saw, and she could see the white flash of the adze as it shaped the beams; the skeleton of a noble ship being covered with its flesh of wood, and veined with iron; the tall masts quivering to their places as the workmen hauled at the pulleys, singing snatches of patois rhymes. She had seen more than one ship launched, and a strange shiver of pleasure and of pain had gone through her; for as the water caught the graceful figure of the vessel, and the wind bellied out the sails, it seemed to her as if some ship of her own hopes were going out between the reefs to the open sea. What would her ship bring back again to her? Or would anything ever come back?

The books of adventure, poetry, history, and mythology she had read with her mother had quickened her mind, sharpened her intuition, had made her temperament still more sensitive—and her heart less peaceful. In her was almost every note of human feeling: home and duty, song and gaiety, daring and neighbourly kindness, love of sky and sea and air and orchards, of the good-smelling earth and wholesome animal life, and all the incidents, tragic, comic, or commonplace, of human existence.

How wonderful love was, she thought! How wonderful that so many millions who had loved had come and gone, and yet of all they felt they had spoken no word that laid bare the exact feeling to her or to any other. The barbarians who raised these very stones she sat on, they had loved and hated, and everything they had dared or suffered was recorded—but where? And who could know exactly what they felt?

She realised the almost keenest pain of life, that universal agony, the trying to speak, to reveal; and the proof, the hourly proof even the wisest and most gifted have, that what they feel they can never quite express, by sound, or by colour, or by the graven stone, or by the spoken word.... But life was good, ah yes! and all that might be revealed to her she would pray for; and Philip—her Philip—would help her to the revelation.

Her Philip! Her heart gave a great throb, for the knowledge that she was a wife came home to her with a pleasant shock. Her name was no longer Guida Landresse de Landresse, but Guida d'Avranche. She had gone from one tribe to another, she had been adopted, changed. A new life was begun.

She rose, slowly made her way down to the sea, and proceeded along the sands and shore-paths to the town. Presently a large vessel, with new sails, beautiful white hull, and gracious form, came slowly round a point. She shaded her eyes to look at it.

"Why, it's the boat Maitre Ranulph was to launch to-day," she said. Then she stopped suddenly. "Poor Ranulph—poor Ro!" she added gently. She knew that he cared for her—loved her. Where had he been these weeks past? She had not seen him once since that great day when they had visited the Ecrehos.

# CHAPTER XV

The house of Elie Mattingley the smuggler stood in the Rue d'Egypte, not far east of the Vier Prison. It had belonged to a jurat of repute, who parted with it to Mattingley not long before he died. There was no doubt as to the validity of the transfer, for the deed was duly registered au greffe, and it said: "In consideration of one livre turnois," etc. Possibly it was a libel against the departed jurat that he and Mattingley had had dealings unrecognised by customs law, crystallising at last into this legacy to the famous pirate-smuggler.

Unlike any other in the street, this house had a high stone wall in front, enclosing a small square paved with flat stones. In one corner was an ivy-covered well, with an antique iron gate, and the bucket, hanging on a hook inside the fern-grown hood, was an old wine-keg—appropriate emblem for a smuggler's house. In one corner, girdled by about five square feet of green earth, grew a pear tree, bearing large juicy pears, reserved for the use of a distinguished lodger, the Chevalier du Champsavoys de Beaumanoir.

In the summer the Chevalier always had his breakfast under this tree. Occasionally one other person breakfasted with him, even Savary dit Detricand, whom however he met less frequently than many people of the town, though they lived in the same house. Detricand was but a fitful lodger, absent at times for a month or so, and running up bills for food and wine, of which payment was never summarily demanded by Mattingley, for some day or other he always paid. When he did, he never questioned the bill, and, what was most important, whether he was sober or "warm as a thrush," he always treated Carterette with respect, though she was not unsparing with her tongue under slight temptation.

Despite their differences and the girl's tempers, when the day came for Detricand to leave for France, Carterette was unhappy. Several things had come at once: his going,—on whom should she lavish her good advice and biting candour now?—yesterday's business in the Vier Marchi with Olivier Delagarde, and the bitter change in Ranulph. Sorrowful reflections and as sorrowful curiosity devoured her.

All day she tortured herself. The late afternoon came, and she could bear it no longer—she would visit Guida. She was about to start, when the door in the garden wall opened and Olivier Delagarde entered. As he doffed his hat to her she thought she had never seen anything more beautiful than the smooth forehead, white hair, and long beard of the returned patriot. That was the first impression; but a closer scrutiny detected the furtive, watery eye, the unwholesome, drooping mouth, the vicious teeth, blackened and irregular. There was, too, something sinister in the yellow stockings, luridly contrasting with the black knickerbockers and rusty blue coat.

At first Carterette was inclined to run towards the prophet-like figure— it was Ranulph's father; next she drew back with dislike—his smile was leering malice under the guise of amiable mirth. But he was old, and he looked feeble, so her mind instantly changed again, and she offered him a seat on a bench beside the arched doorway with the superscription:

"*Nor Poverty nor Riches, but Daily Bread*
*Under Mine Own Fig Tree.*"

After the custom of the country, Carterette at once offered him refreshment, and brought him brandy—good old brandy was always to be got at the house of Elie Mattingley! As he drank she noticed a peculiar, uncanny twitching of the fingers and eyelids. The old man's eyes were continually shifting from place to place. He asked Carterette many questions. He had known the house years before—did the deep stream still run beneath it? Was the round hole still in the floor of the back room, from which water used to be drawn in old days? Carterette replied that it was M. Detricand's bedroom now, and you could plainly hear the stream running beneath the house. Did not the noise of the water worry poor M. Detricand then? And so it still went straight on to the sea—and, of course, much swifter after such a heavy rain as they had had the day before.

Carterette took him into every room in the house save her own and the Chevalier's. In the kitchen and in Detricand's bedroom Olivier Delagarde's eyes were very busy. He saw that the kitchen opened on the garden, which had a gate in the rear wall. He also saw that the lozenge-paned windows swung like doors, and were not securely fastened; and he tried the trap-door in Detricand's bedroom to see the water flowing beneath, just as it did when he was young—Yes, there it was running swiftly away to the sea! Then he babbled all the way to the door that led into the street; for now he would stay no longer.

When he had gone, Carterette sat wondering why it was that Ranulph's father should inspire her with such dislike. She knew that at this moment no man in Jersey was so popular as Olivier Delagarde. The longer she thought the more puzzled she became. No sooner had she got one theory than another forced her to move on. In the language of her people, she did not know on which foot to dance.

As she sat and thought, Detricand entered, loaded with parcels and bundles. These were mostly gifts for her father and herself; and for du Champsavoys there was a fine delft shaving-dish, shaped like a quartermoon to fit the neck. They were distributed, and by the time supper was over, it was quite dark. Then Detricand said his farewells, for it was ten o'clock, and he must be away at three, when his boat was to steal across to Brittany, and land him near to the outposts of the Royalist army under de la Rochejaquelein. There were letters to write and packing yet to do. He set to work gaily.

At last everything was done, and he was stooping over a bag to fasten it. The candle was in the window. Suddenly a hand—a long, skinny hand—reached softly out from behind a large press, and swallowed and crushed out the flame. Detricand raised his head quickly, astonished. There was no wind blowing—the candle had not even flickered when burning. But then, again, he had not heard a sound; perhaps that was because his foot was scraping the floor at the moment the light went out. He looked out of the window, but there was only starlight, and he could not see distinctly. Turning round he went to the door of the outer hall-way, opened it, and stepped into the garden. As he did so, a figure slipped from behind the press in the bedroom, swiftly raised the trap-door in the flooring, then, shadowed by the door leading into the hall-way, waited for him.

Presently his footstep was heard. He entered the hall, stood in the doorway of the bedroom for a moment, while he searched in his pockets for a light, then stepped inside.

Suddenly his attention was arrested. There was the sound of flowing water beneath his feet. This could always be heard in his room, but now how loud it was! Realising that the trap-door must be open, he listened for a second and was instantly conscious of some one in the room. He made a step towards the door, but it suddenly closed softly. He moved swiftly to the window, for the presence was near the door.

What did it mean? Who was it? Was there one, or more? Was murder intended? The silence, the weirdness, stopped his tongue—besides, what was the good of crying out? Whatever was to happen would happen at once. He struck a light, and held it up. As he did so some one or something rushed at him. What a fool he had been—the light had revealed his position! But at the same moment came the instinct to throw himself to one side; which he did as the rush came. In that one flash he had seen—a man's white beard.

Next instant there was a sharp sting in his right shoulder. The knife had missed his breast—the sudden swerving had saved him. Even as it struck, he threw himself on his assailant. Then came a struggle. The long fingers of the man with the white beard clove to the knife like a dead soldier's to the handle of a sword. Twice Detricand's hand was gashed slightly, and then he pinioned the wrist of his enemy, and tripped him up. The miscreant fell half across the opening in the floor. One foot, hanging down, almost touched the running water.

Detricand had his foe at his mercy. There was the first inclination to drop him into the stream, but that was put away as quickly as it came. He gave the wretch a sudden twist, pulling him clear of the hole, and wrenched the knife from his fingers at the same moment.

"Now, monsieur," said he, feeling for a light, "now we'll have a look at you."

The figure lay quiet beneath him. The nervous strength was gone, the body was limp, the breathing was laboured. The light flared. Detricand held it down, and there was revealed the haggard, malicious face of Olivier Delagarde.

"So, monsieur the traitor," said Detricand—"so you'd be a murderer too—eh?"

The old man mumbled an oath.

"Hand of the devil," continued Detricand, "was there ever a greater beast than you! I held my tongue about you these eleven years past, I held it yesterday and saved your paltry life, and you'd repay me by stabbing me in the dark—in a fine old-fashioned way too, with your trap-doors, and blown-out candle, and Italian tricks—"

He held the candle down near the white beard as though he would singe it.

"Come, sit up against the wall there and let me look at you."

Cringing, the old man drew himself over to the wall. Detricand, seating himself in a chair, held the candle up before him.

After a moment he said: "What I want to know is, how could a low-flying cormorant like you beget a gull of the cliffs like Maitre Ranulph?"

The old man did not answer, but sat blinking with malignant yet fearful eyes at Detricand, who continued: "What did you come back for? Why didn't you stay dead? Ranulph had a name as clean as a piece of paper from the mill, and he can't write it now without turning sick, because it's the same name as yours. You're the choice blackamoor of creation, aren't you? Now what have you got to say?"

"Let me go," whined the old man with the white beard. "Let me go, monsieur. Don't send me to prison."

Detricand stirred him with his foot, as one might a pile of dirt.

"Listen," said he. "In the Vier Marchi they're cutting off the ear of a man and nailing it to a post, because he ill-used a cow. What do you suppose they'd do to you, if I took you down there and told them it was through you Rullecour landed, and that you'd have seen them all murdered—eh, maitre cormorant?"

The old man crawled towards Detricand on his knees. "Let me go, let me go," he whined. "I was mad; I didn't know what I was doing; I've not been right in the head since I was in the Guiana prison."

At that moment it struck Detricand that the old man must have had some awful experience in prison, for now his eyes had the most painful terror, the most abject fear. He had never seen so craven a sight.

"What were you in prison for in Guiana, and what did they do to you there?" asked Detricand sternly. Again the old man shivered horribly, and tears streamed down his cheeks, as he whined piteously: "Oh no, no, no—for the mercy of Christ, no!" He threw up his hands as if to ward off a blow.

Detricand saw that this was not acting, that it was a supreme terror, an awful momentary aberration; for the traitor's eyes were wildly staring, the mouth was drawn in agony, the hands were now rigidly clutching an imaginary something, the body stiffened where it crouched.

Detricand understood now. The old man had been tied to a triangle and whipped—how horribly who might know? His mood towards the miserable creature changed: he spoke to him in a firm, quiet tone.

"There, there, you're not going to be hurt. Be quiet now, and you shall not be touched."

Then he stooped over, and quickly undoing the old man's waistcoat, he pulled down the coat and shirt and looked at his back. As far as he could see it was scarred as though by a red-hot iron, and the healed welts were like whipcords on the shrivelled skin. The old man whimpered yet, but he was growing quieter. Detricand lifted him up, and buttoning the shirt and straightening the coat again, he said:

"Now, you're to go home and sleep the sleep of the unjust, and you're to keep the sixth commandment, and you're to tell no more lies. You've made a shameful mess of your son's life, and you're to die now as soon as you can without attracting notice. You're to pray for an accident to take you out of the world: a wind to blow you over a cliff, a roof to fall on you, a boat to go down with you, a hole in the ground to swallow you up, a fever or a plague to end you in a day."

He opened the door to let him go; but suddenly catching his arms held him in a close grip. "Hark!" he said in a mysterious whisper.

There was only the weird sound of the running water through the open trap-door of the floor. He knew how superstitious was every Jerseyman, from highest to lowest, and he would work upon that weakness now.

"You hear that water running to the sea?" he said solemnly. "You tried to kill and drown me to-night. You've heard how when one man has drowned another an invisible stream follows the murderer wherever he goes, and he hears it, hour after hour, month after month, year after year, until suddenly one day it comes on him in a huge flood, and he is found, whether in the road, or in his bed, or at the table, or in the field, drowned, and dead?"

The old man shivered violently.

"You know Manon Moignard the witch? Well, if you don't do what I say—and I shall find out, mind you—she shall bewitch the flood on you. Be still ... listen! That's the sound you'll hear every day of your life, if you break the promise you've got to make to me now."

He spoke the promise with ghostly deliberation, and the old man, all the desperado gone out of him, repeated it in a husky voice. Whereupon Detricand led him into the garden, saw him safe out on the road and watched him disappear. Then rubbing his fingers, as though to rid them of pollution, with an exclamation of disgust he went back to the house.

By another evening—that is, at the hour when Guida arrived home after her secret marriage with Philip d'Avranche—he saw the lights of the army of de la Rochejaquelein in the valley of the Vendee.

# CHAPTER XVI

The night and morning after Guida's marriage came and went. The day drew on to the hour fixed for the going of the Narcissus. Guida had worked all forenoon with a feverish unrest, not trusting herself, though the temptation was sore, to go where she might see Philip's vessel lying in the tide-way. She had resolved that only at the moment fixed for sailing would she go to the shore; yet from her kitchen door she could see a wide acreage of blue water and a perfect sky; and out there was Noirmont Point, round which her husband's ship would go, and be lost to her vision thereafter.

The day wore on. She got her grandfather's dinner, saw him bestowed in the great arm-chair for his afternoon sleep, and, when her household work was done, settled herself at the spinning wheel.

The old man loved to have her spin and sing as he drowsed. To-day his eyes had followed her everywhere. He could not have told why it was, but somehow all at once he seemed to deeply realise her—her beauty, the joy of this innocent living intelligence moving through his home. She had always been necessary to him, but he had taken her presence as a matter of course. She had always been to him the most wonderful child ever given to comfort an old man's life, but now as he abstractedly took a pinch of snuff from the silver box and then forgot to put it to his nose, he seemed suddenly to get that clearness of sight, that perspective, from which he could see her as she really was. He took another pinch of snuff, and again forgot to put it to his nose, but brushed imaginary dust from his coat, as was his wont, and whispered to himself:

"Why now, why now, I had not thought she was so much a woman. Flowers of the sea, but what eyes, what carriage, and what an air! I had not thought—h'm—blind old bat that I am—I had not thought she was grown such a lady. It was only yesterday, surely but yesterday, since I rocked her to sleep. Francois de Mauprat"—he shook his head at himself—"you are growing old. Let me see—why, yes, she was born the day I sold the blue enamelled timepiece to his Highness the Duc de Mauban. The Duc was but putting the watch to his ear when a message comes to say the child there is born. 'Good,' says the Duc de Mauban, when he hears, 'give me the honour, de Mauprat,' says he, 'for the sake of old days in France, to offer a name to the brave innocent—for the sake of old associations,' says de Mauban. 'You knew my wife, de Mauprat,' says he; 'you knew the Duchesse Guida-Guidabaldine. She's been gone these ten years, alas! You were with me when we were married, de Mauprat,' says the Duc; 'I should care to return the compliment if you will allow me to offer a name, eh?' 'Duc,' said I, 'there is no honour I more desire for my grandchild.' 'Then let the name of Guidabaldine be somewhere among others she will carry, and—and I'll not forget her, de Mauprat, I'll not forget her.'... Eh, eh, I wonder—I wonder if he has forgotten the little Guidabaldine there? He sent her a golden cup for the christening, but I wonder—I wonder—if he has forgotten her since? So quick of tongue, so bright of eye, so light of foot, so sweet a face—if one could but be always young! When her grandmother, my wife, my Julie, when she was young—ah, she was fair, fairer than Guida, but not so tall—not quite so tall. Ah!..."

He was slipping away into sleep when he realised that Guida was singing

*"Spin, spin, belle Mergaton!*
*The moon wheels full, and the tide flows high,*
*And your wedding-gown you must put it on*
*Ere the night hath no moon in the sky—*
*Gigoton Mergaton, spin!"*

"I had never thought she was so much a woman," he said drowsily; "I—I wonder why—I never noticed it."

He roused himself again, brushed imaginary snuff from his coat, keeping time with his foot to the wheel as it went round. "I—I suppose she will wed soon.... I had forgotten. But she must marry well, she must marry well—she is the godchild of the Duc de Mauban. How the wheel goes round! I used to hear—her mother—sing that song, 'Gigoton, Mergaton spin-spin-spin.'" He was asleep.

Guida put by the wheel, and left the house. Passing through the Rue des Sablons, she came to the shore. It was high tide. This was the time that Philip's ship was to go. She had dressed herself with as much care as to what might please his eye as though she were going to meet him in person. Not without reason, for, though she could not see him from the land, she knew he could see her plainly through his telescope, if he chose.

She reached the shore. The time had come for him to go, but there was his ship at anchor in the tide-way still. Perhaps the Narcissus was not going; perhaps, after all, Philip was to remain! She laughed with pleasure at the thought of that. Her eyes wandered lovingly over the ship which was her husband's home upon the sea. Just such another vessel Philip would command. At a word from him those guns, like long, black, threatening arms thrust out, would strike for England with thunder and fire.

A bugle call came across the still water, clear, vibrant, and compelling. It represented power. Power—that was what Philip, with his ship, would stand for in the name of England. Danger—oh yes, there would be danger, but Heaven would be good to her; Philip should go safe through storm and war, and some day great honours would be done him. He should be an admiral, and more perhaps; he had said so. He was going to do it as much for her as for himself, and when he had done it, to be proud of it more for her than for himself; he had said so: she believed in him utterly. Since that day upon the Ecrehos it had never occurred to her not to believe him. Where she gave her faith she gave it wholly; where she withdrew it—

The bugle call sounded again. Perhaps that was the signal to set sail. No, a boat was putting out from the Narcissus. It was coming landward. As she watched its approach she heard a chorus of boisterous voices behind her. She turned and saw nearing the shore from the Rue d'Egypte a half-dozen sailors, singing cheerily:

"Get you on, get you on, get you on,
Get you on to your fo'c'stle'ome;
Leave your lassies, leave your beer,
For the bugle what you 'ear
Pipes you on to your fo'c'stle 'ome—
'Ome—'ome—'ome,
Pipes you on to your fo'c'stle 'ome."

Guida drew near.

"The Narcissus is not leaving to-day?" she asked of the foremost sailor.

The man touched his cap. "Not to-day, lady."

"When does she leave?"

"Well, that's more nor I can say, lady, but the cap'n of the main-top, yander, 'e knows."

She approached the captain of the main-top. "When does the Narcissus leave?" she asked.

He looked her up and down, at first glance with something like boldness, but instantly he touched his hat.

"To-morrow, mistress—she leaves at 'igh tide tomorrow."

With an eye for a fee or a bribe, he drew a little away from the others, and said to her in a low tone: "Is there anything what I could do for you, mistress? P'r'aps you wanted some word carried aboard, lady?"

She hesitated an instant, then said: "No-no, thank you."

He still waited, however, rubbing his hand on his hip with mock bashfulness. There was an instant's pause, then she divined his meaning.

She took from her pocket a shilling. She had never given away so much money in her life before, but she seemed to feel instinctively that now she must give freely—now that she was the wife of an officer of the navy. Strange how these sailors to-day seemed so different to her from ever before—she felt as if they all belonged to her. She offered the shilling to the captain of the main-top. His eyes gloated, but he said with an affected surprise:

"No, I couldn't think of it, yer leddyship."

"Ah, but you will take it!" she said. "I—I have a r-relative"—she hesitated at the word—"in the navy."

"'Ave you now, yer leddyship?" he said. "Well, then, I'm proud to 'ave the shilling to drink 'is 'ealth, yer leddyship."

He touched his hat, and was about to turn away. "Stay a little," she said with bashful boldness. The joy of giving was rapidly growing to a vice. "Here's something for them," she added, nodding towards his fellows, and a second shilling came from her pocket. "Just as you say, yer leddyship," he said with owlish gravity; "but for my part I think they've 'ad enough. I don't 'old with temptin' the weak passions of man."

A moment afterwards the sailors were in the boat, rowing towards the Narcissus. Their song came back across the water:

"... O you A.B. sailor-man,

*Wet your whistle while you can,*

*For the piping of the bugle calls you 'ome!*

*'Ome—'ome—'ome,*

*Calls you on to your fo'c'stle 'ome!"*

The evening came down, and Guida sat in the kitchen doorway looking out over the sea, and wondering why Philip had sent her no message. Of course he would not come himself, he must not: he had promised her. But how much she would have liked to see him for just one minute, to feel his arms about her, to hear him say good-bye once more. Yet she loved him the better for not coming.

By and by she became very restless. She would have been almost happier if he had gone that day: he was within call of her, still they were not to see each other.

She walked up and down the garden, Biribi the dog by her side. Sitting down on the bench beneath the appletree, she recalled every word that Philip had said to her two days before. Every tone of his voice, every look he had given her, she went over in her thoughts. There is no reporting in the world so exact, so perfect, as that in a woman's mind, of the words, looks, and acts of her lover in the first days of mutual confession and understanding.

It can come but once, this dream, fantasy, illusion—call it what you will: it belongs to the birth hour of a new and powerful feeling; it is the first sunrise of the heart. What comes after may be the calmer joy of a more truthful, a less ideal emotion, but the transitory glory of the love and passion of youth shoots higher than all other glories into the sky of time. The splendour of youth is its madness, and the splendour of that madness is its unconquerable belief. And great is the strength of it, because violence alone can destroy it. It does not yield to time nor to decay, to the long wash of experience that wears away the stone, nor to disintegration. It is always broken into pieces at a blow. In the morning all is well, and ere the evening come the radiant temple is in ruins.

At night when Guida went to bed she could not sleep at first. Then came a drowsing, a floating between waking and sleeping, in which a hundred swift images of her short past flashed through her mind:

A butterfly darting in the white haze of a dusty road, and the cap of the careless lad that struck it down.... Berry-picking along the hedges beyond the quarries of Mont Mado, and washing her hands in the strange green pools at the bottom of the quarries.... Stooping to a stream and saying of it to a lad: "Ro, won't it never come back?"... From the front doorway watching a poor criminal shrink beneath the lash with which he was being flogged from the Vier Marchi to the Vier Prison... Seeing a procession of bride and bridegroom with young men and women gay in ribbons and pretty cottons, calling from house to house to receive the good wishes of their friends, and drinking cinnamon wine and mulled cider—the frolic, the gaiety of it all. Now, in a room full of people, she was standing on a veille flourished with posies of broom and wildflowers, and Philip was there beside her, and he was holding her hand, and they were waiting and waiting for some one who never came. Nobody took any notice of her and Philip, she thought; they stood there waiting and waiting—why, there was M. Savary dit Detricand in the doorway, waving a handkerchief at her, and saying: "I've found it—I've found it!"—and she awoke with a start.

Her heart was beating hard, and for a moment she was dazed; but presently she went to sleep again, and dreamed once more.

This time she was on a great warship, in a storm which was driving towards a rocky shore. The sea was washing over the deck. She recognised the shore: it was the cliff at Plemont in the north of Jersey, and behind the ship lay the awful Paternosters. They were drifting, drifting on the wall of rock. High above on the land there was a solitary stone hut. The ship came nearer and nearer. The storm increased in strength. In the midst of the violence she looked up and saw a man standing in the doorway of the hut. He turned his face towards her: it was Ranulph Delagarde, and he had a rope in his hand. He saw her and called to her, making ready to throw the rope, but suddenly some one drew her back. She cried aloud, and then all grew black....

And then, again, she knew she was in a small, dark cabin of the ship. She could hear the storm breaking over the deck. Now the ship struck. She could feel her grinding upon the rocks. She seemed to be sinking, sinking— There was a knocking, knocking at the door of the cabin, and a voice calling to her—how far away it seemed!... Was she dying, was she drowning? The words of a nursery rhyme rang in her ears distinctly, keeping time to the knocking. She wondered who should be singing a nursery rhyme on a sinking ship:

> "La main morte,
>
> La main morte,
>
> Tapp' a la porte,
>
> Tapp' a la porte."

She shuddered. Why should the dead hand tap at her door? Yet there it was tapping louder, louder.... She struggled, she tried to cry out, then suddenly she grew quiet, and the tapping got fainter and fainter—her eyes opened: she was awake.

For an instant she did not know where she was. Was it a dream still? For there was a tapping, tapping at her door—no, it was at the window. A shiver ran through her from head to foot. Her heart almost stopped beating. Some one was calling to her.

"Guida! Guida!"

It was Philip's voice. Her cheek had been cold the moment before; now she felt the blood tingling in her face. She slid to the floor, threw a shawl round her, and went to the casement.

The tapping began again. For a moment she could not open the window. She was trembling from head to foot. Philip's voice reassured her a little.

"Guida, Guida, open the window a moment."

She hesitated. She could not—no—she could not do it. He tapped still louder.

"Guida, don't you hear me?" he asked.

She undid the catch, but she had hardly the courage even yet. He heard her now, and pressed the window a little. Then she opened it slowly, and her white face showed.

"O Philip," she said breathlessly, "why have you frightened me so?"

He caught her hand in his own. "Come out into the garden, sweetheart," he said, and he kissed the hand. "Put on a dress and your slippers and come," he urged again.

"Philip," she said, "O Philip, I cannot! It is too late. It is midnight. Do not ask me. Why, why did you come?"

"Because I wanted to speak with you for one minute. I have only a little while. Please come outside and say good-bye to me again. We are sailing to-morrow—there's no doubt about it this time."

"O Philip," she answered, her voice quivering, "how can I? Say good-bye to me here, now."

"No, no, Guida, you must come. I can't kiss you good-bye where you are."

"Must I come to you?" she said helplessly. "Well, then, Philip," she added, "go to the bench by the apple-tree, and I shall be there in a moment."

"Beloved!" he exclaimed ardently. She shut the window slowly.

For a moment he looked about him; then went lightly through the garden, and sat down on the bench under the apple-tree, near to the summer-house. At last he heard her footstep. He rose quickly to meet her, and as she came timidly to him, clasped her in his arms.

"Philip," she said, "this isn't right. You ought not to have come; you have broken your promise."

"Are you not glad to see me?"

"Oh, you know, you know that I'm glad to see you, but you shouldn't have come—hark! what's that?" They both held their breath, for there was a sound outside the garden wall. Clac-clac! clac-clac!—a strange, uncanny footstep. It seemed to be hurrying away—clac-clac! clac-clac!

"Ah, I know," whispered Guida: "it is Dormy Jamais. How foolish of me to be afraid!"

"Of course, of course," said Philip—"Dormy Jamais, the man who never sleeps."

"Philip—if he saw us!"

"Foolish child, the garden wall is too high for that. Besides—"

"Yes, Philip?"

"Besides, you are my wife, Guida!"

"No, no, Philip, no; not really so until all the world is told."

"My beloved Guida, what difference can that make?" She sighed and shook her head. "To me, Philip, it is only that which makes it right—that the whole world knows. Philip, I am so afraid of—of secrecy, and cheating."

"Nonsense-nonsense!" he answered. "Poor little wood-bird, you're frightened at nothing at all. Come and sit by me." He drew her close to him.

Her trembling presently grew less. Hundreds of glow-worms were shimmering in the hedge. The grass-hoppers were whirring in the mielles beyond; a flutter of wings went by overhead. The leaves were rustling gently; a fresh wind was coming up from the sea upon the soft, fragrant dusk.

They talked a little while in whispers, her hands in his, his voice soothing her, his low, hurried words giving her no time to think. But presently she shivered again, though her heart was throbbing hotly.

"Come into the summer-house, Guida; you are cold, you are shivering." He rose, with his arm round her waist, raising her gently at the same time.

"Oh no, Philip dear," she said, "I'm not really cold—I don't know what it is—"

"But indeed you are cold," he answered. "There's a stiff south-easter rising, and your hands are like ice. Come into the arbour for a minute. It's warm there, and then—then we'll say good-bye, sweetheart."

His arm round her, he drew her with him to the summer-house, talking to her tenderly all the time. There was reassurance, comfort, loving care in his very tones.

How brightly the stars shone, how clearly the music of the stream came over the hedge! With what lazy restfulness the distant All's well floated across the mielles from a ship at anchor in the tide-way, how like a slumber-song the wash of the sea rolled drowsily along the wind! How gracious the smell of the earth, drinking up the dew of the affluent air, which the sun, on the morrow, should turn into life-blood for the grass and trees and flowers!

# CHAPTER XVII

Philip was gone. Before breakfast was set upon the table, Guida saw the Narcissus sail round Noirmont Point and disappear.

Her face had taken on a new expression since yesterday. An old touch of dreaminess, of vague anticipation was gone—that look which belongs to youth, which feels the confident charm of the unknown future. Life was revealed; but, together with joy, wonder and pain informed the revelation.

A marvel was upon her. Her life was linked to another's, she was a wife. She was no longer sole captain of herself. Philip would signal, and she must come until either he or she should die. He had taken her hand, and she must never let it go; the breath of his being must henceforth give her new and healthy life, or inbreed a fever which should corrode the heart and burn away the spirit. Young though she was, she realised it—but without defining it. The new-found knowledge was diffused in her character, expressed in her face.

Seldom had a day of Guida's life been so busy. It seemed to her that people came and went far more than usual. She talked, she laughed a little, she answered back the pleasantries of the seafaring folk who passed her doorway or her garden. She was attentive to her grandfather; exact with her household duties. But all the time she was thinking—thinking—thinking. Now and again she smiled, but at times too tears sprang to her eyes, to be quickly dried. More than once she drew in her breath with a quick, sibilant sound, as though some thought wounded her; and she flushed suddenly, then turned pale, then came to her natural colour again.

Among those who chanced to visit the cottage was Maitresse Aimable. She came to ask Guida to go with her and Jean to the island of Sark, twelve miles away, where Guida had never been. They would only be gone one night, and, as Maitresse Aimable said, the Sieur de Mauprat could very well make shift for once.

The invitation came to Guida like water to thirsty ground. She longed to get away from the town, to be where she could breathe; for all this day the earth seemed too small for breath: she gasped for the sea, to be alone there. To sail with Jean Touzel was practically to be alone, for Maitresse Aimable never talked; and Jean knew Guida's ways, knew when she wished to be quiet. In Jersey phrase, he saw beyond his spectacles—great brass-rimmed things, giving a droll, childlike kind of wisdom to his red rotund face.

Having issued her invitation, Maitresse Aimable smiled placidly and seemed about to leave, when, all at once, without any warning, she lowered herself like a vast crate upon the veille, and sat there looking at Guida.

At first the grave inquiry of her look startled Guida. She was beginning to know that sensitive fear assailing those tortured by a secret. How she loathed this secrecy! How guilty she now felt, where, indeed, no guilt was! She longed to call aloud her name, her new name, from the housetops.

The voice of Maitresse Aimable roused her. Her ponderous visitor had made a discovery which had yet been made by no other human being. Her own absurd romance, her ancient illusion, had taught her to know when love lay behind another woman's face. And after her fashion, Maitresse Aimable loved Jean Touzel as it is given to few to love.

"I was sixteen when I fell in love; you're seventeen—you," she said. "Ah bah, so it goes!"

Guida's face crimsoned. What—how much did Maitresse Aimable know? By what necromancy had this fat, silent fisher-wife learned the secret which was the heart of her life, the soul of her being—which was Philip? She was frightened, but danger made her cautious.

"Can you guess who it is?" she asked, without replying directly to the oblique charge.

"It is not Maitre Ranulph," answered her friendly inquisitor; "it is not that M'sieu' Detricand, the vaurien." Guida flushed with annoyance. "It is not that farmer Blampied, with fifty vergees, all potatoes; it is not M'sieu' Janvrin, that bat'd'lagoule of an ecrivain. Ah bah, so it goes!"

"Who is it, then?" persisted Guida. "Eh ben, that is the thing!"

"How can you tell that one is in love, Maitresse Aimable?" persisted Guida.

The other smiled with a torturing placidity, then opened her mouth; but nothing came of it. She watched Guida moving about the kitchen abstractedly. Her eye wandered to the racllyi, with its flitches of bacon, to the dreschiaux and the sanded floor, to the great Elizabethan oak chair, and at last back to Guida, as though through her the lost voice might be charmed up again.

The eyes of the two met now, fairly, firmly; and Guida was conscious of a look in the other's face which she had never seen before. Had then a new sight been given to herself? She saw and understood the look in Maitresse Aimable's face, and instantly knew it to be the same that was in her own.

With a sudden impulse she dropped the bashin she was polishing, and, going over quickly, she silently laid her cheek against her old friend's. She could feel the huge breast heave, she felt the vast face turn hot, she was conscious of a voice struggling back to life, and she heard it say at last:

"Gatd'en'ale, rosemary tea cures a cough, but nothing cures the love— ah bah, so it goes!"

"Do you love Jean?" whispered Guida, not showing her face, but longing to hear the experience of another who suffered that joy called love.

Maitresse Aimable's face grew hotter; she did not speak, but patted Guida's back with her heavy hand and nodded complacently.

"Have you always loved him?" asked Guida again, with an eager inquisition, akin to that of a wayside sinner turned chapel-going saint, hungry to hear what chanced to others when treading the primrose path.

Maitresse Aimable again nodded, and her arm drew closer about Guida. There was a slight pause, then came an unsophisticated question:

"Has Jean always loved you?"

A short silence, and then the voice said with the deliberate prudence of an unwilling witness:

"It is not the man who wears the wedding-ring." Then, as if she had been disloyal in even suggesting that Jean might hold her lightly, she added, almost eagerly—an enthusiasm tempered by the pathos of a half-truth:

"But my Jean always sleeps at home."

This larger excursion into speech gave her courage, and she said more; and even as Guida listened hungrily—so soon had come upon her the apprehensions and wavering moods of loving woman!—she was wondering to hear this creature, considered so dull by all, speak as though out of a watchful and capable mind. What further Maitresse Aimable said was proof that if she knew little and spake little, she knew that little well; and if she had gathered meagrely from life, she had at least winnowed out some small handfuls of grain from the straw and chaff. At last her sagacity impelled her to say:

"If a man's eyes won't see, elder-water can't make him; if he will— ah bah, glad and good!" Both arms went round Guida, and hugged her awkwardly.

Her voice came up but once more that morning. As she left Guida in the doorway, she said with a last effort:

"I will have one bead to pray for you, trejous." She showed her rosary, and, Huguenot though she was, Guida touched the bead reverently. "And if there is war, I will have two beads, trejous. A bi'tot—good-bye!"

Guida stood watching her from the doorway, and the last words of the fisher-wife kept repeating themselves through her brain: "And if there is war, I will have two beads, trejous."

So, Maitresse Aimable knew she loved Philip! How strange it was that one should read so truly without words spoken, or through seeing acts which reveal. She herself seemed to read Maitresse Aimable all at once— read her by virtue, and in the light, of true love, the primitive and consuming feeling in the breast of each for a man. Were not words necessary for speech after all? But here she stopped short suddenly; for if love might find and read love, why was it she needed speech of Philip? Why was it her spirit kept beating up against the hedge beyond which his inner self was, and, unable to see that beyond, needed reassurance by words, by promises and protestations?

All at once she was angry with herself for thinking thus concerning Philip. Of course Philip loved her deeply. Had she not seen the light of true love in his eyes, and felt the arms of love about her? Suddenly she shuddered and grew bitter, and a strange rebellion broke loose in her. Why had Philip failed to keep his promise not to see her again after the marriage, till he should return from Portsmouth? It was selfish, painfully, terribly selfish of him. Why, even though she had been foolish in her request—why had he not done as she wished? Was that love—was it love to break the first promise he had ever made to his wife?

Yet she excused him to herself. Men were different from women, and men did not understand what troubled a woman's heart and spirit; they were not shaken by the same gusts of emotion; they—they were not so fine; they did not think so deeply on what a woman, when she loves, thinks always, and acts upon according to her thought. If Philip were only here to resolve these fears, these perplexities, to quiet the storm in her! And yet, could he— could he? For now she felt that this storm was rooting up something very deep and radical in her. It frightened her, but for the moment she fought it passionately.

She went into her garden; and here among her animals and her flowers it seemed easier to be gay of heart; and she laughed a little, and was most tender and pretty with her grandfather when he came home from spending the afternoon with the Chevalier.

In this manner the first day of her marriage passed—in happy reminiscence and in vague foreboding; in affection yet in reproach as the secret wife; and still as the loving, distracted girl, frightened at her own bitterness, but knowing it to be justified.

The late evening was spent in gaiety with her grandfather and the Chevalier; but at night when she went to bed she could not sleep. She tossed from side to side; a hundred thoughts came and went. She grew feverish, her breath choked her, and she got up and opened the window. It was clear, bright moonlight, and from where she was she could see the mielles and the ocean and the star-sown sky above and beyond. There she sat and thought and thought till morning.

# CHAPTER XVIII

At precisely the same moment in the morning two boats set sail from the south coast of Jersey: one from Grouville Bay, and one from the harbour of St. Heliers. Both were bound for the same point; but the first was to sail round the east coast of the island, and the second round the west coast.

The boat leaving Grouville Bay would have on her right the Ecrehos and the coast of France, with the Dirouilles in her course; the other would have the wide Atlantic on her left, and the Paternosters in her course. The two converging lines should meet at the island of Sark.

The boat leaving Grouville Bay was a yacht carrying twelve swivel-guns, bringing Admiralty despatches to the Channel Islands. The boat leaving St. Heliers harbour was a new yawl-rigged craft owned by Jean Touzel. It was the fruit of ten years' labour, and he called her the Hardi Biaou, which, in plain English, means "very beautiful." This was the third time she had sailed under Jean's hand. She carried two carronades, for war with France was in the air, and it was Jean's whim to make a show of preparation, for, as he said: "If the war-dogs come, my pups can bark too. If they don't, why, glad and good, the Hardi Biaou is big enough to hold the cough-drops."

The business of the yacht Dorset was important that was why so small a boat was sent on the Admiralty's affairs. Had she been a sloop she might have attracted the attention of a French frigate or privateer wandering the seas in the interests of Vive la Nation! The business of the yawl was quite unimportant. Jean Touzel was going to Sark with kegs of wine and tobacco for the seigneur, and to bring over whatever small cargo might be waiting for Jersey. The yacht Dorset had aboard her the Reverend Lorenzo Dow, an old friend of her commander. He was to be dropped at Sark, and was to come back with Jean Touzel in the Hardi Biaou, the matter having been arranged the evening before in the Vier Marchi. The saucy yawl had aboard Maitresse Aimable, Guida, and a lad to assist Jean in working the sails. Guida counted as one of the crew, for there was little in the handling of a boat she did not know.

As the Hardi Biaou was leaving the harbour of St. Heliers, Jean told Guida that Mr. Dow was to join them on the return journey. She had a thrill of excitement, for this man was privy to her secret, he was connected with her life history. But before the little boat passed St. Brelade's Bay she was lost in other thoughts: in picturing Philip on the Narcissus, in inwardly conning the ambitious designs of his career. What he might yet be, who could tell? She had read more than a little of the doings of great naval commanders, both French and British. She knew how simple midshipmen had sometimes become admirals, and afterwards peers of the realm.

Suddenly a new thought came to her. Suppose that Philip should rise to high places, would she be able to follow? What had she seen—what did she know—what social opportunities had been hers? How would she fit with an exalted station?

Yet Philip had said that she could take her place anywhere with grace and dignity; and surely Philip knew. If she were gauche or crude in manners, he would not have cared for her; if she were not intelligent, he would scarcely have loved her. Of course she had read French and English to some purpose; she could speak Spanish—her grandfather had taught her that; she understood Italian fairly—she had read it aloud on Sunday evenings with the Chevalier. Then there were Corneille, Shakespeare, Petrarch, Cervantes—she had read them all; and even Wace, the old Norman trouvere, whose Roman de Rou she knew almost by heart. Was she so very ignorant?

There was only one thing to do: she must interest herself in what interested Philip; she must read what he read; she must study naval history; she must learn every little thing about a ship of war. Then Philip would be able to talk with her of all he did at sea, and she would understand.

When, a few days ago, she had said to him that she did not know how she was going to be all that his wife ought to be, he had answered her: "All I ask is that you be your own sweet self, for it is just you that I want, you with your own thoughts and imaginings, and not a Guida who has dropped her own way of looking at things to take on some one else's—even mine. It's the people who try to be clever who never are; the people who are clever never think of trying to be."

Was Philip right? Was she really, in some way, a little bit clever? She would like to believe so, for then she would be a better companion for him. After all, how little she knew of Philip—now, why did that thought always come up! It made her shudder. They two would really have to begin with the A B C of understanding. To understand was a passion, it was breathing and life to her. She would never, could never, be satisfied with skimming the surface of life as the gulls out there skimmed the water.... Ah, how beautiful the morning was, and how the bracing air soothed her feverishness! All this sky, and light, and uplifting sea were hers, they fed her with their strength— they were all so companionable.

Since Philip had gone—and that was but four days ago—she had sat down a dozen times to write to him, but each time found she could not. She, drew back from it because she wanted to empty out her heart, and yet, somehow, she dared not. She wanted to tell Philip all the feelings that possessed her; but how dared she write just what she felt: love and bitterness, joy and indignation, exaltation and disappointment, all in one? How was it these could all exist in a woman's heart at once? Was it because Love was greater than all, deeper than all, overcame all, forgave all? and was that what women felt and did always? Was that their lot, their destiny? Must they begin in blind faith, then be plunged into the darkness of disillusion, shaken by the storm of emotion, taste the sting in the fruit of the tree of knowledge—and go on again the same, yet not the same?

More or less incoherently these thoughts flitted through Guida's mind. As yet her experiences were too new for her to fasten securely upon their meaning. In a day or two she would write to Philip freely and warmly of her love and of her hopes; for, maybe, by that time nothing but happiness would be left in the caldron of feeling. There was a packet going to England in three days—yes, she would wait for that. And Philip—alas! a letter from him could not reach her for at least a fortnight yet; and then in another month after that he would be with her, and she would be able to tell the whole world that she was the wife of Captain Philip d'Avranche, of the good ship Araminta—for that he was to be when he came again.

She was not sad now, indeed she was almost happy, for her thoughts had brought her so close to Philip that she could feel his blue eyes looking at her, the strong clasp of his hand. She could almost touch the brown hair waving back carelessly from the forehead, untouched by powder, in the fashion of the time; and she could hear his cheery laugh quite plainly, so complete was the illusion.

St. Ouen's Bay, l'Etacq, Plemont, dropped behind them as they sailed. They drew on to where the rocks of the Paternosters foamed to the unquiet sea. Far over between the Nez du Guet and the sprawling granite pack of the Dirouilles, was the Admiralty yacht winging to the nor'-west. Beyond it again lay the coast of France, the tall white cliffs, the dark blue smoky curve ending in Cap de la Hague.

To-day there was something new in this picture of the coast of France. Against the far-off sands were some little black spots, seemingly no bigger than a man's hand. Again and again Jean Touzel had eyed these moving specks with serious interest; and Maitresse Aimable eyed Jean, for Jean never looked so often at anything without good reason. If, perchance, he looked three times at her consecutively, she gaped with expectation, hoping that he would tell her that her face was not so red to-day as usual—a mark of rare affection.

At last Guida noticed Jean's look. "What is it that you see, Maitre Jean?" she said.

"Little black wasps, I think, ma'm'selle-little black wasps that sting."

Guida did not understand.

Jean gave a curious cackle, and continued: "Ah, those wasps—they have a sting so nasty!" He paused an instant, then he added in a lower voice, and not quite so gaily: "Yon is the way that war begins."

Guida's fingers suddenly clinched rigidly upon the tiller. "War? Do—do you think that's a French fleet, Maitre Jean?"

"Steadee—steadee-keep her head up, ma'm'selle," he answered, for Guida had steered unsteadily for the instant. "Steadee—shale ben! that's right—I remember twenty years ago the black wasps they fly on the coast of France like that. Who can tell now?" He shrugged his shoulders. "P'rhaps they are coum out to play, but see you, when there is trouble in the nest it is my notion that wasps come out to sting. Look at France now, they all fight each other there, ma fuifre! When folks begin to slap faces at home, look out when they get into the street. That is when the devil have a grand fete."

Guida's face grew paler as he spoke. The eyes of Maitresse Aimable were fixed on her now, and unconsciously the ponderous good-wife felt in that warehouse she called her pocket for her rosary. An extra bead was there for Guida, and one for another than Guida. But Maltresse Aimable did more: she dived into the well of silence for her voice; and for the first time in her life she showed anger with Jean. As her voice came forth she coloured, her cheeks expanded, and the words sallied out in puffs:

"Nannin, Jean, you smell shark when it is but herring. You cry wasp when the critchett sing. I will believe war when I see the splinters fly—me!"

Jean looked at his wife in astonishment. That was the longest speech he had ever heard her make. It was also the first time that her rasp of criticism had ever been applied to him, and with such asperity too. He could not make it out. He looked from his wife to Guida; then, suddenly arrested by the look in her face, he scratched his shaggy head in despair, and moved about in his seat.

"Sit you still, Jean," said his wife sharply; "you're like peas on a hot griddle."

This confused Jean beyond recovery, for never in his life had Aimable spoken to him like that. He saw there was something wrong, and he did not know whether to speak or hold his tongue; or, as he said to himself, he "didn't know which eye to wink." He adjusted his spectacles, and, pulling himself together, muttered: "Smoke of thunder, what's all this?"

Guida wasn't a wisp of quality to shiver with terror at the mere mention of war with France; but ba su, thought Jean, there was now in her face a sharp, fixed look of pain, in her eyes a bewildered anxiety.

Jean scratched his head still more. Nothing particular came of that. There was no good trying to work the thing out suddenly, he wasn't clever enough. Then out of an habitual good-nature he tried to bring better weather fore and aft.

"Eh ben," said he, "in the dark you can't tell a wasp from a honey-bee till he lights on you; and that's too far off there"—he jerked a finger towards the French shore—"to be certain sure. But if the wasp nip, you make him pay for it, the head and the tail—yes, I think-me.... There's the Eperquerie," he added quickly, nodding in front of him.

The island of Sark lifted a green bosom above her perpendicular cliffs, with the pride of an affluent mother among her brood. Dowered by sun and softened by a delicate haze like an exquisite veil of modesty, this youngest daughter of the isles clustered with her kinsfolk in the emerald archipelago between the great seas.

The outlines of the coast grew plainer as the Hardi Biaou drew nearer and nearer. From end to end there was no harbour upon this southern side. There was no roadway, as it seemed no pathway at all up the overhanging cliffs-ridges of granite and grey and green rock, belted with mist, crowned by sun, and fretted by the milky, upcasting surf. Little islands, like outworks before it, crouched slumberously to the sea, as a dog lays its head in its paws and hugs the ground close, with vague, soft-blinking eyes.

By the shore the air was white with sea-gulls flying and circling, rising and descending, shooting up straight into the air; their bodies smooth and long like the body of a babe in white samite, their feathering tails spread like a fan, their wings expanding on the ambient air. In the tall cliffs were the nests of dried seaweed, fastened to the edge of a rocky bracket on lofty ledges, the little ones within piping to the little ones without. Every point of rock had its sentinel gull, looking-looking out to sea like some watchful defender of a mystic city. Piercing might be the cries of pain or of joy from the earth, more piercing were their cries; dark and dreadful might be the woe of those who went down to the sea in ships, but they shrilled on unheeding, their yellow beaks still yellowing in the sun, keeping their everlasting watch and ward.

Now and again other birds, dark, quick-winged, low-flying, shot in among the white companies of sea-gulls, stretching their long necks, and turning their swift, cowardly eyes here and there, the cruel beak extended, the body gorged with carrion. Black marauders among blithe birds of peace and joy, they watched like sable spirits near the nests, or on some near sea rocks, sombre and alone, blinked evilly at the tall bright cliffs and the lightsome legions nestling there.

These swart loiterers by the happy nests of the young were like spirits of fate who might not destroy, who had no power to harm the living, yet who could not be driven forth: the ever-present death-heads at the feast, the impressive acolytes by the altars of destiny.

As the Hardi Biaou drew near the lofty, inviolate cliffs, there opened up sombre clefts and caverns, honeycombing the island at all points of the compass. She slipped past rugged pinnacles, like buttresses to the island, here trailed with vines, valanced with shrubs of unnameable beauty, and yonder shrivelled and bare like the skin of an elephant.

Some rocks, indeed, were like vast animals round which molten granite had been poured, preserving them eternally. The heads of great dogs, like the dogs of Ossian, sprang out in profile from the repulsing mainland; stupendous gargoyles grinned at them from dark points of excoriated cliff. Farther off, the face of a battered sphinx stared with unheeding look into the vast sea and sky beyond. From the dark depths of mystic crypts came groanings, like the roaring of lions penned beside the caves of martyrs.

Jean had startled Guida with his suggestions of war between England and France. Though she longed to have Philip win glory in some great battle, yet her first natural thought was of danger to the man she loved — and the chance too of his not coming back to her from Portsmouth. But now as she looked at this scene before her, there came again to her face the old charm of blitheness. The tides of temperament in her were fast to flow and quick to ebb. The reaction from pain was in proportion to her splendid natural health.

Her lips smiled. For what can long depress the youthful and the loving when they dream that they are entirely beloved? Lands and thrones may perish, plague and devastation walk abroad with death, misery and beggary crawl naked to the doorway, and crime cower in the hedges; but to the egregious egotism of young love there are only two identities bulking in the crowded universe. To these immensities all other beings are audacious who dream of being even comfortable and obscure — happiness would be a presumption; as though Fate intended each living human being at some one moment to have the whole world to himself. And who shall cry out against that egotism with which all are diseased?

So busy was Guida with her own thoughts that she scarcely noticed they had changed their course, and were skirting the coast westerly, whereby to reach Havre Gosselin on the other side of the island. There on the shore above lay the seigneurie, the destination of the Hardi Biaou.

As they passed the western point of the island, and made their course easterly by a channel between rocky bulwarks opening Havre Gosselin, they suddenly saw a brig rounding the Eperquerie. She was making to the south-east under full sail. Her main and mizzen masts were not visible, and her colours could not be seen, but Jean's quick eye had lighted on something which made him cast apprehensive glances at his wife and Guida. There was a gun in the stern port-hole of the vanishing brig; and he also noted that it was run out for action.

His swift glance at his wife and Guida assured him that they had not noticed the gun.

Jean's brain began working with unusual celerity. He was certain that the brig was a French sloop or a privateer. In other circumstances, that in itself might not have given him much trouble of mind, for more than once French frigates had sailed round the Channel Isles in insulting strength and mockery; but at this moment every man knew that France and England were only waiting to see who should throw the ball first and set the red game going. Twenty French frigates could do little harm to the island of Sark; a hundred men could keep off an army and navy there; but Jean knew that the Admiralty yacht Dorset was sailing at this moment within half a league of the Eperquerie. He would stake his life that the brig was French and hostile and knew it also. At all costs he must follow and learn the fate of the yacht.

If he landed at Havre Gosselin and crossed the island on foot, whatever was to happen would be over and done, and that did not suit the book of Jean Touzel. More than once he had seen a little fighting, and more than once shared in it. If there was to be a fight—he looked affectionately at his carronades—then he wanted to be within seeing or striking distance.

Instead of running into Havre Gosselin, he set for the Bec du Nez, the eastern point of the island. His object was to land upon the rocks of the Eperquerie, where the women would be safe whatever befell. The tide was running strong round the point, and the surf was heavy, so that once or twice the boat was almost overturned; but Jean had measured well the currents and the wind.

This was one of the most exciting moments in his life, for, as they rounded the Bec du Nez, there was the Dorset going about to make for Guernsey, and the brig, under full sail, bearing down upon her. Even as they rounded the point, up ran the tricolour to the brig's mizzen-mast, and the militant shouts of the French sailors came over the water.

Too late had the little yacht with her handful of guns seen the danger and gone about. The wind was fair for her; but it was as fair for the brig, able to outsail her twice over. As the Hardi Biaou neared the landing-place of the Eperquerie, a gun was fired from the privateer across the bows of the Dorset, and Guida realised what was happening.

As they landed another shot was fired, then came a broadside. Guida put her hands before her eyes, and when she looked again the main-mast of the yacht was gone. And now from the heights of Sark above there rang out a cry from the lips of the affrighted islanders: "War—war—war—war!"

Guida sank down upon the rock, and her face dropped into her hands. She trembled violently. Somehow all at once, and for the first time in her life, there was borne in upon her a feeling of awful desolation and loneliness. She was alone—she was alone—she was alone that was the refrain of her thoughts.

The cry of war rang along the cliff tops; and war would take Philip from her. Perhaps she would never see him again. The horror of it, the pity of it, the peril of it.

Shot after shot the twelve-pounders of the Frenchman drove like dun hail at the white timbers of the yacht, and her masts and spars were flying. The privateer now came drawing down to where she lay lurching.

A hand touched Guida upon the shoulder. "Cheer thee, my dee-ar," said Maitresse Aimable's voice. Below, Jean Touzel had eyes only for this sea-fight before him, for, despite the enormous difference, the Englishmen were now fighting their little craft for all that she was capable. But the odds were terribly against her, though she had the windward side, and the firing of the privateer was bad. The carronades on her flush decks were replying valiantly to the twelve-pounders of the brig. At last a chance shot carried away her mizzenmast, and another dismounted her single great gun, killing a number of men. The carronades, good for only a few discharges, soon left her to the fury of her assailant, and presently the Dorset was no better than a battered raisin-box. Her commander had destroyed his despatches, and nothing remained now but to be sunk or surrender.

In not more than twenty minutes from the time the first shot was fired, the commander and his brave little crew yielded to the foe, and the Dorset's flag was hauled down.

When her officers and men were transferred to the Frenchman, her one passenger and guest, the Rev. Lorenzo Dow, passed calmly from the gallant little wreck to the deck of the privateer, with a finger between the leaves of his book of meditations. With as much equanimity as he would have breakfasted with a bishop, made breaches of the rubric, or drunk from a sailor's black-jack, he went calmly into captivity in France, giving no thought to what he left behind; quite heedless that his going would affect for good or ill the destiny of the young wife of Philip d'Avranche.

Guida watched the yacht go down, and the brig bear away towards France where those black wasps of war were as motes against the white sands. Then she remembered that there had gone with it one of the three people in the world who knew her secret, the man who had married her to Philip. She shivered a little, she scarcely knew why, for it did not then seem of consequence to her whether Mr. Dow went or stayed, though he had never given her the marriage certificate. Indeed, was it not better he should go? Thereby one less would know her secret. But still an undefined fear possessed her.

"Cheer thee, cheer thee, my dee-ar, my sweet dormitte," said Maitresse Aimable, patting her shoulder. "It cannot harm thee, ba su! 'Tis but a flash in the pan."

Guida's first impulse was to throw herself into the arms of the slow-tongued, great-hearted woman who hung above her like a cloud of mercy, and tell her whole story. But no, she would keep her word to Philip, till Philip came again. Her love—the love of the young, lonely wife, must be buried deep in her own heart until he appeared and gave her the right to speak.

Jean was calling to them. They rose to go. Guida looked about her. Was it all a dream-all that had happened to her, and around her? The world was sweet to look upon, and yet was it true that here before her eyes there had been war, and that out of war peril must come to her.

A week ago she was free as air, happy as healthy body, truthful mind, simple nature, and tender love can make a human being. She was then only a young, young girl. To-day-she sighed.

Long after they put out to sea again she could still hear the affrighted cry of the peasants from the cliff-or was it only the plaintive echo of her own thoughts?

"War—war—war—war!"

# IN FRANCE—NEAR FIVE MONTHS AFTER

## CHAPTER XIX

### "A moment, monsieur le duc."

The Duke turned at the door, and looked with listless inquiry into the face of the Minister of Marine, who, picking up an official paper from his table, ran an eye down it, marked a point with the sharp corner of his snuff-box, and handed it over to his visitor, saying:

"Our roster of English prisoners taken in the action off Brest."

The Duke, puzzled, lifted his glass and scanned the roll mechanically.

"No, no, Duke, just where I have marked," interposed the Minister.

"My dear Monsieur Dalbarade," remarked the Duke a little querulously, "I do not see what interest—"

He stopped short, however, looked closer at the document, and then lowering it in a sort of amazement, seemed about to speak; but, instead, raised the paper again and fixed his eyes intently on the spot indicated by the Minister.

"Most curious," he said after a moment, making little nods of his head towards Dalbarade; "my own name—and an English prisoner, you say?"

"Precisely so; and he gave our fellows some hard knocks before his frigate went on the reefs."

"Strange that the name should be my own. I never heard of an English branch of our family."

A quizzical smile passed over the face of the Minister, adding to his visitor's mystification. "But suppose he were English, yet French too?" he rejoined.

"I fail to understand the entanglement," answered the Duke stiffly.

"He is an Englishman whose name and native language are French—he speaks as good French as your own."

The Duke peevishly tapped a chair with his stick. "I am no reader of riddles, monsieur," he said acidly, although eager to know more concerning this Englishman of the same name as himself, ruler of the sovereign duchy of Bercy.

"Shall I bid him enter, Prince?" asked the Minister. The Duke's face relaxed a little, for the truth was, at this moment of his long life he was deeply concerned with his own name and all who bore it.

"Is he here then?" he asked, nodding assent.

"In the next room," answered the Minister, turning to a bell and ringing. "I have him here for examination, and was but beginning when I was honoured by your Highness's presence." He bowed politely, yet there was, too, a little mockery in the bow, which did not escape the Duke. These were days when princes received but little respect in France.

A subaltern entered, received an order, and disappeared. The Duke withdrew to the embrasure of a window, and immediately the prisoner was gruffly announced.

The young Englishman stood quietly waiting, his quick eyes going from Dalbarade to the wizened figure by the window, and back again to the Minister. His look carried both calmness and defiance, but the defiance came only from a sense of injury and unmerited disgrace.

"Monsieur," said the Minister with austerity, "in your further examination we shall need to repeat some questions."

The prisoner nodded indifferently, and for a brief space there was silence. The Duke stood by the window, the Minister by his table, the prisoner near the door. Suddenly the prisoner, with an abrupt motion of the hand towards two chairs, said with an assumption of ordinary politeness:

"Will you not be seated?"

The remark was so odd in its coolness and effrontery, that the Duke chuckled audibly. The Minister was completely taken aback. He glanced stupidly at the two chairs—the only ones in the room—and at the prisoner. Then the insolence of the thing began to work upon him, and he was about to burst forth, when the Duke came forward, and politely moving a chair near to the young commander, said:

"My distinguished compliments, monsieur le capitaine. I pray you accept this chair."

With quiet self-possession and a matter-of-course air the prisoner bowed politely, and seated himself, then with a motion of the hand backward towards the door, said to the Duke: "I've been standing five hours with some of those moutons in the ante-room. My profound thanks to monseigneur."

Touching the angry Minister on the arm, the Duke said quietly:

"Dear monsieur, will you permit me a few questions to the prisoner?"

At that instant there came a tap at the door, and an orderly entered with a letter to the Minister, who glanced at it hurriedly, then turned to the prisoner and the Duke, as though in doubt what to do.

"I will be responsible for the prisoner, if you must leave us," said the Duke at once.

"For a little, for a little—a matter of moment with the Minister of War," answered Dalbarade, nodding, and with an air of abstraction left the room.

The Duke withdrew to the window again, and seated himself in the embrasure, at some little distance from the Englishman, who at once got up and brought his chair closer. The warm sunlight of spring, streaming through the window, was now upon his pale face, and strengthened it, giving it fulness and the eye fire.

"How long have you been a prisoner, monsieur?" asked the Duke, at the same time acknowledging the other's politeness with a bow.

"Since March, monseigneur."

"Monseigneur again—a man of judgment," said the Duke to himself, pleased to have his exalted station recognised. "H'm, and it is now June— four months, monsieur. You have been well used, monsieur?"

"Vilely, monseigneur," answered the other; "a shipwrecked enemy should never be made prisoner, or at least he should be enlarged on parole; but I have been confined like a pirate in a sink of a jail."

"Of what country are you?"

Raising his eyebrows in amazement the young man answered:

"I am an Englishman, monseigneur."

"Monsieur is of England, then?"

"Monseigneur, I am an English officer."

"You speak French well, monsieur."

"Which serves me well in France, as you see, monseigneur."

The Duke was a trifle nettled. "Where were you born, monsieur?"

There was a short pause, and then the prisoner, who had enjoyed the other's perplexity, said:

"On the Isle of Jersey, monseigneur."

The petulant look passed immediately from the face of the Duke; the horizon was clear at once.

"Ah, then, you are French, monsieur!"

"My flag is the English flag; I was born a British subject, and I shall die one," answered the other steadily.

"The sentiment sounds estimable," answered the Duke; "but as for life and death, and what we are or what we may be, we are the sport of Fate." His brow clouded. "I myself was born under a monarchy; I shall probably die under a Republic. I was born a Frenchman; I may die—"

His tone had become low and cynical, and he broke off suddenly, as though he had said more than he meant. "Then you are a Norman, monsieur," he added in a louder tone.

"Once all Jerseymen were Normans, and so were many Englishmen, monseigneur."

"I come of Norman stock too, monsieur," remarked the Duke graciously, yet eyeing the young man keenly.

"Monseigneur has not the kindred advantage of being English?" added the prisoner dryly.

The Duke protested with a deprecatory wave of the fingers and a flash of the sharp eyes, and then, after a slight pause, said: "What is your name, monsieur?"

"Philip d'Avranche," was the brief reply; then with droll impudence: "And monseigneur's, by monseigneur's leave?"

The Duke smiled, and that smile relieved the sourness, the fret of a face which had care and discontent written upon every line of it. It was a face that had never known happiness. It had known diversion, however, and unusual diversion it knew at this moment.

"My name," he answered with a penetrating quizzical look, "—my name is Philip d'Avranche."

The young man's quick, watchful eyes fixed themselves like needles on the Duke's face. Through his brain there ran a succession of queries and speculations, and dominating them all one clear question-was he to gain anything by this strange conversation? Who was this great man with a name the same as his own, this crabbed nobleman with skin as yellow as an orange, and body like an orange squeezed dry? He surely meant him no harm, however, for flashes of kindliness had lighted the shrivelled face as he talked. His look was bent in piercing comment upon Philip, who, trying hard to solve the mystery, now made a tentative rejoinder to his strange statement. Rising from his chair and bowing, he said, with shrewd foreknowledge of the effect of his words:

"I had not before thought my own name of such consequence."

The old man grunted amiably. "My faith, the very name begets a towering conceit wherever it goes," he answered, and he brought his stick down on the floor with such vehemence that the emerald and ruby rings rattled on his shrunken fingers.

"Be seated—cousin," he said with dry compliment, for Philip had remained standing, as if with the unfeigned respect of a cadet in the august presence of the head of his house. It was a sudden and bold suggestion, and it was not lost on the Duke. The aged nobleman was too keen an observer not to see the designed flattery, but he was in a mood when flattery was palatable, seeing that many of his own class were arrayed against him for not having joined the army of the Vendee; and that the Revolutionists, with whom he had compromised, for the safety of his lands of d'Avranche and his duchy of Bercy, regarded him with suspicion. Between the two, the old man—at heart most profoundly a Royalist—bided his time, in some peril but with no fear. The spirit of this young Englishman of his own name pleased him; the flattery, patent as it was, gratified him, for in revolutionary France few treated him with deference now. Even the Minister of Marine, with whom he was on good terms, called him "citizen" at times.

All at once it flashed on the younger man that this must be the Prince d'Avranche, Duc de Bercy, of that family of d'Avranche from which his own came in long descent—even from the days of Rollo, Duke of Normandy. He recalled on the instant the token of fealty of the ancient House of d'Avranche—the offering of a sword.

"Your Serene Highness," he said with great deference and as great tact, "I must first offer my homage to the Prince d'Avranche, Duc de Bercy—" Then with a sudden pause, and a whimsical look, he added: "But, indeed, I had forgotten, they have taken away my sword!"

"We shall see," answered the Prince, well pleased, "we shall see about that sword. Be seated." Then, after a short pause: "Tell me now, monsieur, of your family, of your ancestry."

His eyes were bent on Philip with great intentness, and his thin lips tightened in some unaccountable agitation.

Philip instantly responded. He explained how in the early part of the thirteenth century, after the great crusade against the Albigenses, a cadet of the house of d'Avranche had emigrated to England, and had come to place and honour under Henry III, who gave to the son of this d'Avranche certain tracts of land in Jersey, where he settled. Philip was descended in a direct line from this same receiver of king's favours, and was now the only representative of his family.

While Philip spoke the Duke never took eyes from his face—that face so facile in the display of feeling or emotion. The voice also had a lilt of health and vitality which rang on the ears of age pleasantly. As he listened he thought of his eldest son, partly imbecile, all but a lusus naturae, separated from his wife immediately after marriage, through whom there could never be succession—he thought of him, and for the millionth time in his life winced in impotent disdain. He thought too of his beloved second son, lying in a soldier's grave in Macedonia; of the buoyant resonance of that by-gone voice, of the soldierly good spirits like to the good spirits of the prisoner before him, and "his heart yearned towards the young man exceedingly." If that second son had but lived there would be now no compromising with this Republican Government of France; he would be fighting for the white flag with the golden lilies over in the Vendee.

"Your ancestors were mine, then," remarked the Duke gravely, after a pause, "though I had not heard of that emigration to England. However—however! Come, tell me of the engagement in which you lost your ship," he added hurriedly in a low tone. He was now so intent that he did not stir in his seat, but sat rigidly still, regarding Philip kindly. Something in the last few moments' experience had loosened the puckered skin, softened the crabbed look in the face, and Philip had no longer doubt of his friendly intentions.

"I had the frigate Araminta, twenty-four guns, a fortnight out from Portsmouth," responded Philip at once. "We fell in with a French frigate, thirty guns. She was well to leeward of us, and the Araminta bore up under all sail, keen for action. The Frenchman was as ready as ourselves for a brush, and tried to get the weather of us, but, failing, she shortened sail and gallantly waited for us. The Araminta overhauled her on the weather quarter, and hailed. She responded with cheers and defiance—as sturdy a foe as man could wish. We lost no time in getting to work, and, both running before the wind, we fired broadsides as we cracked on. It was tit-for-tat for a while with splinters flying and neither of us in the eye of advantage, but at last the Araminta shot away the main-mast and wheel of the Niobe, and she wallowed like a tub in the trough of the sea. We bore down on her, and our carronades raked her like a comb. Then we fell thwart her hawse, and tore her up through her bowline-ports with a couple of thirty-two-pounders. But before we could board her she veered, lurched, and fell upon us, carrying away our foremast. We cut clear of the tangle, and were making once more to board her, when I saw to windward two French frigates bearing down on us under full sail. And then—"

The Prince exclaimed in surprise: "I had not heard of this," he said. "They did not tell the world of those odds against you."

"Odds and to spare, monsieur le due! We had had all we could manage in the Niobe, though she was now disabled, and we could hurt her no more. If the others came up on our weather we should be chewed like a bone in a mastiff's jaws. If she must fight again, the Araminta would be little fit for action till we cleared away the wreckage; so I sheered off to make all sail. We ran under courses with what canvas we had, and got away with a fair breeze and a good squall whitening to windward, while our decks were cleared for action again. The guns on the main-deck had done good service and kept their places. On the quarter-deck and fo'castle there was more amiss, but as I watched the frigates overhauling us I took heart of grace still. There was the creaking and screaming of the carronade-slides, the rattling of the carriages of the long twelve-pounders amidships as they were shotted and run out again, the thud of the carpenters' hammers as the shot-holes were plugged—good sounds in the ears of a fighter—"

"Of a d'Avranche—of a d'Avranche!" interposed the Prince.

"We were in no bad way, and my men were ready for another brush with our enemies, everything being done that could be done, everything in its place," continued Philip. "When the frigates were a fair gunshot off, I saw that the squall was overhauling us faster than they. This meant good fortune if we wished escape, bad luck if we would rather fight. But I had no time to think of that, for up comes Shoreham, my lieutenant, with a face all white. 'For God's sake, sir,' says he, 'shoal water-shoal water! We're ashore.' So much, monsieur le prince, for Admiralty charts and soundings! It's a hateful thing to see—the light green water, the deadly sissing of the straight narrow ripple like the grooves of a wash-board: and a ship's length ahead the water breaking over the reefs, two frigates behind ready to eat us.

"Up we came to the wind, the sheets were let run, and away flew the halyards. All to no purpose, for a minute later we came broadside on the reef, and were gored on a pinnacle of rock. The end wasn't long in coming. The Araminta lurched off the reef on the swell. We watched our chance as she rolled, and hove overboard our broadside of long twelve-pounders. But it was no use. The swishing of the water as it spouted from the scuppers was a deal louder than the clang of the chain-pumps. It didn't last long. The gale spilled itself upon us, and the Araminta, sick and spent, slowly settled down. The last I saw of her"—Philip raised his voice as though he would hide what he felt behind an unsentimental loudness—"was the white pennant at the main-top gallant masthead. A little while, and then I didn't see it, and—and so good-bye to my first command! Then"—he smiled ironically—"then I was made prisoner by the French frigates, and have been closely confined ever since, against every decent principle of warfare. And now here I am, monsieur le duc."

The Duke had listened with an immovable attention, the grey eyebrows twitching now and then, the arid face betraying a grim enjoyment. When Philip had finished, he still sat looking at him with steady slow-blinking eyes, as though unwilling to break the spell the tale had thrown round him. But an inquisition in the look, a slight cocking of the head as though weighing important things, the ringed fingers softly drumming on the stick before him—all these told Philip that something was at stake concerning himself.

The Duke seemed about to speak, when the door of the room opened and the Minister of Marine entered. The Duke, rising and courteously laying a hand on his arm, drew him over to the window, and engaged him in whispered conversation, of which the subject seemed unwelcome to the Minister, for now and then he interrupted sharply.

As the two stood fretfully debating, the door of the room again opened. There appeared an athletic, adventurous-looking officer in brilliant uniform who was smiling at something called after him from the antechamber. His blue coat was spick and span and very gay with double embroidery at the collar, coat-tails, and pockets. His white waistcoat and trousers were spotless; his netted sash of blue with its stars on the silver tassels had a look of studied elegance. The black three-cornered hat, broidered with gold, and adorned with three ostrich tips of red and a white and blue aigrette, was, however, the glory of his bravery. He seemed young to be a General of Division, for such his double embroideries and aigrette proclaimed him.

He glanced at Philip, and replied to his salute with a half-quizzical smile on his proud and forceful face. "Dalbarade, Dalbarade," said he to the Minister, "I have but an hour—ah, monsieur le prince!" he added suddenly, as the latter came hurriedly towards him, and, grasping his hand warmly, drew him over to Dalbarade at the window. Philip now knew beyond doubt that he was the subject of debate, for all the time that the Duke in a low tone, half cordial, half querulous, spoke to the new-comer, the latter let his eyes wander curiously towards Philip. That he was an officer of great importance was to be seen from the deference paid him by Dalbarade.

All at once he made a polite gesture towards the Duke, and, facing the Minister, said in a cavalier-like tone, and with a touch of patronage: "Yes, yes, Dalbarade; it is of no consequence, and I myself will be surety for both." Then turning to the nobleman, he added: "We are beginning to square accounts, Duke. Last time we met I had a large favour of you, and to-day you have a small favour of me. Pray introduce your kinsman here, before you take him with you," and he turned squarely towards Philip.

Philip could scarcely believe his ears. The Duke's kinsman! Had the Duke then got his release on the ground that they were of kin—a kinship which, even to be authentic, must go back seven centuries for proof?

Yet here he was being introduced to the revolutionary general as "my kinsman of the isles of Normandy." Here, too, was the same General Grandjon-Larisse applauding him on his rare fortune to be thus released on parole through the Duc de Bercy, and quoting with a laugh, half sneer and half raillery, the old Norman proverb: "A Norman dead a thousand years cries Haro! Haro! if you tread on his grave."

So saying, he saluted the Duke with a liberal flourish of the hand and a friendly bow, and turned away to Dalbarade.

A half-hour later Philip was outside with the Duke, walking slowly through the court-yard to an open gateway, where waited a carriage with unliveried coachman and outriders. No word was spoken till they entered the carriage and were driven swiftly away.

"Whither now, your Highness?" asked Philip.

"To the duchy," answered the other shortly, and relapsed into sombre meditation.

# CHAPTER XX

The castle of the Prince d'Avranche, Duc de Bercy, was set upon a vast rock, and the town of Bercy huddled round the foot of it and on great granite ledges some distance up. With fifty defenders the castle, on its lofty pedestal, might have resisted as many thousands; and, indeed, it had done so more times than there were rubies in the rings of the present Duke, who had rescued Captain Philip d'Avranche from the clutches of the Red Government.

Upon the castle, with the flag of the duchy, waved the republican tricolour, where for a thousand years had floated a royal banner. When France's great trouble came to her, and the nobles fled, or went to fight for the King in the Vendee, the old Duke, with a dreamy indifference to the opinion of Europe, had proclaimed alliance with the new Government. He felt himself privileged in being thus selfish; and he had made the alliance that he might pursue, unchecked, the one remaining object of his life.

This object had now grown from a habit into a passion. It was now his one ambition to arrange a new succession excluding the Vaufontaines, a detested branch of the Bercy family. There had been an ancient feud between his family and the Vaufontaines, whose rights to the succession, after his eldest son, were to this time paramount. For three years past he had had a whole monastery of Benedictine monks at work to find some collateral branch from which he might take a successor to Leopold John, his imbecile heir—but to no purpose.

In more than a little the Duke was superstitious, and on the day when he met Philip d'Avranche in the chamber of M. Dalbarade he had twice turned back after starting to make the visit, so great was his dislike to pay homage to the revolutionary Minister. He had nerved himself to the distasteful duty, however, and had gone. When he saw the name of the young English prisoner—his own name—staring him in the face, he had had such a thrill as a miracle might have sent through the veins of a doubting Christian.

Since that minute he, like Philip, had been in a kind of dream; on his part, to find in the young man, if possible, an heir and successor; on Philip's to make real exalted possibilities. There had slipped past two months, wherein Philip had seen a new and brilliant avenue of life opening out before him.

Most like a dream indeed it seemed. He had been shut out from the world, cut off from all connection with England and his past, for M. Dalbarade made it a condition of release that he should send no message or correspond with any one outside Castle Bercy. He had not therefore written to Guida. She seemed an interminable distance away. He was as completely in a new world as though he had been transplanted; he was as wholly in the air of fresh ambitions as though he were beginning the world again—ambitions as gorgeous as bewildering.

For, almost from the first, the old nobleman treated him like a son. He spoke freely to him of the most private family matters, of the most important State affairs. He consulted with him, he seemed to lean upon him. He alluded often, in oblique phrase, to adoption and succession. In the castle Philip was treated as though he were in truth a high kinsman of the Duke. Royal ceremony and state were on every hand. He who had never had a servant of his own, now had a score at his disposal. He had spent his early days in a small Jersey manor-house; here he was walking the halls of a palace with the step of assurance, the most honoured figure in a principality next to the sovereign himself. "Adoption and succession" were words that rang in his ears day and night. The wild dream had laid feverish hands upon him. Jersey, England, the Navy, seemed very far away.

Ambition was the deepest passion in him, even as defeating the hopes of the Vaufontaines was more than a religion with the Duke. By no trickery, but by a persistent good-nature, alertness of speech, avoidance of dangerous topics, and aptness in anecdote, he had hourly made his position stronger, himself more honoured at the Castle Bercy. He had also tactfully declined an offer of money from the Prince—none the less decidedly because he was nearly penniless. The Duke's hospitality he was ready to accept, but not his purse—not yet.

Yet he was not in all acting a part. He was sincere in his liking for the soured, bereaved sovereign, forced to endure alliance with a Government he loathed. He even admired the Duke for his vexing idiosyncrasies, for they came of a strong individuality which, in happier case, should have made him a contented and beloved monarch. As it was, the people of his duchy were loyal to him beyond telling, doing his bidding without cavil: standing for the King of France at his will, declaring for the Republic at his command; for, whatever the Duke was to the world outside, within his duchy he was just and benevolent, if imperious.

All these things Philip had come to know in his short sojourn. He had, with the Duke, mingled freely, yet with great natural dignity, among the people of the duchy, and was introduced everywhere, and at all times, as the sovereign's kinsman—"in a direct line from an ancient branch," as his Highness declared. He had been received gladly, and had made himself an agreeable figure in the duchy, to the delight of the Duke, who watched his every motion, every word, and their effect. He came to know the gossip gone abroad that the Duke had already chosen him for heir. A fantastic rumour, maybe, yet who could tell?

One day the Duke arranged a conference of the civil and military officers of his duchy. He chuckled to see how reluctant they all were at first to concede their homage to his favourite, and how soon they fell under that favourite's influence—all save one man, the Intendant of the duchy. Philip himself was quick to see that this man, Count Carignan Damour, apprehensive for his own selfish ends, was bitterly opposed to him. But Damour was one among many, and the Duke was entirely satisfied, for the common people received Philip with applause.

On this very day was laid before the Duke the result of the long researches of the monks into the genealogy of the d'Avranches, and there, clearly enough, was confirmation of all Philip had said about his ancestors and their relation to the ancient house of d'Avranche. The Duke was overjoyed, and thereupon secretly made ready for Philip's formal adoption and succession. It never occurred to him that Philip might refuse.

On the same afternoon he sent for Philip to come to him in the highest room of the great tower. It was in this room that, many years ago, the Duke's young and noble wife, from the province of Aquitaine, had given birth to the second son of the house of Bercy, and had died a year later, happy that she should at last leave behind a healthy, beautiful child, to do her honour in her lord's eyes.

In this same room the Duke and the brave second son had spent unnumbered hours; and here it had come home to him that the young wife was faultless as to the elder, else she had not borne him this perfect younger son. Thus her memory came to be adored; and thus, when the noble second son, the glory of his house and of his heart, was killed in Macedonia, the Duke still came to the little upper room for his communion of remembrance. Hour after hour he would sit looking from the great window out over the wide green valley, mourning bitterly, and feeling his heart shrivel up within him, his body grow crabbed and cold, and his face sour and scornful.

When Philip now entered this sanctuary, the Duke nodded and motioned him to a chair. In silence he accepted, and in silence they sat for a time. Philip knew the history of this little room—he had learned it first from Frange Pergot, the porter at the castle gates with whom he had made friends. The silence gave him opportunity to recall the whole story.

At length the motionless brown figure huddled in the great chair, not looking at Philip but out over the wide green valley, began to speak in a low, measured tone, as a dreamer might tell his dream, or a priest his vision:

"A breath of life has come again to me through you. Centuries ago our ancestors were brothers—far back in the direct line, brothers—the monks have proved it.

"Now I shall have my spite of the Vaufoutaines, and now shall I have another son—strong, and with good blood in him to beget good blood."

A strange, lean sort of smile passed over his lips, his eyebrows twitched, his hands clinched the arm of the chair wherein he sat, and he made a motion of his jaws as though enjoying a toothsome morsel.

"H'm, Henri Vaufontaine shall see—and all his tribe! They shall not feed upon these lands of the d'Avranches, they shall not carouse at my table when I am gone and the fool I begot has returned to his Maker. The fault of him was never mine, but God's—does the Almighty think we can forget that? I was ever sound and strong. When I was twenty I killed two men with my own sword at a blow; when I was thirty, to serve the King I rode a hundred and forty miles in one day—from Paris to Dracourt it was. We d'Avranches have been men of power always. We fought for Christ's sepulchre in the Holy Land, and three bishops and two archbishops have gone from us to speak God's cause to the world. And my wife, she came of the purest stock of Aquitaine, and she was constant, in her prayers. What discourtesy was it then, for God, who hath been served well by us, to serve me in return with such mockery: to send me a bloodless zany, whom his wife left ere the wedding meats were cold."

His foot tapped the floor in anger, his eyes wandered restlessly out over the green expanse. Suddenly a dove perched upon the window-sill before him. His quick, shifting gaze settled on it and stayed, softening and quieting.

After a slight pause, he turned to Philip and spoke in a still lower tone. "Last night in the chapel I spake to God and I said: 'Lord God, let there be fair speech between us. Wherefore hast Thou nailed me like a malefactor to the tree? Why didst Thou send me a fool to lead our house, and afterwards a lad as fine and strong as Absalom, and then lay him low like a wisp of corn in the wind, leaving me wifeless—with a prince to follow me, the by-word of men, the scorn of women—and of the Vaufontaines?'"

He paused again, and his eyes seemed to pierce Philip's, as though he would read if each word was burning its way into his brain.

"As I stood there alone, a voice spoke to me as plainly as now I speak to you, and it said: 'Have done with railing. That which was the elder's shall be given to the younger. The tree hath grown crabbed and old, it beareth no longer. Behold the young sapling by thy door—I have planted it there. The seed is the seed of the old tree. Cherish it, lest a grafted tree flourish in thy house.'".... His words rose triumphantly. "Yes, yes, I heard it with my own ears, the Voice. The crabbed tree, that is the main line, dying in me; the grafted tree is the Vaufontaine, the interloper and the mongrel; and the sapling from the same seed as the crabbed old tree"—he reached out as though to clutch Philip's arm, but drew back, sat erect in his chair, and said with ringing decision: "the sapling is Philip d'Avranche, of the Jersey Isle."

For a moment there was silence between the two. A strong wind came rushing up the valley through the clear sunlight, the great trees beneath the castle swayed, and the flapping of the tricolour could be heard within. From the window-sill the dove, caught up on the wave of wind, sailed away down the widening glade.

Philip's first motion was to stand up and say: "I dare not think your Highness means in very truth to make me your kinsman in the succession."

"And why not, why not?" testily answered the Duke, who liked not to be imperfectly apprehended. Then he added more kindly: "Why not—come, tell me that, cousin? Is it then distasteful?"

Philip's heart gave a leap and his face flushed. "I have no other kinsman," he answered in a low tone of feeling. "I knew I had your august friendship—else all the tokens of your goodness to me were mockery; but I had scarce let myself count on the higher, more intimate honour—I, a poor captain in the English navy."

He said the last words slowly, for, whatever else he was, he was a loyal English sailor, and he wished the Duc de Bercy to know it, the more convincingly the better for the part he was going to play in this duchy, if all things favoured.

"Tut, tut, what has that to do with it?" answered the Duke. "What has poverty to do with blood? Younger sons are always poor, younger cousins poorer. As for the captaincy of an English warship, that's of no consequence where greater games are playing—eh?"

He eyed Philip keenly, yet too there was an unasked question in his look. He was a critic of human nature, he understood the code of honour, none better; his was a mind that might be wilfully but never crassly blind. He was selfish where this young gentleman was concerned, yet he knew well how the same gentleman ought to think, speak, and act.

The moment of the great test was come.

Philip could not read behind the strange, shrivelled face. Instinct could help him much, but it could not interpret that parchment. He did not know whether his intended reply would alienate the Duke or not, but if it did, then he must bear it. He had come, as he thought, to the crux of this adventure. All in a moment he was recalled again to his real position. The practical facts of his life possessed him. He was standing between a garish dream and commonplace realities. Old feelings came back—the old life. The ingrain loyalty of all his years was his again. Whatever he might be, he was still an English officer, and he was not the man to break the code of professional honour lightly. If the Duke's favour and adoption must depend on the answer he must now give, well, let it be; his last state could not be worse than his first.

So, still standing, he answered the Duke boldly, yet quietly, his new kinsman watching him with a grim curiosity.

"Monsieur le prince," said Philip, "I am used to poverty, that matters little; but whatever you intend towards me—and I am persuaded it is to my great honour and happiness—I am, and must still remain, an officer of the English navy."

The Duke's brow contracted, and his answer came cold and incisive: "The navy—that is a bagatelle; I had hoped to offer you heritage. Pooh, pooh, commanding a frigate is a trade—a mere trade!"

Philip's face did not stir a muscle. He was in spirit the born adventurer, the gamester who could play for life's largest stakes, lose all, draw a long breath—and begin the world again.

"It's a busy time in my trade now, as Monsieur Dalbarade would tell you, Duke."

The Duke's lips compressed as though in anger. "You mean to say, monsieur, that you would let this wretched war between France and England stand before our own kinship and alliance? What are you and I in this great shuffle of events? Have less egotism, less vanity, monsieur. You are no more than a million others—and I—I am nothing. Come, come, there is more than one duty in the life of every man, and sometime he must choose between one and the other. England does not need you"—his voice and manner softened, he leaned towards Philip, the eyes almost closing as he peered into his face—"but you are needed by the House of Bercy."

"I was commissioned to a warship in time of war," answered Philip quietly, "and I lost that warship. When I can, it is my duty to go back to the powers that sent me forth. I am still an officer in full commission. Your Highness knows well what honour claims of me."

"There are hundreds of officers to take your place; in the duchy of Bercy there is none to stand for you. You must choose between your trade and the claims of name and blood, older than the English navy, older than Norman England."

Philip's colour was as good, his manner as easy as if nothing were at stake; but in his heart he felt that the game was lost—he saw a storm gathering in the Duke's eyes, the disappointment presently to break out into wrath, the injured vanity to burst into snarling disdain. But he spoke boldly nevertheless, for he was resolved that, even if he had to return from this duchy to prison, he would go with colours flying.

"The proudest moment of my life was when the Duc de Bercy called me kinsman," he responded; "the best" (had he then so utterly forgotten the little church of St. Michael's?) "was when he showed me friendship. Yet, if my trade may not be reconciled with what he may intend for me, I must ask to be sent back to Monsieur Dalbarade." He smiled hopelessly, yet with stoical disregard of consequences, and went on: "For my trade is in full swing these days, and I stand my chance of being exchanged and earning my daily bread again. At the Admiralty I am a master workman on full pay, but I'm not earning my salt here. With Monsieur Dalbarade my conscience would be easier."

He had played his last card. Now he was prepared for the fury of a jaundiced, self-willed old man, who could ill brook being thwarted. He had quickly imagined it all, and not without reason, for surely a furious disdain was at the grey lips, lines of anger were corrugating the forehead, the rugose parchment face was fiery with distemper.

But what Philip expected did not come to pass. Rising quickly to his feet, the Duke took him by the shoulders, kissed him on both cheeks, and said:

"My mind is made up—is made up. Nothing can change it. You have no father, cousin—well, I will be your father. You shall retain your post in the English navy-officer and patriot you shall be if you choose. A brave man makes a better ruler. But now there is much to do. There is the concurrence of the English King to secure; that shall be—has already been—my business. There is the assent of Leopold John to achieve; that I shall command. There are the grave formalities of adoption to arrange; these I shall expedite. You shall see, Master Insolence—you, who'd throw me and my duchy over for your trade; you shall see how the Vaufontaines will gnash their teeth!"

In his heart Philip was exultant, though outwardly he was calm. He was, however, unprepared for what followed. Suddenly the Duke, putting a hand on his shoulder, said:

"One thing, cousin, one thing: you must marry in our order, and at once. There shall be no delay. Succession must be made sure. I know the very woman—the Comtesse Chantavoine—young, rich, amiable. You shall meet her to-morrow-to-morrow."

# CHAPTER XXI

"The Comtesse Chantavoine, young, rich, amiable. You shall meet her to-morrow"...!—Long after Philip left the Duke to go to his own chamber, these words rang in his ears. He suddenly felt the cords of fate tightening round him. So real was the momentary illusion that, as he passed through the great hall where hung the portraits of the Duke's ancestors, he made a sudden outward motion of his arms as though to free himself from a physical restraint. Strange to say, he had never foreseen or reckoned with this matter of marriage in the designs of the Duke. He had forgotten that sovereign dukes must make sure their succession even unto the third and fourth generation. His first impulse had been to tell the Duke that to introduce him to the Countess would be futile, for he was already married. But the instant warning of the mind that his Highness could never and would never accept the daughter of a Jersey ship-builder restrained him. He had no idea that Guida's descent from the noble de Mauprats of Chambery would weigh with the Duke, who would only see in her some apple-cheeked peasant stumbling over her court train.

It was curious that the Duke had never even hinted at the chance of his being already married—yet not so curious either, since complete silence concerning a wife was in itself declaration enough that he was unmarried. He felt in his heart that a finer sense would have offered Guida no such humiliation, for he knew the lie of silence to be as evil as the lie of speech.

He had not spoken, partly because he had not yet become used to the fact that he really was married. It had never been brought home to him by the ever-present conviction of habit. One day of married life, or, in reality, a few hours of married life, with Guida had given the sensation more of a noble adventure than of a lasting condition. With distance from that noble adventure, something of the glow of a lover's relations had gone, and the subsequent tender enthusiasm of mind and memory was not vivid enough to make him daring or—as he would have said—reckless for its sake. Yet this same tender enthusiasm was sincere enough to make him accept the fact of his marriage without discontent, even in the glamour of new and alluring ambitions.

If it had been a question of giving up Guida or giving up the duchy of Bercy—if that had been put before him as the sole alternative, he would have decided as quickly in Guida's favour as he did when he thought it was a question between the duchy and the navy. The straightforward issue of Guida or the duchy he had not been called upon to face. But, unfortunately for those who are tempted, issues are never put quite so plainly by the heralds of destiny and penalty. They are disguised as delectable chances: the toss-up is always the temptation of life. The man who uses trust-money for three days, to acquire in those three days a fortune, certain as magnificent, would pull up short beforehand if the issue of theft or honesty were put squarely before him. Morally he means no theft; he uses his neighbour's saw until his own is mended: but he breaks his neighbour's saw, his own is lost on its homeward way; and having no money to buy another, he is tried and convicted on a charge of theft. Thus the custom of society establishes the charge of immorality upon the technical defect. But not on that alone; upon the principle that what is committed in trust shall be held inviolate, with an exact obedience to the spirit as to the letter of the law.

The issue did not come squarely to Philip. He had not openly lied about Guida: so far he had had no intention of doing so. He even figured to himself with what surprise Guida would greet his announcement that she was henceforth Princesse Guida d'Avranche, and in due time would be her serene highness the Duchesse de Bercy. Certainly there was nothing immoral in his ambitions. If the reigning Prince chose to establish him as heir, who had a right to complain?

Then, as to an officer of the English navy accepting succession in a sovereign duchy in suzerainty to the present Government of France, while England was at war with her, the Duke had more than once, in almost so many words, defined the situation. Because the Duke himself, with no successor assured, was powerless to side with the Royalists against the Red Government, he was at the moment obliged, for the very existence of his duchy, to hoist the tricolour upon the castle with his own flag. Once the succession was secure beyond the imbecile Leopold John, then he would certainly declare against the present fiendish Government and for the overthrown dynasty.

Now England was fighting France, not only because she was revolutionary France, but because of the murder of Louis XVI and for the restoration of the overthrown dynasty. Also she was in close sympathy with the war of the Vendee, to which she would lend all possible assistance. Philip argued that if it was his duty, as a captain in the English navy, to fight against the revolutionaries from without, he would be beyond criticism if, as the Duc de Bercy, he also fought against them from within.

Indeed, it was with this plain statement of the facts that the second military officer of the duchy had some days before been sent to the Court of St. James to secure its intervention for Philip's freedom by exchange of prisoners. This officer was also charged with securing the consent of the English King for Philip's acceptance of succession in the duchy, while retaining his position in the English navy. The envoy had been instructed by the Duke to offer his sympathy with England in the war and his secret adherence to the Royalist cause, to become open so soon as the succession through Philip was secured.

To Philip's mind all that side of the case was in his favour, and sorted well with his principles of professional honour. His mind was not so acutely occupied with his private honour. To tell the Duke now of his marriage would be to load the dice against himself: he felt that the opportunity for speaking of it had passed.

He seated himself at a table and took from his pocket a letter of Guida's written many weeks before, in which she had said firmly that she had not announced the marriage, and would not; that he must do it, and he alone; that the letter written to her grandfather had not been received by him, and that no one in Jersey knew their secret.

In reading this letter again a wave of feeling rushed over him. He realised the force and strength of her nature: every word had a clear, sharp straightforwardness and the ring of truth.

A crisis was near, and he must prepare to meet it.

The Duke had said that he must marry; a woman had already been chosen for him, and he was to meet her to-morrow. But, as he said to himself, that meant nothing. To meet a woman was not of necessity to marry her.

Marry—he could feel his flesh creeping! It gave him an ugly, startled sensation. It was like some imp of Satan to drop into his ear the suggestion that princes, ere this, had been known to have two wives—one of them unofficial. He could have struck himself in the face for the iniquity of the suggestion; he flushed from the indecency of it; but so have sinners ever flushed as they set forth on the garish road to Avernus. Yet—yet somehow he must carry on the farce of being single until the adoption and the succession had been formally arranged.

Vexed with these unbidden and unwelcome thoughts, he got up and walked about his chamber restlessly. "Guida—poor Guida!" he said to himself many times. He was angry, disgusted that those shameful, irresponsible thoughts should have come to him. He would atone for all that—and more—when he was Prince and she Princess d'Avranche. But, nevertheless, he was ill at ease with himself. Guida was off there alone in Jersey—alone. Now, all at once, another possibility flashed into his mind. Suppose, why, suppose—thoughtless scoundrel that he had been—suppose that there might come another than himself and Guida to bear his name! And she there alone, her marriage still kept secret—the danger of it to her good name. But she had said nothing in her letters, hinted nothing. No, in none had there been the most distant suggestion. Then and there he got them, one and all, and read every word, every line, all through to the end. No; there was not one hint. Of course it could not be so; she would have— but no, she might not have! Guida was unlike anybody else.

He read on and on again. And now, somehow, he thought he caught in one of the letters a new ring, a pensive gravity, a deeper tension, which were like ciphers or signals to tell him of some change in her. For a moment he was shaken. Manhood, human sympathy, surged up in him. The flush of a new sensation ran through his veins like fire. The first instinct of fatherhood came to him, a thrilling, uplifting feeling. But as suddenly there shot through his mind a thought which brought him to his feet with a spring.

But suppose—suppose that it was so—suppose that through Guida the further succession might presently be made sure, and suppose he went to the Prince and told him all; that might win his favour for her; and the rest would be easy. That was it, as clear as day. Meanwhile he would hold his peace, and abide the propitious hour.

For, above all else—and this was the thing that clinched the purpose in his mind—above all else, the Duke had, at best, but a brief time to live. Only a week ago the Court physician had told him that any violence or mental shock might snap the thread of existence. Clearly, the thing was to go on as before, keep his marriage secret, meet the Countess, apparently accede to all the Duke proposed, and wait—and wait.

With this clear purpose in his mind colouring all that he might say, yet crippling the freedom of his thought, he sat down to write to Guida. He had not yet written to her, according to his parole: this issue was clear; he could not send a letter to Guida until he was freed from that condition. It had been a bitter pill to swallow; and many times he had had to struggle with himself since his arrival at the castle. For whatever the new ambitions and undertakings, there was still a woman in the lonely distance for whose welfare he was responsible, for whose happiness he had yet done nothing, unless to give her his name under sombre conditions was happiness for her. All that he had done to remind him of the wedded life he had so hurriedly, so daringly, so eloquently entered upon, was to send his young wife fifty pounds. Somehow, as this fact flashed to his remembrance now, it made him shrink; it had a certain cold, commercial look which struck him unpleasantly. Perhaps, indeed, the singular and painful shyness—chill almost—with which Guida had received the fifty pounds now communicated itself to him by the intangible telegraphy of the mind and spirit.

All at once that bare, glacial fact of having sent her fifty pounds acted as an ironical illumination of his real position. He felt conscious that Guida would have preferred some simple gift, some little thing that women love, in token and remembrance, rather than this contribution to the common needs of existence. Now that he came to think of it, since he had left her in Jersey, he had never sent her ever so small a gift. He had never given her any gifts at all save the Maltese cross in her childhood—and her wedding-ring. As for the ring, it had never occurred to him that she could not wear it save in the stillness of the night, unseen by any eye save her own. He could not know that she had been wont to go to sleep with the hand clasped to her breast, pressing close to her the one outward token she had of a new life, begun with a sweetness which was very bitter and a bitterness only a little sweet.

Philip was in no fitting mood to write a letter. Too many emotions were in conflict in him at once. They were having their way with him; and, perhaps, in this very complexity of his feelings he came nearer to being really and acutely himself than he had ever been in his life. Indeed, there was a moment when he was almost ready to consign the Duke and all that appertained to the devil or the deep sea, and to take his fate as it came. But one of the other selves of him calling down from the little attic where dark things brood, told him that to throw up his present chances would bring him no nearer and no sooner to Guida, and must return him to the prison whence he came.

Yet he would write to Guida now, and send the letter when he was released from parole. His courage grew as the sentences spread out before him; he became eloquent. He told her how heavily the days and months went on apart from her. He emptied out the sensations of absence, loneliness, desire, and affection. All at once he stopped short. It flashed upon him now that always his letters had been entirely of his own doings; he had pictured himself always: his own loneliness, his own grief at separation. He had never yet spoken of the details of her life, questioned her of this and of that, of all the little things which fill the life of a woman—not because she loves them, but because she is a woman, and the knowledge and governance of little things is the habit of her life. His past egotism was borne in upon him now. He would try to atone for it. Now he asked her many questions in his letter. But one he did not ask. He knew not how to speak to her of it. The fact that he could not was a powerful indictment of his relations towards her, of his treatment of her, of his headlong courtship and marriage.

So portions of this letter of his had not the perfect ring of truth, not the conviction which unselfish love alone can beget. It was only at the last, only when he came to a close, that the words went from him with the sharp photography of his own heart. It came, perhaps, from a remorse which, for the instant, foreshadowed danger ahead; from an acute pity for her; or perchance from a longing to forego the attempt upon an exalted place, and get back to the straightforward hours, such as those upon the Ecrehos, when he knew that he loved her. But the sharpness of his feelings rendered more intense now the declaration of his love. The phrases were wrung from him. "Good-bye—no, a la bonne heure, my dearest," he wrote. "Good days are coming—brave, great days, when I shall be free to strike another blow for England, both from within and from without France; when I shall be, if all go well, the Prince d'Avranche, Duc de Bercy, and you my perfect Princess. Good-bye! Thy Philip, qui t'aime toujours."

He had hardly written the last words when there came a knocking at his door, and a servant entered. "His Highness offers his compliments to monsieur, and will monsieur descend to meet the Marquis Grandjon-Larisse and the Comtesse Chantavoine, who have just arrived."

For an instant Philip could scarce compose himself, but he sent a message of obedience to the Duke's command, and prepared to go down.

So it was come—not to-morrow, but to-day. Already the deep game was on. With a sigh which was half bitter and mocking laughter, he seized the pouncebox, dried his letter to Guida, and put it in his pocket. As he descended the staircase, the last words of it kept assailing his mind, singing in his brain: "Thy Philip, qui t'aime toujours!"

# CHAPTER XXII

Not many evenings after Philip's first interview with the Comtesse Chantavoine, a visitor arrived at the castle. From his roundabout approach up the steep cliff in the dusk it was clear he wished to avoid notice. Of gallant bearing, he was attired in a fashion unlike the citizens of Bercy, or the Republican military often to be seen in the streets of the town. The whole relief of the costume was white: white sash, white cuffs turned back, white collar, white rosette and band, white and red bandeau, and the faint glitter of a white shirt. In contrast were the black hat and plume, black top boots with huge spurs, and yellow breeches. He carried a gun and a sword, and a pistol was stuck in the white sash. But one thing caught the eye more than all else: a white square on the breast of the long brown coat, strangely ornamented with a red heart and a cross. He was evidently a soldier of high rank, but not of the army of the Republic.

The face was that of a devotee, not of peace but of war—of some forlorn crusade. It had deep enthusiasm, which yet to the trained observer would seem rather the tireless faith of a convert than the disposition of the natural man. It was somewhat heavily lined for one so young, and the marks of a hard life were on him, but distinction and energy were in his look and in every turn of his body.

Arriving at the castle, he knocked at the postern. At first sight of him the porter suspiciously blocked the entrance with his person, but seeing the badge upon his breast, stood at gaze, and a look of keen curiosity crossed over his face. On the visitor announcing himself as a Vaufontaine, this curiosity gave place to as keen surprise; he was admitted with every mark of respect, and the gates closed behind him.

"Has his Highness any visitors?" he asked as he dismounted.

The porter nodded assent.

"Who are they?" He slipped a coin into the porter's hand.

"One of the family—for so his Serene Highness calls him."

"H'm, indeed! A Vaufontaine, friend?"

"No, monsieur, a d'Avranche."

"What d'Avranche? Not Prince Leopold John?"

"No, monsieur, the name is the same as his Highness's."

"Philip d'Avranche? Ah, from whence?"

"From Paris, monsieur, with his Highness."

The visitor, whistling softly to himself, stood thinking a moment.
Presently he said:

"How old is he?"

"About the same age as monsieur."

"How does he occupy himself?"

"He walks, rides, talks with his Highness, asks questions of the people, reads in the library, and sometimes shoots and fishes."

"Is he a soldier?"

"He carries no sword, and he takes long aim with a gun."

A sly smile was lurking about the porter's mouth. The visitor drew from his pocket a second gold piece, and, slipping it into the other's hand, said:

"Tell it all at once. Who is the gentleman, and what is his business here? Is he, perhaps, on the side of the Revolution, or does he—keep better company?"

He looked keenly into the eyes of the porter, who screwed up his own, returning the gaze unflinchingly. Handing back the gold piece, the man answered firmly:

"I have told monsieur what every one in the duchy knows; there's no charge for that. For what more his Highness and—and those in his Highness's confidence know," he drew himself up with brusque importance, "there's no price, monsieur."

"Body o' me, here's pride and vainglory!" answered the other. "But I know you, my fine Pergot, I knew you almost too well years ago; and then you were not so sensitive; then you were a good Royalist like me, Pergot."

This time he fastened the man's look with his own and held it until Pergot dropped his head before it.

"I don't remember monsieur," he answered, perturbed.

"Of course not. The fine Pergot has a bad memory, like a good Republican, who by law cannot worship his God, or make the sign of the Cross, or, ask the priest to visit him when he's dying. A red Revolutionist is our Pergot now!"

"I'm as good a Royalist as monsieur," retorted the man with some asperity. "So are most of us. Only—only his Highness says to us—"

"Don't gossip of what his Highness says, but do his bidding, Pergot. What a fool are you to babble thus! How d'ye know but I'm one of Fouche's or Barere's men? How d'ye know but there are five hundred men beyond waiting for my whistle?"

The man changed instantly. His hand was at his side like lightning. "They'd never hear that whistle, monsieur, though you be Vaufontaine or no Vaufontaine!"

The other, smiling, reached out and touched him on the shoulder kindly.

"My dear Frange Pergot," said he, "that's the man I knew once, and the sort of man that's been fighting with me for the Church and for the King these months past in the Vendee. Come, come, don't you know me, Pergot? Don't you remember the scapegrace with whom, for a jape, you waylaid my uncle the Cardinal and robbed him, then sold him back his jewelled watch for a year's indulgences?"

"But no, no," answered the man, crossing himself quickly, and by the dim lanthorn light peering into the visitor's face, "it is not possible, monsieur. The Comte Detricand de Tournay—God rest him!—died in the Jersey Isle, with him they called Rullecour."

"Well, well, you might at least remember this," rejoined the other, and with a smile he showed an old scar in the palm of his hand.

A little later was ushered into the library of the castle the Comte Detricand de Tournay, who, under the name of Savary dit Detricand, had lived in the Isle of Jersey for many years. There he had been a dissipated idler, a keeper of worthless company, an alien coolly accepting the hospitality of a country he had ruthlessly invaded as a boy. Now, returned from vagabondage, he was the valiant and honoured heir of the House of Vaufontaine, and heir-presumptive of the House of Bercy.

True to his intention, Detricand had joined de la Rochejaquelein, the intrepid, inspired leader of the Vendee, whose sentiments became his own—"If I advance, follow me; if I retreat, kill me; if I fall, avenge me."

He had proven himself daring, courageous, resourceful. His unvarying gaiety of spirits infected the simple peasants with a rebounding energy; his fearlessness inspired their confidence; his kindness to the wounded, friend or foe, his mercy to prisoners, the respect he showed devoted priests who shared with the peasants the perils of war, made him beloved.

From the first all the leaders trusted him, and he sprang in a day, as had done the peasants Cathelineau, d'Elbee, and Stofflet, or gentlemen like Lescure and Bonchamp, and noble fighters like d'Antichamp and the Prince of Talmont, to an outstanding position in the Royalist army. Again and again he had been engaged in perilous sorties and leading forlorn hopes. He had now come from the splendid victory at Saumur to urge his kinsman, the Duc de Bercy, to join the Royalists.

He had powerful arguments to lay before a nobleman the whole traditions of whose house were of constant alliance with the Crown of France, whose very duchy had been the gift of a French monarch. Detricand had not seen the Duke since he was a lad at Versailles, and there would be much in his favour, for of all the Vaufontaines the Duke had reason to dislike him least, and some winning power in him had of late grown deep and penetrating.

When the Duke entered upon him in the library, he was under the immediate influence of a stimulating talk with Philip d'Avranche and the chief officers of the duchy. With the memory of past feuds and hatreds in his mind, and predisposed against any Vaufontaine, his greeting was courteously disdainful, his manner preoccupied.

Remarking that he had but lately heard of monsieur le comte's return to France, he hoped he had enjoyed his career in—was it then England or America? But yes, he remembered, it began with an expedition to take the Channel Isles from England, an insolent, a criminal business in time of peace, fit only for boys or buccaneers. Had monsieur le comte then spent all these years in the Channel Isles—a prisoner perhaps? No? Fastening his eyes cynically on the symbol of the Royalist cause on Detricand's breast, he asked to what he was indebted for the honour of this present visit. Perhaps, he added drily, it was to inquire after his own health, which, he was glad to assure monsieur le comte and all his cousins of Vaufontaine, was never better.

The face was like a leather mask, telling nothing of the arid sarcasm in the voice. The shoulders were shrunken, the temples fallen in, the neck behind was pinched, and the eyes looked out like brown beads alive with fire, and touched with the excitement of monomania. His last word had a delicate savagery of irony, though, too, there could be heard in the tone a defiance, arguing apprehension, not lost upon his visitor.

Detricand had inwardly smiled during the old man's monologue, broken only by courteous, half-articulate interjections on his own part. He knew too well the old feud between their houses, the ambition that had possessed many a Vaufontaine to inherit the dukedom of Bercy, and the Duke's futile revolt against that possibility. But for himself, now heir to the principality of Vaufontaine, and therefrom, by reversion, to that of Bercy, it had no importance.

He had but one passion now, and it burned clear and strong, it dominated, it possessed him. He would have given up any worldly honour to see it succeed. He had idled and misspent too many years, been vaurien and ne'er-do-well too long to be sordid now. Even as the grievous sinner, come from dark ways, turns with furious and tireless strength to piety and good works, so this vagabond of noble family, wheeling suddenly in his tracks, had thrown himself into a cause which was all sacrifice, courage, and unselfish patriotism—a holy warfare. The last bitter thrust of the Duke had touched no raw flesh, his withers were unwrung. Gifted to thrust in return, and with warrant to do so, he put aside the temptation, and answered his kinsman with daylight clearness.

"Monsieur le duc," said he, "I am glad your health is good—it better suits the purpose of this interview. I am come on business, and on that alone. I am from Saumur, where I left de la Rochejaquelein, Stofflet, Cathelineau, and Lescure masters of the city and victors over Coustard's army. We have taken eleven thousand prisoners, and—"

"I have heard a rumour—" interjected the Duke impatiently.

"I will give you fact," continued Detricand, and he told of the series of successes lately come to the army of the Vendee. It was the heyday of the cause.

"And how does all this concern me?" asked the Duke.

"I am come to beg you to join us, to declare for our cause, for the Church and for the King. Yours is of the noblest names in France. Will you not stand openly for what you cannot waver from in your heart? If the Duc de Bercy declares for us, others will come out of exile, and from submission to the rebel government, to our aid. My mission is to beg you to put aside whatever reasons you may have had for alliance with this savage government, and proclaim for the King."

The Duke never took his eyes from Detricand's.

What was going on behind that parchment face, who might say?

"Are you aware," he answered Detricand at last, "that I could send you straight from here to the guillotine?"

"So could the porter at your gates, but he loves France almost as well as does the Duc de Bercy."

"You take refuge in the fact that you are my kinsman," returned the Duke acidly.

"The honour is stimulating, but I should not seek salvation by it. I have the greater safety of being your guest," answered Detricand with dignity.

"Too premature a sanctuary for a Vaufontaine!" retorted the Duke, fighting down growing admiration for a kinsman whose family he would gladly root out, if it lay in his power.

Detricand made a gesture of impatience, for he felt that his appeal had availed nothing, and he had no heart for a battle of words. His wit had been tempered in many fires, his nature was non-incandescent to praise or gibe. He had had his share of pastime; now had come his share of toil, and the mood for give and take of words was not on him.

He went straight to the point now. Hopelessly he spoke the plain truth.

"I want nothing of the Prince d'Avranche but his weight and power in a cause for which the best gentlemen of France are giving their lives. I fasten my eyes on France alone: I fight for the throne of Louis, not for the duchy of Bercy. The duchy of Bercy may sink or swim for all of me, if so be it does not stand with us in our holy war."

The Duke interjected a disdainful laugh. Suddenly there shot into Detricand's mind a suggestion, which, wild as it was, might after all belong to the grotesque realities of life. So he added with deliberation:

"If alliance must still be kept with this evil government of France, then be sure there is no Vaufontaine who would care to inherit a duchy so discredited. To meet that peril the Duc de Bercy will do well to consult his new kinsman—Philip d'Avranche."

For a moment there was absolute silence in the room. The old nobleman's look was like a flash of flame in a mask of dead flesh. The short upper lip was arrested in a sort of snarl, the fingers, half-closed, were hooked like talons, and the whole man was a picture of surprise, fury, and injured pride. The Duc de Bercy to be harangued to his duty, scathed, measured, disapproved, and counselled, by a stripling Vaufontaine—it was monstrous.

It had the bitterness of aloes also, for in his own heart he knew that Detricand spoke truth. The fearless appeal had roused him, for a moment at least, to the beauty and righteousness of a sombre, all but hopeless, cause, while the impeachment had pierced every sore in his heart. He felt now the smarting anger, the outraged vanity of the wrong-doer who, having argued down his own conscience, and believing he has blinded others as himself, suddenly finds that himself and his motives are naked before the world.

Detricand had known regretfully, even as he spoke, that the Duke, no matter what the reason, would not now ally himself with the Royalists; though, had his life been in danger, he still would have spoken the truth. So he had been human enough to try and force open the door of mystery by a biting suggestion; for he had a feeling that in the presence of the mysterious kinsman, Philip d'Avranche, lay the cause of the Duke's resistance to his prayer. Who was this Philip d'Avranche? At the moment it seemed absurd to him that his mind should travel back to the Isle of Jersey.

The fury of the Duke was about to break forth, when the door of the chamber opened and Philip stepped inside. The silence holding two men now held three, and a curious, cold astonishment possessed the two younger. The Duke was too blind with anger to see the start of recognition his visitors gave at sight of each other, and by a concurrence of feeling neither Detricand nor Philip gave sign of acquaintance. Wariness was Philip's cue, wondering caution Detricand's attitude.

The Duke spoke first. Turning from Philip, he said to Detricand with malicious triumph:

"It will disconcert your pious mind to know I have yet one kinsman who counts it no shame to inherit Bercy. Monsieur le comte, I give you here the honour to know Captain Philip d'Avranche."

Something of Detricand's old buoyant self came back to him. His face flushed with sudden desire to laugh, then it paled in dumb astonishment. So this man, Philip d'Avranche, was to be set against him even in the heritage of his family, as for one hour in a Jersey kitchen they had been bitter opposites. For the heritage of the Houses of Vaufontaine and Bercy he cared little—he had deeper ambitions; but this adventuring sailor roused in him again the private grudge he had once begged him to remember. Recovering himself, he answered meaningly, bowing low:

"The honour is memorable—and monstrous." Philip set his teeth, but replied: "I am overwhelmed to meet one whose reputation is known—in every taproom."

Neither had chance to say more, for the Duke, though not conceiving the cause or meaning of the biting words, felt the contemptuous suggestion in Detricand's voice, and burst out in anger:

"Go tell the prince of Vaufontaine that the succession is assured to my house. Monsieur my cousin, Captain Philip d'Avranche, is now my adopted son; a wife is chosen for him, and soon, monsieur le comte, there will be still another successor to the title."

"The Duc de Bercy should add inspired domestic prophecy to the family record in the 'Almanach de Gotha,'" answered Detricand.

"God's death!" cried the old nobleman, trembling with rage, and stretching towards the bell-rope, "you shall go to Paris and the Temple. Fouche will take care of you."

"Stop, monsieur le duc!" Detricand's voice rang through the room. "You shall not betray even the humblest of your kinsmen, like that monster d'Orleans who betrayed the highest of his. Be wise: there are hundreds of your people who still will pass a Royalist on to safety."

The Duke's hand dropped from the bell-rope. He knew that Detricand's words were true. Ruling himself to quiet, he said with cold hatred:

"Like all your breed, crafty and insolent. But I will make you pay for it one day."

Glancing towards Philip as though to see if he could move him, Detricand answered: "Make no haste on my behalf; years are not of such moment to me as to your Highness."

Philip saw Detricand's look, and felt his moment and his chance had come. "Monsieur le comte!" he exclaimed threateningly.

The Duke glanced proudly at Philip. "You will collect the debt, cousin," said he, and the smile on his face was wicked as he again turned towards Detricand.

"With interest well compounded," answered Philip firmly.

Detricand smiled. "I have drawn the Norman-Jersey cousin, then?" said he. "Now we can proceed to compliments." Then with a change of manner he added quietly: "Your Highness, may the House of Bercy have no worse enemy than I! I came only to plead the cause which, if it give death, gives honour too. And I know well that at least you are not against us in heart. Monsieur d'Avranche"—he turned to Philip, and his words were slow and deliberate—"I hope we may yet meet in the Place du Vier Prison—but when and where you will; and you shall find me in the Vendee when you please." So saying, he bowed, and, turning, left the room.

"What meant the fellow by his Place du Vier Prison?" asked the Duke.

"Who knows, monsieur le duc?" answered Philip. "A fanatic like all the Vaufontaines—a roysterer yesterday, a sainted chevalier to-morrow," said the Duke irritably. "But they still have strength and beauty—always!" he added reluctantly. Then he looked at the strong and comely frame before him, and was reassured. He laid a hand on Philip's broad shoulder, and said admiringly:

"You will of course have your hour with him, cousin: but not—not till you are a d'Avranche of Bercy."

"Not till I am a d'Avranche of Bercy," responded Philip in a low voice.

# CHAPTER XXIII

With what seemed an unnecessary boldness Detricand slept that night at the inn, "The Golden Crown," in the town of Bercy: a Royalist of the Vendee exposing himself to deadly peril in a town sworn to alliance with the Revolutionary Government. He knew that the town, even the inn, might be full of spies; but one other thing he also knew: the innkeeper of "The Golden Crown" would not betray him, unless he had greatly changed since fifteen years ago. Then they had been friends, for his uncle of Vaufontaine had had a small estate in Bercy itself, in ironical proximity to the castle.

He walked boldly into the inn parlour. There were but four men in the room—the landlord, two stout burghers, and Frange Pergot, the porter of the castle, who had lost no time carrying his news: not to betray his old comrade in escapade, but to tell a chosen few, Royalists under the rose, that he had seen one of those servants of God, an officer of the Vendee.

At sight of the white badge with the red cross on Detricand's coat, the four stood up and answered his greeting with devout respect; and he had speedy assurance that in this inn he was safe from betrayal. Presently he learned that three days hence a meeting of the States of Bercy was to be held for setting the seal upon the Duke's formal adoption of Philip, and to execute a deed of succession. It was deemed certain that, ere this, the officer sent to England would have returned with Philip's freedom and King George's licence to accept the succession in the duchy. From interest in these matters alone Detricand would not have remained at Bercy, but he thought to use the time for secretly meeting officers of the duchy likely to favour the cause of the Royalists.

During these three days of waiting he heard with grave concern a rumour that the great meeting of the States would be marked by Philip's betrothal with the Comtesse Chantavoine. He cared naught for the succession, but there was ever with him the remembrance of Guida Landresse de Landresse, and what touched Philip d'Avranche he had come to associate with her. Of the true relations between Guida and Philip he knew nothing, but from that last day in Jersey he did know that Philip had roused in her emotions, perhaps less vital than love but certainly less equable than friendship.

Now in his fear that Guida might suffer, the more he thought of the Comtesse Chantavoine as the chosen wife of Philip the more it troubled him. He could not shake off oppressive thoughts concerning Guida and this betrothal. They interwove themselves through all his secret business with the Royalists of Bercy. For his own part, he would have gone far and done much to shield her from injury. He had seen and known in her something higher than Philip might understand—a simple womanliness, a profound depth of character. His pledge to her had been the key-note of his new life. Some day, if he lived and his cause prospered, he would go back to Jersey—too late perhaps to tell her what was in his heart, but not too late to tell her the promise had been kept.

It was a relief when the morning of the third day came, bright and joyous, and he knew that before the sun went down he should be on his way back to Saumur.

His friend the innkeeper urged him not to attend the meeting of the States of Bercy, lest he should be recognised by spies of government. He was, however, firm in his will to go, but he exchanged his coat with the red cross for one less conspicuous.

With this eventful morn came the news that the envoy to England had returned with Philip's freedom by exchange of prisoners, and with the needful licence from King George. But other news too was carrying through the town: the French Government, having learned of the Duke's intentions towards Philip, had despatched envoys from Paris to forbid the adoption and deed of succession.

Though the Duke would have defied them, it behoved him to end the matter, if possible, before these envoys' arrival. The States therefore was hurriedly convened two hours before the time appointed, and the race began between the Duke and the emissaries of the French Government.

It was a perfect day, and as the brilliant procession wound down the great rock from the castle, in ever-increasing, glittering line, the effect was mediaeval in its glowing splendour. All had been ready for two days, and the general enthusiasm had seized upon the occasion with an adventurous picturesqueness, in keeping with this strange elevation of a simple British captain to royal estate. This buoyant, clear-faced, stalwart figure had sprung suddenly out of the dark into the garish light of sovereign place, and the imagination of the people had been touched. He was so genial too, so easy-mannered, this d'Avranche of Jersey, whose genealogy had been posted on a hundred walls and carried by a thousand mouths through the principality. As Philip rode past on the left of the exulting Duke, the crowds cheered him wildly. Only on the faces of Comte Carignan Damour and his friends was discontent, and they must perforce be still. Philip himself was outwardly calm, with that desperate quiet which belongs to the most perilous, most adventurous achieving. Words he had used many years ago in Jersey kept ringing in his ears—"'Good-bye, Sir Philip'—I'll be more than that some day."

The Assembly being opened, in a breathless silence the Governor-General of the duchy read aloud the licence of the King of England for Philip d'Avranche, an officer in his navy, to assume the honours to be conferred upon him by the Duke and the States of Bercy. Then, by command of the Duke, the President of the States read aloud the new order of succession:

"1. To the Hereditary Prince Leopold John and his heirs male; in default of which to

"2. The Prince successor, Philip d'Avranche and his heirs male; in default of which to

"3. The heir male of the House of Vaufontaine."

Afterwards came reading of the deed of gift by which the Duke made over to Prince Philip certain possessions in the province of d'Avranche. To all this the assent of Prince Leopold John had been formally secured. After the Assembly and the chief officers of the duchy should have ratified these documents and the Duke signed them, they were to be enclosed in a box with three locks and deposited with the Sovereign Court at Bercy. Duplicates were also to be sent to London and registered in the records of the College of Arms. Amid great enthusiasm, the States, by unanimous vote, at once ratified the documents. The one notable dissentient was the Intendant, Count Carignan Damour, the devout ally of the French Government. It was he who had sent Fouche word concerning Philip's adoption; it was also he who had at last, through his spies, discovered Detricand's presence in the town, and had taken action thereupon. In the States, however, he had no vote, and wisdom kept him silent, though he was watchful for any chance to delay events against the arrival of the French envoys.

They should soon be here, and, during the proceedings in the States, he watched the doors anxiously. Every minute that passed made him more restless, less hopeful. He had a double motive in preventing this new succession. With Philip as adopted son and heir there would be fewer spoils of office; with Philip as duke there would be none at all, for the instinct of distrust and antipathy was mutual. Besides, as a Republican, he looked for his reward from Fouche in good time.

Presently it was announced by the President that the signatures to the acts of the States would be set in private. Thereupon, with all the concourse standing, the Duke, surrounded by the law, military, and civil officers of the duchy, girded upon Philip the jewelled sword which had been handed down in the House of d'Avranche from generation to generation. The open function being thus ended, the people were enjoined to proceed at once to the cathedral, where a Te Deum would be sung.

The public then retired, leaving the Duke and a few of the highest officials of the duchy to formally sign and seal the deeds. When the outer doors were closed, one unofficial person remained—Comte Detricand de Tournay, of the House of Vaufontaine. Leaning against a pillar, he stood looking calmly at the group surrounding the Duke at the great council-table.

Suddenly the Duke turned to a door at the right of the President's chair, and, opening it, bowed courteously to some one beyond. An instant afterwards there entered the Comtesse Chantavoine, with her uncle the Marquis Grandjon-Larisse, an aged and feeble but distinguished figure. They advanced towards the table, the lady on the Duke's arm, and Philip, saluting them gravely, offered the Marquis a chair. At first the Marquis declined it, but the Duke pressed him, and in the subsequent proceedings he of all the number was seated.

Detricand apprehended the meaning of the scene. This was the lady whom the Duke had chosen as wife for the new Prince. The Duke had invited the Comtesse to witness the final act which was to make Philip d'Avranche his heir in legal fact as by verbal proclamation; not doubting that the romantic nature of the incident would impress her. He had even hoped that the function might be followed by a formal betrothal in the presence of the officials; and the situation might still have been critical for Philip had it not been for the pronounced reserve of the Comtesse herself.

Tall, of gracious and stately carriage, the curious quietness of the face of the Comtesse would have been almost an unbecoming gravity were it not that the eyes, clear, dark, and strong, lightened it. The mouth had a somewhat set sweetness, even as the face was somewhat fixed in its calm. In her bearing, in all her motions, there was a regal quality; yet, too, something of isolation, of withdrawal, in her self-possession and unruffled observation. She seemed, to Detricand, a figure apart, a woman whose friendship would be everlasting, but whose love would be more an affectionate habit than a passion; and in whom devotion would be strong because devotion was the key-note of her nature. The dress of a nun would have turned her into a saint; of a peasant would have made her a Madonna; of a Quaker, would have made her a dreamer and a devote; of a queen, would have made her benign yet unapproachable. It struck him all at once as he looked, that this woman had one quality in absolute kinship with Guida Landresse—honesty of mind and nature; only with this young aristocrat the honesty would be without passion. She had straight-forwardness, a firm if limited intellect, a clear-mindedness belonging somewhat to narrowness of outlook, but a genuine capacity for understanding the right and the wrong of things. Guida, so Detricand thought, might break her heart and live on; this woman would break her heart and die: the one would grow larger through suffering, the other shrink to a numb coldness.

So he entertained himself by these flashes of discernment, presently merged in wonderment as to what was in Philip's mind as he stood there, destiny hanging in that drop of ink at the point of the pen in the Duke's fingers!

Philip was thinking of the destiny, but more than all else just now he was thinking of the woman before him and the issue to be faced by him regarding her. His thoughts were not so clear nor so discerning as Detricand's. No more than he understood Guida did he understand this clear-eyed, still, self-possessed woman. He thought her cold, unsympathetic, barren of that glow which should set the pulses of a man like himself bounding. It never occurred to him that these still waters ran deep, that to awaken this seemingly glacial nature, to kindle a fire on this altar, would be to secure unto his life's end a steady, enduring flame of devotion. He revolted from her; not alone because he had a wife, but because the Comtesse chilled him, because with her, in any case, he should never be able to play the passionate lover as he had done with Guida; and with Philip not to be the passionate lover was to be no lover at all. One thing only appealed to him: she was the Comtesse Chantavoine, a fitting consort in the eyes of the world for a sovereign duke. He was more than a little carried off his feet by the marvel of the situation. He could think of nothing quite clearly; everything was confused and shifting in his mind.

The first words of the Duke were merely an informal greeting to his council and the high officers present. He was about to speak further when some one drew his attention to Detricand's presence. An order was given to challenge the stranger, but Detricand, without waiting for the approach of the officer, advanced towards the table, and, addressing the Duke, said:

"The Duc de Bercy will not forbid the presence of his cousin, Detricand de Tournay, at this impressive ceremony?"

The Duke, dumfounded, though he preserved an outward calm, could not answer for an instant. Then with a triumphant, vindictive smile which puckered his yellow cheeks like a wild apple, he said:

"The Comte de Tournay is welcome to behold an end of the ambitions of the Vaufontaines." He looked towards Philip with an exulting pride.

"Monsieur le Comte is quite right," he added, turning to his council—"he may always claim the privileges of a relative of the Bercys; but the hospitality goes not beyond my house and my presence, and monsieur le comte will understand my meaning."

At that moment Detricand caught the eye of Damour the Intendant, and he understood perfectly. This man, the innkeeper had told him, was known to be a Revolutionary, and he felt he was in imminent danger.

He came nearer, however, bowing to all present, and, making no reply to the Duke save a simple, "I thank your Highness," took a place near the council-table.

The short ceremony of signing the deeds immediately followed. A few formal questions were asked of Philip, to which he briefly replied, and afterwards he made the oath of allegiance to the Duke, with his hand upon the ancient sword of the d'Avranches. These preliminaries ended, the Duke was just stooping to put his pen to the paper for signature, when the Intendant, as much to annoy Philip as still to stay the proceedings against the coming of Fouche's men, said:

"It would appear that one question has been omitted in the formalities of this Court." He paused dramatically. He was only aiming a random shot; he would make the most of it.

The Duke looked up perturbed, and said sharply: "What is that—what is that, monsieur?"

"A form, monsieur le duc, a mere form. Monsieur"—he bowed towards Philip politely—"monsieur is not already married? There is no—" He paused again.

For an instant there was absolute stillness. Philip had felt his heart give one great thump of terror: Did the Intendant know anything? Did Detricand know anything.

Standing rigid for a moment, his pen poised, the Duke looked sharply at the Intendant and then still more sharply at Philip. The progress of that look had granted Philip an instant's time to recover his composure. He was conscious that the Comtesse Chantavoine had given a little start, and then had become quite still and calm. Now her eyes were intently fixed upon him.

He had, however, been too often in physical danger to lose his nerve at this moment. The instant was big with peril; it was the turning point of his life, and he felt it. His eyes dropped towards the spot of ink at the point of the pen the Duke held. It fascinated him, it was destiny.

He took a step nearer to the table, and, drawing himself up, looked his princely interlocutor steadily in the eyes.

"Of course there is no marriage—no woman?" asked the Duke a little hoarsely, his eyes fastened on Philip's. With steady voice Philip replied: "Of course, monsieur le duc."

There was another stillness. Some one sighed heavily. It was the Comtesse Chantavoine.

The next instant the Duke stooped, and wrote his signature three times hurriedly upon the deeds.

A moment afterwards, Detricand was in the street, making towards "The Golden Crown." As he hurried on he heard the galloping of horses ahead of him. Suddenly some one plucked him by the arm from a doorway.

"Quick—within!" said a voice. It was that of the Duke's porter, Frange Pergot. Without hesitation or a word, Detricand did as he was bid, and the door clanged to behind him.

"Fouche's men are coming down the street; spies have betrayed you," whispered Pergot. "Follow me. I will hide you till night, and then you must away."

Pergot had spoken the truth. But Detricand was safely hidden, and Fouche's men came too late to capture the Vendean chief or to forbid those formal acts which made Philip d'Avranche a prince.

Once again at Saumur, a week later, Detricand wrote a long letter to Carterette Mattingley, in Jersey, in which he set forth these strange events at Bercy, and asked certain questions concerning Guida.

# CHAPTER XXIV

Since the day of his secret marriage with Guida, Philip had been carried along in the gale of naval preparation and incidents of war as a leaf is borne onward by a storm—no looking back, to-morrow always the goal. But as a wounded traveller nursing carefully his hurt seeks shelter from the scorching sun and the dank air, and travels by little stages lest he never come at all to friendly hostel, so Guida made her way slowly through the months of winter and of spring.

In the past, it had been February to Guida because the yellow Lenten lilies grew on all the sheltered cotils; March because the periwinkle and the lords-and-ladies came; May when the cliffs were a blaze of golden gorse and the perfume thereof made all the land sweet as a honeycomb.

Then came the other months, with hawthorn trees and hedges all in blow; the honeysuckle gladdening the doorways, the lilac in bloomy thickets; the ox-eyed daisy of Whitsuntide; the yellow rose of St. Brelade that lies down in the sand and stands up in the hedges; the "mergots" which, like good soldiers, are first in the field and last out of it; the unscented dog-violets, orchises and celandines; the osier beds, the ivy on every barn; the purple thrift in masses on the cliff; the sea-thistle in its glaucous green—"the laughter of the fields whose laugh was gold." And all was summer.

Came a time thereafter, when the children of the poor gathered blackberries for preserves and home made wine; when the wild stock flowered in St. Ouen's Bay; when the bracken fern was gathered from every cotil, and dried for apple-storing, for bedding for the cherished cow, for back-rests for the veilles, and seats round the winter fire; when peaches, apricots, and nectarines made the walls sumptuous red and gold; when the wild plum and crab-apple flourished in secluded roadways, and the tamarisk dropped its brown pods upon the earth. And all this was autumn.

At last, when the birds of passage swept aloft, snipe and teal and barnacle geese, and the rains began; when the green lizard with its turquoise-blue throat vanished; when the Jersey crapaud was heard croaking no longer in the valleys and the ponds; and the cows were well blanketed—then winter had come again.

Such was the association of seasons in Guida's mind until one day of a certain year, when for a few hours a man had called her his wife, and then had sailed away. There was no log that might thereafter record the days and weeks unwinding the coils of an endless chain into that sea whither Philip had gone.

Letters she had had, two letters, one in January, one in March. How many times, when a Channel-packet came in, did she go to the doorway and watch for old Mere Rossignol, making the rounds with her hand basket, chanting the names of those for whom she had letters; and how many times did she go back to the kitchen, choking down a sob!

The first letter from Philip was at once a blessing and a blow; it was a reassurance and it was a misery. It spoke of bread, as it were, yet offered a stone. It eloquently, passionately told of his love; but it also told, with a torturing ease, that the Araminta was commissioned with sealed orders, and he did not know when he should see her nor when he should be able to write again. War had been declared against France, and they might not touch a port nor have chance to send a letter by a homeward vessel for weeks, and maybe months. This was painful, of course, but it was fate, it was his profession, and it could not be helped. Of course—she must understand—he would write constantly, telling her, as through a kind of diary, what he was doing every day, and then when the chance came the big budget should go to her.

A pain came to Guida's heart as she read the flowing tale of his buoyant love. Had she been the man and he the woman, she could never have written so smoothly of "fate," and "profession," nor told of this separation with so complaisant a sorrow. With her the words would have been wrenched forth from her heart, scarred into the paper with the bitterness of a spirit tried beyond enduring.

With what enthusiasm did Philip, immediately after his heart-breaking news, write of what the war might do for him; what avenues of advancement it might open up, what splendid chances it would offer for success in his career! Did he mean that to comfort her, she asked herself. Did he mean it to divert her from the pain of the separation, to give her something to hope for? She read the letter over and over again—yet no, she could not, though her heart was so willing, find that meaning in it. It was all Philip, Philip full of hope, purpose, prowess, ambition. Did he think—did he think that that could ease the pain, could lighten the dark day settling down on her? Could he imagine that anything might compensate for his absence in the coming months, in this year of all years in her life? His lengthened absence might be inevitable, it might be fate, but could he not see the bitter cruelty of it? He had said that he would be back with her again in two months; and now—ah, did he not know!

As the weeks came and went again she felt that indeed he did not know—or care, maybe.

Some natures cling to beliefs long after conviction has been shattered. These are they of the limited imagination, the loyal, the pertinacious, and the affectionate, the single-hearted children of habit; blind where they do not wish to see, stubborn where their inclinations lie, unamenable to reason, wholly held by legitimate obligations.

But Guida was not of these. Her brain and imagination were as strong as her affections. Her incurable honesty was the deepest thing in her; she did not know even how to deceive herself. As her experience deepened under the influence of a sorrow which still was joy, and a joy that still was sorrow, her vision became acute and piercing. Her mind was like some kaleidoscope. Pictures of things, little and big, which had happened to her in her life, flashed by her inner vision in furious procession. It was as if, in the photographic machinery of the brain, some shutter had slipped from its place, and a hundred orderless and ungoverned pictures, loosed from natural restraint, rushed by.

Five months had gone since Philip had left her: two months since she had received his second letter, months of complexity of feeling; of tremulousness of discovery; of hungry eagerness for news of the war; of sudden little outbursts of temper in her household life—a new thing in her experience; of passionate touches of tenderness towards her grandfather; of occasional biting comments in the conversations between the Sieur and the Chevalier, causing both gentlemen to look at each other in silent amaze; of as marked lapses into listless disregard of any talk going on around her.

She had been used often to sit still, doing nothing, in a sort of physical content, as the Sieur and his visitors talked; now her hands were always busy, knitting, sewing, or spinning, the steady gaze upon the work showing that her thoughts were far away. Though the Chevalier and her grandfather vaguely noted these changes, they as vaguely set them down to her growing womanhood. In any case, they held it was not for them to comment upon a woman or upon a woman's ways. And a girl like Guida was an incomprehensible being, with an orbit and a system all her own; whose sayings and doings were as little to be reduced to their understandings as the vagaries of any star in the Milky Way or the currents in St. Michael's Basin.

One evening she sat before the fire thinking of Philip. Her grandfather had retired earlier than usual. Biribi lay asleep on the veille. There was no sound save the ticking of the clock on the mantel above her head, the dog's slow breathing, the snapping of the log on the fire, and a soft rush of heat up the chimney. The words of Philip's letters, from which she had extracted every atom of tenderness they held, were always in her ears. At last one phrase kept repeating itself to her like some plaintive refrain, torturing in its mournful suggestion. It was this: "But you see, beloved, though I am absent from you I shall have such splendid chances to get on. There's no limit to what this war may do for me."

Suddenly Guida realised how different was her love from Philip's, how different her place in his life from his place in her life. She reasoned with herself, because she knew that a man's life was work in the world, and that work and ambition were in his bones and in his blood, had been carried down to him through centuries of industrious, ambitious generations of men: that men were one race and women were another. A man was bound by the conditions governing the profession by which he earned his bread and butter and played his part in the world, while striving to reach the seats of honour in high places. He must either live by the law, fulfil to the letter his daily duties in the business of life, or drop out of the race; while a woman, in the presence of man's immoderate ambition, with bitterness and tears, must learn to pray, "O Lord, have mercy upon us, and incline our hearts to keep this law."

Suddenly the whole thing resolved itself in Guida's mind, and her thinking came to a full stop. She understood now what was the right and what the wrong; and, child as she was in years, woman in thought and experience, yielding to the impulse of the moment, she buried her face in her hands and burst into tears.

"O Philip, Philip, Philip," she sobbed aloud, "it was not right of you to marry me; it was wicked of you to leave me!" Then in her mind she carried on the impeachment and reproach. If he had married her openly and left her at once, it would have been hard to bear, but in the circumstances it might have been right. If he had married her secretly and left her at the altar, so keeping the vow he had made her when she promised to become his wife, that might have been pardonable. But to marry her as he did, and then, breaking his solemn pledge, leave her—it was not right in her eyes; and if not right in the eyes of her who loved him, in whose would it be right?

To these definitions she had come at last.

It is an eventful moment, a crucial ordeal for a woman, when she forces herself to see the naked truth concerning the man she has loved, yet the man who has wronged her. She is born anew in that moment: it may be to love on, to blind herself, and condone and defend, so lowering her own moral tone; or to congeal in heart, become keener in intellect, scornful and bitter with her own sex and merciless towards the other, indifferent to blame and careless of praise, intolerant, judging all the world by her own experience, incredulous of any true thing. Or again she may become stronger, sadder, wiser; condoning nothing, minimising nothing, deceiving herself in nothing, and still never forgiving at least one thing—the destruction of an innocent faith and a noble credulity; seeing clearly the whole wrong; with a strong intelligence measuring perfectly the iniquity; but out of a largeness of nature and by virtue of a high sense of duty, devoting her days to the salvation of a man's honour, to the betterment of one weak or wicked nature.

Of these last would have been Guida.

"O Philip, Philip, you have been wicked to me!" she sobbed.

Her tears fell upon the stone hearth, and the fire dried them. Every teardrop was one girlish feeling and emotion gone, one bright fancy, one tender hope vanished. She was no longer a girl. There were troubles and dangers ahead of her, but she must now face them dry-eyed and alone.

In his second letter Philip had told her to announce the marriage, and said that he would write to her grandfather explaining all, and also to the Rev. Lorenzo Dow. She had waited and watched for that letter to her grandfather, but it had not come. As for Mr. Dow, he was a prisoner with the French; and he had never given her the marriage certificate.

There was yet another factor in the affair. While the island was agog over Mr. Dow's misfortune, there had been a bold robbery at St. Michael's Rectory of the strong-box containing the communion plate, the parish taxes for the year, and—what was of great moment to at least one person—the parish register of deaths, baptisms, and marriages. Thus it was that now no human being in Jersey could vouch that Guida had been married.

Yet these things troubled her little. How easily could Philip set all right! If he would but come back—that at first was her only thought; for what matter a ring, or any proof or proclamation without Philip!

It did not occur to her at first that all these things were needed to save her from shame in the eyes of the world. If she had thought of them apprehensively, she would have said to herself, how easy to set all right by simply announcing the marriage! And indeed she would have done so when war was declared and Philip received his new command, but that she had wished the announcement to come from him. Well, that would come in any case when his letter to her grandfather arrived. No doubt it had missed the packet by which hers came, she thought.

But another packet and yet another arrived; and still there was no letter from Philip for the Sieur de Mauprat. Winter had come, and spring had gone, and now summer was at hand. Haymaking was beginning, the wild strawberries were reddening among the clover, and in her garden, apples had followed the buds on the trees beneath which Philip had told his fateful tale of love.

At last a third letter arrived, but it brought little joy to her heart. It was extravagant in terms of affection, but somehow it fell short of the true thing, for its ardour was that of a mind preoccupied, and underneath all ran a current of inherent selfishness. It delighted in the activity of his life, it was full of hope, of promise of happiness for them both in the future, but it had no solicitude for Guida in the present. It chilled her heart—so warm but a short season ago—that Philip to whom she had once ascribed strength, tenderness, profound thoughtfulness, should concern himself so little in the details of her life. For the most part, his letters seemed those of an ardent lover who knew his duty and did it gladly, but with a self-conscious and flowing eloquence, costing but small strain of feeling.

In this letter he was curious to know what the people in Jersey said about their marriage. He had written to Lorenzo Dow and her grandfather, he said, but had heard afterwards that the vessel carrying the letters had been taken by a French privateer; and so they had not arrived in Jersey. But of course she had told her grandfather and all the island of the ceremony performed at St. Michael's. He was sending her fifty pounds, his first contribution to their home; and, the war over, a pretty new home she certainly should have. He would write to her grandfather again, though this day there was no time to do so.

Guida realised now that she must announce the marriage at once. But what proofs of it had she? There was the ring Philip had given her, inscribed with their names; but she was sophisticated enough to know that this would not be adequate evidence in the eyes of her Jersey neighbours. The marriage register of St. Michael's, with its record, was stolen, and that proof was gone. Lastly, there were Philip's letters; but no—a thousand times no!—she would not show Philip's letters to any human being; even the thought of it hurt her delicacy, her self-respect. Her heart burned with fresh bitterness to think that there had been a secret marriage. How hard it was at this distance of time to tell the world the tale, and to be forced to prove it by Philip's letters. No, no, in spite of all, she could not do it—not yet. She would still wait the arrival of his letter to her grandfather. If it did not come soon, then she must be brave and tell her story.

She went to the Vier Marchi less now. Also fewer folk stood gossiping with her grandfather in the Place du Vier Prison, or by the well at the front door—so far he had not wondered why. To be sure, Maitresse Aimable came oftener; but, since that notable day at Sark, Guida had resolutely avoided reference, however oblique, to Philip and herself. In her dark days the one tenderly watchful eye upon her was that of the egregiously fat old woman called the "Femme de Ballast," whose thick tongue clave to the roof of her mouth, whose outer attractions were so meagre that even her husband's chief sign of affection was to pull her great toe, passing her bed of a morning to light the fire.

Carterette Mattingley also came, but another friend who had watched over Guida for years before Philip appeared in the Place du Vier Prison never entered her doorway now. Only once or twice since that day on the Ecrehos, so fateful to them both, had Guida seen Ranulph. He had withdrawn to St. Aubin's Bay, where his trade of ship-building was carried on, and having fitted up a small cottage, lived a secluded life with his father there. Neither of them appeared often in St. Heliers, and they were seldom or never seen in the Vier Marchi.

Carterette saw Ranulph little oftener than did Guida, but she knew what he was doing, being anxious to know, and every one's business being every one else's business in Jersey. In the same way Ranulph knew of Guida. What Carterette was doing Ranulph was not concerned to know, and so knew little; and Guida knew and thought little of how Ranulph fared: which was part of the selfishness of love.

But one day Carterette received a letter from France which excited her greatly, and sent her off hot-foot to Guida. In the same hour Ranulph heard a piece of hateful gossip which made him fell to the ground the man who told him, and sent him with white face, and sick, yet indignant heart, to the cottage in the Place du Vier Prison.

# CHAPTER XXV

Guida was sitting on the veille reading an old London paper she had bought of the mate of the packet from Southampton. One page contained an account of the execution of Louis XVI; another reported the fight between the English thirty-six gun frigate Araminta and the French Niobe. The engagement had been desperate, the valiant Araminta having been fought, not alone against odds as to her enemy, but against the irresistible perils of a coast upon which the Admiralty charts gave cruelly imperfect information. To the Admiralty we owed the fact, the journal urged, that the Araminta was now at the bottom of the sea, and its young commander confined in a French fortress, his brave and distinguished services lost to the country. Nor had the government yet sought to lessen the injury by arranging a cartel for the release of the unfortunate commander.

The Araminta! To Guida the letters of the word seemed to stand out from the paper like shining hieroglyphs on a misty grey curtain. The rest of the page was resolved into a filmy floating substance, no more tangible than the ashy skeleton on which writing still lives when the paper itself has been eaten by flame, and the flame swallowed by the air.

Araminta—this was all her eyes saw, that familiar name in the flaring handwriting of the Genius of Life, who had scrawled her destiny in that one word.

Slowly the monstrous ciphers faded from the grey hemisphere of space, and she saw again the newspaper in her trembling fingers, the kitchen into which the sunlight streamed from the open window, the dog Biribi basking in the doorway. That living quiet which descends upon a house when the midday meal and work are done came suddenly home to her, in contrast to the turmoil in her mind and being.

So that was why Philip had not written to her! While her heart was daily growing more bitter against him, he had been fighting his vessel against great odds, and at last had been shipwrecked and carried off a prisoner. A strange new understanding took possession of her. Her life suddenly widened. She realised all at once how the eyes of the whole world might be fixed upon a single ship, a few cannon, and some scores of men. The general of a great army leading tens of thousands into the clash of battle—that had been always within her comprehension; but this was almost miraculous, this sudden projection of one ship and her commander upon the canvas of fame. Philip had left her, unknown save to a few. With the nations turned to see, he had made a gallant and splendid fight, and now he was a prisoner in a French fortress.

This then was why her grandfather had received no letter from him concerning the marriage. Well, now she must speak for herself; she must announce it. Must she show Philip's letters?—No, no, she could not.... Suddenly a new suggestion came to her: there was one remaining proof. Since no banns had been published, Philip must have obtained a license from the Dean of the island, and he would have a record of it. All she had to do now was to get a copy of this record—but no, a license to marry was no proof of marriage; it was but evidence of intention.

Still, she would go to the Dean this very moment.

It was not right that she should wait longer: indeed, in waiting so long she had already done great wrong to herself—and to Philip perhaps.

She rose from the veille with a sense of relief. No more of this secrecy, making her innocence seem guilt; no more painful dreams of punishment for some intangible crime; no starting if she heard a sudden footstep; no more hurried walk through the streets, looking neither to right nor to left; no more inward struggles wearing away her life.

To-morrow—to-morrow—no, this very night, her grandfather and one other, even Maitresse Aimable, should know all; and she should sleep quietly—oh, so quietly to-night!

Looking into a mirror on the wall—it had been a gift from her grandfather—she smiled at herself. Why, how foolish of her it had been to feel so much and to imagine terrible things! Her eyes were shining now, and her hair, catching the sunshine from the window, glistened like burnished copper. She turned to see how it shone on the temple and the side of her head. Philip had praised her hair. Her look lingered for a moment placidly on herself-then she started suddenly. A wave of feeling, a shiver, passed through her, her brow gathered, she flushed deeply.

Turning away from the mirror, she went and sat down again on the edge of the veille. Her mind had changed. She would go to the Dean's—but not till it was dark. She suddenly thought it strange that the Dean had never said anything about the license. Why, again, perhaps he had. How should she know what gossip was going on in the town! But no, she was quick to feel, and if there had been gossip she would have felt it in the manner of her neighbours. Besides, gossip as to a license to marry was all on the right side.

She sighed—she had sighed so often of late—to think what a tangle it all was, of how it would be smoothed out tomorrow, of what—

There was a click of the garden-gate, a footstep on the walk, a half-growl from Biribi, and the face of Carterette Mattingley appeared in the kitchen doorway. Seeing Guida seated on the veille, she came in quickly, her dancing dark eyes heralding great news.

"Don't get up, ma couzaine," she said, "please no. Sit just there, and I'll sit beside you. Ah, but I have the most wonderfuls!"

Carterette was out of breath. She had hurried here from her home. As she said herself, her two feet weren't in one shoe on the way, and that with her news made her quiver with excitement.

At first, bursting with mystery, she could do no more than sit and look in Guida's face. Carterette was quick of instinct in her way, but yet she had not seen any marked change in her friend during the past few months. She had been so busy thinking of her own particular secret that she was not observant of others. At times she met Ranulph, and then she was uplifted, to be at once cast down again; for she saw that his old cheerfulness was gone, that a sombreness had settled on him. She flattered herself, however, that she could lighten his gravity if she had the right and the good opportunity; the more so that he no longer visited the cottage in the Place du Vier Prison.

This drew her closer to Guida also, for, in truth, Carterette had no loftiness of nature. Like most people, she was selfish enough to hold a person a little dearer for not standing in her own especial light. Long ago she had shrewdly guessed that Guida's interest lay elsewhere than with Ranulph, and a few months back she had fastened upon Philip as the object of her favour. That seemed no weighty matter, for many sailors had made love to Carterette in her time, and knowing it was here to-day and away to-morrow with them, her heart had remained untouched. Why then should she think Guida would take the officer seriously where she herself held the sailor lightly? But at the same time she felt sure that what concerned Philip must interest Guida, she herself always cared to hear the fate of an old admirer, and this was what had brought her to the cottage to-day.

"Guess who's wrote me a letter?" she asked of Guida, who had taken up some sewing, and was now industriously regarding the stitches.

At Carterette's question, Guida looked up and said with a smile, "Some one you like, I see."

Carterette laughed gaily. "Ba su, I should think I did—in a way. But what's his name? Come, guess, Ma'm'selle Dignity."

"Eh ben, the fairy godmother," answered Guida, trying not to show an interest she felt all too keenly; for nowadays it seemed to her that all news should be about Philip. Besides, she was gaining time and preparing herself for—she knew not what.

"O my grief!" responded the brown-eyed elf, kicking off a red slipper, and thrusting her foot into it again, "never a fairy godmother had I, unless it's old Manon Moignard the witch:

> "'Sas, son, bileton,
>
> My grand'methe a-fishing has gone:
>
> She'll gather the fins to scrape my jowl,
>
> And ride back home on a barnyard fowl!'

"Nannin, ma'm'selle, 'tis plain to be seen you can't guess what a cornfield grows besides red poppies." Laughing in sheer delight at the mystery she was making, she broke off again into a whimsical nursery rhyme:

> "'Coquelicot, j'ai mal au de
>
> Coquelicot, qu'est qui l'a fait?
>
> Coquelicot, ch'tai mon valet.'"

She kicked off the red slipper again. Flying half-way across the room, it alighted on the table, and a little mud from the heel dropped on the clean scoured surface. With a little moue of mockery, she got slowly up and tiptoed across the floor, like a child afraid of being scolded. Gathering the dust carefully, and looking demurely askance at Guida the while, she tiptoed over again to the fireplace and threw it into the chimney.

"Naughty Carterette," she said at herself with admiring reproach, as she looked in Guida's mirror, and added, glancing with farcical approval round the room, "and it all shines like peacock's feather, too!"

Guida longed to snatch the letter from Carterette's hand and read it, but she only said calmly, though the words fluttered in her throat:

"You're as gay as a chaffinch, Garcon Carterette." Garcon Carterette! Instantly Carterette sobered down. No one save Ranulph ever called her Garcon Carterette. Guida used Ranulph's name for Carterette, knowing that it would change the madcap's mood. Carterette, to hide a sudden flush, stooped and slowly put on her slipper. Then she came back to the veille, and sat down again beside Guida, saying as she did so:

"Yes, I'm gay as a chaffinch—me."

She unfolded the letter slowly, and Guida stopped sewing, but mechanically began to prick the linen lying on her knee with the point of the needle.

"Well," said Carterette deliberately, "this letter's from a pend'loque of a fellow—at least, we used to call him that—though if you come to think, he was always polite as mended porringer. Often he hadn't two sous to rub against each other. And—and not enough buttons for his clothes."

Guida smiled. She guessed whom Carterette meant. "Has Monsieur Detricand more buttons now?" she asked with a little whimsical lift of the eyebrows.

"Ah bidemme, yes, and gold too, all over him—like that!" She made a quick sweeping gesture which would seem to make Detricand a very spangle of buttons. "Come, what do you think—he's a general now."

"A general!" Instantly Guida thought of Philip and a kind of envy shot into her heart that this idler Detricand should mount so high in a few months—a man whose past had held nothing to warrant such success. "A general—where?" she asked.

"In the Vendee army, fighting for the new King of France—you know the rebels cut off the last King's head."

At another time Guida's heart would have throbbed with elation, for the romance of that Vendee union of aristocrat and peasant fired her imagination; but she only said in the tongue of the people: "Ma fuifre, yes, I know!"

Carterette was delighted to thus dole out her news, and get due reward of astonishment. "And he's another name," she added. "At least it's not another, he always had it, but he didn't call himself by it. Pardi, he's more than the Chevalier; he's the Comte Detricand de Tournay—ah, then, believe me if you choose, there it is!"

She pointed to the signature of the letter, and with a gush of eloquence explained how it all was about Detricand the vaurien and Detricand the Comte de Tournay.

"Good riddance to Monsieur Savary dit Detricand, and good welcome to the Comte de Tournay," answered Guida, trying hard to humour Carterette, that she should sooner hear the news yet withheld. "And what follows after?"

Carterette was half sorry that her great moment had come. She wished she could have linked out the suspense longer. But she let herself be comforted by the anticipated effect of her "wonderfuls."

"I'll tell you what comes after—ah, but see then what a news I have for you! You know that Monsieur d'Avranche—well, what do you think has come to him?"

Guida felt as if a monstrous hand had her heart in its grasp, crushing it. Presentiment seized her. Carterette was busy running over the pages of the letter, and did not notice her colourless face. She had no thought that Guida had any vital interest in Philip, and ruthlessly, though unconsciously, she began to torture the young wife as few are tortured in this world.

She read aloud Detricand's description of his visit to the Castle of Bercy, and of the meeting with Philip. "'See what comes of a name!'" wrote Detricand. "'Here was a poor prisoner whose ancestor, hundreds of years ago, may or mayn't have been a relative of the d'Avranches of Clermont, when a disappointed duke, with an eye open for heirs, takes a fancy to the good-looking face of the poor prisoner, and voila! you have him whisked off to a palace, fed on milk and honey, and adopted into the family. Then a pedigree is nicely grown on a summer day, and this fine young Jersey adventurer is found to be a green branch from the old root; and there's a great blare of trumpets, and the States of the duchy are called together to make this English officer a prince—and that's the Thousand and One Nights in Arabia, Ma'm'selle Carterette.'"

Guida was sitting rigid and still. In the slight pause Carterette made, a hundred confused torturing thoughts swam through her mind and presently floated into the succeeding sentences of the letter:

"'As for me, I'm like Rabot's mare, I haven't time to laugh at my own foolishness. I'm either up to my knees in grass or clay fighting Revolutionists, or I'm riding hard day and night till I'm round-backed like a wood-louse, to make up for all the good time I so badly lost in your little island. You wouldn't have expected that, my friend with the tongue that stings, would you? But then, Ma'm'selle of the red slippers, one is never butted save by a dishorned cow—as your father used to say.'"

Carterette paused again, saying in an aside: "That is M'sieu' all over, all so gay. But who knows? For he says, too, that the other day a-fighting Fontenay, five thousand of his men come across a cavalry as they run to take the guns that eat them up like cabbages, and they drop on their knees, and he drops with them, and they all pray to God to help them, while the cannon balls whiz-whiz over their heads. And God did hear them, for they fell down flat when the guns was fired and the cannon balls never touched 'em."

During this interlude, Guida, sick with anxiety, could scarcely sit still. She began sewing again, though her fingers trembled so she could hardly make a stitch. But Carterette, the little egoist, did not notice her agitation; her own flurry dimmed her sight.

She began reading again. The first few words had little or no significance for Guida, but presently she was held as by the fascination of a serpent.

"'And Ma'm'selle Carterette, what do you think this young captain, now Prince Philip d'Avranche, heir to the title of Bercy—what do you think he is next to do? Even to marry a countess of great family the old Duke has chosen for him; so that the name of d'Avranche may not die out in the land. And that is the way that love begins.... Wherefore, I want you to write and tell me—'"

What he wanted Carterette to tell him Guida never heard, though it concerned herself, for she gave a moan like a dumb animal in agony, and sat rigid and blanched, the needle she had been using embedded in her finger to the bone, but not a motion, not a sign of animation in face or figure.

All at once, some conception of the truth burst upon the affrighted Carterette. The real truth she imagined as little as had Detricand.

But now when she saw the blanched face, the filmy eyes and stark look, the finger pierced by the needle, she knew that a human heart had been pierced too, with a pain worse than death—truly it was worse, for she had seen death, and she had never seen anything like this in its dire misery and horror. She caught the needle quickly from the finger, wrapped her kerchief round the wound, threw away the sewing from Guida's lap, and running an arm about her waist, made as if to lay a hot cheek against the cold brow of her friend. Suddenly, however, with a new and painful knowledge piercing her intelligence, and a face as white and scared as Guida's own, she ran to the dresser, caught up a hanap, and brought some water. Guida still sat as though life had fled, and the body, arrested in its activity, would presently collapse.

Carterette, with all her seeming lightsomeness, had sense and self-possession. She tenderly put the water to Guida's lips, with comforting words, though her own brain was in a whirl, and dark forebodings flashed through her mind.

"Ah, man gui, man pethe!" she said in the homely patois. "There, drink, drink, dear, dear couzaine." Guida's lips opened, and she drank slowly, putting her hand to her heart with a gesture of pain. Carterette put down the hanap and caught her hands. "Come, come, these cold hands—pergui, but we must stop that! They are so cold." She rubbed them hard. "The poor child of heaven—what has come over you? Speak to me... ah, but see, everything will come all right by and by! God is good. Nothing's as bad as what it seems. There was never a grey wind but there's a greyer. Nanningia, take it not so to heart, my couzaine; thou shalt have love enough in the world.... Ah, grand doux d'la vie, but I could kill him!" she added under her breath, and she rubbed Guida's hands still, and looked frankly, generously into her eyes.

Yet, try as she would in that supreme moment, Carterette could not feel all she once felt concerning Guida. There is something humiliating in even an undeserved injury, something which, to the human eye, lessens the worthiness of its victim. To this hour Carterette had looked upon her friend as a being far above her own companionship. All in a moment, in this new office of comforter the relative status was altered. The plane on which Guida had moved was lowered. Pity, while it deepened Carterette's tenderness, lessened the gap between them.

Perhaps something of this passed through Guida's mind, and the deep pride and courage of her nature came to her assistance. She withdrew her hands and mechanically smoothed back her hair, then, as Carterette sat watching her, folded up the sewing and put it in the work-basket hanging on the wall.

There was something unnatural in her governance of herself now. She seemed as if doing things in a dream, but she did them accurately and with apparent purpose. She looked at the clock, then went to the fire to light it, for it was almost time to get her grandfather's tea. She did not seem conscious of the presence of Carterette, who still sat on the veille, not knowing quite what to do. At last, as the flame flashed up in the chimney, she came over to her friend, and said:

"Carterette, I am going to the Dean's. Will you run and ask Maitresse Aimable to come here to me soon?" Her voice had the steadiness of despair—that steadiness coming to those upon whose nerves has fallen a great numbness, upon whose sensibilities has settled a cloud that stills them as the thick mist stills the ripples on the waters of a fen.

All the glamour of Guida's youth had dropped away. She had deemed life good, and behold, it was not good; she had thought her dayspring was on high, and happiness had burnt into darkness like quick-consuming flax. But all was strangely quiet in her heart and mind. Nothing more that she feared could happen to her; the worst had fallen, and now there came down on her the impermeable calm of the doomed.

Carterette was awed by her face, and saying that she would go at once to Maitresse Aimable, she started towards the door, but as quickly stopped and came back to Guida. With none of the impulse that usually marked her actions, she put her arms round Guida's neck and kissed her, saying with a subdued intensity:

"I'd go through fire and water for you. I want to help you every way I can—me."

Guida did not say a word, but she kissed the hot cheek of the smuggler-pirate's daughter, as in dying one might kiss the face of a friend seen with filmy eyes.

When she had gone Guida drew herself up with a shiver. She was conscious that new senses and instincts were born in her, or were now first awakened to life. They were not yet under control, but she felt them, and in so far as she had power to think, she used them.

Leaving the house and stepping into the Place du Vier Prison, she walked quietly and steadily up the Rue d'Driere. She did not notice that people she met glanced at her curiously, and turned to look after her as she hurried on.

# CHAPTER XXVI

It had been a hot, oppressive day, but when, a half-hour later, Guida hastened back from a fruitless visit to the house of the Dean, who was absent in England, a vast black cloud had drawn up from the south-east, dropping a curtain of darkness upon the town. As she neared the doorway of the cottage, a few heavy drops began to fall, and, in spite of her bitter trouble, she quickened her footsteps, fearing that her grandfather had come back, to find the house empty and no light or supper ready.

M. de Mauprat had preceded her by not more than five minutes. His footsteps across the Place du Vier Prison had been unsteady, his head bowed, though more than once he raised it with a sort of effort, as it were in indignation or defiance. He muttered to himself as he opened the door, and he paused in the hall-way as though hesitating to go forward. After a moment he made a piteous gesture of his hand towards the kitchen, and whispered to himself in a kind of reassurance. Then he entered the room and stood still. All was dark save for the glimmer of the fire.

"Guida! Guida!" he said in a shaking, muffled voice. There was no answer. He put by his hat and stick in the corner, and felt his way to the great chair-he seemed to have lost his sight. Finding the familiar, worn arm of the chair, he seated himself with a heavy sigh. His lips moved, and he shook his head now and then, as though in protest against some unspoken thought.

Presently he brought his clinched hand down heavily on the table, and said aloud:

"They lie—they lie! The Connetable lies! Their tongues shall be cut out. ... Ah, my little, little child!... The Connetable dared—he dared—to tell me this evil gossip—of the little one—of my Guida!"

He laughed contemptuously, but it was a crackling, dry laugh, painful in its cheerlessness. He drew his snuff-box from his pocket, opened it, and slowly taking a pinch, raised it towards his nose, but the hand paused half-way, as though a new thought arrested it.

In the pause there came the sound of the front door opening, and then footsteps in the hall.

The pinch of snuff fell from the fingers of the old man on to the white stuff of his short-clothes, but as Guida entered the room and stood still a moment, he did not stir in his seat. The thundercloud had come still lower and the room was dark, the coals in the fireplace being now covered with grey ashes.

"Grandpethe! Grandpethe!" Guida said.

He did not answer. His heart was fluttering, his tongue clove to the roof of his mouth, dry and thick. Now he should know the truth, now he should be sure that they had lied about his little Guida, those slanderers of the Vier Marchi. Yet, too, he had a strange, depressing fear, at variance with his loving faith and belief that in Guida there was no wrong: such belief as has the strong swimmer that he can reach the shore through wave and tide; yet also with strange foreboding, prelude to the cramp that makes powerless, defying youth, strength, and skill. He could not have spoken if it had been to save his own life—or hers.

Getting no answer to her words, Guida went first to the hearth and stirred the fire, the old man sitting rigid in his chair and regarding her with fixed, watchful eyes. Then she found two candles and lighted them, placing them on the mantel, and turning to the crasset hanging by its osier rings from a beam, slowly lighted it. Turning round, she was full in the light of the candles and the shooting flames of the fire.

De Mauprat's eyes had followed her every motion, unconscious of his presence as she was. This—this was not the Guida he had known! This was not his grandchild, this woman with the pale, cold face, and dark, unhappy eyes; this was not the laughing girl who but yesterday was a babe at his knee. This was not—

The truth, which had yet been before his blinded eyes how long! burst upon him. The shock of it snapped the filmy thread of being. As the escaping soul found its wings, spread them, and rose from that dun morass called Life, the Sieur de Mauprat, giving a long, deep sigh, fell back in his great arm-chair dead, and the silver snuff-box rattled to the floor.

Guida turned round with a sharp cry. Running to him, she lifted up the head that lay over on his shoulder. She felt his pulse, she called to him. Opening his waistcoat, she put her ear to his heart; but it was still—still.

A mist, a blackness, came over her own eyes, and without a cry or a word, she slid to the floor unconscious, as the black thunderstorm broke upon the Place du Vier Prison.

The rain was like a curtain let down between the prying, clattering world without and the strange peace within: the old man in his perfect sleep; the young, misused wife in that passing oblivion borrowed from death and as tender and compassionate while it lasts.

As though with merciful indulgence, Fate permitted no one to enter upon the dark scene save a woman in whom was a deep motherhood which had never nourished a child, and to whom this silence and this sorrow gave no terrors. Silence was her constant companion, and for sorrow she had been granted the touch that assuages the sharpness of pain and the love called neighbourly kindness. Maitresse Aimable came.

Unto her it was given to minister here. As the night went by, and the offices had been done for the dead, she took her place by the bedside of the young wife, who lay staring into space, tearless and still, the life consuming away within her.

In the front room of the cottage, his head buried in his hands, Ranulph Delagarde sat watching beside the body of the Sieur de Mauprat.

# CHAPTER XXVII

In the Rue d'Driere, the undertaker and his head apprentice were right merry. But why should they not be? People had to die, quoth the undertaker, and when dead they must be buried. Burying was a trade, and wherefore should not one—discreetly—be cheerful at one's trade? In undertaking there were many miles to trudge with coffins in a week, and the fixed, sad, sympathetic look long custom had stereotyped was wearisome to the face as a cast of plaster-of-paris. Moreover, the undertaker was master of ceremonies at the house of bereavement as well. He not only arranged the funeral, he sent out the invitations to the "friends of deceased, who are requested to return to the house of the mourners after the obsequies for refreshment." All the preparations for this feast were made by the undertaker—Master of Burials he chose to be called.

Once, after a busy six months, in which a fever had carried off many a Jersiais, the Master of Burials had given a picnic to his apprentices, workmen, and their families. At this buoyant function he had raised his glass and with playful plaintiveness proposed: "The day we celebrate!"

He was in a no less blithesome mood this day. The head apprentice was reading aloud the accounts for the burials of the month, while the master checked off the items, nodding approval, commenting, correcting or condemning with strange expletives.

"Don't gabble, gabble next one slowlee!" said the Master of Burials, as the second account was laid aside, duly approved. "Eh ben, now let's hear the next—who is it?"

"That Josue Anquetil," answered the apprentice. The Master of Burials rubbed his hands together with a creepy sort of glee. "Ah, that was a clever piece of work! Too little of a length and a width for the box, but let us be thankful—it might have been too short, and it wasn't."

"No danger of that, pardingue!" broke in the apprentice. "The first it belonged to was a foot longer than Josue—he."

"But I made the most of Josue," continued the Master. "The mouth was crooked, but he was clean, clean—I shaved him just in time. And he had good hair for combing to a peaceful look, and he was light to carry—O my good! Go on, what has Josue the centenier to say for himself?"

With a drawling dull indifference, the lank, hatchet-faced servitor of the master servitor of the grave read off the items:

*The Relict of Josue Anquetil, Centenier, in account with*

*Etienne Mahye, Master of Burials.*

Item: Livres. Sols. Farth. Paid to Gentlemen of Vingtaine, who carried him to his grave.................. 4 4 0 Ditto to me, Etienne Mahye, for proper gloves of silk and cotton................. 1 0 0 Ditto to me, E. M., for laying of him out and all that appertains.............. 0 7 0 Ditto to me, E. M., for coffin........... 4 0 0 Ditto to me, E. M., for divers............ 0 4 0

The Master of Burials interrupted. "Bat'dlagoule, you've forgot blacking for coffin!"

The apprentice made the correction without deigning reply, and then went on

*Livres. Sols. Farth.*

Ditto to me, E. M., for black for blacking coffin.................................... 0 3 0 Ditto to me, E. M., paid out for supper after obs'quies.......................... 3 2 0 Ditto to me, E. M., paid out for wine (3 pots and 1 pt. at a shilling) for ditto..................................... 2 5 6 Ditto to me, E. M., paid out for oil and candle..................................... 0 7 0 Ditto to me, E. M., given to the poor, as fitting station of deceased.............. 4 0 0

The apprentice stopped. "That's all," he said.

There was a furious leer on the face of the Master of Burials. So, after all his care, apprentices would never learn to make mistakes on his side. "O my grief, always on the side of the corpse, that can thank nobody for naught!" was his snarling comment.

"What about those turnips from Denise Gareau, numskull?" he grunted, in a voice between a sneer and a snort.

The apprentice was unmoved. He sniffed, rubbed his nose with a forefinger, laboriously wrote for a moment, and then added:

Ditto to Madame Denise Gareau for turnips for supper after obs'quies ..................... 10 sols

"Saperlote, leave out the Madame, calf-lugs—, you!"

The apprentice did not move a finger. Obstinacy sat enthroned on him. In a rage, the Master made a snatch at a metal flower-wreath to throw at him. "Shan't! She's my aunt. I knows my duties to my aunt—me," said the apprentice stolidly.

The Master burst out in a laugh of scorn. "Gaderabotin, here's family pride for you! I'll go stick dandelines in my old sow's ear—respe d'la compagnie."

The apprentice was still calm. "If you want to flourish yourself, don't mind me," said he, and picking up the next account, he began reading:

*Mademoiselle Landresse, in the matter of the Burial of*

*the Sieur de Mauprat, to Etienne Mahye, &c. Item—*

The first words read by the apprentice had stilled the breaking storm of the Master's anger. It dissolved in a fragrant dew of proud reminiscence, profit, and scandal.

He himself had no open prejudices. He was an official of the public—or so he counted himself—and he very shrewdly knew his duty in that walk of life to which it had pleased Heaven to call him. The greater the notoriety of the death, the more in evidence was the Master and all his belongings. Death with honour was an advantage to him; death with disaster a boon; death with scandal was a godsend. It brought tears of gratitude to his eyes when the death and the scandal were in high places. These were the only real tears he ever shed. His heart was in his head, and the head thought solely of Etienne Mahye. Though he wore an air of sorrow and sympathy in public, he had no more feeling than a hangman. His sympathy seemed to say to the living, "I wonder how soon you'll come into my hands," and to the dead, "What a pity you can only die once—and second-hand coffins so hard to get!"

*Item: paid to me, Etienne Mahye,*

droned the voice of the apprentice,

*for rosewood coffin—*

"O my good," interrupted the Master of Burials with a barren chuckle, and rubbing his hands with glee, "O my good, that was a day in a lifetime! I've done fine work in my time, but upon that day—not a cloud above, no dust beneath, a flowing tide, and a calm sea. The Royal Court, too, caught on a sudden marching in their robes, turns to and joins the cortegee, and the little birds a-tweeting-tweeting, and two parsons at the grave. Pardingue, the Lord was—with me that day, and—"

The apprentice laughed—a dry, mirthless laugh of disbelief and ridicule. "Ba su, master, the Lord was watching you. There was two silver bits inside that coffin, on Sieur's eyes."

"Bigre!" The Master was pale with rage. His lips drew back, disclosing long dark teeth and sickly gums, in a grimace of fury. He reached out to seize a hammer lying at his hand, but the apprentice said quickly:

"Sapri—that's the cholera hammer!"

The Master of Burials dropped the hammer as though it were at white heat, and eyed it with scared scrutiny. This hammer had been used in nailing down the coffins of six cholera patients who had died in one house at Rozel Bay a year before. The Master would not himself go near the place, so this apprentice had gone, on a promise from the Royal Court that he should have for himself—this he demanded as reward—free lodging in two small upper rooms of the Cohue Royale, just under the bell which said to the world, "Chicane—chicane! Chicane—chicane!"

This he asked, and this he got, and he alone of all Jersey went out to bury three people who had died of cholera; and then to watch three others die, to bury them scarce cold, and come back, with a leer of satisfaction, to claim his price. At first people were inclined to make a hero of him, but that only made him grin the more, and at last the island reluctantly decided that he had done the work solely for fee and reward.

The hammer used in nailing the coffins, he had carried through the town like an emblem of terror and death, and henceforth he only, in the shop of the Master, touched it.

"It won't hurt you if you leave it alone," said the apprentice grimly to the Master of Burials. "But, if you go bothering, I'll put it in your bed, and it'll do after to nail down your coffin."

Then he went on reading with a malicious calmness, as though the matter were the dullest trifle:

Item: one dozen pairs of gloves for mourners.

"Par made, that's one way of putting it!" commented the apprentice, "for what mourners was there but Ma'm'selle herself, and she quiet as a mice, and not a teardrop, and all the island necks end to end for look at her, and you, master, whispering to her: 'The Lord is the Giver and Taker,' and the Femme de Ballast t'other side, saying 'My dee-ar, my dee-ar, bear thee up, bear thee up—thee.'"

"And she looking so steady in front of her, as if never was shame about her—and her there soon to be; and no ring of gold upon her hand, and all the world staring!" broke in the Master, who, having edged away from the cholera hammer, was launched upon a theme that stirred his very soul. "All the world staring, and good reason," he added.

"And she scarce winking, eh?" said the apprentice. "True that—her eyes didn't feel the cold," said the Master of Burials with a leer, for to his sight as to that of others, only as boldness had been Guida's bitter courage, the blank, despairing gaze, coming from eyes that turn their agony inward.

The apprentice took up the account again, and prepared to read it. The Master, however, had been roused to a genial theme. "Poor fallen child of Nature!" said he. "For what is birth or what is looks of virtue like a summer flower! It is to be brought down by hand of man." He was warmed to his text. Habit had long made him so much hypocrite, that he was sentimentalist and hard materialist in one. "Some pend'loque has brought her beauty to this pass, but she must suffer—and also his time will come, the sulphur, the torment, the worm that dieth not—and no Abraham for parched tongue—misery me! They that meet in sin here shall meet hereafter in burning fiery furnace."

The cackle of the apprentice rose above the whining voice. "Murder, too—don't forget the murder, master. The Connetable told the old Sieur de Mauprat what people were blabbing, and in half-hour dead he is—he."

"Et ben, the Sieur's blood it is upon their heads," continued the Master of Burials; "it will rise up from the ground—"

The apprentice interrupted. "A good thing if the Sieur himself doesn't rise, for you'd get naught for coffin or obs'quies. It was you tells the Connetable what folks babbled, and the Connetable tells the Sieur, and the Sieur it kills him dead. So if he rised, he'd not pay you for murdering him—no, bidemme! And 'tis a gobbly mouthful—this," he added, holding up the bill.

The undertaker's lips smacked softly, as though in truth he were waiting for the mouthful. Rubbing his hands, and drawing his lean leg up till it touched his nose, he looked over it with avid eyes, and said: "How much—don't read the items, but come to total debit—how much she pays me?"

Ma'm'selle Landresse, debtor in all for one hundred and twenty livres, eleven sols and two farthings.

"Shan't you make it one hundred and twenty-one livres?" added the apprentice.

"God forbid, the odd sols and farthings are mine—no more!" returned the Master of Burials. "Also they look exact; but the courage it needs to be honest! O my grief, if—"

"'Sh!" said the apprentice, pointing, and the Master of Burials, turning, saw Guida pass the window. With a hungry instinct for the morbid they stole to the doorway and looked down the Rue d'Driere after her. The Master was sympathetic, for had he not in his fingers at that moment a bill for a hundred and twenty livres odd? The way the apprentice craned his neck, and tightened the forehead over his large, protuberant eyes, showed his intense curiosity, but the face was implacable. It was like that of some strong fate, superior to all influences of sorrow, shame, or death. Presently he laughed—a crackling cackle like new-lighted kindling wood; nothing could have been more inhuman in sound. What in particular aroused this arid mirth probably he himself did not know. Maybe it was a native cruelty which had a sort of sardonic pleasure in the miseries of the world. Or was it only the perception, sometimes given to the dullest mind, of the futility of goodness, the futility of all? This perhaps, since the apprentice shared with Dormy Jamais his rooms at the top of the Cohue Royale; and there must have been some natural bond of kindness between the blank, sardonic undertaker's apprentice and the poor beganne, who now officially rang the bell for the meetings of the Royal Court.

The dry cackle of the apprentice as he looked after Guida roused a mockery of indignation in the Master. "Sacre matin, a back-hander on the jaw'd do you good, slubberdegullion—you! Ah, get go scrub the coffin blacking from your jowl!" he rasped out with furious contempt.

The apprentice seemed not to hear, but kept on looking after Guida, a pitiless leer on his face. "Dame, lucky for her the Sieur died before he had chance to change his will. She'd have got ni fiche ni bran from him."

"Support d'en haut, if you don't stop that I'll give you a coffin before your time, keg of nails—you. Sorrow and prayer at the throne of grace that she may have a contrite heart"—he clutched the funeral bill tighter in his fingers—"is what we must feel for her. The day the Sieur died and it all came out, I wept. Bedtime come I had to sop my eyes with elder-water. The day o' the burial mine eyes were so sore a-draining I had to put a rotten sweet apple on 'em over-night—me."

"Ah bah, she doesn't need rosemary wash for her hair!" said the apprentice admiringly, looking down the street after Guida as she turned into the Rue d'Egypte.

Perhaps it was a momentary sympathy for beauty in distress which made the Master say, as he backed from the doorway with stealthy step:

"Gatd'en'ale, 'tis well she has enough to live on, and to provide for what's to come!"

But if it was a note of humanity in the voice it passed quickly, for presently, as he examined the bill for the funeral of the Sieur de Mauprat, he said shrilly:

"Achocre, you've left out the extra satin for his pillow—you."

"There wasn't any extra satin," drawled the apprentice.

With a snarl the Master of Burials seized a pen and wrote in the account:

Item: To extra satin for pillow, three livres.

# CHAPTER XXVIII

Guida's once blithe, rose-coloured face was pale as ivory, the mouth had a look of deep sadness, and the step was slow; but the eye was clear and steady, and her hair, brushed under the black crape of the bonnet as smoothly as its nature would admit, gave to the broad brow a setting of rare attraction and sombre nobility. It was not a face that knew inward shame, but it carried a look that showed knowledge of life's cruelties and a bitter sensitiveness to pain. Above all else it was fearless, and it had no touch of the consciousness or the consequences of sin; it was purity itself.

It alone should have proclaimed abroad her innocence, though she said no word in testimony. To most people, however, her dauntless sincerity only added to her crime and to the scandalous mystery. Yet her manner awed some, while her silence held most back. The few who came to offer sympathy, with curiousness in their eyes and as much inhumanity as pity in their hearts, were turned back gently but firmly, more than once with proud resentment.

So it chanced that soon only Maitresse Aimable came—she who asked no questions, desired no secrets—and Dormy Jamais.

Dormy had of late haunted the precincts of the Place du Vier Prison, and was the only person besides Maitresse Aimable whom Guida welcomed. His tireless feet went clac-clac past her doorway, or halted by it, or entered in when it pleased him. He was more a watch-dog than Biribi; he fetched and carried; he was silent and sleepless—always sleepless. It was as if some past misfortune had opened his eyes to the awful bitterness of life, and they had never closed again.

The Chevalier had not been with her, for on the afternoon of the very day her grandfather died, he had gone a secret voyage to St. Malo, to meet the old solicitor of his family. He knew nothing of his friend's death or of Guida's trouble. As for Carterette, Guida would not let her come—for her own sake.

Nor did Maitre Ranulph visit her after the funeral of the Sieur de Mauprat. The horror of the thing had struck him dumb, and his mind was one confused mass of conflicting thoughts. There—there were the terrifying facts before him; yet, with an obstinacy peculiar to him, he still went on believing in her goodness and in her truth. Of the man who had injured her he had no doubt, and his course was clear, in the hour when he and Philip d'Avranche should meet. Meanwhile, from a spirit of delicacy, avoiding the Place du Vier Prison, he visited Maitresse Aimable, and from day to day learned all that happened to Guida. As of old, without her knowledge, he did many things for her through the same Maitresse Aimable. And it quickly came to be known in the island that any one who spoke ill of Guida in his presence did so at no little risk. At first there had been those who marked him as the wrongdoer, but somehow that did not suit with the case, for it was clear he loved Guida now as he had always done; and this the world knew, as it had known that he would have married her all too gladly. Presently Detricand and Philip were the only names mentioned, but at last, as by common consent, Philip was settled upon, for such evidence as there was pointed that way. The gossips set about to recall all that had happened when Philip was in Jersey last. Here one came forward with a tittle of truth, and there another with tattle of falsehood, and at last as wild a story was fabricated as might be heard in a long day.

But in bitterness Guida kept her own counsel.

This day when she passed the undertaker's shop she had gone to visit the grave of her grandfather. He had died without knowing the truth, and her heart was hardened against him who had brought misery upon her. Reaching the cottage in the Place du Vier Prison now, she took from a drawer the letter Philip had written her on the day he first met the Comtesse Chantavoine. She had received it a week ago. She read it through slowly, shuddering a little once or twice. When she had finished, she drew paper to her and began a reply.

The first crisis of her life was passed. She had met the shock of utter disillusion; her own perfect honesty now fathomed the black dishonesty of the man she had loved. Death had come with sorrow and unmerited shame. But an innate greatness, a deep courage supported her. Out of her wrongs and miseries now she made a path for her future, and in that path Philip's foot should never be set. She had thought and thought, and had come to her decision. In one month she had grown years older in mind. Sorrow gave her knowledge, it threw her back on her native strength and goodness. Rising above mere personal wrongs she grew to a larger sense of womanhood, to a true understanding of her position and its needs. She loved no longer, but Philip was her husband by the law, and even as she had told him her whole mind and heart in the days of their courtship and marriage, she would tell him her whole mind and heart now. Once more, to satisfy the bond, to give full reasons for what she was about to do, she would open her soul to her husband, and then no more! In all she wrote she kept but two things back, her grandfather's death—and one other. These matters belonged to herself alone.

> No, Philip d'Avranche, [she wrote], your message came too late. All
> that you might have said and done should have been said and done
> long ago, in that past which I believe in no more. I will not ask
> you why you acted as you did towards me. Words can alter nothing
> now. Once I thought you true, and this letter you send would have
> me still believe so. Do you then think so ill of my intelligence?
> In the light of the past it may be you have reason, for you know
> that I once believed in you! Think of it—believed in you!
>
> How bad a man are you! In spite of all your promises; in spite of
> the surrender of honest heart and life to you; in spite of truth and
> every call of honour, you denied me—dared to deny me, at the very
> time you wrote this letter.
>
> For the hopes and honours of this world, you set aside, first by
> secrecy, and then by falsehood, the helpless girl to whom you once
> swore undying love. You, who knew the open book of her heart, you
> threw it in the dust. "Of course there is no wife?" the Duc de
> Bercy said to you before the States of Bercy. "Of course," you
> answered. You told your lie without pity.
>
> Were you blind that you did not see the consequences? Or did you
> not feel the horror of your falsehood?—to play shuttlecock with a
> woman's life, with the soul of your wife; for that is what your
> conduct means. Did you not realise it, or were you so wicked that
> you did not care? For I know that before you wrote me this letter,
> and afterwards when you had been made prince, and heir to the duchy,
> the Comtesse Chantavoine was openly named by the Duc de Bercy for
> your wife.
>
> Now read the truth. I understand all now. I am no longer the

*thoughtless, believing girl whom you drew from her simple life to
give her so cruel a fate. Yesterday I was a child, to-day— —Oh,
above all else, do you think I can ever forgive you for having
killed the faith, the joy of life that was in me! You have spoiled
for me for ever my rightful share of the joyous and the good. My
heart is sixty though my body is not twenty. How dared you rob me
of all that was my birthright, of all that was my life, and give me
nothing—nothing in return!*

*Do you remember how I begged you not to make me marry you;
but you
urged me, and because I loved you and trusted you, I did? how I
entreated you not to make me marry you secretly, but you insisted,
and loving you, I did? how you promised you would leave me at
the
altar and not see me till you came again to claim me openly for
your
wife, and you broke that sacred promise? Do you remember—my
husband!*

*Do you remember that night in the garden when the wind came
moaning
up from the sea? Do you remember how you took me in your arms,
and
even while I listened to your tender and assuring words, in that
moment—ah, the hurt and the wrong and the shame of it!
Afterwards
in the strange confusion, in my blind helplessness I tried to say,
"But he loved me," and I tried to forgive you. Perhaps in time I
might have made myself believe I did; for then I did not know you
as
you are—and were; but understanding all now I feel that in that
hour I really ceased to love you; and when at last I knew you had
denied me, love was buried for ever.*

*Your worst torment is to come, mine has already been with me. When*
*my miseries first fell upon me, I thought that I must die. Why*
*should I live on—why should I not die? The sea was near, and it*
*buries deep. I thought of all the people that live on the great*
*earth, and I said to myself that the soul of one poor girl could not*
*count, that it could concern no one but myself. It was clear to me*
*—I must die and end all.*

*But there came to me a voice in the night which said: "Is thy life*
*thine own to give or to destroy?" It was clearer than my own*
*thinking. It told my heart that death by one's own hand meant*
*shame; and I saw then that to find rest I must drag unwilling feet*
*over the good name and memory of my dead loved ones. Then I*
*remembered my mother. If you had remembered her perhaps you would*
*have guarded the gift of my love and not have trampled it under your*
*feet—I remembered my mother, and so I live still.*

*I must go on alone, with naught of what makes life bearable; you*
*will keep climbing higher by your vanity, your strength, and your*
*deceit. But yet I know however high you climb you will never find*
*peace. You will remember me, and your spirit will seek in vain for*
*rest. You will not exist for me, you will not be even a memory; but*
*even against your will I shall always be part of you: of your brain,*
*of your heart, of your soul—the thought of me your torment in your*
*greatest hour. Your passion and your cowardice have lost me all;*
*and God will punish you, be sure of that.*

*There is little more to say. If it lies in my power I shall never*
*see you again while I live. And you will not wish it. Yes, in*
*spite of your eloquent letter lying here beside me, you do not wish*
*it, and it shall not be. I am not your wife save by the law; and*
*little have you cared for law! Little, too, would the law help you*

*in this now; for which you will rejoice. For the ease of your mind I hasten to tell you why.*

*First let me inform you that none in this land knows me to be your wife. Your letter to my grandfather never reached him, and to this hour I have held my peace. The clergyman who married us is a prisoner among the French, and the strong-box which held the register of St. Michael's Church was stolen. The one other witness, Mr. Shoreham, your lieutenant—as you tell me—went down with the Araminta. So you are safe in your denial of me. For me, I would endure all the tortures of the world rather than call you husband ever again. I am firmly set to live my own life, in my own way, with what strength God gives. At last I see beyond the Hedge.*

*Your course is clear. You cannot turn back now. You have gone too far. Your new honours and titles were got at the last by a falsehood. To acknowledge it would be ruin, for all the world knows that Captain Philip d'Avranche of the King's navy is now the adopted son of the Duc de Bercy. Surely the house of Bercy has cause for joy, with an imbecile for the first in succession and a traitor for the second!*

*I return the fifty pounds you sent me—you will not question why ....And so all ends. This is a last farewell between us.*

*Do you remember what you said to me on the Ecrehos? "If ever I deceive you, may I die a black, dishonourable death, abandoned and alone. I should deserve that if ever I deceived you, Guida."*
*Will you ever think of that, in your vain glory hereafter?*

*GUIDA LANDRESSE DE LANDRESSE.*

# IN JERSEY FIVE YEARS LATER

## CHAPTER XXIX

On a map the Isle of Jersey has the shape and form of a tiger on the prowl.

The fore-claws of this tiger are the lacerating pinnacles of the Corbiere and the impaling rocks of Portelet Bay and Noirmont; the hind-claws are the devastating diorite reefs of La Motte and the Banc des Violets. The head and neck, terrible and beautiful, are stretched out towards the west, as it were to scan the wild waste and jungle of the Atlantic seas. The nose is L'Etacq, the forehead Grosnez, the ear Plemont, the mouth the dark cavern by L'Etacq, and the teeth are the serried ledges of the Foret de la Brequette. At a discreet distance from the head and the tail hover the jackals of La Manche: the Paternosters, the Dirouilles, and the Ecrehos, themselves destroying where they may, or filching the remains of the tiger's feast of shipwreck and ruin. In truth, the sleek beast, with its feet planted in fearsome rocks and tides, and its ravening head set to defy the onslaught of the main, might, but for its ensnaring beauty, seem some monstrous foot-pad of the deep.

To this day the tiger's head is the lonely part of Jersey; a hundred years ago it was as distant from the Vier Marchi as is Penzance from Covent Garden. It would almost seem as if the people of Jersey, like the hangers-on of the king of the jungle, care not to approach too near the devourer's head. Even now there is but a dwelling here and there upon the lofty plateau, and none at all near the dark and menacing headland. But as if the ancient Royal Court was determined to prove its sovereignty even over the tiger's head, it stretched out its arms from the Vier Marchi to the bare neck of the beast, putting upon it a belt of defensive war; at the nape, a martello tower and barracks; underneath, two other martello towers like the teeth of a buckle.

The rest of the island was bristling with armament. Tall platforms were erected at almost speaking distance from each other, where sentinels kept watch for French frigates or privateers. Redoubts and towers were within musket-shot of each other, with watch-houses between, and at intervals every able-bodied man in the country was obliged to leave his trade to act as sentinel, or go into camp or barracks with the militia for months at a time.

British cruisers sailed the Channel: now a squadron under Barrington, again under Bridport, hovered upon the coast, hoping that a French fleet might venture near.

But little of this was to be seen in the western limits of the parish of St. Ouen's. Plemont, Grosnez, L'Etacq, all that giant headland could well take care of itself—the precipitous cliffs were their own defence. A watch-house here and there sufficed. No one lived at L'Etacq, no one at Grosnez; they were too bleak, too distant and solitary. There were no houses, no huts.

If you had approached Plemont from Vinchelez-le-Haut, making for the sea, you would have said that it also had no habitation. But when at last you came to a hillock near Plemont point, looking to find nothing but sky and sea and distant islands, suddenly at your very feet you saw a small stone dwelling. Its door faced the west, looking towards the Isles of Guernsey and Sark. Fronting the north was a window like an eye, ever watching the tireless Paternosters. To the east was another tiny window like a deep loop-hole or embrasure set towards the Dirouilles and the Ecrehos.

The hut had but one room, of moderate size, with a vast chimney. Between the chimney and the western wall was a veille, which was both lounge and bed. The eastern side was given over to a few well-polished kitchen utensils, a churn, and a bread-trough. The floor was of mother earth alone, but a strip of handmade carpet was laid down before the fireplace, and there was another at the opposite end. There were also a table, a spinning-wheel, and a shelf of books.

It was not the hut of a fisherman, though upon the wall opposite the books there hung fishing-tackle, nets, and cords, while outside, on staples driven in the jutting chimney, were some lobster-pots. Upon two shelves were arranged a carpenter's and a cooper's tools, polished and in good order. And yet you would have said that neither a cooper nor a carpenter kept them in use. Everywhere there were signs of man's handicraft as well as of woman's work, but upon all was the touch of a woman. Moreover, apart from the tools there was no sign of a man's presence in the hut. There was no coat hanging behind the door, no sabots for the fields or oilskins for the sands, no pipe laid upon a ledge, no fisherman's needle holding a calendar to the wall. Whatever was the trade of the occupant, the tastes were above those of the ordinary dweller in the land. That was to be seen in a print of Raphael's "Madonna and Child" taking the place of the usual sampler upon the walls of Jersey homes; in the old clock nicely bestowed between a narrow cupboard and the tool shelves; in a few pieces of rare old china and a gold-handled sword hanging above a huge, well-carved oak chair. The chair relieved the room of anything like commonness, and somehow was in sympathy with the simple surroundings, making for dignity and sweet quiet. It was clear that only a woman could have arranged so perfectly this room and all therein. It was also clear that no man lived here.

Looking in at the doorway of this hut on a certain autumn day of the year 1797, the first thing to strike your attention was a dog lying asleep on the hearth. Then a suit of child's clothes on a chair before the fire of vraic would have caught the eye. The only thing to distinguish this particular child's dress from that of a thousand others in the island was the fineness of the material. Every thread of it had been delicately and firmly knitted, till it was like perfect soft blue cloth, relieved by a little red silk ribbon at the collar.

The hut contained as well a child's chair, just so high that when placed by the windows commanding the Paternosters its occupant might see the waves, like panthers, beating white paws against the ragged granite pinnacles; the currents writhing below at the foot of the cliffs, or at half-tide rushing up to cover the sands of the Greve aux Langons, and like animals in pain, howling through the caverns in the cliffs; the great nor'wester of November come battering the rocks, shrieking to the witches who boiled their caldrons by the ruins of Grosnez Castle that the hunt of the seas was up.

Just high enough was the little chair that of a certain day in the year its owner might look out and see mystic fires burning round the Paternosters, and lighting up the sea with awful radiance. Scarce a rock to be seen from the hut but had some legend like this: the burning Russian ship at the Paternosters, the fleet of boats with tall prows and long oars drifting upon the Dirouilles and going down to the cry of the Crusaders' Dahindahin! the Roche des Femmes at the Ecrehos, where still you may hear the cries of women in terror of the engulfing sea.

On this particular day, if you had entered the hut, no one would have welcomed you; but had you tired of waiting, and followed the indentations of the coast for a mile or more by a deep bay under tall cliffs, you would have seen a woman and a child coming quickly up the sands. Slung upon the woman's shoulders was a small fisherman's basket. The child ran before, eager to climb the hill and take the homeward path.

A man above was watching them. He had ridden along the cliff, had seen the woman in her boat making for the shore, had tethered his horse in the quarries near by, and now awaited her. He chuckled as she came on, for he had ready a surprise for her. To make it more complete he hid himself behind some boulders, and as she reached the top sprang out with an ugly grinning.

The woman looked at him calmly and waited for him to speak. There was no fear on her face, not even surprise; nothing but steady inquiry and quiet self-possession. With an air of bluster the man said:

"Aha, my lady, I'm nearer than you thought—me!" The child drew in to its mother's side and clasped her hand. There was no fear in the little fellow's look, however; he had something of the same self-possession as the woman, and his eyes were like hers, clear, unwavering, and with a frankness that consumed you. They were wells of sincerity; open-eyed, you would have called the child, wanting a more subtle description.

"I'm not to be fooled—me! Come now, let's have the count," said the man, as he whipped a greasy leather-covered book from his pocket. "Sapristi, I'm waiting. Stay yourself!" he added roughly as she moved on, and his greyish-yellow face had an evil joy at thought of the brutal work in hand.

"Who are you?" she asked, but taking her time to speak.

"Dame! you know who I am."

"I know what you are," she answered quietly.

He did not quite grasp her meaning, but the tone sounded contemptuous, and that sorted little with his self-importance.

"I'm the Seigneur's bailiff—that's who I am. Gad'rabotin, don't you put on airs with me! I'm for the tribute, so off with the bag and let's see your catch."

"I have never yet paid tribute to the seigneur of the manor."

"Well, you'll begin now. I'm the new bailiff, and if you don't pay your tale, up you come to the court of the fief to-morrow."

She looked him clearly in the eyes. "If I were a man, I should not pay the tribute, and I should go to the court of the fief to-morrow, but being a woman—"

She clasped the hand of the child tightly to her for an instant, then with a sigh she took the basket from her shoulders and, opening it, added:

"But being a woman, the fish I caught in the sea that belongs to God and to all men I must divide with the Seigneur whose bailiff spies on poor fisher-folk."

The man growled an oath and made a motion as though he would catch her by the shoulder in anger, but the look in her eyes stopped him. Counting out the fish, and giving him three out of the eight she had caught, she said:

"It matters not so much to me, but there are others poorer than I, they suffer."

With a leer the fellow stooped, and, taking up the fish, put them in the pockets of his queminzolle, all slimy from the sea as they were.

"Ba su, you haven't got much to take care of, have you? It don't take much to feed two mouths—not so much as it does three, Ma'm'selle."

Before he had ended, the woman, without reply to the insult, took the child by the hand and moved along her homeward path towards Plemont.

"A bi'tot, good-bye!" the bailiff laughed brutally. Standing with his legs apart and his hands fastened on the fish in the pockets of his long queminzolle, he called after her in sneering comment: "Ma fistre, your pride didn't fall—ba su!" Then he turned on his heel.

"Eh ben, here's mackerel for supper," he added as he mounted his horse.

The woman was Guida Landresse, the child was her child, and they lived in the little house upon the cliff at Plemont. They were hastening thither now.

# CHAPTER XXX

A visitor was awaiting Guida and the child: a man who, first knocking at the door, then looking in and seeing the room empty, save for the dog lying asleep by the fire, had turned slowly away, and going to the cliff edge, looked out over the sea. His movements were deliberate, his body moved slowly; the whole appearance was of great strength and nervous power. The face was preoccupied, the eyes were watchful, dark, penetrating. They seemed not only to watch but to weigh, to meditate, even to listen—as it were, to do the duty of all the senses at once. In them worked the whole forces of his nature; they were crucibles wherein every thought and emotion were fused. The jaw was set and strong, yet it was not hard. The face contradicted itself. While not gloomy it had lines like scars telling of past wounds. It was not despairing, it was not morbid, and it was not resentful; it had the look of one both credulous and indomitable. Belief was stamped upon it; not expectation or ambition, but faith and fidelity. You would have said he was a man of one set idea, though the head had a breadth sorting little with narrowness of purpose. The body was too healthy to belong to a fanatic, too powerful to be that of a dreamer alone, too firm for other than a man of action.

Several times he turned to look towards the house and up the pathway leading from the hillock to the doorway. Though he waited long he did not seem impatient; patience was part of him, and not the least part. At last he sat down on a boulder between the house and the shore, and scarcely moved, as minute after minute passed, and then an hour and more, and no one came. Presently there was a soft footstep beside him, and he turned. A dog's nose thrust itself into his hand.

"Biribi, Biribi!" he said, patting its head with his big hand. "Watching and waiting, eh, old Biribi?" The dog looked into his eyes as if he knew what was said, and would speak—or, indeed, was speaking in his own language. "That's the way of life, Biribi—watching and waiting, and watching—always watching."

Suddenly the dog caught its head away from his hand, gave a short joyful bark, and ran slowly up the hillock.

"Guida and the child," the man said aloud, moving towards the house—"Guida and the child!"

He saw her and the little one before they saw him. Presently the child said: "See, maman," and pointed. Guida started. A swift flush passed over her face, then she smiled and made a step forward to meet her visitor.

"Maitre Ranulph—Ranulph!" she said, holding out her hand. "It's a long time since we met."

"A year," he answered simply, "just a year." He looked down at the child, then stooped, caught him up in his arms and said: "He's grown. Es-tu gentiment?" he added to the child—"es-tu gentiment, m'sieu'?"

The child did not quite understand. "Please?" it said in true Jersey fashion—at which the mother was troubled.

"O Guilbert, is that what you should say?" she asked. The child looked up quaintly at her, and with the same whimsical smile which Guida had given to another so many years ago, he looked at Ranulph and said: "Pardon, monsieur."

"Coum est qu'on etes, m'sieu'?" said Ranulph in another patois greeting.

Guida shook her head reprovingly. The child glanced swiftly at his mother as though asking permission to reply as he wished, then back at Ranulph, and was about to speak, when Guida said: "I have not taught him the Jersey patois, Ranulph; only English and French."

Her eyes met his clearly, meaningly. Her look said to him as plainly as words, The child's destiny is not here in Jersey. But as if he knew that in this she was blinding herself, and that no one can escape the influences of surroundings, he held the child back from him, and said with a smile: "Coum est qu'on vos portest?"

Now the child with elfish sense of the situation replied in Jersey English: "Naicely, thenk you."

"You see," said Ranulph to Guida, "there are things in us stronger than we are. The wind, the sea, and people we live with, they make us sing their song one way or another. It's in our bones."

A look of pain passed over Guida's face, and she did not reply to his remark, but turned almost abruptly to the doorway, saying, with just the slightest hesitation: "You will come in?"

There was no hesitation on his part. "Oui-gia!" he said, and stepped inside.

She hastily hung up the child's cap and her own, and as she gathered in the soft, waving hair, Ranulph noticed how the years had only burnished it more deeply and strengthened the beauty of the head. She had made the gesture unconsciously, but catching the look in his eye a sudden thrill of anxiety ran through her. Recovering herself, however, and with an air of bright friendliness, she laid a hand upon the great arm-chair, above which hung the ancient sword of her ancestor, the Comte Guilbert Mauprat de Chambery, and said: "Sit here, Ranulph."

Seating himself he gave a heavy sigh—one of those passing breaths of content which come to the hardest lives now and then: as though the Spirit of Life itself, in ironical apology for human existence, gives moments of respite from which hope is born again. Not for over four long years had Ranulph sat thus quietly in the presence of Guida. At first, when Maitresse Aimable had told him that Guida was leaving the Place du Vier Prison to live in this lonely place with her newborn child, he had gone to entreat her to remain; but Maitresse Aimable had been present then, and all that he could say—all that he might speak out of his friendship, out of the old love, now deep pity and sorrow—was of no avail. It had been borne in upon him then that she was not morbid, but that her mind had a sane, fixed purpose which she was intent to fulfil. It was as though she had made some strange covenant with a little helpless life, with a little face that was all her face; and that covenant she would keep.

So he had left her, and so to do her service had been granted elsewhere. The Chevalier, with perfect wisdom and nobility, insisted on being to Guida what he had always been, accepting what was as though it had always been, and speaking as naturally of her and the child as though there had always been a Guida and the child. Thus it was that he counted himself her protector, though he sat far away in the upper room of Elie Mattingley's house in the Rue d'Egypte, thinking his own thoughts, biding the time when she should come back to the world, and mystery be over, and happiness come once more; hoping only that he might live to see it.

Under his directions, Jean Touzel had removed the few things that Guida took with her to Plemont; and instructed by him, Elie Mattingley sold her furniture. Thus Guida had settled at Plemont, and there over four years of her life were passed.

"Your father—how is he?" she asked presently. "Feeble," replied Ranulph; "he goes abroad but little now."

"It was said the Royal Court was to make him a gift, in remembrance of the Battle of Jersey." Ranulph turned his head away from her to the child, and beckoned him over. The child came instantly.

As Ranulph lifted him on his knee he answered Guida: "My father did not take it."

"Then they said you were to be constable—the grand monsieur." She smiled at him in a friendly way.

"They said wrong," replied Ranulph.

"Most people would be glad of it," rejoined Guida. "My mother used to say you would be Bailly one day."

"Who knows—perhaps I might have been!"

She looked at him half sadly, half curiously. "You—you haven't any ambitions now, Maitre Ranulph?" It suddenly struck her that perhaps she was responsible for the maiming of this man's life—for clearly it was maimed. More than once she had thought of it, but it came home to her to-day with force. Years ago Ranulph Delagarde had been spoken of as one who might do great things, even to becoming Bailly. In the eyes of a Jerseyman to be Bailly was to be great, with jurats sitting in a row on either side of him and more important than any judge in the Kingdom. Looking back now Guida realised that Ranulph had never been the same since that day on the Ecrehos when his father had returned and Philip had told his wild tale of love.

A great bitterness suddenly welled up in her. Without intention, without blame, she had brought suffering upon others. The untoward happenings of her life had killed her grandfather, had bowed and aged the old Chevalier, had forced her to reject the friendship of Carterette Mattingley, for the girl's own sake; had made the heart of one fat old woman heavy within her; and, it would seem, had taken hope and ambition from the life of this man before her. Love in itself is but a bitter pleasure; when it is given to the unworthy it becomes a torture—and so far as Ranulph and the world knew she was wholly unworthy. Of late she had sometimes wondered if, after all, she had had the right to do as she had done in accepting the public shame, and in not proclaiming the truth: if to act for one's own heart, feelings, and life alone, no matter how perfect the honesty, is not a sort of noble cruelty, or cruel nobility; an egotism which obeys but its own commandments, finding its own straight and narrow path by first disbarring the feelings and lives of others. Had she done what was best for the child? Misgiving upon this point made her heart ache bitterly. Was life then but a series of trist condonings at the best, of humiliating compromises at the worst?

She repeated her question to Ranulph now. "You haven't ambition any longer?"

"I'm busy building ships," he answered evasively. "I build good ships, they tell me, and I am strong and healthy. As for being connetable, I'd rather help prisoners free than hale them before the Royal Court. For somehow when you get at the bottom of most crimes—the small ones leastways—you find they weren't quite meant. I expect—I expect," he added gravely, "that half the crimes oughtn't to be punished at all; for it's queer that things which hurt most can't be punished by law."

"Perhaps it evens up in the long end," answered Guida, turning away from him to the fire, and feeling her heart beat faster as she saw how the child nestled in Ranulph's arms—her child which had no father. "You see," she added, "if some are punished who oughtn't to be, there are others who ought to be that aren't, and the worst of it is, we care so little for real justice that we often wouldn't punish if we could. I have come to feel that. Sometimes if you do exactly what's right, you hurt some one you don't wish to hurt, and if you don't do exactly what's right, perhaps that some one else hurts you. So, often, we would rather be hurt than hurt."

With the last words she turned from the fire and involuntarily faced him. Their eyes met. In hers were only the pity of life, the sadness, the cruelty of misfortune, and friendliness for him. In his eyes was purpose definite, strong.

He went over and put the child in its high chair. Then coming a little nearer to Guida, he said:

"There's only one thing in life that really hurts—playing false."

Her heart suddenly stopped beating. What was Ranulph going to say? After all these years was he going to speak of Philip? But she did not reply according to her thought.

"Have people played false in your life—ever?" she asked.

"If you'll listen to me I'll tell you how," he answered. "Wait, wait," she said in trepidation. "It—it has nothing to do with me?"

He shook his head. "It has only to do with my father and myself. When I've told you, then you must say whether you will have anything to do with it, or with me.... You remember," he continued, without waiting for her to speak, "you remember that day upon the Ecrehos—five years ago? Well, that day I had made up my mind to tell you in so many words what I hoped you had always known, Guida. I didn't—why? Not because of another man—no, no, I don't mean to hurt you, but I must tell you the truth now—not because of another man, for I should have bided my chance with him."

"Ranulph, Ranulph," she broke in, "you must not speak of this now! Do you not see it hurts me? It is not like you. It is not right of you—"

A sudden emotion seized him, and his voice shook. "Not right! You should know that I'd never say one word to hurt you, or do one thing to wrong you. But I must speak to-day-I must tell you everything. I've thought of it for four long years, and I know now that what I mean to do is right."

She sat down in the great arm-chair. A sudden weakness came upon her: she was being brought face to face with days of which she had never allowed herself to think, for she lived always in the future now.

"Go on," she said helplessly. "What have you to say, Ranulph?"

"I will tell you why I didn't speak of my love to you that day we went to the Ecrehos. My father came back that day."

"Yes, yes," she said; "of course you had to think of him."

"Yes, I had to think of him, but not in the way you mean. Be patient a little while," he added.

Then in a few words he told her the whole story of his father's treachery and crime, from the night before the Battle of Jersey up to their meeting again upon the Ecrehos.

Guida was amazed and moved. Her heart filled with pity. "Ranulph— poor Ranulph!" she said, half rising in her seat.

"No, no—wait," he rejoined. "Sit where you are till I tell you all. Guida, you don't know what a life it has been for me these four years. I used to be able to look every man in the face without caring whether he liked me or hated me, for then I had never lied, I had never done a mean thing to any man; I had never deceived—nannin-gia, never! But when my father came back, then I had to play a false game. He had lied, and to save him I either had to hold my peace or tell his story. Speaking was lying or being silent was lying. Mind you, I'm not complaining, I'm not saying it because I want any pity. No, I'm saying it because it's the truth, and I want you to know the truth. You understand what it means to feel right in your own mind—if you feel that way, the rest of life is easy. Eh ben, what a thing it is to get up in the morning, build your fire, make your breakfast, and sit down facing a man whose whole life's a lie, and that man your own father! Some morning perhaps you forget, and you go out into the sun, and it all seems good; and you take your tools and go to work, and the sea comes washing up the shingle, and you think that the shir-r-r-r of the water on the pebbles and the singing of the saw and the clang of the hammer are the best music in the world. But all at once you remember—and then you work harder, not because you love work now for its own sake, but because it uses up your misery and makes you tired; and being tired you can sleep, and in sleep you can forget. Yet nearly all the time you're awake it fairly kills you, for you feel some one always at your elbow whispering, 'you'll never be happy again, you'll never be happy again!' And when you tell the truth about anything, that some one at your elbow laughs and says: 'Nobody believes— your whole life's a lie!' And if the worst man you know passes you by, that some one at your elbow says: 'You can wear a mask, but you're no better than he, no better, no—'"

While Ranulph spoke Guida's face showed a pity and a kindness as deep as the sorrow which had deepened her nature. She shook her head once or twice as though to say, Surely, what suffering! and now this seemed to strike Ranulph, to convict him of selfishness, for he suddenly stopped. His face cleared, and, smiling with a little of his old-time cheerfulness, he said:

"Yet one gets used to it and works on because one knows it will all come right sometime. I'm of the kind that waits."

She looked up at him with her old wide-eyed steadfastness and replied: "You are a good man, Ranulph." He stood gazing at her a moment without remark, then he said:

"No, ba su, no! but it's like you to say I am." Then he added suddenly: "I've told you the whole truth about myself and about my father. He did a bad thing, and I've stood by him. At first, I nursed my troubles and my shame. I used to think I couldn't live it out, that I had no right to any happiness. But I've changed my mind about that-oui-gia! As I hammered away at my ships month in month out, year in year out, the truth came home to me at last. What right had I to sit down and brood over my miseries? I didn't love my father, but I've done wrong for him, and I've stuck to him. Well, I did love—and I do love—some one else, and I should only be doing right to tell her, and to ask her to let me stand with her against the world."

He was looking down at her with all his story in his face. She put out her hand quickly as if in protest and said:

"Ranulph—ah no, Ranulph—"

"But yes, Guida," he replied with stubborn tenderness, "it is you I mean—it is you I've always meant. You have always been a hundred times more to me than my father, but I let you fight your fight alone. I've waked up now to my mistake. But I tell you true that though I love you better than anything in the world, if things had gone well with you I'd never have come to you. I never came, because of my father, and I'd never have come because you are too far above me always—too fine, too noble for me. I only come now because we're both apart from the world and lonely beyond telling; because we need each other. I have just one thing to say: that we two should stand together. There's none ever can be so near as those that have had hard troubles, that have had bitter wrongs. And when there's love too, what can break the bond! You and I are apart from the world, a black loneliness no one understands. Let us be lonely no longer. Let us live our lives together. What shall we care for the rest of the world if we know we mean to do good and no wrong? So I've come to ask you to let me care for you and the child, to ask you to make my home your home. My father hasn't long to live, and when he is gone we could leave this island for ever. Will you come, Guida?"

She had never taken her eyes from his face, and as his story grew her face lighted with emotion, the glow of a moment's content, of a fleeting joy. In spite of all, this man loved her, he wanted to marry her—in spite of all. Glad to know that such men lived—and with how dark memories contrasting with this bright experience-she said to him once again: "You are a good man, Ranulph."

Coming near to her, he said in a voice husky with feeling: "Will you be my wife, Guida?"

She stood up, one hand resting on the arm of the great chair, the other half held out in pitying deprecation.

"No, Ranulph, no; I can never, never be your wife—never in this world."

For an instant he looked at her dumfounded, then turned away to the fireplace slowly and heavily. "I suppose it was too much to hope for," he said bitterly. He realised now how much she was above him, even in her sorrow and shame.

"You forget," she answered quietly, and her hand went out suddenly to the soft curls of the child, "you forget what the world says about me."

There was a kind of fierceness in his look as he turned to her again.

"Me—I have always forgotten—everything," he answered. "Have you thought that for all these years I've believed one word? Secours d'la vie, of what use is faith, what use to trust, if you thought I believed! I do not know the truth, for you have not told me; but I do know, as I know I have a heart in me—I do know that there never was any wrong in you. It is you who forget," he added quickly—"it is you who forget. I tried to tell you all this before; three years ago I tried to tell you. You stopped me, you would not listen. Perhaps you've thought I did not know what has happened to you every week, almost every day of your life? A hundred times I have walked here and you haven't seen me—when you were asleep, when you were fishing, when you were working like a man in the fields and the garden; you who ought to be cared for by a man, working like a slave at man's work. But, no, no, you have not thought well of me, or you would have known that every day I cared, every day I watched, and waited, and hoped—and believed!"

She came to him slowly where he stood, his great frame trembling with his passion and the hurt she had given him, and laying her hand upon his arm, she said:

"Your faith was a blind one, Ro. I was either a girl who—who deserved nothing of the world, or I was a wife. I had no husband, had I? Then I must have been a girl who deserved nothing of the world, or of you. Your faith was blind, Ranulph, you see it was blind."

"What I know is this," he repeated with dogged persistence—"what I know is this: that whatever was wrong, there was no wrong in you. My life a hundred times on that!"

She smiled at him, the brightest smile that had been on her face these years past, and she answered softly: "'I did not think there was so great faith—no, not in Israel!'" Then the happiness passed from her lips to her eyes. "Your faith has made me happy, Ro—I am selfish, you see. Your love in itself could not make me happy, for I have no right to listen, because—"

She paused. It seemed too hard to say: the door of her heart enclosing her secret opened so slowly, so slowly. A struggle was going on in her. Every feeling, every force of her nature was alive. Once, twice, thrice she tried to speak and could not. At last with bursting heart and eyes swimming with tears she said solemnly:

"I can never marry you, Ranulph, and I have no right to listen to your words of love, because—because I am a wife."

Then she gave a great sigh of relief; like some penitent who has for a lifetime hidden a sin or a sorrow and suddenly finds the joy of a confessional which relieves the sick heart, takes away the hand of loneliness that clamps it, and gives it freedom again; lifting the poor slave from the rack of secrecy, the cruelest inquisition of life and time. She repeated the words once more, a little louder, a little clearer. She had vindicated herself to God, now she vindicated herself to man—though to but one.

"I can never marry you; because I am a wife," she said again. There was a slight pause, and then the final word was said: "I am the wife of Philip d'Avranche."

Ranulph did not speak. He stood still and rigid, looking with eyes that scarcely saw.

"I had not intended telling any one until the time should come"—once more her hand reached out and tremblingly stroked the head of the child—"but your faith has forced it from me. I couldn't let you go from me now, ignorant of the truth, you whose trust is beyond telling. Ranulph, I want you to know that I am at least no worse than you thought me."

The look in his face was one of triumph, mingled with despair, hatred, and purpose—hatred of Philip d'Avranche, and purpose concerning him. He gloried now in knowing that Guida might take her place among the honest women of this world,—as the world terms honesty,—but he had received the death-blow to his every hope. He had lost her altogether, he who had watched and waited; who had served and followed, in season and out of season; who had been the faithful friend, keeping his eye fixed only upon her happiness; who had given all; who had poured out his heart like water, and his life like wine before her.

At first he only grasped the fact that Philip d'Avranche was the husband of the woman he loved, and that she had been abandoned. Then sudden remembrance stunned him: Philip d'Avranche, Duc de Bercy, had another wife. He remembered—it had been burned into his brain the day he saw it first in the Gazette de Jersey—that he had married the Comtesse Chantavoine, niece of the Marquis Grandjon-Larisse, upon the very day, and but an hour before, the old Duc de Bercy suddenly died. It flashed across his mind now what he had felt then. He had always believed that Philip had wronged Guida; and long ago he would have gone in search of him—gone to try the strength of his arm against this cowardly marauder, as he held him—but his father's ill-health had kept him where he was, and Philip was at sea upon the nation's business. So the years had gone on until now.

His brain soon cleared. All that he had ever thought upon the matter now crystallised itself into the very truth of the affair. Philip had married Guida secretly; but his new future had opened up to him all at once, and he had married again—a crime, but a crime which in high places sometimes goes unpunished. How monstrous it was that such vile wickedness should be delivered against this woman before him, in whom beauty, goodness, power were commingled! She was the real Princess Philip d'Avranche, and this child of hers—now he understood why she allowed Guilbert to speak no patois.

They scarcely knew how long they stood silent, she with her hand stroking the child's golden hair, he white and dazed, looking, looking at her and the child, as the thing resolved itself to him. At last, in a voice which neither he nor she could quite recognise as his own, he said:

"Of course you live now only for Guilbert."

How she thanked him in her heart for the things he had left unsaid, those things which clear-eyed and great-minded folk, high or humble, always understand. There was no selfish lamenting, no reproaches, none of the futile banalities of the lover who fails to see that it is no crime for a woman not to love him. The thing he had said was the thing she most cared to hear.

"Only for that, Ranulph," she answered.

"When will you claim the child's rights?"

She shook her head sadly. "I do not know," she answered with hesitation. "I will tell you all about it."

Then she told him of the lost register of St. Michael's, and about the Reverend Lorenzo Dow, but she said nothing as to why she had kept silence. She felt that, man though he was, he might divine something of the truth. In any case he knew that Philip had deserted her.

After a moment he said: "I'll find Mr. Dow if he is alive, and the register too. Then the boy shall have his rights."

"No, Ranulph," she answered firmly, "it shall be in my own time. I must keep the child with me. I know not when I shall speak; I am biding my day. Once I thought I never should speak, but then I did not see all, did not wholly see my duty towards Guilbert. It is so hard to find what is wise and just."

"When the proofs are found your child shall have his rights," he said with grim insistence.

"I would never let him go from me," she answered, and, leaning over, she impulsively clasped the little Guilbert in her arms.

"There'll be no need for Guilbert to go from you," he rejoined, "for when your rights come to you, Philip d'Avranche will not be living."

"Will not be living!" she said in amazement. She did not understand.

"I mean to kill him," he answered sternly.

She started, and the light of anger leaped into her eyes. "You mean to kill Philip d'Avranche—you, Maitre Ranulph Delagarde!" she exclaimed. "Whom has he wronged? Myself and my child only—his wife and his child. Men have been killed for lesser wrongs, but the right to kill does not belong to you. You speak of killing Philip d'Avranche, and yet you dare to say you are my friend!"

In that moment Ranulph learned more than he had ever guessed of life's subtle distinctions and the workings of a woman's mind; and he knew that she was right. Her father, her grandfather, might have killed Philip d'Avranche—any one but himself, he the man who had but now declared his love for her. Clearly his selfishness had blinded him. Right was on his side, but not the formal codes by which men live. He could not avenge Guida's wrongs upon her husband, for all men knew that he himself had loved her for years.

"Forgive me," he said in a low tone. Then a new thought came to him. "Do you think your not speaking all these years was best for the child?" he asked.

Her lips trembled. "Oh, that thought," she said, "that thought has made me unhappy so often! It comes to me at night as I lie sleepless, and I wonder if my child will grow up and turn against me one day. Yet I did what I thought was right, Ranulph, I did the only thing I could do. I would rather have died than—"

She stopped short. No, not even to this man who knew all could she speak her whole mind; but sometimes the thought came to her with horrifying acuteness: was it possible that she ought to have sunk her own disillusions, misery, and contempt of Philip d'Avranche, for the child's sake? She shuddered even now as the reflection of that possibility came to her—to live with Philip d'Avranche!

Of late she had felt that a crisis was near. She had had premonitions that her fate, good or bad, was closing in upon her; that these days in this lonely spot with her child, with her love for it and its love for her, were numbered; that dreams must soon give way for action, and this devoted peace would be broken, she knew not how.

Stooping, she kissed the little fellow upon the forehead and the eyes, and his two hands came up and clasped both her cheeks.

"Tu m'aimes, maman?" the child asked. She had taught him the pretty question.

"Comme la vie, comme la vie!" she answered with a half sob, and caught up the little one to her bosom. Now she looked towards the window. Ranulph followed her look, and saw that the shades of night were falling.

"I have far to walk," he said; "I must be going." As he held out his hand to Guida the child leaned over and touched him on the shoulder. "What is your name, man?" he asked.

He smiled, and, taking the warm little hand in his own, he said: "My name is Ranulph, little gentleman. Ranulph's my name, but you shall call me Ro."

"Good-night, Ro, man," the child answered with a mischievous smile.

The scene brought up another such scene in Guida's life so many years ago. Instinctively she drew back with the child, a look of pain crossing her face. But Ranulph did not see; he was going. At the doorway he turned and said:

"You know you can trust me. Good-bye."

# CHAPTER XXXI

When Ranulph returned to his little house at St. Aubin's Bay night had fallen. Approaching he saw there was no light in the windows. The blinds were not drawn, and no glimmer of fire came from the chimney. He hesitated at the door, for he instinctively felt that something must have happened to his father. He was just about to enter, however, when some one came hurriedly round the corner of the house.

"Whist, boy," said a voice; "I've news for you." Ranulph recognised the voice as that of Dormy Jamais. Dormy plucked at his sleeve. "Come with me, boy," said he.

"Come inside if you want to tell me something," answered Ranulph.

"Ah bah, not for me! Stone walls have ears. I'll tell only you and the wind that hears and runs away."

"I must speak to my father first," answered Ranulph.

"Come with me, I've got him safe," Dormy chuckled to himself.

Ranulph's heavy hand dropped on his shoulder. "What's that you're saying—my father with you! What's the matter?"

As though oblivious of Ranulph's hand Dormy went on chuckling.

"Whoever burns me for a fool 'll lose their ashes. Des monz a fous—I have a head! Come with me." Ranulph saw that he must humour the shrewd natural, so he said:

"Et ben, put your four shirts in five bundles and come along." He was a true Jerseyman at heart, and speaking to such as Dormy Jamais he used the homely patois phrases. He knew there was no use hurrying the little man, he would take his own time.

"There's been the devil to pay," said Dormy as he ran towards the shore, his sabots going clac—clac, clac—clac. "There's been the devil to pay in St. Heliers, boy." He spoke scarcely above a whisper.

"Tcheche—what's that?" said Ranulph. But Dormy was not to uncover his pot of roses till his own time. "That connetable's got no more wit than a square bladed knife," he rattled on. "But gache-a-penn, I'm hungry!" And as he ran he began munching a lump of bread he took from his pocket.

For the next five minutes they went on in silence. It was quite dark, and as they passed up Market Hill—called Ghost Lane because of the Good Little People who made it their highway—Dormy caught hold of Ranulph's coat and trotted along beside him. As they went, tokens of the life within came out to them through doorway and window. Now it was the voice of a laughing young mother:

"*Si tu as faim*

*Manges ta main*

*Et gardes l'autre pour demain;*

*Et ta tete*

*Pour le jour de fete;*

*Et ton gros ortee*

*Pour le Jour Saint Norbe*"

And again:

"*Let us pluck the bill of the lark,*

*The lark from head to tail—*"

He knew the voice. It was that of a young wife of the parish of St. Saviour: married happily, living simply, given a frugal board, after the manner of her kind, and a comradeship for life. For the moment he felt little but sorrow for himself. The world seemed to be conspiring against him: the chorus of Fate was singing behind the scenes, singing of the happiness of others in sardonic comment on his own final unhappiness. Yet despite the pain of finality there was on him something of the apathy of despair.

From another doorway came fragments of a song sung at a veille. The door was open, and he could see within the happy gathering of lads and lassies in the light of the crasset. There was the spacious kitchen, its beams and rafters dark with age, adorned with flitches of bacon, huge loaves resting in the racllyi beneath the centre beam, the broad open hearth, the flaming fire of logs, and the great brass pan shining like fresh-coined gold, on its iron tripod over the logs. Lassies in their short woollen petticoats, and bedgones of blue and lilac, with boisterous lads, were stirring the contents of the vast bashin—many cabots of apples, together with sugar, lemon-peel, and cider; the old ladies in mob-caps tied under the chin, measuring out the nutmeg and cinnamon to complete the making of the black butter: a jocund recreation for all, and at all times.

In one corner was a fiddler, and on the veille, flourished for the occasion with satinettes and fern, sat two centeniers and the prevot, singing an old song in the patois of three parishes.

Ranulph looked at the scene lingeringly. Here he was, with mystery and peril to hasten his steps, loitering at the spot where the light of home streamed out upon the roadway. But though he lingered, somehow he seemed withdrawn from all these things; they were to him now as pictures of a distant past.

Dormy plucked at his coat. "Come, come, lift your feet, lift your feet," said he; "it's no time to walk in slippers. The old man will be getting scared, oui-gia!" Ranulph roused himself. Yes, yes, he must hurry on. He had not forgotten his father, but something held him here; as though Fate were whispering in his ear. What does it matter now? While yet you may, feed on the sight of happiness. So the prisoner going to execution seizes one of the few moments left to him for prayer, to look lingeringly upon what he leaves, as though to carry into the dark a clear remembrance of it all.

Moving on quietly in a kind of dream, Ranulph was roused again by Dormy's voice: "On Sunday I saw three magpies, and there was a wedding that day. Tuesday I saw two—that's for joy—and fifty Jersey prisoners of the French comes back on Jersey that day. This morning one I saw. One magpie is for trouble, and trouble's here. One doesn't have eyes for naught—no, bidemme!"

Ranulph's patience was exhausted.

"Bachouar," he exclaimed roughly, "you make elephants out of fleas! You've got no more news than a conch-shell has music. A minute and you'll have a back-hander that'll put you to sleep, Maitre Dormy."

If he had been asked his news politely Dormy would have been still more cunningly reticent. To abuse him in his own argot was to make him loose his bag of mice in a flash.

"Bachouar yourself, Maitre Ranulph! You'll find out soon. No news— no trouble—eh! Par made, Mattingley's gone to the Vier Prison—he! The baker's come back, and the Connetable's after Olivier Delagarde. No trouble, pardingue, if no trouble, Dormy Jamais's a batd'lagoule and no need for father of you to hide in a place that only Dormy knows—my good!"

So at last the blow had fallen; after all these years of silence, sacrifice, and misery. The futility of all that he had done and suffered for his father's sake came home to Ranulph. Yet his brain was instantly alive. He questioned Dormy rapidly and adroitly, and got the story from him in patches.

The baker Carcaud, who, with Olivier Delagarde, betrayed the country into the hands of Rullecour years ago, had, with a French confederate of Mattingley's, been captured in attempting to steal Jean Touzel's boat, the Hardi Biaou. At the capture the confederate had been shot. Before dying he implicated Mattingley in several robberies, and a notorious case of piracy of three months before, committed within gunshot of the men-of-war lying in the tide-way. Carcaud, seriously wounded, to save his life turned King's evidence, and disclosed to the Royal Court in private his own guilt and Olivier Delagarde's treason.

Hidden behind the great chair of the Bailly himself, Dormy Jamais had heard the whole business. This had brought him hot-foot to St. Aubin's Bay, whence he had hurried Olivier Delagarde to a hiding-place in the hills above the bay of St. Brelade. The fool had travelled more swiftly than Jersey justice, whose feet are heavy. Elie Mattingley was now in the Vier Prison. There was the whole story.

The mask had fallen, the game was up. Well, at least there would be no more lying, no more brutalising inward shame. All at once it appeared to Ranulph madness that he had not taken his father away from Jersey long ago. Yet too he knew that as things had been with Guida he could never have stayed away.

Nothing was left but action. He must get his father clear of the island and that soon. But how? and where should they go? He had a boat in St. Aubin's Bay: getting there under cover of darkness he might embark with his father and set sail—whither? To Sark—there was no safety there. To Guernsey— that was no better. To France—yes, that was it, to the war of the Vendee, to join Detricand. No need to find the scrap of paper once given him in the Vier Marchi. Wherever Detricand might be, his fame was the highway to him. All France knew of the companion of de la Rochejaquelein, the fearless Comte de Tournay. Ranulph made his decision. Shamed and dishonoured in Jersey, in that holy war of the Vendee he would find something to kill memory, to take him out of life without disgrace. His father must go with him to France, and bide his fate there also.

By the time his mind was thus made up, they had reached the lonely headland dividing Portelet Bay from St. Brelade's. Dark things were said of this spot, and the country folk of the island were wont to avoid it. Beneath the cliffs in the sea was a rocky islet called Janvrin's Tomb. One Janvrin, ill of a fell disease, and with his fellows forbidden by the Royal Court to land, had taken refuge here, and died wholly neglected and without burial. Afterwards his body lay exposed till the ravens and vultures devoured it, and at last a great storm swept his bones off into the sea. Strange lights were to be seen about this rock, and though wise men guessed them mortal glimmerings, easily explained, they sufficed to give the headland immunity from invasion.

To a cave at this point Dormy Jamais had brought the trembling Olivier Delagarde, unrepenting and peevish, but with a craven fear of the Royal Court and a furious populace quickening his footsteps. This hiding-place was entered at low tide by a passage from a larger cave. It was like a little vaulted chapel floored with sand and shingle. A crevice through rock and earth to the world above let in the light and out the smoke.

Here Olivier Delagarde sat crouched over a tiny fire, with some bread and a jar of water at his hand, gesticulating and talking to himself. The long white hair and beard, with the benevolent forehead, gave him the look of some latter-day St. Helier, grieving for the sins and praying for the sorrows of mankind; but from the hateful mouth came profanity fit only for the dreadful communion of a Witches' Sabbath.

Hearing the footsteps of Ranulph and Dormy, he crouched and shivered in terror, but Ranulph, who knew too well his revolting cowardice, called to him reassuringly. On their approach he stretched out his talon-like fingers in a gesture of entreaty.

"You'll not let them hang me, Ranulph—you'll save me," he whimpered.

"Don't be afraid, they shall not hang you," Ranulph replied quietly, and began warming his hands at the fire. "You'll swear it, Ranulph—on the Bible?"

"I've told you they shall not hang you. You ought to know by now whether I mean what I say," his son answered more sharply.

Assuredly Ranulph meant that his father should not be hanged. Whatever the law was, whatever wrong the old man had done, it had been atoned for; the price had been paid by both. He himself had drunk the cup of shame to the dregs, but now he would not swallow the dregs. An iron determination entered into him. He had endured all that he would endure from man. He had set out to defend Olivier Delagarde from the worst that might happen, and he was ready to do so to the bitter end. His scheme of justice might not be that of the Royal Court, but he would defend it with his life. He had suddenly grown hard—and dangerous.

# CHAPTER XXXII

The Royal Court was sitting late. Candles had been brought to light the long desk or dais where sat the Bailly in his great chair, and the twelve scarlet-robed jurats. The Attorney-General stood at his desk, mechanically scanning the indictment read against prisoners charged with capital crimes. His work was over, and according to his lights he had done it well. Not even the Undertaker's Apprentice could have been less sensitive to the struggles of humanity under the heel of fate and death. A plaintive complacency, a little righteous austerity, and an agreeable expression of hunger made the Attorney-General a figure in godly contrast to the prisoner awaiting his doom in the iron cage opposite.

There was a singular stillness in this sombre Royal Court, where only a tallow candle or two and a dim lanthorn near the door filled the room with flickering shadows-great heads upon the wall drawing close together, and vast lips murmuring awful secrets. Low whisperings came through the dusk like mournful nightwinds carrying tales of awe through a heavy forest. Once in the long silence a figure rose up silently, and stealing across the room to a door near the jury box, tapped upon it with a pencil. A moment's pause, the door opened slightly, and another shadowy figure appeared, whispered, and vanished. Then the first figure closed the door again silently, and came and spoke softly up to the Bailly, who yawned in his hand, sat back in his chair, and drummed his fingers upon the arm. Thereupon the other—the greffier of the court—settled down at his desk beneath the jurats, and peered into an open book before him, his eyes close to the page, reading silently by the meagre light of a candle from the great desk behind him.

Now a fat and ponderous avocat rose up and was about to speak, but the Bailly, with a peevish gesture, waved him down, and he settled heavily into place again.

At last the door at which the greffier had tapped opened, and a gaunt figure in a red robe came out. Standing in the middle of the room he motioned towards the great pew opposite the Attorney-General. Slowly the twenty-four men of the grand jury following him filed into place and sat themselves down in the shadows. Then the gaunt figure—the Vicomte or high sheriff—bowing to the Bailly and the jurats, went over and took his seat beside the Attorney-General. Whereupon the Bailly leaned forward and droned a question to the Grand Enquete in the shadow. One rose up from among the twenty-four, and out of the dusk there came in reply to the Judge a squeaking voice:

"We find the Prisoner at the Bar more Guilty than Innocent."

A shudder ran through the court. But some one not in the room shuddered still more violently. From the gable window of a house in the Rue des Tres Pigeons, a girl had sat the livelong day, looking, looking into the court-room. She had watched the day decline, the evening come, and the lighting of the crassets and the candles, and had waited to hear the words that meant more to her than her own life. At last the great moment came, and she could hear the foreman's voice whining the fateful words, "More Guilty than Innocent."

It was Carterette Mattingley, and the prisoner at the bar was her father.

# CHAPTER XXXIII

Mattingley's dungeon was infested with rats and other vermin, he had only straw for his bed, and his food and drink were bread and water. The walls were damp with moisture from the Fauxbie running beneath, and a mere glimmer of light came through a small barred window. Superstition had surrounded the Vier Prison with horrors. As carts passed under the great archway, its depth multiplied the sounds so powerfully, the echoes were so fantastic, that folk believed them the roarings of fiendish spirits. If a mounted guard hurried through, the reverberation of the drum-beats and the clatter of hoofs were so uncouth that children stopped their ears and fled in terror. To the ignorant populace the Vier Prison was the home of noisome serpents and the rendezvous of the devil and his witches of Rocbert.

When therefore the seafaring merchant of the Vier Marchi, whose massive, brass-studded bahue had been as a gay bazaar where the gentry of Jersey refreshed their wardrobes, with one eye closed—when he was transferred to the Vier Prison, little wonder he should become a dreadful being round whom played the lightnings of dark fancy. Elie Mattingley the popular sinner, with insolent gold rings in his ears, unchallenged as to how he came by his merchandise, was one person; Elie Mattingley, a torch for the burning, and housed amid the terrors of the Vier Prison, was another.

Few people in Jersey slept the night before his execution. Here and there kind-hearted women or unimportant men lay awake through pity, and a few through a vague sense of loss; for, henceforth, the Vier Marchi would lack a familiar interest; but mostly the people of Mattingley's world were wakeful through curiosity. Morbid expectation of the hanging had for them a gruesome diversion. The thing itself would break the daily monotony of life and provide hushed gossip for vraic gatherings and veilles for a long time to come. Thus Elie Mattingley would not die in vain!

Here was one sensation, but there was still another. Olivier Delagarde had been unmasked, and the whole island had gone tracking him down. No aged toothless tiger was ever sported through the jungle by an army of shikarris with hungrier malice than was this broken traitor by the people he had betrayed. Ensued, therefore, a commingling of patriotism with lust of man-hunting and eager expectation of to-morrow's sacrifice.

Nothing of this excitement disturbed Mattingley. He did not sleep, but that was because he was still watching for a means of escape. He felt his chances diminish, however, when about midnight an extra guard was put round the prison. Something had gone amiss in the matter of his rescue.

Three things had been planned.

Firstly, he was to try escape by the small window of the dungeon.

Secondly, Carterette was to bring Sebastian Alixandre to the prison disguised as a sorrowing aunt of the condemned. Alixandre was suddenly to overpower the jailer, Mattingley was to make a rush for freedom, and a few bold spirits without would second his efforts and smuggle him to the sea. The directing mind and hand in the business were Ranulph Delagarde's. He was to have his boat waiting to respond to a signal from the shore, and to make sail for France, where he and his father were to be landed. There he was to give Mattingley, Alixandre, and Carterette his craft to fare across the seas to the great fishing-ground of Gaspe in Canada.

Lastly, if these plans failed, the executioner was to be drugged with liquor, his besetting weakness, on the eve of the hanging.

The first plan had been found impossible, the window being too small for even Mattingley's head to get through. The second had failed because the righteous Royal Court forbade Carterette the prison, intent that she should no longer be contaminated by so vile a wretch as her father. For years this same Christian solicitude had looked down from the windows of the Cohue Royale upon this same criminal in the Vier Marchi, with one blind eye for himself the sinner and an open one for his merchandise.

Mattingley could hear the hollow sound of the sentinels' steps under the archway of the Vier Prison. He was quite stoical. If he had to die, then he had to die. Death could only be a little minute of agony; and for what came after—well, he had not thought fearfully of that, and he had no wish to think of it at all. The visiting chaplain had talked, and he had not listened. He had his own ideas about life, and death, and the beyond, and they were not ungenerous. The chaplain had found him patient but impossible, kindly but unresponsive, sometimes even curious, but without remorse.

"You should repent with sorrow and a contrite heart," said the clergyman. "You have done many evil things in your life, Mattingley."

Mattingley had replied: "Ma fuifre, I can't remember them! I know I never done them, for I never done anything but good all my life—so much for so much." He had argued it out with himself and he believed he was a good man. He had been open-handed, had stood by his friends, and, up to a few days ago, was counted a good citizen; for many had come to profit through him. His trade—a little smuggling, a little piracy? Was not the former hallowed by distinguished patronage, and had it not existed from immemorial time? It was fair fight for gain, an eye for an eye and a tooth for a tooth. If he hadn't robbed others on the high seas, they would probably have robbed him—and sometimes they did. His spirit was that of the Elizabethan admirals; he belonged to a century not his own. As for the crime for which he was to suffer, it had been the work of another hand, and very bad work it was, to try and steal Jean Touzel's Hardi Biaou, and then bungle it. He had had nothing to do with it, for he and Jean Touzel were the best of friends, as was proved by the fact that while he lay in his dungeon, Jean wandered the shore sorrowing for his fate.

Thinking now of the whole business and of his past life, Mattingley suddenly had a pang. Yes, remorse smote him at last. There was one thing on his conscience—only one. He had respect for the feelings of others, and where the Church was concerned this was mingled with a droll sort of pity, as of the greater for the lesser, the wise for the helpless. For clergymen he had a half-affectionate contempt. He remembered now that when, five years ago, his confederate who had turned out so badly—he had trusted him, too! had robbed the church of St. Michael's, carrying off the great chest of communion plate, offertories, and rents, he had piously left behind in Mattingley's house the vestry-books and parish-register; a nice definition in rogues' ethics. Awaiting his end now, it smote Mattingley's soul that these stolen records had not been returned to St. Michael's. Next morning he must send word to Carterette to restore the books. Then his conscience would be clear once more. With this resolve quieting his mind, he turned over on his straw and went peacefully to sleep.

Hours afterwards he waked with a yawn. There was no start, no terror, but the appearance of the jailer with the chaplain roused in him disgust for the coming function at the Mont es Pendus. Disgust was his chief feeling. This was no way for a man to die! With a choice of evils he should have preferred walking the plank, or even dying quietly in his bed, to being stifled by a rope. To dangle from a cross-tree like a half-filled bag offended all instincts of picturesqueness, and first and last he had been picturesque.

He asked at once for pencil and paper. His wishes were obeyed with deference. On the whole he realised by the attentions paid him—the brandy and the food offered by the jailer, the fluttering kindness of the chaplain— that in the life of a criminal there is one moment when he commands the situation. He refused the brandy, for he was strongly against spirits in the early morning, but asked for coffee. Eating seemed superfluous—and a man might die more gaily on an empty stomach. He assured the chaplain that he had come to terms with his conscience and was now about to perform the last act of a well-intentioned life.

There and then he wrote to Carterette, telling her about the vestry-books of St. Michael's, and begging that she should restore them secretly. There were no affecting messages; they understood each other. He knew that when it was possible she would never fail to come to the mark where he was concerned, and she had equal faith in him. So the letter was sealed, addressed with flourishes, he was proud of his handwriting, and handed to the chaplain for Carterette.

He had scarcely drunk his coffee when there was a roll of drums outside. Mattingley knew that his hour was come, and yet to his own surprise he had no violent sensations. He had a shock presently, however, for on the jailer announcing the executioner, who should be there before him but the Undertaker's Apprentice! In politeness to the chaplain Mattingley forbore profanity. This was the one Jerseyman for whom he had a profound hatred, this youth with the slow, cold, watery blue eye, a face that never wrinkled either with mirth or misery, the square-set teeth always showing a little—an involuntary grimace of cruelty. Here was insult.

"Devil below us, so you're going to do it—you!" broke out Mattingley.

"The other man was drunk," said the Undertaker's Apprentice. "He's been full as a jug three days. He got drunk too soon." The grimace seemed to widen. "O my good!" said Mattingley, and he would say no more. To him words were like nails—of no use unless they were to be driven home by acts.

To Mattingley the procession of death was stupidly slow. As it issued from the archway of the Vier Prison between mounted guards, and passed through a long lane of moving spectators, he looked round coolly. One or two bold spirits cried out: "Head up to the wind, Maitre Elie!"

"Oui-gia," he replied; "devil a top-sail in!" and turned a look of contempt on those who hooted him. He realised now that there was no chance of rescue. The militia and the town guard were in ominous force, and although his respect for the island military was not devout, a bullet from the musket of a fool might be as effective as one from Bonapend's—as Napoleon Bonaparte was disdainfully called in Jersey. Yet he could not but wonder why all the plans of Alixandre, Carterette, and Ranulph had gone for nothing; even the hangman had been got drunk too soon! He had a high opinion of Ranulph, and that he should fail him was a blow to his judgment of humanity.

He was thoroughly disgusted. Also they had compelled him to put on a white shirt, he who had never worn linen in his life. He was ill at ease in it. It made him conspicuous; it looked as though he were aping the gentleman at the last. He tried to resign himself, but resignation was hard to learn so late in life. Somehow he could not feel that this was really the day of his death. Yet how could it be otherwise? There was the Vicomte in his red robe, there was the sinister Undertaker's Apprentice, ready to do his hangman's duty. There, as they crossed the mielles, while the sea droned its sing-song on his left, was the parson droning his sing-song on the right "In the midst of life we are in death," etc. There were the grumbling drums, and the crowd morbidly enjoying their Roman holiday; and there, looming up before him, were the four stone pillars on the Mont es Pendus from which he was to swing. His disgust deepened. He was not dying like a seafarer who had fairly earned his reputation.

His feelings found vent even as he came to the foot of the platform where he was to make his last stand, and the guards formed a square about the great pillars, glooming like Druidic altars. He burst forth in one phrase expressive of his feelings.

"Sacre matin—so damned paltry!" he said, in equal tribute to two races.

The Undertaker's Apprentice, thinking this a reflection upon his arrangements, said, with a wave of the hand to the rope:

"Nannin, ch'est tres ship-shape, Maitre!"

The Undertaker's Apprentice was wrong. He had made everything ship-shape, as he thought, but a gin had been set for him. The rope to be used at the hanging had been measured and approved by the Vicomte, and the Undertaker's Apprentice had carried it to his room at the top of the Cohue Royale. In the dead of night, however, Dormy Jamais drew it from under the mattress whereon the deathman slept, and substituted one a foot longer. This had been Ranulph's idea as a last resort, for he had a grim wish to foil the law even at the twelfth hour.

The great moment had come. The shouts and hootings ceased. Out of the silence there arose only the champing of a horse's bit or the hysterical giggle of a woman. The high painful drone of the chaplain's voice was heard.

Then came the fatal "Maintenant!" from the Vicomte, the platform fell, and Elie Mattingley dropped the length of the rope.

What was the consternation of the Vicomte and the hangman, and the horror of the crowd, to see that Mattingley's toes just touched the ground! The body shook and twisted. The man was being slowly strangled, not hanged.

The Undertaker's Apprentice was the only person who kept a cool head. The solution of the problem of the rope for afterwards, but he had been sent there to hang a man, and a man he would hang somehow. Without more ado he jumped upon Mattingley's shoulders and began to drag him down.

That instant Ranulph Delagarde burst through the mounted guard and the militia. Rushing to the Vicomte, he exclaimed:

"Shame! The man was to be hung, not strangled. This is murder. Stop it, or I'll cut the rope." He looked round on the crowd. "Cowards—cowards," he cried, "will you see him murdered?"

He started forward to drag away the deathmann, but the Vicomte, thoroughly terrified at Ranulph's onset, himself seized the Undertaker's Apprentice, who, drawing off with unruffled malice, watched what followed with steely eyes.

Dragged down by the weight of the Apprentice, Mattingley's feet were now firmly on the ground. While the excited crowd tried to break through the cordon of mounted guards, Mattingley, by a twist and a jerk, freed his corded hands. Loosing the rope at his neck he opened his eyes and looked around him, dazed and dumb.

The Apprentice came forward. "I'll shorten the rope oui-gia! Then you shall see him swing," he grumbled viciously to the Vicomte.

The gaunt Vicomte was trembling with excitement. He looked helplessly around him.

The Apprentice caught hold of the rope to tie knots in it and so shorten it, but Ranulph again appealed to the Vicomte.

"You've hung the man," said he; "you've strangled him and you didn't kill him. You've got no right to put that rope round his neck again."

Two jurats who had waited on the outskirts of the crowd, furtively watching the effect of their sentence, burst in, as distracted as the Vicomte.

"Hang the man again and the whole world will laugh at you," Ranulph said. "If you're not worse than fools or Turks you'll let him go. He has had death already. Take him back to the prison then, if you're afraid to free him." He turned on the crowd fiercely. "Have you nothing to say to this butchery?" he cried. "For the love of God, haven't you anything to say?"

Half the crowd shouted "Let him go free!" and the other half, disappointed in the working out of the gruesome melodrama, groaned and hooted.

Meanwhile Mattingley stood as still as ever he had stood by his bahue in the Vier Marchi, watching—waiting.

The Vicomte conferred nervously with the jurats for a moment, and then turned to the guard.

"Take the prisoner to the Vier Prison," he said. Mattingley had been slowly solving the problem of his salvation. His eye, like a gimlet, had screwed its way through Ranulph's words into what lay behind, and at last he understood the whole beautiful scheme. It pleased him: Carterette had been worthy of herself, and of him. Ranulph had played his game well too. He only failed to do justice to the poor beganne, Dormy Jamais. But then the virtue of fools is its own reward. As the procession started back with the Undertaker's Apprentice now following after Mattingley, not going before, Mattingley turned to him, and with a smile of malice said:

"Ch'est tres ship-shape, Maitre-eh!" and he jerked his head back towards the inadequate rope.

He was not greatly troubled about the rest of this grisly farce. He was now ready for breakfast, and his appetite grew as he heard how the crowd hooted and snarled yah! at the Undertaker's Apprentice. He was quite easy about the future. What had been so well done thus far could not fail in the end.

# CHAPTER XXXIV

Events proved Mattingley right. Three days after, it was announced that he had broken prison. It is probable that the fury of the Royal Court at the news was not quite sincere, for it was notable that the night of his evasion, suave and uncrestfallen, they dined in state at the Tres Pigeons. The escape gave them happy issue from a quandary.

The Vicomte officially explained that Mattingley had got out by the dungeon window. People came to see the window, and there, ba su, the bars were gone! But that did not prove the case, and the mystery was deepened by the fact that Jean Touzel, whose head was too small for Elie's hat, could not get that same head through the dungeon window. Having proved so much, Jean left the mystery there, and returned to his Hardi Biaou.

This happened on the morning after the dark night when Mattingley, Carterette, and Alixandre hurried from the Vier Prison, through the Rue des Sablons to the sea, and there boarded Ranulph's boat, wherein was Olivier Delagarde the traitor.

Accompanying Carterette to the shore was a little figure that moved along beside them like a shadow, a little grey figure that carried a gold-headed cane. At the shore this same little grey figure bade Mattingley good-bye with a quavering voice. Whereupon Carterette, her face all wet with tears, kissed him upon both cheeks, and sobbed so that she could scarcely speak. For now when it was all done—all the horrible ordeal over—the woman in her broke down before the little old gentleman, who had been like a benediction in the house where the ten commandments were imperfectly upheld. But she choked down her sobs, and thinking of another more than of herself, she said:

"Dear Chevalier, do not forget the book—that register—I gave you to-night. Read it—read the last writing in it, and then you will know—ah, bidemme—but you will know that her we love—ah, but you must read it and tell nobody till—till the right time comes! She hasn't held her tongue for naught, and it's only fair to do as she's done all along, and hold ours. Pardingue, but my heart hurts me!" she added suddenly, and catching the hand that held the little gold cane she kissed it with impulsive ardour. "You have been so good to me—oui-gia!" she said with a gulp, and then she dropped the hand and turned and fled to the boat rocking in the surf.

The little Chevalier watched the boat glide out into the gloom of night, and waited till he knew that they must all be aboard Ranulph's schooner and making for the sea. Then he turned and went back to the empty house in the Rue d'Egypte.

Opening the book Carterette had placed in his hands before they left the house, he turned up and scanned closely the last written page. A moment after, he started violently, his eyes dilating, first with wonder, then with a bewildered joy; and then, Protestant though he was, with the instinct of long-gone forefathers, he made the sacred gesture, and said:

"Now I have not lived and loved in vain, thanks be to God!"

Even as joy opened wide the eyes of the Chevalier, who had been sorely smitten through the friends of his heart, out at sea Night and Death were closing the eyes of another wan old man who had been a traitor to his country.

For the boat of the fugitives had scarcely cleared reefs and rocks, and reached the open Channel, when Olivier Delagarde, uttering the same cry as when Ranulph and the soldiers had found him wounded in the Grouville road sixteen years before, suddenly started up from where he had lain mumbling, and whispering incoherently, "Ranulph—they've killed me!" fell back dead.

True to the instinct which had kept him faithful to one idea for sixteen years, and in spite of the protests of Mattingley and Carterette—of the despairing Carterette who felt the last thread of her hopes snap with his going—Ranulph made ready to leave them. Bidding them good-bye, he placed his father's body in the rowboat, and pulling back to the shore of St. Aubin's Bay with his pale freight, carried it on his shoulders up to the little house where he had lived so many years. There he kept the death-watch alone.

# CHAPTER XXXV

Guida knew nothing of the arrest and trial of Mattingley until he had been condemned to death. Nor until then did she know anything of what had happened to Olivier Delagarde; for soon after her interview with Ranulph she had gone a-marketing to the Island of Sark, with the results of half a year's knitting. Her return had been delayed by ugly gales from the south east. Several times a year she made this journey, landing at the Eperquerie Rocks as she had done one day long ago, and selling her beautiful wool caps and jackets to the farmers and fisher-folk, getting in kind for what she gave.

When she made these excursions to Sark, Dormy Jamais had always remained at the little house, milking her cow, feeding her fowls, and keeping all in order—as perfect a sentinel as old Biribi, and as faithful. For the first time in his life, however, Dormy Jamais was unfaithful. On the day that Carcaud the baker and Mattingley were arrested, he deserted the hut at Plemont to exploit, with Ranulph, the adventure which was at last to save Olivier Delagarde and Mattingley from death. But he had been unfaithful only in the letter of his bond. He had gone to the house of Jean Touzel, through whose Hardi Biaou the disaster had come, and had told Mattresse Aimable that she must go to Plemont in his stead—for a fool must keep his faith whate'er the worldly wise may do. So the fat Femme de Ballast, puffing with every step, trudged across the island to Plemont, and installed herself as keeper of the house.

One day Mattresse Aimable's quiet was invaded by two signalmen who kept watch, not far from Guida's home, for all sail, friend or foe, bearing in sight. They were now awaiting the new Admiral of the Jersey station and his fleet. With churlish insolence they entered Guida's hut before Maitresse Aimable could prevent it. Looking round, they laughed meaningly, and then told her that the commander coming presently to lie with his fleet in Grouville Bay was none other than the sometime Jersey midshipman, now Admiral Prince Philip d'Avranche, Duc de Bercy. Understanding then the meaning of their laughter, and the implied insult to Guida, Maitresse Aimable's voice came ravaging out of the silence where it lay hid so often and so long, and the signalmen went their ways shamefacedly.

She could not make head or tail of her thoughts now, nor see an inch before her nose; all she could feel was an aching heart for Guida. She had heard strange tales of how Philip had become Prince Philip d'Avranche, and husband of the Comtesse Chantavoine, and afterwards Duc de Bercy. Also she had heard how Philip, just before he became the Duc de Bercy, had fought his ship against a French vessel off Ushant, and, though she had heavier armament than his own, had destroyed her. For this he had been made an admiral. Only the other day her Jean had brought the Gazette de Jersey in which all these things were related, and had spelled them out for her. And now this same Philip d'Avranche with his new name and fame was on his way to defend the Isle of Jersey.

Mattresse Aimable's muddled mind could not get hold of this new Philip. For years she had thought him a monster, and here he was, a great and valiant gentleman to the world. He had done a thing that Jean would rather have cut off his hand—both hands—than do, and yet here he was, an admiral, a prince, and a sovereign duke, and men like Jean were as dust beneath his feet. The real Philip she knew: he was the man who had spoiled the life of a woman; this other Philip—she could read about him, she could think about him, just as she could think about William and his horse' in Boulay Bay, or the Little Bad Folk of Rocbert; but she could not realise him as a thing of flesh and blood and actual being. The more she tried to realise him the more mixed she became.

As in her mental maze she sat panting her way to enlightenment, she saw Guida's boat entering the little harbour. Now the truth must be told—but how?

After her first exclamation of welcome to mother and child, Maitresse Aimable struggled painfully for her voice. She tried to find words in which to tell Guida the truth, but, stopping in despair, she suddenly began rocking the child back and forth, saying only: "Prince Admiral he—and now to come! O my good—O my good!" Guida's sharp intuition found the truth.

"Philip d'Avranche!" she said to herself. Then aloud, in a shaking voice—"Philip d'Avranche!"

She could not think clearly for a moment. It was as if her brain had received a blow, and in her head was a singing numbness, obscuring eyesight, hearing, speech.

When she had recovered a little she took the child from Maitresse Aimable, and pressing him to her bosom placed him in the Sieur de Mauprat's great arm-chair. This action, ordinary as it seemed, was significant of what was in her mind. The child himself realised something unusual, and he sat perfectly still, two small hands spread out on the big arms.

"You always believed in me, 'tresse Aimable," Guida said at last in a low voice.

"Oui-gia, what else?" was the instant reply. The quick responsiveness of her own voice seemed to confound the Femme de Ballast, and her face suffused.

Guida stooped quickly and kissed her on the cheek. "You'll never regret that. And you will have to go on believing still, but you'll not be sorry in the end, 'tresse Aimable," she said, and turned away to the fireplace. An hour afterwards Mattresse Aimable was upon her way to St. Heliers, but now she carried her weight more easily and panted less. Twice within the last month Jean had given her ear a friendly pinch, and now Guida had kissed her—surely she had reason to carry her weight more lightly.

That afternoon and evening Guida struggled with herself: the woman in her shrinking from the ordeal at hand. But the mother in her pleaded, commanded, ruled confused emotions to quiet. Finality of purpose once determined, a kind of peace came over her sick spirit, for with finality there is quiescence if not peace.

When she looked at the little Guilbert, refined and strong, curiously observant, and sensitive in temperament like herself, her courage suddenly leaped to a higher point than it had ever known. This innocent had suffered enough. What belonged to him he had not had. He had been wronged in much by his father, and maybe—and this was the cruel part of it—had been unwittingly wronged, alas! how unwilling, by her! If she gave her own life many times, it still could be no more than was the child's due.

A sudden impulse seized her, and with a quick explosion of feeling she dropped on her knees, and looking into his eyes, as though hungering for the words she so often yearned to hear, she said:

"You love your mother, Guilbert? You love her, little son?"

With a pretty smile and eyes brimming with affectionate fun, but without a word, the child put out a tiny hand and drew the fingers softly down his mother's face.

"Speak, little son, tell your mother that you love her." The tiny hand pressed itself over her eyes, and a gay little laugh came from the sensitive lips, then both arms ran round her neck. The child drew her head to him impulsively, and kissing her, a little upon the hair and a little upon the forehead, so indefinite was the embrace, he said:

"Si, maman, I loves you best of all," then added: "Maman, can't I have the sword now?"

"You shall have the sword too some day," she answered, her eyes flashing.

"But, maman, can't I touch it now?"

Without a word she took down the sheathed goldhandled sword and laid it across the chair-arms.

"I can't take the sword out, can I, maman?" he asked.

She could not help smiling. "Not yet, my son, not yet."

"I has to be growed up so the blade doesn't hurt me, hasn't I, maman?"

She nodded and smiled again, and went about her work.

He nodded sagely. "Maman—" he said. She turned to him; the little figure was erect with a sweet importance. "Maman, what am I now—with the sword?" he asked, with wide-open, amazed eyes.

A strange look passed across her face. Stooping, she kissed his curly hair.

"You are my prince," she said.

A little later the two were standing on that point of land called Grosnez— the brow of the Jersey tiger. Not far from them was a signal-staff which telegraphed to another signal-staff inland. Upon the staff now was hoisted a red flag. Guida knew the signals well. The red flag meant warships in sight. Then bags were hoisted that told of the number of vessels: one, two, three, four, five, six, then one next the upright, meaning seven. Last of all came the signal that a flag-ship was among them.

This was a fleet in command of an admiral. There, not far out, between Guernsey and Jersey, was the squadron itself. Guida watched it for a long while, her heart hardening; but seeing that the men by the signal-staff were watching her, she took the child and went to a spot where they were shielded from any eyes. Here she watched the fleet draw nearer and nearer.

The vessels passed almost within a stone's throw of her. She could see the St. George's Cross flying at the fore of the largest ship. That was the admiral's flag—that was the flag of Admiral Prince Philip d'Avranche, Duc de Bercy.

She felt her heart stand still suddenly, and with a tremor, as of fear, she gathered her child close to her. "What is all those ships, maman?" asked the child. "They are ships to defend Jersey," she said, watching the Imperturbable and its flotilla range on.

"Will they affend us, maman?"

"Perhaps-at the last," she said.

# CHAPTER XXXVI

Off Grouville Bay lay the squadron of the Jersey station. The St. George's Cross was flying at the fore of the Imperturbable, and on every ship of the fleet the white ensign flapped in the morning wind. The wooden-walled three-decked flag-ship, with her 32-pounders, and six hundred men, was not less picturesque and was more important than the Castle of Mont Orgueil near by, standing over two hundred feet above the level of the sea: the home of Philip d'Avranche, Duc de Bercy, and the Comtesse Chantavoine, now known to the world as the Duchesse de Bercy.

The Comtesse had arrived in the island almost simultaneously with Philip, although he had urged her to remain at the ducal palace of Bercy. But the duchy of Bercy was in hard case. When the imbecile Duke Leopold John died and Philip succeeded, the neutrality of Bercy had been proclaimed, but this neutrality had since been violated, and there was danger at once from the incursions of the Austrians and the ravages of the French troops. In Philip's absence the valiant governor-general of the duchy, aided by the influence and courage of the Comtesse Chantavoine, had thus far saved it from dismemberment, in spite of attempted betrayals by Damour the Intendant, who still remained Philip's enemy.

But when the Marquis Grandjon-Larisse, the uncle of the Comtesse, died, her cousin, General Grandjon-Larisse of the Republican army—whose word with Dalbarade had secured Philip's release years before for her own safety, first urged and then commanded her temporary absence from the duchy. So far he had been able to protect it from the fury of the Republicans and the secret treachery of the Jacobins. But a time of great peril was now at hand. Under these anxieties and the lack of other inspiration than duty, her health had failed, and at last she obeyed her cousin, joining Philip at the Castle of Mont Orgueil.

More than a year had passed since she had seen him, but there was no emotion, no ardour in their present greeting. From the first there had been nothing to link them together. She had married, hoping that she might love thereafter; he in choler and bitterness, and in the stress of a desperate ambition. He had avoided the marriage so long as he might, in hope of preventing it until the Duke should die, but with the irony of fate the expected death had come two hours after the ceremony. Then, shortly afterwards, came the death of the imbecile Leopold John; and Philip found himself the Duc de Bercy, and within a year, by reason of a splendid victory for the Imperturbable, an admiral.

Truth to tell, in this battle he had fought for victory for his ship and a fall for himself: for the fruit he had plucked was turning to dust and ashes. He was haunted by the memory of a wronged woman, as she herself had foretold. Death, with the burial of private dishonour under the roses of public victory—that had come to be his desire. But he had found that Death is wilful and chooseth her own time; that she may be lured, but she will not come with shouting. So he had stoically accepted his fate, and could even smile with a bitter cynicism when ordered to proceed to the coast of Jersey, where collision with a French squadron was deemed certain.

Now, he was again brought face to face with his past; with the imminent memory of Guida Landresse de Landresse. Where was Guida now? What had happened to her? He dared not ask, and none told him. Whichever way he turned—night or day—her face haunted him. Looking out from the windows of Mont Orgueil Castle, or from the deck of the Imperturbable, he could see—and he could scarce choose but see—the lonely Ecrehos. There, with a wild eloquence, he had made a girl believe he loved her, and had taken the first step in the path which should have led to true happiness and honour. From this good path he had violently swerved—and now?

From all that could be seen, however, the world went very well with him. He was the centre of authority. Almost any morning one might have seen a boat shoot out from below the Castle wall, carrying a flag with the blue ball of a Vice-Admiral of the White in the canton, and as the Admiral himself stepped upon the deck of the Imperturbable between saluting guards, across the water came a gay march played in his honour.

Jersey herself was elate, eager to welcome one of her own sons risen to such high estate. When, the very day after his arrival, he passed through the Vier Marchi on his way to visit the Lieutenant-Governor, the redrobed jurats impulsively turned out to greet him. They were ready to prove that memory is a matter of will and cultivation. There is no curtain so opaque as that which drops between the mind of man and the thing it is advantageous to forget. But how closely does the ear of self-service listen for the footfall of a most distant memory, when to do so is to share even a reflected glory!

A week had gone since Philip had landed on the island. Memories pursued him. If he came by the shore of St. Clement's Bay, he saw the spot where he had stood with her the evening he married her, and she said to him: "Philip, I wonder what we will think of this day a year from now!... To-day is everything to you, but to-morrow is very much to me." He remembered Shoreham sitting upon the cromlech above singing the legend of the gui-l'annee—and Shoreham was lying now a hundred fathoms deep.

As he walked through the Vier Marchi with his officers, there flashed before his eyes the scene of sixteen years ago, when, through the grime and havoc of battle, he had run to save Guida from the scimitar of the garish Turk. Walking through the Place du Vier Prison, he recalled the morning when he had rescued Ranulph from the hands of the mob. Where was Ranulph now?

If he had but known it, that very morning as he passed Mattingley's house Ranulph had looked down at him with infinite scorn and loathing—but with triumph too, for the Chevalier had just shown him a certain page in a certain parish-register long lost, left with him by Carterette Mattingley. Philip knew naught of Ranulph save the story babbled by the islanders. He cared to hear of no one but Guida, and who was now to mention her name to him? It was long—so long since he had seen her face. How many years ago was it? Only five, and yet it seemed twenty.

He was a boy then; now his hair was streaked with grey. He was light-hearted then, and he was still buoyant with his fellows, still alert and vigorous, quick of speech and keen of humour—but only before the world. In his own home he was fitful of mood, impatient of the grave, meditative look of his wife, of her resolute tenacity of thought and purpose, of her unvarying evenness of mood, through which no warmth played. It seemed to him that if she had defied him—given him petulance for petulance, impatience for impatience, it would have been easier to bear. If—if he could only read behind those passionless eyes, that clear, unwrinkled forehead! But he knew her no better now than he did the day he married her. Unwittingly she chilled him, and he felt he had no right to complain, for he had done her the greatest wrong which can be done a woman. Whatever chanced, Guida was still his wife; and there was in him yet the strain of Calvinistic morality of the island race that bred him. He had shrunk from coming here, but it had been far worse than he had looked for.

One day, in a nervous, bitter moment, after an impatient hour with the Comtesse, he had said: "Can you—can you not speak? Can you not tell me what you think?" She had answered quietly:

"It would do no good. You would not understand. I know you in some ways better than you know yourself. I cannot tell what it is, but there is something wrong in your nature, something that poisons your life. And not myself only has felt that. I never told you—but you remember the day the old Duke died, the day we were married? You had gone from the room a moment. The Duke beckoned me to him, and whispered 'Don't be afraid— don't be afraid—' and then he died. That meant that he was afraid, that death had cleared his sight as to you in some way. He was afraid—of what? And I have been afraid—of what? I do not know. Things have not gone well somehow. You are strong, you are brave, and I come of a family that have been strong and brave. We ought to be near: yet, yet we are lonely and far apart, and we shall never be nearer or less lonely. That I know."

To this he had made no reply and this anger vanished. Something in her words had ruled him to her own calmness, and at that moment he had the first flash of understanding of her nature and its true relation to his own.

Passing through the Rue d'Egypte this day he met Dormy Jamais. Forgetful of everything save that this quaint foolish figure had interested him when a boy, he called him by name; but Dormy Jamais swerved away, eyeing him askance.

At that instant he saw Jean Touzel standing in the doorway of his house. A wave of remorseful feeling rushed over him. He could wait no longer: he would ask Jean Touzel and his wife about Guida. He instantly bethought him of an excuse for the visit. His squadron needed another pilot; he would approach Jean in the matter.

Bidding his flag-lieutenant go on to Elizabeth Castle whither they were bound, and await him there, he crossed over to Jean. By the time he reached the doorway, however, Jean had retreated to the veille by the chimney behind Maitresse Aimable, who sat in a great stave-chair mending a net.

Philip knocked and stepped inside. When Mattresse Aimable saw who it was she was so startled that she dropped her work, and made vague clutches to recover it. Stooping, however, was a great effort for her. Philip instantly stepped forward and picked up the net. Politely handing it to her, he said:

"Ah, Maitresse Aimable, it is as if you had never stirred all these years!" Then turning to her husband "I have come looking for a good pilot, Jean." Mattresse Aimable had at first flushed to a purple, had afterwards gone pale, then recovered herself, and now returned Philip's look with a downright steadiness. Like Jean, she knew well enough he had not come for a pilot—that was not the business of a Prince Admiral.

She did not even rise. Philip might be whatever the world chose to call him, but her house was her own, and he had come uninvited, and he was unwelcome.

She kept her seat, but her fat head inclined once in greeting, and she waited for him to speak again. She knew why he had come; and somehow the steady look in these slow, brown eyes, and the blinking glance behind Jean's brass-rimmed spectacles, disconcerted Philip. Here were people who knew the truth about him, knew the sort of man he really was. These poor folk who had had nothing of the world but what they earned, they would never hang on any prince's favours.

He read the situation rightly. The penalties of his life were teaching him a discernment which could never have come to him through good fortune alone. Having at last discovered his real self a little, he was in the way of knowing others.

"May I shut the door?" he asked quietly. Jean nodded. Closing it he turned to them again. "Since my return I have heard naught concerning Mademoiselle Landresse," he said. "I want to ask you about her now. Does she still live in the Place du Vier Prison?"

Both Jean and Aimable shook their heads. They had spoken no word since his entrance.

"She—she is not dead?" he asked. They shook their heads again.

"Her grandfather"—he paused—"is he living?" Once more they shook their heads in negation. "Where is mademoiselle?" he asked, sick at heart.

Jean looked at his wife; neither moved nor answered. "Where does she live?" urged Philip. Still there was no motion, no reply. "You might as well tell me." His tone was half pleading, half angry—little like a sovereign duke, very like a man in trouble. "You must know I shall find out from some one else, then," he continued. "But it is better for you to tell me. I mean her no harm, and I would rather know about her from her friends."

He took off his hat now. Something in the dignity of these two honest folk rebuked the pride of place and spirit in him. As plainly as though heralds had proclaimed it, he understood that these two knew the abatements on the shield of his honour-argent, a plain point tenne, due to him "that tells lyes to his Prince or General," and argent, a gore sinister tenne, due for flying from his colours.

Maitresse Aimable turned and looked towards Jean, but Jean turned away his head. Then she did not hesitate. The voice so oft eluding her will responded readily now. Anger—plain primitive rage-possessed her. She had had no child, but as the years had passed all the love that might have been given to her own was bestowed upon Guida, and in that mind she spoke.

"O my grief, to think you have come here-you!" she burst forth. "You steal the best heart in the world—there is none like her, nannin-gia. You promise her, you break her life, you spoil her, and then you fly away—ah coward you! Man pethe benin, was there ever such a man like you! If my Jean there had done a thing as that I would sink him in the sea—he would sink himself, je me crais! But you come back here, O my Mother of God, you come back here with your sword, with your crown-ugh, it is like a black cat in heaven—you!"

She got to her feet more nimbly than she had ever done in her life, and the floor seemed to heave as she came towards Philip. "You speak to me with soft words," she said harshly—"but you shall have the good hard truth from me. You want to know now where she is—I ask where you have been these five years? Your voice it tremble when you speak of her now. Oh ho! it has been nice and quiet these five years. The grand pethe of her drop dead in his chair when he know. The world turn against her, make light of her, when they know. All alone—she is all alone, but for one fat old fool like me. She bear all the shame, all the pain, for the crime of you. All alone she take her child and go on to the rock of Plemont to live these five years. But you, you go and get a crown and be Amiral and marry a grande comtesse—marry, oh, je crais ben! This is no world for such men like you. You come to my house, to the house of Jean Touzel, to ask this and that—well, you have the truth of God, ba su! No good will come to you in the end, nannin-gia! When you go to die, you will think and think and think of that beautiful Guida Landresse; you will think and think of the heart you kill, and you will call, and she will not come. You will call till your throat rattle, but she will not come, and the child of sorrow you give her will not come—no, bidemme! E'fin, the door you shut you can open now, and you can go from the house of Jean Touzel. It belong to the wife of an honest man—maint'nant!"

In the moment's silence that ensued, Jean took a step forward. "Ma femme, ma bonne femme!" he said with a shaking voice. Then he pointed to the door. Humiliated, overwhelmed by the words of the woman, Philip turned mechanically towards the door without a word, and his fingers fumbled for the latch, for a mist was before his eyes. With a great effort he recovered himself, and passed slowly out into the Rue d'Egypte.

"A child—a child!" he said brokenly. "Guida's child—my God! And I—have never—known. Plemont—Plemont, she is at Plemont!" He shuddered. "Guida's child—and mine," he kept saying to himself, as in a painful dream he passed on to the shore.

In the little fisherman's cottage he had left, a fat old woman sat sobbing in the great chair made of barrel-staves, and a man, stooping, kissed her twice on the cheek—the first time in fifteen years. And then she both laughed and cried.

# CHAPTER XXXVII

Guida sat by the fire sewing, Biribi the dog at her feet. A little distance away, to the right of the chimney, lay Guilbert asleep. Twice she lowered the work to her lap to look at the child, the reflected light of the fire playing on his face. Stretching out her hand, she touched him, and then she smiled. Hers was an all-devouring love; the child was her whole life; her own present or future was as nothing; she was but fuel for the fire of his existence.

A storm was raging outside. The sea roared in upon Plemont and Grosnez, battering the rocks in futile agony. A hoarse nor'-easter ranged across the tiger's head in helpless fury: a night of awe to inland folk, and of danger to seafarers. To Guida, who was both of the sea and of the land, fearless as to either, it was neither terrible nor desolate to be alone with the storm. Storm was but power unshackled, and power she loved and understood. She had lived so long in close commerce with storm and sea that something of their keen force had entered into her, and she was kin with them. Each wind to her was intimate as a friend, each rock and cave familiar as her hearthstone; and the ungoverned ocean spoke in terms intelligible. So heavy was the surf that now and then the spray of some foiled wave broke on the roof, but she only nodded at that, as though the sea were calling her to come forth, tapping on her rooftree in joyous greeting.

But suddenly she started and bent her head. It seemed as if her whole body were hearkening. Now she rose quickly to her feet, dropped her work upon the table near by, and rested herself against it, still listening. She was sure she heard a horse's hoofs. Turning swiftly, she drew the curtain of the bed before her sleeping child, and then stood quiet waiting—waiting. Her hand went to her heart once as though its fierce throbbing hurt her. Plainly as though she could look through these stone walls into clear sunlight, she saw some one dismount, and she heard a voice.

The door of the but was unlocked and unbarred. If she feared, it was easy to shoot the bolt and lock the door, to drop the bar across the little window, and be safe and secure. But no bodily fear possessed her—only that terror of the spirit when its great trial comes suddenly and it shrinks back, though the mind be of faultless courage.

She waited. There came a knocking at the door. She did not move from where she stood.

"Come in," she said. She was composed and resolute now.

The latch clicked, the door opened, and a cloaked figure entered, the shriek of the storm behind. The door closed again. The intruder took a step forward, his hat came off, the cloak was loosed and dropped upon the floor. Guida's premonition had been right: It was Philip.

She did not speak. A stone could have been no colder as she stood in the light of the fire, her face still and strong, the eyes darkling, luminous. There was on her the dignity of the fearless, the pure in heart.

"Guida!" Philip said, and took a step nearer, and paused.

He was haggard, he had the look of one who had come upon a desperate errand. When she did not answer he said pleadingly:

"Guida, won't you speak to me?"

"The Duc de Bercy chooses a strange hour for his visit," she said quietly.

"But see," he answered hurriedly; "what I have to say to you—" he paused, as though to choose the thing he should say first.

"You can say nothing I need hear," she answered, looking him steadily in the eyes.

"Ah, Guida," he cried, disconcerted by her cold composure, "for God's sake listen to me! To-night we have to face our fate. To-night you have to say—"

"Fate was faced long ago. I have nothing to say."

"Guida, I have repented of all. I have come now only to speak honestly of the wrong I did you. I have come to—"

Scorn sharpened her words, though she spoke calmly: "You have forced yourself upon a woman's presence—and at this hour!"

"I chose the only hour possible," he answered quickly. "Guida, the past cannot be changed, but we have the present and the future still. I have not come to justify myself, but to find a way to atone."

"No atonement is possible."

"You cannot deny me the right to confess to you that—"

"To you denial should not seem hard usage," she answered slowly, "and confession should have witnesses—"

She paused suggestively. The imputation that he of all men had the least right to resent denial; that, dishonest still, he was willing to justify her privately though not publicly; that repentance should have been open to the world—it all stung him.

He threw out his hands in a gesture of protest. "As many witnesses as you will, but not now, not this hour, after all these years. Will you not at least listen to me, and then judge and act? Will you not hear me, Guida?"

She had not yet even stirred. Now that it had come, this scene was all so different from what she might have imagined. But she spoke out of a merciless understanding, an unchangeable honesty. Her words came clear and pitiless:

"If you will speak to the point and without a useless emotion, I will try to listen. Common kindness should have prevented this intrusion—by you!"

Every word she said was like a whip-lash across his face. A devilish light leapt into his eye, but it faded as quickly as it came.

"After to-night, to the public what you will," he repeated with dogged persistence, "but it was right we should speak alone to each other at least this once before the open end. I did you wrong, yet I did not mean to ruin your life, and you should know that. I ought not to have married you secretly; I acknowledge that. But I loved you—"

She shook her head, and with a smile of pitying disdain—he could so little see the real truth, his real misdemeanour—she said: "Oh no, never—never! You were not capable of love; you never knew what it means. From the first you were too untrue ever to love a woman. There was a great fire of emotion, you saw shadows on the wall, and you fell in love with them. That was all."

"I tell you that I loved you," he answered with passionate energy. "But as you will. Let it be that it was not real love: at least it was all there was in me to give. I never meant to desert you. I never meant to disavow our marriage. I denied you, you will say. I did. In the light of what came after, it was dishonourable—I grant that; but I did it at a crisis and for the fulfilment of a great ambition—and as much for you as for me."

"That was the least of your evil work. But how little you know what true people think or feel!" she answered with a kind of pain in her voice, for she felt that such a nature could never even realise its own enormities. Well, since it had gone so far she would speak openly, though it hurt her sense of self-respect.

"For that matter, do you think that I or any good woman would have had place or power, been princess or duchess, at the price? What sort of mind have you?" She looked him straight in the eyes. "Put it in the clear light of right and wrong, it was knavery. You—you talk of not meaning to do me harm. You were never capable of doing me good. It was not in you. From first to last you are untrue. Were it otherwise, were you not from first to last unworthy, would you have—but no, your worst crime need not be judged here. Yet had you one spark of worthiness would you have made a mock marriage—it is no more—with the Comtesse Chantavoine? No matter what I said or what I did in anger, or contempt of you, had you been an honest man you would not have so ruined another life. Marriage, alas! You have wronged the Comtesse worse than you have wronged me. One day I shall be righted, but what can you say or do to right her wrongs?"

Her voice had now a piercing indignation and force. "Yes, Philip d'Avranche, it is as I say, justice will come to me. The world turned against me because of you; I have been shamed and disgraced. For years I have suffered in silence. But I have waited without fear for the end. God is with me. He is stronger than fortune or fate. He has brought you to Jersey once more, to right my wrongs, mine and my child's."

She saw his eyes flash to the little curtained bed. They both stood silent and still. He could hear the child breathing. His blood quickened. An impulse seized him. He took a step towards the bed, as though to draw the curtain, but she quickly moved between.

"Never," she said in a low stern tone; "no touch of yours for my Guilbert—for my son! Every minute of his life has been mine. He is mine— all mine—and so he shall remain. You who gambled with the name, the fame, the very soul of your wife, you shall not have one breath of her child's life."

It was as if the outward action of life was suspended in them for a moment, and then came the battle of two strong spirits: the struggle of fretful and indulged egotism, the impulse of a vigorous temperament, against a deep moral force, a high purity of mind and conscience, and the invincible love of the mother for the child. Time, bitterness, and power had hardened Philip's mind, and his long-restrained emotions, breaking loose now, made him a passionate and wilful figure. His force lay in the very unruliness of his spirit, hers in the perfect command of her moods and emotions. Well equipped by the thoughts and sufferings of five long years, her spirit was trained to meet this onset with fiery wisdom. They were like two armies watching each other across a narrow stream, between one conflict and another.

For a minute they stood at gaze. The only sounds in the room were the whirring of the fire in the chimney and the child's breathing. At last Philip's intemperate self-will gave way. There was no withstanding that cold, still face, that unwavering eye. Only brutality could go further. The nobility of her nature, her inflexible straight-forwardness came upon him with overwhelming force. Dressed in molleton, with no adornment save the glow of a perfect health, she seemed at this moment, as on the Ecrehos, the one being on earth worth living and caring for. What had he got for all the wrong he had done her? Nothing. Come what might, there was one thing that he could yet do, and even as the thought possessed him he spoke.

"Guida," he said with rushing emotion, "it is not too late. Forgive the past-the wrong of it, the shame of it. You are my wife; nothing can undo that. The other woman—she is nothing to me. If we part and never meet again she will suffer no more than she suffers to go on with me. She has never loved me, nor I her. Ambition did it all, and of ambition God knows I have had enough! Let me proclaim our marriage, let me come back to you. Then, happen what will, for the rest of our lives I will try to atone for the wrong I did you. I want you, I want our child. I want to win your love again. I can't wipe out what I have done, but I can put you right before the world, I can prove to you that I set you above place and ambition. If you shrink from doing it for me, do it"—he glanced towards the bed—"do it for our child. To-morrow—to-morrow it shall be, if you will forgive. To-morrow let us start again—Guida—Guida!"

She did not answer at once; but at last she said "Giving up place and ambition would prove nothing now. It is easy to repent when our pleasures have palled. I told you in a letter four years ago that your protests came too late. They are always too late. With a nature like yours nothing is sure or lasting. Everything changes with the mood. It is different with me: I speak only what I truly mean. Believe me, for I tell you the truth, you are a man that a woman could forget but could never forgive. As a prince you are much better than as a plain man, for princes may do what other men may not. It is their way to take all and give nothing. You should have been born a prince, then all your actions would have seemed natural. Yet now you must remain a prince, for what you got at such a price to others you must pay for. You say you would come down from your high place, you would give up your worldly honours, for me. What madness! You are not the kind of man with whom a woman could trust herself in the troubles and changes of life. Laying all else aside, if I would have had naught of your honours and your duchy long ago, do you think I would now share a disgrace from which you could never rise? For in my heart I feel that this remorse is but caprice. It is to-day; it may not—will not—be tomorrow."

"You are wrong, you are wrong. I am honest with you now," he broke in.

"No," she answered coldly, "it is not in you to be honest. Your words have no ring of truth in my ears, for the note is the same as I heard once upon the Ecrehos. I was a young girl then and I believed; I am a woman now, and I should still disbelieve though all the world were on your side to declare me wrong. I tell you"—her voice rose again, it seemed to catch the note of freedom and strength of the storm without—"I tell you, I will still live as my heart and conscience prompt me. The course I have set for myself I will follow; the life I entered upon when my child was born I will not leave. No word you have said has made my heart beat faster. You and I can never have anything to say to each other in this life, beyond"—her voice changed, she paused—"beyond one thing—"

Going to the bed where the child lay, she drew the curtain softly, and pointing, she said:

"There is my child. I have set my life to the one task, to keep him to myself, and yet to win for him the heritage of the dukedom of Bercy. You shall yet pay to him the price of your wrong-doing."

She drew back slightly so that he could see the child lying with its rosy face half buried in its pillow, the little hand lying like a flower upon the coverlet.

Once more with a passionate exclamation he moved nearer to the child.

"No farther!" she said, stepping before him.

When she saw the wild impulse in his face to thrust her aside, she added: "It is only the shameless coward that strikes the dead. You had a wife—Guida d'Avranche, but Guida d'Avranche is dead. There only lives the mother of this child, Guida Landresse de Landresse."

She looked at him with scorn, almost with hatred. Had he touched her—but she would rather pity than loathe!

Her words roused all the devilry in him. The face of the child had sent him mad.

"By Heaven, I will have the child—I will have the child!" he broke out harshly. "You shall not treat me like a dog. You know well I would have kept you as my wife, but your narrow pride, your unjust anger threw me over. You have wronged me. I tell you you have wronged me, for you held the secret of the child from me all these years."

"The whole world knew!" she exclaimed indignantly. "I will break your pride," he said, incensed and unable to command himself. "Mark you, I will break your pride. And I will have my child too!"

"Establish to the world your right to him," she answered keenly. "You have the right to acknowledge him, but the possession shall be mine."

He was the picture of impotent anger and despair. It was the irony of penalty that the one person in the world who could really sting him was this unacknowledged, almost unknown woman. She was the only human being that had power to shatter his egotism and resolve him into the common elements of a base manhood. Of little avail his eloquence now! He had cajoled a sovereign dukedom out of an aged and fatuous prince; he had cajoled a wife, who yet was no wife, from among the highest of a royal court; he had cajoled success from Fate by a valour informed with vanity and ambition; years ago, with eloquent arts he had cajoled a young girl into a secret marriage—but he could no longer cajole the woman who was his one true wife. She knew him through and through.

He was so wild with rage he could almost have killed her as she stood there, one hand stretched out to protect the child, the other pointing to the door.

He seized his hat and cloak and laid his hand upon the latch, then suddenly turned to her. A dark project came to him. He himself could not prevail with her; but he would reach her yet, through the child. If the child were in his hands, she would come to him.

"Remember, I will have the child," he said, his face black with evil purpose.

She did not deign reply, but stood fearless and still, as, throwing open the door, he rushed out into the night. She listened until she heard his horse's hoofs upon the rocky upland. Then she went to the door, locked it, and barred it. Turning, she ran with a cry as of hungry love to the little bed. Crushing the child to her bosom, she buried her face in his brown curls.

"My son, my own, own son!" she said.

# CHAPTER XXXVIII

If at times it would seem that Nature's disposition of the events of a life or a series of lives is illogical, at others she would seem to play them with an irresistible logic—loosing them, as it were, in a trackless forest of experience, and in some dramatic hour, by an inevitable attraction, drawing them back again to a destiny fulfilled. In this latter way did she seem to lay her hand upon the lives of Philip d'Avranche and Guida Landresse.

At the time that Elie Mattingley, in Jersey, was awaiting hanging on the Mont es Pendus, and writing his letter to Carterette concerning the stolen book of church records, in a town of Brittany the Reverend Lorenzo Dow lay dying. The army of the Vendee, under Detricand Comte de Tournay, had made a last dash at a small town held by a section of the Republican army, and captured it. On the prisons being opened, Detricand had discovered in a vile dungeon the sometime curate of St. Michael's Church in Jersey. When they entered on him, wasted and ragged he lay asleep on his bed of rotten straw, his fingers between the leaves of a book of meditations. Captured five years before and forgotten alike by the English and French Governments, he had apathetically pined and starved to these last days of his life.

Recognising him, Detricand carried him in his strong arms to his own tent. For many hours the helpless man lay insensible, but at last the flickering spirit struggled back to light for a little space. When first conscious of his surroundings, the poor captive felt tremblingly in the pocket of his tattered vest. Not finding what he searched for, he half started up. Detricand hastened forward with a black leather-covered book in his hand. Mr. Dow's thin trembling fingers clutched eagerly—it was his only passion—at this journal of his life. As his grasp closed on it, he recognised Detricand, and at the same time he saw the cross and heart of the Vendee on his coat.

A victorious little laugh struggled in his throat. "The Lord hath triumphed gloriously—I could drink some wine, monsieur," he added in the same quaint clerical monotone.

Having drunk the wine he lay back murmuring thanks and satisfaction, his eyes closed. Presently they opened. He nodded at Detricand.

"I have not tasted wine these five years," he said; then added, "You—you took too much wine in Jersey, did you not, monsieur? I used to say an office for you every Litany day, which was of a Friday."

His eyes again caught the cross and heart on Detricand's coat, and they lighted up a little. "The Lord hath triumphed gloriously," he repeated, and added irrelevantly, "I suppose you are almost a captain now?"

"A general—almost," said Detricand with gentle humour.

At that moment an orderly appeared at the tent-door, bearing a letter for Detricand.

"From General Grandjon-Larisse of the Republican army, your highness," said the orderly, handing the letter. "The messenger awaits an answer."

As Detricand hastily read, a look of astonishment crossed over his face, and his brows gathered in perplexity. After a minute's silence he said to the orderly:

"I will send a reply to-morrow."

"Yes, your highness." The orderly saluted and retired.

Mr. Dow half raised himself on his couch, and the fevered eyes swallowed Detricand.

"You—you are a prince, monsieur?" he said. Detricand glanced up from the letter he was reading again, a grave and troubled look on his face.

"Prince of Vaufontaine they call me, but, as you know, I am only a vagabond turned soldier," he said. The dying man smiled to himself,—a smile of the sweetest vanity this side of death,—for it seemed to him that the Lord had granted him this brand from the burning, and in supreme satisfaction, he whispered: "I used to say an office for you every Litany—which was a Friday, and twice, I remember, on two Saints' days."

Suddenly another thought came to him, and his lips moved—he was murmuring to himself. He would leave a goodly legacy to the captive of his prayers.

Taking the leather-covered journal of his life in both hands, he held it out.

"Highness, highness—" said he. Death was breaking the voice in his throat.

Detricand stooped and ran an arm round his shoulder, but raising himself up Mr. Dow gently pushed him back. The strength of his supreme hour was on him.

"Highness," said he, "I give you the book of five years of my life—not of its every day, but of its moments, its great days. Read it," he added, "read it wisely. Your own name is in it—with the first time I said an office for you." His breath failed him, he fell back, and lay quiet for several minutes.

"You used to take too much wine," he said half wildly, starting up again. "Permit me your hand, highness."

Detricand dropped on his knee and took the wasted hand. Mr. Dow's eyes were glazing fast. With a last effort he spoke—his voice like a squeaking wind in a pipe:

"The Lord hath triumphed gloriously—" and he leaned forward to kiss Detricand's hand.

But Death intervened, and his lips fell instead upon the red cross on Detricand's breast, as he sank forward lifeless.

That night, after Lorenzo Dow was laid in his grave, Detricand read the little black leather-covered journal bequeathed to him. Of the years of his captivity the records were few; the book was chiefly concerned with his career in Jersey. Detricand read page after page, more often with a smile than not; yet it was the smile of one who knew life and would scarce misunderstand the eccentric and honest soul of the Reverend Lorenzo Dow.

Suddenly, however, he started, for he came upon these lines:

*I have, in great privacy and with halting of spirit, married, this*
*twenty-third of January, Mr. Philip d'Avranche of His Majesty's ship*
*"Narcissus," and Mistress Guida Landresse de Landresse, both*
*of this*
*Island of Jersey; by special license of the Bishop of Winchester.*

To this was added in comment:

*Unchurchmanlike, and most irregular. But the young gentleman's*
*tongue is gifted, and he pressed his cause heartily. Also Mr.*
*Shoreham of the Narcissus—"Mad Shoreham of Galway" his*
*father was*
*called—I knew him—added his voice to the request also. Troubled*
*in conscience thereby, yet I did marry the twain gladly, for I think*
*a worthier maid never lived than this same Mistress Guida*
*Landresse*
*de Landresse, of the ancient family of the de Mauprats. Yet I like*

*not secrecy, though it be but for a month or two months—on my vow,*
*I like it not for one hour.*

*Note: At leisure read of the family history of the de Mauprats and*
*the d'Avranches.*

*N.: No more secret marriages nor special licenses—most uncanonical*
*privileges!*

*N.: For ease of conscience write to His Grace at Lambeth upon the*
*point.*

Detricand sprang to his feet. So this was the truth about Philip d'Avranche, about Guida, alas!

He paced the tent, his brain in a whirl. Stopping at last, he took from his pocket the letter received that afternoon from General Grandjon-Larisse, and read it through again hurriedly. It proposed a truce, and a meeting with himself at a village near, for conference upon the surrender of Detricand's small army.

"A bitter end to all our fighting," said Detricand aloud at last. "But he is right. It is now a mere waste of life. I know my course.... Even to-night," he added, "it shall be to-night."

Two hours later Detricand, Prince of Vaufontaine, was closeted with General Grandjon-Larisse at a village half-way between the Republican army and the broken bands of the Vendee.

As lads Detricand and Grandjon-Larisse had known each other well. But since the war began Grandjon-Larisse had gone one way, and he had gone the other, bitter enemies in principle but friendly enough at heart.

They had not seen each other since the year before Rullecour's invasion of Jersey.

"I had hoped to see you by sunset, monseigneur," said Grandjon-Larisse after they had exchanged greetings.

"It is through a melancholy chance you see me at all," replied Detricand heavily.

"To what piteous accident am I indebted?" Grandjon-Larisse replied in an acid tone, for war had given his temper an edge. "Were not my reasons for surrender sound? I eschewed eloquence—I gave you facts."

Detricand shook his head, but did not reply at once. His brow was clouded.

"Let me speak fully and bluntly now," Grandjon-Larisse went on. "You will not shrink from plain truths, I know. We were friends ere you went adventuring with Rullecour. We are soldiers too; and you will understand I meant no bragging in my letter."

He raised his brows inquiringly, and Detricand inclined his head in assent.

Without more ado, Grandjon-Larisse laid a map on the table. "This will help us," he said briefly, then added: "Look you, Prince, when war began the game was all with you. At Thouars here"—his words followed his finger—"at Fontenay, at Saumur, at Torfou, at Coron, at Chateau-Gonthier, at Pontorson, at Dol, at Antrain, you had us by the heels. Victory was ours once to your thrice. Your blood was up. You had great men—great men," he repeated politely.

Detricand bowed. "But see how all is changed," continued the other. "See: by this forest of Vesins de la Rochejaquelein fell. At Chollet"—his finger touched another point—"Bonchamp died, and here d'Elbee and Lescure were mortally wounded. At Angers Stofflet was sent to his account, and Charette paid the price at Nantes." He held up his fingers. "One—two—three—four—five—six great men gone!"

He paused, took a step away from the table, and came back again.

Once more he dropped his finger on the map. "Tinteniac is gone, and at Quiberon Peninsula your friend Sombreuil was slain. And look you here," he added in a lower voice, "at Laval my old friend the Prince of Talmont was executed at his own chateau, where I had spent many an hour with him."

Detricand's eyes flashed fire. "Why then permit the murder, monsieur le general?"

Grandjon-Larisse started, his voice became hard at once. "It is not a question of Talmont, or of you, or of me, monseigneur. It is not a question of friendship, not even of father, or brother, or son—but of France."

"And of God and the King," said Detricand quickly.

Grandjon-Larisse shrugged his shoulders. "We see with different eyes. We think with different minds," and he stooped over the map again.

"We feel with different hearts," said Detricand. "There is the difference between us—between your cause and mine. You are all for logic and perfection in government, and to get it you go mad, and France is made a shambles—"

"War is cruelty, and none can make it gentle," interrupted Grandjon-Larisse. He turned to the map once more. "And see, monseigneur, here at La Vie your uncle the Prince of Vaufontaine died, leaving you his name and a burden of hopeless war. Now count them all over—de la Rochejaquelein, Bonchamp, d'Elbee, Lescure, Stofflet, Charette, Talmont, Tinteniac, Sombreuil, Vaufontaine—they are all gone, your great men. And who of chieftains and armies are left? Detricand of Vaufontaine and a few brave men—no more. Believe me, monseigneur, your game is hopeless—by your grace, one moment still," he added, as Detricand made an impatient gesture. "Hoche destroyed your army and subdued the country two years ago. You broke out again, and Hoche and I have beaten you again. Fight on, with your doomed followers—brave men I admit—and Hoche will have no mercy. I can save your peasants if you will yield now.

"We have had enough of blood. Let us have peace. To proceed is certain death to all, and your cause worse lost. On my honour, monseigneur, I do this at some risk, in memory of old days. I have lost too many friends," he added in a lower voice.

Detricand was moved. "I thank you for this honest courtesy. I had almost misread your letter," he answered. "Now I will speak freely. I had hoped to leave my bones in Brittany. It was my will to fight to the last, with my doomed followers as you call them—comrades and lovers of France I say. And it was their wish to die with me. Till this afternoon I had no other purpose. Willing deaths ours, for I am persuaded, for every one of us that dies, a hundred men will rise up again and take revenge upon this red debauch of government!"

"Have a care," said Grandjon-Larisse with sudden anger, his hand dropping upon the handle of his sword.

"I ask leave for plain beliefs as you asked leave for plain words. I must speak my mind, and I will say now that it has changed in this matter of fighting and surrender. I will tell you what has changed it," and Detricand drew from his pocket Lorenzo Dow's journal. "It concerns both you and me."

Grandjon-Larisse flashed a look of inquiry at him. "It concerns your cousin the Comtesse Chantavoine and Philip d'Avranche, who calls himself her husband and Duc de Bercy."

He opened the journal, and handed it to Grandjon-Larisse. "Read," he said.

As Grandjon-Larisse read, an oath broke from him. "Is this authentic, monseigneur?" he said in blank astonishment "and the woman still lives?"

Detricand told him all he knew, and added:

"A plain duty awaits us both, monsieur le general. You are concerned for the Comtesse Chantavoine; I am concerned for the Duchy of Bercy and for this poor lady—this poor lady in Jersey," he added.

Grandjon-Larisse was white with rage. "The upstart! The English brigand!" he said between his teeth.

"You see now," said Detricand, "that though it was my will to die fighting your army in the last trench—"

"Alone, I fear," interjected Grandjon-Larisse with curt admiration.

"My duty and my purpose go elsewhere," continued Detricand. "They take me to Jersey. And yours, monsieur?"

Grandjon-Larisse beat his foot impatiently on the floor. "For the moment I cannot stir in this, though I would give my life to do so," he answered bitterly. "I am but now recalled to Paris by the Directory."

He stopped short in his restless pacing and held out his hand.

"We are at one," he said—"friends in this at least. Command me when and how you will. Whatever I can I will do, even at risk and peril. The English brigand!" he added bitterly. "But for this insult to my blood, to the noble Chantavoine, he shall pay the price to me—yes, by the heel of God!"

"I hope to be in Jersey three days hence," said Detricand.

# CHAPTER XXXIX

The bell on the top of the Cohue Royale clattered like the tongue of a scolding fishwife. For it was the fourth of October, and the opening of the Assise d'Heritage.

This particular session of the Court was to proceed with unusual spirit and importance, for after the reading of the King's Proclamation, the Royal Court and the States were to present the formal welcome of the island to Admiral Prince Philip d'Avranche, Duc de Bercy; likewise to offer a bounty to all Jerseymen enlisting under him.

The island was en fete. There had not been such a year of sensations since the Battle of Jersey. Long before chicane—chicane ceased clanging over the Vier Marchi the body of the Court was filled. The Governor, the Bailly, the jurats, the seigneurs and the dames des fiefs, the avocats with their knowledge of the ancient custom of Normandy and the devious inroads made upon it by the customs of Jersey, the military, all were in their places; the officers of the navy had arrived, all save one and he was to be the chief figure of this function. With each arrival the people cheered and the trumpets blared. The islanders in the Vier Marchi turned to the booths for refreshments, or to the printing-machine set up near La Pyramide, and bought halfpenny chapsheets telling of recent defeats of the French; though mostly they told in ebullient words of the sea-fight which had made Philip d'Avranche an admiral, and of his elevation to a sovereign dukedom. The crowds restlessly awaited his coming now.

Inside the Court there was more restlessness still. It was now many minutes beyond the hour fixed. The Bailly whispered to the Governor, the Governor to his aide, and the aide sought the naval officers present; but these could give no explanation of the delay. The Comtesse Chantavoine was in her place of honour beside the Attorney-General—but Prince Philip and his flag-lieutenant came not.

The Comtesse Chantavoine was the one person outwardly unmoved. What she thought, who could tell? Hundreds of eyes scanned her face, yet she seemed unconscious of them, indifferent to them. What would not the Bailly have given for her calmness! What would not the Greffier have given for her importance! She drew every eye by virtue of something which was more than the name of Duchesse de Bercy. The face, the bearing, had an unconscious dignity, a living command and composure: the heritage, perhaps, of a race ever more fighters than courtiers, rather desiring good sleep after good warfare than luxurious peace.

The silence, the tension grew painful. A whole half hour had the Court waited beyond its time. At last, however, cheers arose outside, and all knew that the Prince was coming. Presently the doors were thrown open, two halberdiers stepped inside, and an officer of the Court announced Admiral his Serene Highness Prince Philip d'Avranche, Duc de Bercy.

"Oui-gia, think of that!" said a voice from somewhere in the hall.

Philip heard it, and he frowned, for he recognised Dormy Jamais's voice. Where it came from he knew not, nor did any one; for the daft one was snugly bestowed above a middle doorway in what was half balcony, half cornice.

When Philip had taken his place beside the Comtesse Chantavoine, came the formal opening of the Cour d'Heritage.

The Comtesse's eyes fixed themselves upon Philip. There was that in his manner which puzzled and evaded her clear intuition. Some strange circumstance must have delayed him, for she saw that his flag-lieutenant was disturbed, and this she felt sure was not due to delay alone. She was barely conscious that the Bailly had been addressing Philip, until he had stopped and Philip had risen to reply.

He had scarcely begun speaking when the doors were suddenly thrown open again, and a woman came forward quickly. The instant she entered Philip saw her, and stopped speaking. Every one turned.

It was Guida. In the silence, looking neither to right nor left, she advanced almost to where the Greffier sat, and dropping on her knee and looking up to the Bailly and the jurats, stretched out her hands and cried:

"Haro, haro! A l'aide, mon Prince, on me fait tort!"

If one rose from the dead suddenly to command them to an awed obedience, Jerseymen could not be more at the mercy of the apparition than at the call of one who cries in their midst, "Haro! Haro!"—that ancient relic of the custom of Normandy and Rollo the Dane. To this hour the Jerseyman maketh his cry unto Rollo, and the Royal Court—whose right to respond to this cry was confirmed by King John and afterwards by Charles—must listen, and every one must heed. That cry of Haro makes the workman drop his tools, the woman her knitting, the militiaman his musket, the fisherman his net, the schoolmaster his birch, and the ecrivain his babble, to await the judgment of the Royal Court.

Every jurat fixed his eye upon Guida as though she had come to claim his life. The Bailly's lips opened twice as though to speak, but no words came. The Governor sat with hands clinched upon his chairarm. The crowd breathed in gasps of excitement. The Comtesse Chantavoine looked at Philip, looked at Guida, and knew that here was the opening of the scroll she had not been able to unfold. Now she should understand that something which had made the old Duc de Bercy with his last breath say, Don't be afraid!

Philip stood moveless, his eyes steady, his face bitter, determined. Yet there was in his look, fixed upon Guida, some strange mingling of pity and purpose. It was as though two spirits were fighting in his face for mastery. The Countess touched him upon the arm, but he took no notice. Drawing back in her seat she looked at him and at Guida, as one might watch the balances of justice weighing life and death. She could not read this story, but one glance at the faces of the crowd round her made her aware that here was a tale of the past which all knew in little or in much.

"Haro! haro! A l'aide, mon Prince, on me fait tort!" What did she mean, this woman with the exquisite face, alive with power and feeling, indignation and appeal? To what prince did she cry?—for what aid? who trespassed upon her?

The Bailly now stood up, a frown upon his face. He knew what scandal had said concerning Guida and Philip. He had never liked Guida, for in the first days of his importance she had, for a rudeness upon his part meant as a compliment, thrown his hat—the Lieutenant-Bailly's hat—into the Fauxbie by the Vier Prison. He thought her intrusive thus to stay these august proceedings of the Royal Court, by an appeal for he knew not what.

"What is the trespass, and who the trespasser?" asked the Bailly sternly.

Guida rose to her feet.

"Philip d'Avranche has trespassed," she said. "What Philip d'Avranche, mademoiselle?" asked the Bailly in a rough, ungenerous tone.

"Admiral Philip d'Avranche, known as his Serene Highness the Duc de Bercy, has trespassed on me," she answered.

She did not look at Philip, her eyes were fixed upon the Bailly and the jurats.

The Bailly whispered to one or two jurats. "Wherein is the trespass?" asked the Bailly sharply. "Tell your story."

After an instant's painful pause, Guida told her tale.

"Last night at Plemont," she said in a voice trembling a little at first but growing stronger as she went on, "I left my child, my Guilbert, in his bed, with Dormy Jamais to watch beside him, while I went to my boat which lies far from my hut. I left Dormy Jamais with the child because I was afraid— because I had been afraid, these three days past, that Philip d'Avranche would steal him from me. I was gone but half an hour; it was dark when I returned. I found the door open, I found Dormy Jamais lying unconscious on the floor, and my child's bed empty. My child was gone. He was stolen from me by Philip d'Avranche, Duc de Bercy."

"What proof have you that it was the Duc de Bercy?" asked the Bailly.

"I have told your honour that Dormy Jamais was there. He struck Dormy Jamais to the ground, and rode off with my child."

The Bailly sniffed.

"Dormy Jamais is a simpleton—an idiot."

"Then let the Prince speak," she answered quickly. She turned and looked Philip in the eyes. He did not answer a word. He had not moved since she entered the court-room. He kept his eyes fixed on her, save for one or two swift glances towards the jurats. The crisis of his life had come. He was ready to meet it now: anything would be better than all he had gone through during the past ten days. In mad impulse he had stolen the child, with the wild belief that through it he could reach Guida, could bring her to him. For now this woman who despised him, hated him, he desired more than all else in the world. Ambition has her own means of punishing. For her gifts of place or fortune she puts some impossible hunger in the soul of the victim which leads him at last to his own destruction. With all the world conquered there is still some mystic island of which she whispers, and to gain this her votary risks all—and loses all.

The Bailly saw by Philip's face that Guida had spoken truth. But he whispered with the jurats eagerly, and presently he said with brusque decision:

"Our law of Haro may only apply to trespass upon property. Its intent is merely civil."

Which having said he opened and shut his mouth with gusto, and sat back as though expecting Guida to retire.

"Your law of Haro, monsieur le Bailly!" Guida answered with flashing eyes, her voice ringing out fearlessly. "Your law of Haro! The law of Haro comes from the custom of Normandy, which is the law of Jersey. You make its intent this, you make it that, but nothing can alter the law, and what has been done in its name for generations. Is it so, that if Philip d'Avranche trespass on my land, or my hearth, I may cry Haro, haro! and you will take heed? But when it is blood of my blood, bone of my bone, flesh of my flesh that he has wickedly seized; when it is the head I have pillowed on my breast for four years—the child that has known no father, his mother's only companion in her unearned shame, the shame of an outcast—then is it so that your law of Haro may not apply? Messieurs, it is the justice of Haro that I ask, not your lax usage of it. From this Prince Philip I appeal to the spirit of Prince Rollo who made this law. I appeal to the law of Jersey which is the Custom of Normandy. There are precedents enough, as you well know, messieurs. I demand—I demand—my child."

The Bailly and the jurats were in a hopeless quandary. They glanced furtively at Philip. They were half afraid that she was right, and yet were timorous of deciding against the Prince.

She saw their hesitation. "I call on you to fulfil the law. I have cried Haro, haro! and what I have cried men will hear outside this Court, outside this Isle of Jersey; for I appeal against a sovereign duke of Europe." The Bailly and the jurats were overwhelmed by the situation. Guida's brain was a hundred times clearer than theirs. Danger, peril to her child, had aroused in her every force of intelligence; she had the daring, the desperation of the lioness fighting for her own.

Philip himself solved the problem. Turning to the bench of jurats, he said quietly:

"She is quite right; the law of Haro is with her. It must apply."

The Court was in a greater maze than ever. Was he then about to restore to Guida her child? After an instant's pause Philip continued:

"But in this case there was no trespass, for the child—is my own."

Every eye in the Cohue Royale fixed itself upon him, then upon Guida, then upon her who was known as the Duchesse de Bercy. The face of the Comtesse Chantavoine was like snow, white and cold. As the words were spoken a sigh broke from her, and there came to Philip's mind that distant day in the council chamber at Bercy when for one moment he was upon his trial; but he did not turn and look at her now. It was all pitiable, horrible; but this open avowal, insult as it was to the Comtesse Chantavoine, could be no worse than the rumours which would surely have reached her one day. So let the game fare on. He had thrown down the glove now, and he could not see the end; he was playing for one thing only—for the woman he had lost, for his own child. If everything went by the board, why, it must go by the board. It all flashed through his brain: to-morrow he must send in his resignation to the Admiralty—so much at once. Then Bercy—come what might, there was work for him to do at Bercy. He was a sovereign duke of Europe, as Guida had said. He would fight for the duchy for his son's sake. Standing there he could feel again the warm cheek of the child upon his own, as last night he felt it riding across the island from Plemont to the village near Mont Orgueil. That very morning he had hurried down to a little cottage in the village and seen it lying asleep, well cared for by a peasant woman. He knew that to-morrow the scandal of the thing would belong to the world, but he was not dismayed. He had tossed his fame as an admiral into the gutter, but Bercy still was left. All the native force, the stubborn vigour, the obdurate spirit of the soil of Jersey of which he was, its arrogant self-will, drove him straight into this last issue. What he had got at so much cost he would keep against all the world. He would—

But he stopped short in his thoughts, for there now at the court-room door stood Detricand, the Chouan chieftain.

He drew his hand quickly across his eyes. It seemed so wild, so fantastic, that of all men, Detricand should be there. His gaze was so fixed that every one turned to see—every one save Guida.

Guida was not conscious of this new figure in the scene. In her heart was fierce tumult. Her hour had come at last, the hour in which she must declare that she was the wife of this man. She had no proofs. No doubt he would deny it now, for he knew how she loathed him. But she must tell her tale.

She was about to address the Bailly, but, as though a pang of pity shot, through her heart, she turned instead and looked at the Comtesse Chantavoine. She could find it in her to pause in compassion for this poor lady, more wronged than herself had been. Their eyes met. One instant's flash of intelligence between the souls of two women, and Guida knew that the look of the Comtesse Chantavoine had said: "Speak for your child."

Thereupon she spoke.

"Messieurs, Prince Philip d'Avranche is my husband."

Every one in the court-room stirred with excitement. Some weak-nerved woman with a child at her breast began to cry, and the little one joined its feeble wail to hers.

"Five years ago," Guida continued, "I was married to Philip d'Avranche by the Reverend Lorenzo Dow in the church of St. Michael's—"

The Bailly interrupted with a grunt. "H'm—Lorenzo Dow is well out of the way-have done."

"May I not then be heard in my own defence?" Guida cried in indignation. "For years I have suffered silently slander and shame. Now I speak for myself at last, and you will not hear me! I come to this court of justice, and my word is doubted ere I can prove the truth. Is it for judges to assail one so? Five years ago I was married secretly, in St. Michael's Church—secretly, because Philip d'Avranche urged it, pleaded for it. An open marriage, he said, would hinder his promotion. We were wedded, and he left me. War broke out. I remained silent according to my promise to him. Then came the time when in the States of Bercy he denied that he had a wife. From the hour I knew he had done so I denied him. My child was born in shame and sorrow, I myself was outcast in this island. But my conscience was clear before Heaven. I took myself and my child out from among you and went to Plemont. I waited, believing that God's justice was surer than man's. At last Philip d'Avranche—my husband—returned here. He invaded my home, and begged me to come with my child to him as his wife—he who had so evilly wronged me, and wronged another more than me. I refused. Then he stole my child from me. You ask for proofs of my marriage. Messieurs, I have no proofs.

"I know not where Lorenzo Dow may be found. The register of St. Michael's Church, as you all know, was stolen. Mr. Shoreham, who witnessed the marriage, is dead. But you must believe me. There is one witness left, if he will but speak—even the man who married me, the man that for one day called me his wife. I ask him now to tell the truth."

She turned towards Philip, her clear eyes piercing him through and through.

What was going on in his mind neither she nor any in that Court might ever know, for in the pause, the Comtesse Chantavoine rose up, and passing steadily by Philip, came to Guida. Looking her in the eyes with an incredible sorrow, she took her hand, and turned towards Philip with infinite scorn.

A strange, thrilling silence fell upon all the Court. The jurats shifted in their seats with excitement. The Bailly, in a hoarse, dry voice, said:

"We must have proof. There must be record as well as witness."

From near the great doorway came a voice saying: "The record is here," and Detricand stepped forward, in his uniform of the army of the Vendee.

A hushed murmur ran round the room. The jurats whispered to each other.

"Who are you, monsieur?" said the Bailly.

"I am Detricand, Prince of Vaufontaine," he replied, "for whom the Comtesse Chantavoine will vouch," he added in a pained voice, and bowed low to her and to Guida. "I am but this hour landed. I came to Jersey on this very matter."

He did not wait for the Bailly to reply, but began to tell of the death of Lorenzo Dow, and, taking from his pocket the little black journal, opened it and read aloud the record written therein by the dead clergyman. Having read it, he passed it on to the Greffier, who handed it up to the Bailly. Another moment's pause ensued. To the most ignorant and casual of the onlookers the strain was great; to those chiefly concerned it was supreme. The Bailly and the jurats whispered together. Now at last a spirit of justice was roused in them. But the law's technicalities were still to rule.

The Bailly closed the book, and handed it back to the Greffier with the words: "This is not proof though it is evidence."

Guida felt her heart sink within her. The Comtesse Chantavoine, who still held her hand, pressed it, though herself cold as ice with sickness of spirit.

At that instant, and from Heaven knows where—as a bird comes from a bush—a little grey man came quickly among them all, carrying spread open before him a book almost as big as himself. Handing it up to the Bailly, he said:

"Here is the proof, Monsieur le Bailly—here is the whole proof."

The Bailly leaned over and drew up the book. The jurats crowded near and a dozen heads gathered about the open volume.

At last the Bailly looked up and addressed the Court solemnly.

"It is the lost register of St. Michael's," he said. "It contains the record of the marriage of Lieutenant Philip d'Avranche and Guida Landresse de Landresse, both of the Isle of Jersey, by special license of the Bishop of Winchester."

"Precisely so, precisely so," said the little grey figure—the Chevalier Orvillier du Champsavoys de Beaumanoir. Tears ran down his cheeks as he turned towards Guida, but he was smiling too.

Guida's eyes were upon the Bailly. "And the child?" she cried with a broken voice—"the child?"

"The child goes with its mother," answered the Bailly firmly.

# DURING ONE YEAR LATER

## CHAPTER XL

The day that saw Guida's restitution in the Cohue Royale brought but further trouble to Ranulph Delagarde. The Chevalier had shown him the lost register of St. Michael's, and with a heart less heavy, he left the island once more. Intending to join Detricand in the Vendee, he had scarcely landed at St. Malo when he was seized by a press-gang and carried aboard a French frigate commissioned to ravage the coasts of British America. He had stubbornly resisted the press, but had been knocked on the head, and there was an end on it.

In vain he protested that he was an Englishman. They laughed at him. His French was perfect, his accent Norman, his was a Norman face— evidence enough. If he was not a citizen of France he should be, and he must be. Ranulph decided that it was needless to throw away his life. It was better to make a show of submission. So long as he had not to fight British ships, he could afford to wait. Time enough then for him to take action. When the chance came he would escape this bondage; meanwhile remembering his four years' service with the artillery at Elizabeth Castle, he asked to be made a gunner, and his request was granted.

The Victoire sailed the seas battle-hungry, and presently appeased her appetite among Dutch and Danish privateers. Such excellent work did Ranulph against the Dutchmen, that Richambeau, the captain, gave him a gun for himself, and after they had fought the Danes made him a master-gunner. Of the largest gun on the Victoire Ranulph grew so fond that at last he called her ma couzaine.

Days and weeks passed, until one morning came the cry of "Land! Land!" and once again Ranulph saw British soil—the tall cliffs of the peninsula of Gaspe. Gaspe—that was the ultima Thule to which Mattingley and Carterette had gone.

Presently, as the Victoire came nearer to the coast, he could see a bay and a great rock in the distance, and, as they bore in now, the rock seemed to stretch out like a vast wall into the gulf. As he stood watching and leaning on ma couzaine, a sailor near him said that the bay and the rock were called Perce.

Perce Bay—that was the exact point for which Elie Mattingley and Carterette had sailed with Sebastian Alixandre. How strange it was! He had bidden Carterette good-bye for ever, yet fate had now brought him to the very spot whither she had gone.

The Rock of Perce was a wall, three hundred feet high, and the wall was an island that had once been a long promontory like a battlement, jutting out hundreds of yards into the gulf. At one point it was pierced by an archway. It was almost sheer; its top was flat and level. Upon the sides there was no verdure; upon the top centuries had made a green field. The wild geese as they flew northward, myriad flocks of gulls, gannets, cormorants, and all manner of fowl of the sea, had builded upon the summit until it was rich with grass and shrubs. The nations of the air sent their legions here to bivouac, and the discord of a hundred languages might be heard far out to sea, far in upon the land. Millions of the races of the air swarmed there; at times the air above was darkened by clouds of them. No fog-bell on a rock-bound coast might warn mariners more ominously than these battalions of adventurers on the Perce Rock.

No human being had ever mounted to this eyrie. Generations of fishermen had looked upon the yellowish-red limestone of the Perce Rock with a valorous eye, but it would seem that not even the tiny clinging hoof of a chamois or wild goat might find a foothold upon the straight sides of it.

Ranulph was roused out of the spell Perce cast over him by seeing the British flag upon a building by the shore of the bay they were now entering. His heart gave a great bound. Yes, it was the English flag defiantly flying. And more—there were two old 12 pounders being trained on the French squadron. For the first time in years a low laugh burst from his lips.

"O mai grand doux," he said in the Jersey patois, "only one man in the world would do that. Only Elie Mattingley!"

At that moment, Mattingley now issued from a wooden fishing-shed with Sebastian Alixandre and three others armed with muskets, and passed to the little fort on which flew the British and Jersey flags. Ranulph heard a guffaw behind. Richambeau, the captain, confronted him.

"That's a big splutter in a little pot, gunner," said he. He put his telescope to his eye. "The Lord protect us," he cried, "they're going to fight my ship!" He laughed again till the tears came. "Son of Peter, but it is droll that—a farce au diable! They have humour, these fisher-folk, eh, gunner?"

"Mattingley will fight you just the same," answered Ranulph coolly.

"Oh ho, you know these people, my gunner?" asked Richambeau.

"All my life," answered Ranulph, "and, by your leave, I will tell you how."

Not waiting for permission, after the manner of his country, he told Richambeau of his Jersey birth and bringing up, and how he was the victim of the pressgang.

"Very good," said Richambeau. "You Jersey folk were once Frenchmen, and now that you're French again, you shall do something for the flag. You see that 12-pounder yonder to the right? Very well, dismount it. Then we'll send in a flag of truce, and parley with this Mattingley, for his jests are worth attention and politeness. There's a fellow at the gun—no, he has gone. Dismount the right-hand gun at one shot. Ready now. Get a good range."

The whole matter went through Ranulph's mind as the captain spoke. If he refused to fire, he would be strung up to the yardarm; if he fired and missed, perhaps other gunners would fire, and once started they might raze the fishing-post. If he dismounted the gun, the matter would probably remain only a jest, for such as yet Richambeau regarded it.

Ranulph ordered the tackle and breechings cast away, had off the apron, pricked a cartridge, primed, bruised the priming, and covered the vent. Then he took his range steadily, quietly. There was a brisk wind blowing from the south—he must allow for that; but the wind was stopped somewhat in its course by the Perch Rock—he must allow for that.

All was ready. Suddenly a girl came running round the corner of the building.

It was Carterette. She was making for the right-hand gun. Ranulph started, the hand that held the match trembled.

"Fire, you fool, or you'll kill the girl!" cried Richambeau.

Ranulph laid a hand on himself as it were. Every nerve in his body tingled, his legs trembled, but his eye was steady. He took the sight once more coolly, then blew on the match. Now the girl was within thirty feet of the gun.

He quickly blew on the match again, and fired. When the smoke cleared away he saw that the gun was dismounted, and not ten feet from it stood Carterette looking at it dazedly.

He heard a laugh behind him. There was Richambeau walking away, telescope under arm, even as the other 12-pounder on shore replied impudently to the gun he had fired.

"A good aim," he heard Richambeau say, jerking a finger backward towards him.

Was it then? said Ranulph to himself; was it indeed? Ba su, it was the last shot he would ever fire against aught English, here or elsewhere.

Presently he saw a boat drawing away with the flag of truce in the hands of a sous-lieutenant. His mind was made up; he would escape to-night. His place was there beside his fellow-countrymen. He motioned away the men of the gun. He would load ma couzaine himself for the last time.

As he sponged the gun he made his plans. Swish-swash the sponge-staff ran in and out—he would try to steal away at dog-watch. He struck the sponge smartly on ma couzaine's muzzle, cleansing it—he would have to slide into the water like a rat and swim very softly to the shore. He reached for a fresh cartridge, and thrust it into the throat of the gun, and as the seam was laid downwards he said to himself that he could swim under water, if discovered as he left the Victoire. As he unstopped the touch-hole and tried with the priming-wire whether the cartridge was home, he was stunned by a fresh thought.

Richambeau would send a squad of men to search for him, and if he was not found they would probably raze the Post, or take its people prisoners. As he put the apron carefully on ma couzaine, he determined that he could not take refuge with the Mattingleys. Neither would it do to make for the woods of the interior, for still Richambeau might revenge himself on the fishing-post. What was to be done? He turned his eyes helplessly on Perce Rock.

As he looked, a new idea came to him. If only he could get to the top of that massive wall, not a hundred fleets could dislodge him. One musket could defeat the forlorn hope of any army. Besides, if he took refuge on the rock, there could be no grudge against Perce village or the Mattingleys, and Richambeau would not injure them.

He eyed the wall closely. The blazing sunshine showed it up in a hard light, and he studied every square yard of it with a telescope. At one point the wall was not quite perpendicular. There were also narrow ledges, lumps of stone, natural steps and little pinnacles which the fingers could grip and where man might rest. Yes, he would try it.

It was the last quarter of the moon, and the neaptide was running low when he let himself softly down into the water from the Victoire. The blanket tied on his head held food kept from his rations, with stone and flint and other things. He was not seen, and he dropped away quietly astern, getting clear of the Victoire while the moon was partially obscured.

Now it was a question when his desertion would be discovered. All he asked was two clear hours. By that time the deed would be done, if he could climb Perce Rock at all.

He touched bottom. He was on Perce sands. The blanket on his head was scarcely wetted. He wrung the water out of his clothes, and ran softly up the shore. Suddenly he was met by a cry of Qui va la! and he stopped short at the point of Elie Mattingley's bayonet. "Hush!" said Ranulph, and gave his name.

Mattingley nearly dropped his musket in surprise. He soon knew the tale of Ranulph's misfortunes, but he had not yet been told of his present plans when there came a quick footstep, and Carterette was at her father's side. Unlike Mattingley, she did drop her musket at the sight of Ranulph. Her lips opened, but at first she could not speak—this was more than she had ever dared hope for, since those dark days in Jersey. Ranulph here! She pressed her hands to her heart to stop its throbbing.

Presently she was trembling with excitement at the story of how Ranulph had been pressed at St. Malo, and, all that came after until this very day.

"Go along with Carterette," said Mattingley. "Alixandre is at the house; he'll help you away into the woods."

As Ranulph hurried away with Carterette, he told her his design. Suddenly she stopped short, "Ranulph Delagarde," she said vehemently, "you can't climb Perch Rock. No one has ever done it, and you must not try. Oh, I know you are a great man, but you mustn't think you can do this. You will be safe where we shall hide you. You shall not climb the rock-ah no, ba su!"

He pointed towards the Post. "They wouldn't leave a stick standing there if you hid me. No, I'm going to the top of the rock."

"Man doux terrible!" she said in sheer bewilderment, and then was suddenly inspired. At last her time had come.

"Pardingue," she said, clutching his arm, "if you go to the top of Perch Rock, so will I!"

In spite of his anxiety he almost laughed.

"But see—but see," he said, and his voice dropped; "you couldn't stay up there with me all alone, garcon Carterette. And Richambeau would be firing on you too!"

She was very angry, but she made no reply, and he continued quickly:

"I'll go straight to the rock now. When they miss me there'll be a pot boiling, you may believe. If I get up," he added, "I'll let a string down for a rope you must get for me. Once on top they can't hurt me.... Eh ben, A bi'tot, gargon Carterette!"

"O my good! O my good!" said the girl with a sudden change of mood. "To think you have come like this, and perhaps—" But she dashed the tears from her eyes, and bade him go on.

The tide was well out, the moon shining brightly. Ranulph reached the point where, if the rock was to be scaled at all, the ascent must be made. For a distance there was shelving where foothold might be had by a fearless man with a steady head and sure balance. After that came about a hundred feet where he would have to draw himself up by juttings and crevices hand over hand, where was no natural pathway. Woe be to him if head grew dizzy, foot slipped, or strength gave out; he would be broken to pieces on the hard sand below. That second stage once passed, the ascent thence to the top would be easier; for though nearly as steep, it had more ledges, and offered fair vantage to a man with a foot like a mountain goat. Ranulph had been aloft all weathers in his time, and his toes were as strong as another man's foot, and surer.

He started. The toes caught in crevices, held on to ledges, glued themselves on to smooth surfaces; the knees clung like a rough-rider's to a saddle; the big hands, when once they got a purchase, fastened like an air-cup.

Slowly, slowly up, foot by foot, yard by yard, until one-third of the distance was climbed. The suspense and strain were immeasurable. But he struggled on and on, and at last reached a sort of flying pinnacle of rock, like a hook for the shields of the gods.

Here he ventured to look below, expecting to see Carterette, but there was only the white sand, and no sound save the long wash of the gulf. He drew a horn of arrack from his pocket and drank. He had two hundred feet more to climb, and the next hundred would be the great ordeal.

He started again. This was travail indeed. His rough fingers, his toes, hard as horn almost, began bleeding. Once or twice he swung quite clear of the wall, hanging by his fingers to catch a surer foothold to right or left, and just getting it sometimes by an inch or less. The tension was terrible. His head seemed to swell and fill with blood: on the top it throbbed till it was ready to burst. His neck was aching horribly with constant looking up, the skin of his knees was gone, his ankles bruised. But he must keep on till he got to the top, or until he fell.

The Battle Of The Strong—Complete | 271

He was fighting on now in a kind of dream, quite apart from all usual feelings of this world. The earth itself seemed far away, and he was toiling among vastnesses, himself a giant with colossal frame and huge, sprawling limbs. It was like a gruesome vision of the night, when the body is an elusive, stupendous mass that falls into space after a confused struggle with immensities. It was all mechanical, vague, almost numb, this effort to overcome a mountain. Yet it was precise and hugely expert too; for though there was a strange mist on the brain, the body felt its way with a singular certainty, as might some molluscan dweller of the sea, sensitive like a plant, intuitive like an animal. Yet at times it seemed that this vast body overcoming the mountain must let go its hold and slide away into the darkness of the depths.

Now there was a strange convulsive shiver in every nerve—God have mercy, the time was come!... No, not yet. At the very instant when it seemed the panting flesh and blood would be shaken off by the granite force repelling it, the fingers, like long antennae, touched horns of rock jutting out from ledges on the third escarpment of the wall. Here was the last point of the worst stage of the journey. Slowly, heavily, the body drew up to the shelf of limestone, and crouched in an inert bundle. There it lay for a long time.

While the long minutes went by, a voice kept calling up from below; calling, calling, at first eagerly, then anxiously, then with terror. By and by the bundle of life stirred, took shape, raised itself, and was changed into a man again, a thinking, conscious being, who now understood the meaning of this sound coming up from the earth below—or was it the sea? A human voice had at last pierced the awful exhaustion of the deadly labour, the peril and strife, which had numbed the brain while the body, in its instinct for existence, still clung to the rocky ledges. It had called the man back to earth—he was no longer a great animal, and the rock a monster with skin and scales of stone.

"Ranulph! Maitre Ranulph! Ah, Ranulph!" called the voice.

Now he knew, and he answered down: "All right, all right, garche Carterette!"

"Are you at the top?"

"No, but the rest is easy."

"Hurry, hurry, Ranulph. If they should come before you reach the top!"

"I'll soon be there."

"Are you hurt, Ranulph?"

"No, but my fingers are in rags. I am going now. A bi'tot, Carterette!"

"Ranulph!"

"'Sh, 'sh, do not speak. I am starting."

There was silence for what seemed hours to the girl below. Foot by foot the man climbed on, no less cautious because the ascent was easier, for he was now weaker. But he was on the monster's neck now, and soon he should set his heel on it: he was not to be shaken off.

At last the victorious moment came. Over a jutting ledge he drew himself up by sheer strength and the rubber-like grip of his lacerated fingers, and now he lay flat and breathless upon the ground.

How soft and cool it was! This was long sweet grass touching his face, making a couch like down for the battered, wearied body. Surely such travail had been more than mortal. And what was this vast fluttering over his head, this million-voiced discord round him, like the buffetings and cries of spirits welcoming another to their torment? He raised his head and laughed in triumph. These were the cormorants, gulls, and gannets on the Perch Rock.

Legions of birds circled over him with cries so shrill that at first he did not hear Carterette's voice calling up to him. At last, however, remembering, he leaned over the cliff and saw her standing in the moonlight far below.

Her voice came up to him indistinctly because of the clatter of the birds. "Maitre Ranulph! Ranulph!" She could not see him, for this part of the rock was in shadow.

"Ah bah, all right!" he said, and taking hold of one end of the twine he had brought, he let the roll fall. It dropped almost at Carterette's feet. She tied to the end of it three loose ropes she had brought from the Post. He drew them up quickly, tied them together firmly, and let the great coil down. Ranulph's bundle, a tent and many things Carterette had brought were drawn up.

"Ranulph! Ranulph!" came Carterette's voice again.

"Garcon Carterette!"

"You must help Sebastian Alixandre up," she said.

"Sebastian Alixandre—is he there? Why does he want to come?"

"That is no matter," she called softly. "He is coming. He has the rope round his waist. Pull away!" It was better, Ranulph thought to himself, that he should be on Perch Rock alone, but the terrible strain had bewildered him, and he could make no protest now.

"Don't start yet," he called down; "I'll pull when all's ready."

He fell back from the edge to a place in the grass where, tying the rope round his body, and seating himself, he could brace his feet against a ledge of rock. Then he pulled on the rope. It was round Carterette's waist!

Carterette had told her falsehood without shame, for she was of those to whom the end is more than the means. She began climbing, and Ranulph pulled steadily. Twice he felt the rope suddenly jerk when she lost her footing, but it came in evenly still, and he used a nose of rock as a sort of winch.

The climber was nearly two-thirds of the way up when a cannon-shot boomed out over the water, frightening again the vast covey of birds which shrieked and honked till the air was a maelstrom of cries. Then came another cannon-shot.

Ranulph's desertion was discovered. The fight was begun between a single Jersey shipwright and a French war-ship.

His strength, however, could not last much longer. Every muscle of his body had been strained and tortured, and even this lighter task tried him beyond endurance. His legs stiffened against the ledge of rock, the tension numbed his arms. He wondered how near Alixandre was to the top. Suddenly there was a pause, then a heavy jerk. Love of God—the rope was shooting through his fingers, his legs were giving way! He gathered himself together, and then with teeth, hands, and body rigid with enormous effort, he pulled and pulled. Now he could not see. A mist swam before his eyes. Everything grew black, but he pulled on and on.

He never knew how the climber reached the top. But when the mist cleared away from his eyes, Carterette was bending over him, putting rum to his lips.

"Carterette-garcon Carterette!" he murmured, amazed. Then as the truth burst upon him he shook his head in a troubled sort of way.

"What a cat I was!" said Carterette. "What a wild cat I was to make you haul me up! It was bad for me with the rope round me, it must have been awful for you, my poor esmanus—poor scarecrow Ranulph."

Scarecrow indeed he looked. His clothes were nearly gone, his hair was tossed and matted, his eyes bloodshot, his big hands like pieces of raw meat, his feet covered with blood.

"My poor scarecrow!" she repeated, and she tenderly wiped the blood from his face where his hands had touched it. Meanwhile bugle-calls and cries of command came up to them, and in the first light of morning they could see French officers and sailors, Mattingley, Alixandre, and others, hurrying to and fro.

When day came clear and bright, it was known that Carterette as well as Ranulph had vanished. Mattingley shook his head stoically, but Richambeau on the Victoire was as keen to hunt down one Jersey-Englishman as he had ever been to attack an English fleet. More so, perhaps.

Meanwhile the birds kept up a wild turmoil and shrieking. Never before had any one heard them so clamorous. More than once Mattingley had looked at Perch Rock curiously, but whenever the thought of it as a refuge came to him, he put it away. No, it was impossible.

Yet, what was that? Mattingley's heart thumped. There were two people on the lofty island wall—a man and a woman. He caught' the arm of a French officer near him. "Look, look!" he said. The officer raised his glass.

"It's the gunner," he cried and handed the glass to the old man.

"It's Carterette," said Mattingley in a hoarse voice. "But it's not possible. It's not possible," he added helplessly. "Nobody was ever there. My God, look at it—look at it!"

It was a picture indeed. A man and a woman were outlined against the clear air, putting up a tent as calmly as though on a lawn, thousands of birds wheeling over their heads, with querulous cries.

A few moments later, Elie Mattingley was being rowed swiftly to the Victoire, where Richambeau was swearing viciously as he looked through his telescope. He also had recognised the gunner.

He was prepared to wipe out the fishing-post if Mattingley did not produce Ranulph—well, "here was Ranulph duly produced and insultingly setting up a tent on this sheer rock, with some snippet of the devil," said Richambeau, and defying a great French war-ship. He would set his gunners to work. If he only had as good a marksman as Ranulph himself, the deserter should drop at the first shot "death and the devil take his impudent face!"

He was just about to give the order when Mattingley was brought to him. The old man's story amazed him beyond measure.

"It is no man, then!" said Richambeau, when Mattingley had done. "He must be a damned fly to do it. And the girl—sacre moi! he drew her up after him. I'll have him down out of that though, or throw up my flag," he added, and turning fiercely, gave his orders.

For hours the Victoire bombarded the lonely rock from the north. The white tent was carried away, but the cannon-balls flew over or merely battered the solid rock, the shells were thrown beyond, and no harm was done. But now and again the figure of Ranulph appeared, and a half-dozen times he took aim with his musket at the French soldiers on the shore. Twice his shots took effect; one man was wounded, and one killed. Then whole companies of marines returned a musketry fire at him, to no purpose. At his ease he hid himself in the long grass at the edge of the cliff, and picked off two more men.

Here was a ridiculous thing: one man and a slip of a girl fighting and defying a battle-ship. The smoke of battle covered miles of the great gulf. Even the seabirds shrieked in ridicule.

This went on for three days at intervals. With a fine chagrin Richambeau and his men saw a bright camp-fire lighted on the rock, and knew that Ranulph and the girl were cooking their meals in peace. A flag-staff too was set up, and a red cloth waved defiantly in the breeze. At last Richambeau, who had watched the whole business from the deck of the Victoire, burst out laughing, and sent for Elie Mattingley. "Come, I've had enough," said Richambeau.

"There never was a wilder jest, and I'll not spoil the joke. He has us on his toasting-fork. He shall have the honour of a flag of truce."

And so it was that the French battle-ship sent a flag of truce to the foot of Perch Rock, and a French officer, calling up, gave his captain's word of honour that Ranulph should suffer nothing at the hands of a court-martial, and that he should be treated as an English prisoner of war, not as a French deserter.

There was no court-martial. After Ranulph, at Richambeau's command, had told the tale of the ascent, the Frenchman said:

"No one but an Englishman could be fool enough to try such a thing, and none but a fool could have had the luck to succeed. But even a fool can get a woman to follow him, and so this flyaway followed you, and—"

Carterette made for Richambeau as though to scratch his eyes out, but Ranulph held her back. "—And you are condemned, gunner," continued Richambeau dryly, "to marry the said maid before sundown, or be carried out to sea a prisoner of war." So saying, he laughed, and bade them begone to the wedding.

Ranulph left Richambeau's ship bewildered and perturbed. For hours he paced the shore, and at last his thoughts began to clear. The new life he had led during the last few months had brought many revelations. He had come to realise that there are several sorts of happiness, but that all may be divided into two kinds: the happiness of doing good to ourselves, and that of doing good to others. It opened out clearly to him now as he thought of Carterette in the light of Richambeau's coarse jest.

For years he had known in a sort of way that Carterette preferred him to any other man. He knew now that she had remained single because of him. For him her impatience had been patience, her fiery heart had spilled itself in tenderness for his misfortunes. She who had lightly tossed lovers aside, her coquetry appeased, had to himself shown sincerity without coquetry, loyalty without selfishness. He knew well that she had been his champion in dark days, that he had received far more from her than he had ever given—even of friendship. In his own absorbing love for Guida Landresse, during long years he had been unconsciously blind to a devotion which had lived on without hope, without repining, with untiring cheerfulness.

In those three days spent on the top of the Perch Rock how blithe garcon Carterette had been! Danger had seemed nothing to her. She had the temper of a man in her real enjoyment of the desperate chances of life. He had never seen her so buoyant; her animal spirits had never leapt so high. And yet, despite the boldness which had sent her to the top of Perch Rock with him, there had been in her whole demeanour a frank modesty free from self-consciousness. She could think for herself, she was sure of herself, and she would go to the ends of the earth for him. Surely he had not earned such friendship, such affection.

He recalled how, the night before, as he sat by their little camp-fire, she had come and touched him on the shoulder, and, looking down at him, said:

"I feel as if I was beginning my life all over again, don't you, Maitre Ranulph?"

Her black eyes had been fixed on his, and the fire in them was as bright and full of health and truth as the fire at his feet.

And he had answered her: "I think I feel that too, garcon Carterette."

To which she had replied: "It isn't hard to forget here—not so very hard, is it?"

She did not mean Guida, nor what he had felt for Guida, but rather the misery of the past. He had nodded his head in reply, but had not spoken; and she, with a quick: "A bi'tot," had taken her blanket and gone to that portion of the rock set apart for her own. Then he had sat by the fire thinking through the long hours of night until the sun rose. That day Richambeau had sent his flag of truce, and the end of their stay on Perch Rock was come.

Yes, he would marry Carterette. Yet he was not disloyal, even in memory. What had belonged to Guida belonged to her for ever, belonged to a past life with which henceforth he should have naught to do. What had sprung up in his heart for Carterette belonged to the new life. In this new land there was work to do—what might he not accomplish here? He realised that within one life a man may still live several lives, each loyal and honest after its kind. A fate stronger than himself had brought him here; and here he would stay with fate. It had brought him to Carterette, and who could tell what good and contentment might not yet come to him, and how much to her!

That evening he went to Carterette and asked her to be his wife. She turned pale, and, looking up into his eyes with a kind of fear, she said brokenly:

"It's not because you feel you must? It's not because you know I love you, Ranulph—is it? It's not for that alone?"

"It is because I want you, garcon Carterette," he answered tenderly, "because life will be nothing without you."

"I am so happy—par made, I am so happy!" she answered, and she hid her face on his breast.

# CHAPTER XLI

Detricand, Prince of Vaufontaine, was no longer in the Vendee. The whole of Brittany was in the hands of the victorious Hoche, the peasants were disbanded, and his work for a time at least was done.

On the same day of that momentous scene in the Cohue Royale when Guida was vindicated, Detricand had carried to Granville the Comtesse Chantavoine, who presently was passed over to the loving care of her kinsman General Grandjon-Larisse. This done, he proceeded to England.

From London he communicated with Grandjon-Larisse, who applied himself to secure from the Directory leave for the Chouan chieftain to return to France, with amnesty for his past "rebellion." This was got at last through the influence of young Bonaparte himself. Detricand was free now to proceed against Philip.

He straightway devoted himself to a thing conceived on the day that Guida was restored to her rightful status as a wife. His purpose now was to wrest from Philip the duchy of Bercy. Philip was heir by adoption only, and the inheritance had been secured at the last by help of a lie—surely his was a righteous cause!

His motives had not their origin in hatred of Philip alone, nor in desire for honours and estates for himself, nor in racial antagonism, for had he not been allied with England in this war against the Government? He hated Philip the man, but he hated still more Philip the usurper who had brought shame to the escutcheon of Bercy. There was also at work another and deeper design to be shown in good time. Philip had retired from the English navy, and gone back to his duchy of Bercy. Here he threw himself into the struggle with the Austrians against the French. Received with enthusiasm by the people, who as yet knew little or nothing of the doings in the Cohue Royale, he now took over command of the army and proved himself almost as able in the field as he had been at sea. Of these things Detricand knew, and knew also that the lines were closing in round the duchy; that one day soon Bonaparte would send a force which should strangle the little army and its Austrian allies. The game then would be another step nearer the end. Free to move at will, he visited the Courts of Prussia, Russia, Spain, Italy, and Austria, and laid before them his claims to the duchy, urging an insistence on its neutrality, and a trial of his cause against Philip. Ceaselessly, adroitly, with persistence and power, he toiled towards his end, the way made easier by tales told of his prowess in the Vendee. He had offers without number to take service in foreign armies, but he was not to be tempted. Gossip of the Courts said that there was some strange romance behind this tireless pursuit of an inheritance, but he paid no heed. If at last there crept over Europe wonderful tales of Detricand's past life in Jersey, of the real Duchesse de Bercy, and of the new Prince of Vaufontaine, Detricand did not, or feigned not to, hear them; and the Comtesse Chantavoine had disappeared from public knowledge. The few who guessed his romance were puzzled to understand his cause: for if he dispossessed Philip, Guida must also be dispossessed. This, certainly, was not lover-like or friendly.

But Detricand was not at all puzzled; his mind and purpose were clear. Guida should come to no injury through him—Guida who, as they left the Cohue Royale that day of days, had turned on him a look of heavenly trust and gratitude; who, in the midst of her own great happenings, found time to tell him by a word how well she knew he had kept his promise to her, even beyond belief. Justice for her was now the supreme and immediate object of his life. There were others ready also to care for France, to fight for her, to die for her, to struggle towards the hour when the King should come to his own; but there was only one man in the world who could achieve Guida's full justification, and that was himself, Detricand of Vaufontaine.

He was glad to turn to the Chevalier's letters from Jersey. It was from the Chevalier's lips he had learned the whole course of Guida's life during the four years of his absence from the island. It was the Chevalier who drew for him pictures of Guida in her new home, none other than the house of Elie Mattingley, which the Royal Court having confiscated now handed over to her as an act of homage. The little world of Jersey no longer pointed the finger of scorn at Guida Landresse de Landresse, but bent the knee to Princess Guida d'Avranche.

Detricand wrote many letters to the Chevalier, and they with their cheerful and humorous allusions were read aloud to Guida—all save one concerning Philip. Writing of himself to the Chevalier on one occasion, he laid bare with a merciless honesty his nature and his career. Concerning neither had he any illusions.

> I do not mistake myself, Chevalier [he wrote], nor these late doings
> of mine. What credit shall I take to myself for coming to place and
> some little fame? Everything has been with me: the chance of
> inheritance, the glory of a cause as hopeless as splendid, and more
> splendid because hopeless; and the luck of him who loads the dice—

*for all my old comrades, the better men, are dead, and I, the least of them all, remain, having even outlived the cause. What praise shall I take for this? None—from all decent fellows of the earth, none at all. It is merely laughable that I should be left, the monument of a sacred loyalty greater than the world has ever known.*

*I have no claims—But let me draw the picture, dear Chevalier. Here was a discredited, dissolute fellow whose life was worth a pin to nobody. Tired of the husks and the swine, and all his follies grown stale by over-use, he takes the advice of a good gentleman, and joins the standard of work and sacrifice. What greater luxury shall man ask? If this be not running the full scale of life's enjoyment, pray you what is? The world loves contrasts. The deep-dyed sinner raising the standard of piety is picturesque. If, charmed by his own new virtues, he is constant in his enthusiasm, behold a St. Augustine! Everything is with the returned prodigal—the more so if he be of the notorious Vaufontaines, who were ever saints turned sinners, or sinners turned saints.*

*Tell me, my good friend, where is room for pride in me? I am getting far more out of life than I deserve; it is not well that you and others should think better of me than I do of myself. I do not pretend that I dislike it, it is as balm to me. But it would seem that the world is monstrously unjust. One day when I'm grown old—I*

*cannot imagine what else Fate has spared me for—I shall write the Diary of a Sinner, the whole truth. I shall tell how when my peasant fighters were kneeling round me praying for success, even thanking God for me, I was smiling in my glove—in scorn of myself,*

*not of them, Chevalier, no,—no, not of them! The peasant's is the true greatness. Everything is with the aristocrat; he has to kick the great chances from his path; but the peasant must go hunting them in peril. Hardly snatching sustenance from Fate, the peasant*

*fights into greatness; the aristocrat may only win to it by*
*rejecting Fate's luxuries. The peasant never escapes the austere*
*teaching of hard experience, the aristocrat the languor of good*
*fortune. There is the peasant and there am I. Voila! enough of*
*Detricand of Vaufontaine.... The Princess Guida and the*
*child, are they—*

So the letter ran, and the Chevalier read it aloud to Guida up to the point where her name was writ. Afterwards Guida would sit and think of what Detricand had said, and of the honesty of nature that never allowed him to deceive himself. It pleased her also to think she had in some small way helped a man to the rehabilitation of his life. He had said that she had helped him, and she believed him; he had proved the soundness of his aims and ambitions; his career was in the world's mouth.

The one letter the Chevalier did not read to Guida referred to Philip. In it Detricand begged the Chevalier to hold himself in readiness to proceed at a day's notice to Paris.

So it was that when, after months of waiting, the Chevalier suddenly left St. Heliers to join Detricand, Guida did not know the object of his journey. All she knew was that he had leave from the Directory to visit Paris. Imagining this to mean some good fortune for him, with a light heart she sent him off in charge of Jean Touzel, who took him to St. Malo in the Hardi Biaou, and saw him safely into the hands of an escort from Detricand.

# CHAPTER XLII

Three days later there was opened in one of the chambers of the Emperor's palace at Vienna a Congress of four nations—Prussia, Russia, Austria, and Sardinia. Detricand's labours had achieved this result at last. Grandjon-Larisse, his old enemy in battle, now his personal friend and colleague in this business, had influenced Napoleon, and the Directory through him, to respect the neutrality of the duchy of Bercy, for which the four nations of this Congress declared. Philip himself little knew whose hand had secured the neutrality until summoned to appear at the Congress, to defend his rights to the title and the duchy against those of Detricand Prince of Vaufontaine. Had he known that Detricand was behind it all he would have fought on to the last gasp of power and died on the battle-field. He realised now that such a fate was not for him—that he must fight, not on the field of battle like a prince, but in a Court of Nations like a doubtful claimant of sovereign honours.

His whole story had become known in the duchy, and though it begot no feeling against him in war-time, now that Bercy was in a neutral zone of peace there was much talk of the wrongs of Guida and the Countess Chantavoine. He became moody and saturnine, and saw few of his subjects save the old Governor-General and his whilom enemy, now his friend, Count Carignan Damour. That at last he should choose to accompany him to Vienna the man who had been his foe during the lifetime of the old Duke, seemed incomprehensible. Yet, to all appearance, Damour was now Philip's zealous adherent. He came frankly repenting his old enmity, and though Philip did not quite believe him, some perverse temper, some obliquity of vision which overtakes the ablest minds at times, made him almost eagerly accept his new partisan. One thing Philip knew: Damour had no love for Detricand, who indeed had lately sent him word that for his work in sending Fouche's men to attempt his capture in Bercy, he would have him shot, if the Court of Nations upheld his rights to the duchy. Damour was able, even if Damour was not honest. Damour, the able, the implacable and malignant, should accompany him to Vienna.

The opening ceremony of the Congress was simple, but it was made notable by the presence of the Emperor of Austria, who addressed a few words of welcome to the envoys, to Philip, and, very pointedly, to the representative of the French Nation, the aged Duc de Mauban, who, while taking no active part in the Congress, was present by request of the Directory. The Duke's long residence in Vienna and freedom from share in the civil war in France had been factors in the choice of him when the name was submitted to the Directory by General Grandjon-Larisse, upon whom in turn it had been urged by Detricand.

The Duc de Mauban was the most marked figure of the Court, the Emperor not excepted. Clean shaven, with snowy linen and lace, his own natural hair, silver white, tied in a queue behind, he had large eloquent wondering eyes that seemed always looking, looking beyond the thing he saw. At first sight of him at his court, the Emperor had said: "The stars have frightened him." No fanciful supposition, for the Duc de Mauban was as well known an astronomer as student of history and philanthropist.

When the Emperor mentioned de Mauban's name Philip wondered where he had heard it before. Something in the sound of it was associated with his past, he knew not how. He had a curious feeling too that those deliberate, searching dark eyes saw the end of this fight, this battle of the strong. The face fascinated him, though it awed him. He admired it, even as he detested the ardent strength of Detricand's face, where the wrinkles of dissipation had given way to the bronzed carven look of the war-beaten soldier.

It was fair battle between these two, and there was enough hatred in the heart of each to make the fight deadly. He knew—and he had known since that day, years ago, in the Place du Vier Prison—that Detricand loved the girl whom he himself had married and dishonoured. He felt also that Detricand was making this claim to the duchy more out of vengeance than from desire to secure the title for himself. He read the whole deep scheme: how Detricand had laid his mine at every Court in Europe to bring him to this pass.

For hours Philip's witnesses were examined, among them the officers of his duchy and Count Carignan Damour. The physician of the old Duke of Bercy was examined, and the evidence was with Philip. The testimony of Dalbarade, the French ex-Minister of Marine, was read and considered. Philip's story up to the point of the formal signature by the old Duke was straightforward and clear. So far the Court was in his favour.

Detricand, as natural heir of the duchy, combated each step in the proceedings from the stand-point of legality, of the Duke's fatuity concerning Philip, and his personal hatred of the House of Vaufontaine. On the third day, when the Congress would give its decision, Detricand brought the Chevalier to the palace. At the opening of the sitting he requested that Damour be examined again. The Count was asked what question had been put to Philip immediately before the deeds of inheritance were signed. It was useless for Damour to evade the point, for there were other officers of the duchy present who could have told the truth. Yet this truth, of itself, need not ruin Philip. It was no phenomenon for a prince to have one wife unknown, and, coming to the throne, to take to himself another more exalted.

Detricand was hoping that the nice legal sense of mine and thine should be suddenly weighted in his favour by a prepared tour de force. The sympathies of the Congress were largely with himself, for he was of the order of the nobility, and Philip's descent must be traced through centuries of yeoman blood; yet there was the deliberate adoption by the Duke to face, with the formal assent of the States of Bercy, but little lessened in value by the fact that the French Government had sent its emissaries to Bercy to protest against it. The Court had come to a point where decision upon the exact legal merits of the case was difficult.

After Damour had testified to the question the Duke asked Philip when signing the deeds at Bercy, Detricand begged leave to introduce another witness, and brought in the Chevalier. Now he made his great appeal. Simply, powerfully, he told the story of Philip's secret marriage with Guida, and of all that came after, up to the scene in the Cohue Royale when the marriage was proved and the child given back to Guida; when the Countess Chantavoine, turning from Philip, acknowledged to Guida the justice of her claim. He drove home the truth with bare unvarnished power—the wrong to Guida, the wrong to the Countess, the wrong to the Dukedom of Bercy, to that honour which should belong to those in high estate. Then at the last he told them who Guida was: no peasant girl, but the granddaughter of the Sieur Larchant de Mauprat of de Mauprats of Chambery: the granddaughter of an exile indeed, but of the noblest blood of France.

The old Duc de Mauban fixed his look on him intently, and as the story proceeded his hand grasped the table before him in strong emotion. When at last Detricand turned to the Chevalier and asked him to bear witness to the truth of what he had said, the Duke, in agitation, whispered to the President.

All that Detricand had said moved the Court powerfully, but when the withered little flower of a man, the Chevalier, told in quaint brief sentences the story of the Sieur de Mauprat, his sufferings, his exile, and the nobility of his family, which had indeed, far back, come of royal stock, and then at last of Guida and the child, more than one member of the Court turned his head away with misty eyes.

It remained for the Duc de Mauban to speak the word which hastened and compelled the end. Rising in his place, he addressed to the Court a few words of apology, inasmuch as he was without real power there, and then he turned to the Chevalier.

"Monsieur le chevalier," said he, "I had the honour to know you in somewhat better days for both of us. You will allow me to greet you here with my profound respect. The Sieur Larchant de Mauprat"—he turned to the President, his voice became louder—"the Sieur de Mauprat was my friend. He was with me upon the day I married the Duchess Guidabaldine. Trouble, exile came to him. Years passed, and at last in Jersey I saw him again. It was the very day his grandchild was born. The name given to her was Guidabaldine—the name of the Duchese de Mauban. She was Guidabaldine Landresse de Landresse, she is my godchild. There is no better blood in France than that of the de Mauprats of Chambery, and the grandchild of my friend, her father being also of good Norman blood, was worthy to be the wife of any prince in Europe. I speak in the name of our order, I speak for Frenchmen, I speak for France. If Detricand, Prince of Vaufontaine, be not secured in his right of succession to the dukedom of Bercy, France will not cease to protest till protest hath done its work. From France the duchy of Bercy came. It was the gift of a French king to a Frenchman, and she hath some claims upon the courtesy of the nations."

For a moment after he took his seat there was absolute silence. Then the President wrote upon a paper before him, and it was passed to each member of the Court sitting with him. For a moment longer there was nothing heard save the scratching of a quill. Philip recalled that day at Bercy when the Duke stooped and signed his name upon the deed of adoption and succession three times-three fateful times.

At last the President, rising in his place, read the pronouncement of the Court: that Detricand, Prince of Vaufontaine, be declared true inheritor of the duchy of Bercy, the nations represented here confirming him in his title.

The President having spoken, Philip rose, and, bowing to the Congress with dignity and composure, left the chamber with Count Carignan Damour.

As he passed from the portico into the grounds of the palace, a figure came suddenly from behind a pillar and touched him on the arm. He turned quickly, and received upon the face a blow from a glove.

The owner of the glove was General Grandjon-Larisse.

# CHAPTER XLIII

**"You understand, monsieur?" said Grandjon-Larisse.**

"Perfectly—and without the glove, monsieur le general," answered Philip quietly. "Where shall my seconds wait upon you?" As he spoke he turned with a slight gesture towards Damour.

"In Paris, monsieur, if it please you."

"I should have preferred it here, monsieur le general—but Paris, if it is your choice."

"At 22, Rue de Mazarin, monsieur." Then he made an elaborate bow to Philip. "I bid you good-day, monsieur."

"Monseigneur, not monsieur," Philip corrected. "They may deprive me of my duchy, but I am still Prince Philip d'Avranche. I may not be robbed of my adoption."

There was something so steady, so infrangible in Philip's composure now, that Grandjon-Larisse, who had come to challenge a great adventurer, a marauder of honour, found his furious contempt checked by some integral power resisting disdain. He intended to kill Philip—he was one of the most expert swordsmen in France—yet he was constrained to respect a composure not sangfroid and a firmness in misfortune not bravado. Philip was still the man who had valiantly commanded men; who had held of the high places of the earth. In whatever adventurous blood his purposes had been conceived, or his doubtful plans accomplished, he was still, stripped of power, a man to be reckoned with: resolute in his course once set upon, and impulsive towards good as towards evil. He was never so much worth respect as when, a dispossessed sovereign with an empty title, discountenanced by his order, disbarred his profession, he held himself ready to take whatever penalty now came.

In the presence of General Grandjon-Larisse, with whom was the might of righteous vengeance, he was the more distinguished figure. To Philip now there came the cold quiet of the sinner, great enough to rise above physical fear, proud enough to say to the world: "Come, I pay the debt I owe. We are quits. You have no favours to give, and I none to take. You have no pardon to grant, and I none to ask."

At parting Grandjon-Larisse bowed to Philip with great politeness, and said: "In Paris then, monsieur le prince."

Philip bowed his head in assent.

When they met again, it was at the entrance to the Bois de Boulogne near the Maillot gate.

It was a damp grey morning immediately before sunrise, and at first there was scarce light enough for the combatants to see each other perfectly, but both were eager and would not delay.

As they came on guard the sun rose. Philip, where he stood, was full in its light. He took no heed, and they engaged at once. After a few passes Grandjon-Larisse said: "You are in the light, monseigneur; the sun shines full upon you," and he pointed to the shade of a wall near by. "It is darker there."

"One of us must certainly be in the dark-soon," answered Philip grimly, but he removed to the wall. From the first Philip took the offensive. He was more active, and he was quicker and lighter of fence than his antagonist. But Grandjon-Larisse had the surer eye, and was invincibly certain of hand and strong of wrist. At length Philip wounded his opponent slightly in the left breast, and the seconds came forward to declare that honour was satisfied. But neither would listen or heed; their purpose was fixed to fight to the death. They engaged again, and almost at once the Frenchman was slightly wounded in the wrist. Suddenly taking the offensive and lunging freely, Grandjon-Larisse drove Philip, now heated and less wary, backwards upon the wall. At last, by a dexterous feint, he beat aside Philip's guard and drove the sword through his right breast at one fierce lunge.

With a moan Philip swayed and fell forward into the arms of Damour, still grasping his weapon. Grandjon-Larisse stooped to the injured man. Unloosing his fingers from the sword, Philip stretched up a hand to his enemy.

"I am hurt to death," he said. "Permit my compliments to the best swordsman I have ever known." Then with a touch of sorry humour he added: "You cannot doubt their sincerity."

Grandjon-Larisse was turning away when Philip called him back. "Will you carry my profound regret to the Countess Chantavoine?" he whispered. "Say that it lies with her whether Heaven pardon me."

Grandjon-Larisse hesitated an instant, then answered:

"Those who are in heaven, monseigneur, know best what Heaven may do."

Philip's pale face took on a look of agony. "She is dead—she is dead!" he gasped.

Grandjon-Larisse inclined his head, then after a moment, gravely said:

"What did you think was left for a woman—for a Chantavoine? It is not the broken heart that kills, but broken pride, monseigneur."

So saying, he bowed again to Philip and turned upon his heel.

# CHAPTER XLIV

Philip lay on a bed in the unostentatious lodging in the Rue de Vaugirard where Damour had brought him. The surgeon had pronounced the wound mortal, giving him but a few hours to live. For long after he was gone Philip was silent, but at length he said "You heard what Grandjon-Larisse said—It is broken pride that kills, Damour." Then he asked for pen, ink, and paper. They were brought to him. He tried the pen upon the paper, but faintness suddenly seized him, and he fell back unconscious.

When he came to himself he was alone in the room. It was cold and cheerless—no fire on the hearth, no light save that flaring from a lamp in the street outside his window. He rang the bell at his hand. No one answered. He called aloud: "Damour! Damour!"

Damour was far beyond earshot. He had bethought him that now his place was in Bercy, where he might gather up what fragments of good fortune remained, what of Philip's valuables might be secured. Ere he had fallen back insensible, Philip, in trying the pen, had written his own name on a piece of paper. Above this Damour wrote for himself an order upon the chamberlain of Bercy to enter upon Philip's private apartments in the castle; and thither he was fleeing as Philip lay dying in the dark room of the house in the Rue de Vaugirard.

The woman of the house, to whose care Philip was passed over by Damour, had tired of watching, and had gone to spend one of his gold pieces for supper with her friends.

Meanwhile in the dark comfortless room, the light from without flickering upon his blanched face, Philip was alone with himself, with memory, and with death. As he lay gasping, a voice seemed to ring through the silent room, repeating the same words again and again—and the voice was his own voice. It was himself—some other outside self of him—saying, in tireless repetition: "May I die a black, dishonourable death, abandoned and alone, if ever I deceive you. I should deserve that if I deceived you, Guida!... " "A black, dishonourable death, abandoned and alone": it was like some horrible dirge chanting in his ear.

Pictures flashed before his eyes, strange imaginings. Now he was passing through dark corridors, and the stone floor beneath was cold—so cold! He was going to some gruesome death, and monks with voices like his own voice were intoning: "Abandoned and alone. Alone—alone—abandoned and alone."... And now he was fighting, fighting on board the Araminta. There was the roar of the great guns, the screaming of the carronade slides, the rattle of musketry, the groans of the dying, the shouts of his victorious sailors, the crash of the main-mast as it fell upon the bulwarks. Then the swift sissing ripple of water, the thud of the Araminta as she struck, and the cold chill of the seas as she went down. How cold was the sea—ah, how it chilled every nerve and tissue of his body!

He roused to consciousness again. Here was still the blank cheerless room, the empty house, the lamplight flaring through the window upon his stricken face, upon the dark walls, upon the white paper lying on the table beside him.

Paper—that was it—he must write, he must write while he had strength. With the last courageous effort of life, his strenuous will forcing the declining powers into obedience for a final combat, he drew the paper near, and began to write. The light flickered, wavered, he could just see the letters that he formed—no more.

> Guida [he began], on the Ecrehos I said to you: "If I deceive you
> may I die a black, dishonourable death, abandoned and alone!" It
> has all come true. You were right, always right, and I was always
> wrong. I never started fair with myself or with the world. I was
> always in too great a hurry; I was too ambitious, Guida. Ambition
> has killed me, and it has killed her—the Comtesse. She is gone.
> What was it he said—if I could but remember what Grandjon-Larisse
> said—ah yes, yes!—after he had given me my death-wound, he said:
> "It is not the broken heart that kills, but broken pride." There is
> the truth. She is in her grave, and I am going out into the dark.

He lay back exhausted for a moment, in desperate estate. The body was fighting hard that the spirit might confess itself before the vital spark died down for ever. Seizing a glass of cordial near, he drank of it. The broken figure in its mortal defeat roused itself again, leaned over the paper, and a shaking hand traced on the brief piteous record of a life.

> I climbed too fast. Things dazzled me. I thought too much of
> myself—myself, myself was everything always; and myself has
> killed

*me. In wanton haste I came to be admiral and sovereign duke, and it has all come to nothing—nothing. I wronged you, I denied you, there was the cause of all. There is no one to watch with me now to the one moment of life that counts. In this hour the clock of time fills all the space between earth and heaven. It will strike soon— the awful clock. It will soon strike twelve: and then it will be twelve of the clock for me always—always.*

*I know you never wanted revenge on me, Guida, but still you have it here. My life is no more now than vraic upon a rock. I cling, I cling, but that is all, and the waves break over me. I am no longer an admiral, I am no more a duke—I am nothing. It is all done. Of no account with men I am going to my judgment with God. But you remain, and you are Princess Philip d'Avranche, and your son—your son—will be Prince Guilbert d'Avranche. But I can leave him naught, neither estates nor power. There is little honour in the title now. So it may be you will not use it. But you will have a new life: with my death happiness may begin again for you. That thought makes death easier. I was never worthy of you, never. I understand myself now, and I know that you have read me all these years, read me through and through. The letter you wrote me, never a day or night has passed but, one way or another, it has come home to me.*

There was a footfall outside his window. A roysterer went by in the light of the flaring lamp. He was singing a ribald song. A dog ran barking at his heels. The reveller turned, drew his sword, and ran the dog through, then staggered on with his song. Philip shuddered, and with a supreme effort bent to the table again, and wrote on.

*You were right: you were my star, and I was so blind with selfishness and vanity I could not see. I am speaking the truth to you now, Guida. I believe I might have been a great man if I had thought less of myself and more of others, more of you. Greatness, I was mad for that, and my madness has brought me to this desolate end—alone. Go tell Maitresse Aimable that she too was a good prophet. Tell her that, as she foresaw, I called your name in*

*death, and you did not come. One thing before all: teach your boy
never to try to be great, but always to live well and to be just.
Teach him too that the world means better by him than he thinks, and
that he must never treat it as his foe; he must not try to force its
benefits and rewards. He must not approach it like the highwayman.
Tell him never to flatter. That is the worst fault in a gentleman,
for flattery makes false friends and the flatterer himself false.
Tell him that good address is for ease and courtesy of life, but it
must not be used to one's secret advantage as I have used mine to
mortal undoing. If ever Guilbert be in great temptation, tell him
his father's story, and read him these words to you, written, as you
see, with the cramped fingers of death.*

He could scarcely hold the pen now, and his eyes were growing dim.

*... I am come to the end of my strength. I thought I loved
you, Guida, but I know now that it was not love—not real love. Yet
it was all a twisted manhood had to give. There are some things of
mine that you will keep for your son, if you forgive me dead whom
you despised living. Detricand Duke of Bercy will deal honourably
by you. All that is mine at the Castle of Bercy he will secure to
you. Tell him I have written it so; though he will do it of
himself, I know. He is a great man. As I have gone downwards he
has come upwards. There has been a star in his sky too. I know it,
I know it, Guida, and he—he is not blind. The light is going, I
cannot see. I can only—*

He struggled fiercely for breath, but suddenly collapsed upon the table,
and his head fell forward upon the paper; one cheek lying in the wet ink of
his last written words, the other, cold and stark, turned to the window. The
light from the lamp without flickered on it in gruesome sportiveness. The
eyes stared and stared from the little dark room out into the world. But they
did not see.

The night wore on. At last came a knocking, knocking at the door-
tap! tap! tap! But he did not hear. A moment of silence, and again came a
knocking—knocking—knocking...!

# CHAPTER XLV

The white and red flag of Jersey was flying half-mast from the Cohue Royale, and the bell of the parish church was tolling. It was Saturday, but little business was being done in the Vier Marchi. Chattering people were gathered at familiar points, and at the foot of La Pyramide a large group surrounded two sailor-men just come from Gaspe, bringing news of adventuring Jersiais—Elie Mattingley, Carterette and Ranulph Delagarde. This audience quickly grew, for word was being passed on from one little group to another. So keen was interest in the story told by the home-coming sailors, that the great event which had brought them to the Vier Marchi was, for the moment, almost neglected.

Presently, however, a cannon-shot, then another, and another, roused the people to remembrance. The funeral cortege of Admiral Prince Philip d'Avranche was about to leave the Cohue Royale, and every eye was turned to the marines and sailors lining the road from the court-house to the church.

The Isle of Jersey, ever stubbornly loyal to its own—even those whom the outside world contemned or cast aside—jealous of its dignity even with the dead, had come to bury Philip d'Avranche with all good ceremony. There had been abatements to his honour, but he had been a strong man and he had done strong things, and he was a Jerseyman born, a Norman of the Normans. The Royal Court had judged between him and Guida, doing tardy justice to her, but of him they had ever been proud; and where conscience condemned here, vanity commended there. In any event they reserved the right, independent of all non-Jersiais, to do what they chose with their dead.

For what Philip had been as an admiral they would do his body reverence now; for what he had done as a man, that belonged to another tribunal. It had been proposed by the Admiral of the station to bury him from his old ship, the Imperturbable, but the Royal Court made its claim, and so his body had lain in state in the Cohue Royale. The Admiral joined hands with the island authorities. In both cases it was a dogged loyalty. The sailors of England knew Philip d'Avranche as a fighter, even as the Royal Court knew him as a famous and dominant Jerseyman. A battle-ship is a world of its own, and Jersey is a world of its own. They neither knew nor cared for the comment of the world without; or, knowing, refused to consider it.

When the body of Philip was carried from the Cohue Royale signals were made to the Imperturbable in the tide-way. From all her ships in company forty guns were fired funeral-wise and the flags were struck halfmast.

Slowly the cortege uncoiled itself to one long unbroken line from the steps of the Cohue Royale to the porch of the church. The Jurats in their red robes, the officers, sailors, and marines, added colour to the pageant. The coffin was covered by the flag of Jersey with the arms of William the Conqueror in the canton. Of the crowd some were curious, some stoical; some wept, some essayed philosophy.

"Et ben," said one, "he was a brave admiral!"

"Bravery was his trade," answered another: "act like a sheep and you'll be eaten by the wolf."

"It was a bad business about her that was Guida Landresse," remarked a third.

"Every man knows himself, God knows all men," snuffled the fanatical barber who had once delivered a sermon from the Pompe des Brigands.

"He made things lively while he lived, ba su!" droned the jailer of the Vier Prison. "But he has folded sails now."

"Ma fe, yes, he sleeps like a porpoise now, and white as a wax he looked up there in the Cohue Royale," put in a centenier standing by.

A voice came shrilly over the head of the centenier. "As white as you'll look yellow one day, bat'd'lagoule! Yellow and green, oui-gia—yellow like a bad apple, and cowardly green as a leek." This was Manon Moignard the witch.

"Man doux d'la vie, where's the Master of Burials?" babbled the jailer. "The apprentice does the obs'quies to-day."

"The Master's sick of a squinzy," grunted the centenier. "So hatchet-face and bundle-o'-nails there brings dust to dust, amen."

All turned now to the Undertaker's Apprentice, a grim, saturnine figure with his grey face, protuberant eyes, and obsequious solemnity, in which lurked a callous smile. The burial of the great, the execution of the wicked, were alike to him. In him Fate seemed to personify life's revenges, its futilities, its calculating ironies. The flag-draped coffin was just about to pass, and the fanatical barber harked back to Philip. "They say it was all empty honours with him afore he died abroad."

"A full belly's a full belly if it's only full of straw," snapped Manon Moignard.

"Who was it brought him home?" asked the jailer. "None that was born on Jersey, but two that lived here," remarked Maitre Damian, the schoolmaster from St. Aubins.

"That Chevalier of Champsavoys and the other Duc de Bercy," interposed the centenier.

Maitre Damian tapped his stick upon the ground, and said oracularly: "It is not for me to say, but which is the rightful Duke and which is not, there is the political question!"

"Pardi, that's it," answered the centenier. "Why did Detricand Duke turn Philip Duke out of duchy, see him killed, then fetch him home to Jersey like a brother? Ah, man pethe benin, that's beyond me!"

"Those great folks does things their own ways; oui-gia," remarked the jailer.

"Why did Detricand Duke go back to France?" asked Maitre Damian, cocking his head wisely; "why did he not stay for obsequies—he?"

"That's what I say," answered the jailer, "those great folks does things their own ways."

"Ma fistre, I believe you," ejaculated the centenier. "But for the Chevalier there, for a Frenchman, that is a man after God's own heart—and mine."

"Ah then, look at that," said Manon Moignard, with a sneer, "when one pleases you and God it is a ticket to heaven, diantre!"

But in truth what Detricand and the Chevalier had done was but of human pity. The day after the duel, Detricand had arrived in Paris to proceed thence to Bercy. There he heard of Philip's death and of Damour's desertion. Sending officers to Bercy to frustrate any possible designs of Damour, he, with the Chevalier, took Philip's body back to Jersey, delivering it to those who would do it honour.

Detricand did not see Guida. For all that might be said to her now the Chevalier should be his mouthpiece. In truth there could be no better mouthpiece for him. It was Detricand—Detricand—Detricand, like a child, in admiration and in affection. If Guida did not understand all now, there should come a time when she would understand. Detricand would wait. She should find that he was just, that her honour and the honour of her child were safe with him.

As for Guida, it was not grief she felt in the presence of this tragedy. No spark of love sprang up, even when remembrance was now brought to its last vital moment. But a fathomless pity stirred her heart, that Philip's life had been so futile and that all he had done was come to naught. His letter, blotched and blotted by his own dead cheek, she read quietly. Yet her heart ached bitterly—so bitterly that her face became pinched with pain; for here in this letter was despair, here was the final agony of a broken life, here were the last words of the father of her child to herself. She saw with a sudden pang that in writing of Guilbert he only said your child, not ours. What a measureless distance there was between them in the hour of his death, and how clearly the letter showed that he understood at last!

The evening before the burial she went with the Chevalier to the Cohue Royale. As she looked at Philip's dead face bitterness and aching compassion were quieted within her. The face was peaceful—strong. There was on it no record of fret or despair. Its impassive dignity seemed to say that all accounts had been settled, and in this finality there was quiet; as though he had paid the price, as though the long account against him in the markets of life was closed and cancelled, and the debtor freed from obligation for ever. Poignant impulses in her stilled, pity lost its wounding acuteness. She shed no tears, but at last she stretched out her hand and let it rest upon his forehead for a moment.

"Poor Philip!" she said.

Then she turned and slowly left the room, followed by the Chevalier, and by the noiseless Dormy Jamais, who had crept in behind them. As Dormy Jamais closed the door, he looked back to where the coffin lay, and in the compassion of fools he repeated Guida's words:

"Poor Philip!" he said.

Now, during Philip's burial, Dormy Jamais sat upon the roof of the Cohue Royale, as he had done on the day of the Battle of Jersey, looking down on the funeral cortege and the crowd. He watched it all until the ruffle of drums at the grave told that the body was being lowered—four ruffles for an admiral.

As the people began to disperse and the church bell ceased tolling, Dormy turned to another bell at his elbow, and set it ringing to call the Royal Court together. Sharp, mirthless, and acrid it rang:

Chicane—chicane! Chicane—chicane! Chicane—chicane!

# IN JERSEY-A YEAR LATER

## CHAPTER XLVI

"What is that for?" asked the child, pointing. Detricand put the watch to the child's ear. "It's to keep time. Listen. Do you hear it-tic-tic, tic-tic?"'

The child nodded his head gleefully, and his big eyes blinked with understanding. "Doesn't it ever stop?" he asked.

"This watch never stops," replied Detricand. "But there are plenty of watches that do."

"I like watches," said the child sententiously.

"Would you like this one?" asked Detricand.

The child drew in a gurgling breath of pleasure. "I like it. Why doesn't mother have a watch?"

The man did not answer the last question. "You like it?" he said again, and he nodded his head towards the little fellow. "H'm, it keeps good time, excellent time it keeps," and he rose to meet the child's mother, who having just entered the room, stood looking at them. It was Guida. She had heard the last words, and she glanced towards the watch curiously. Detricand smiled in greeting, and said to her: "Do you remember it?" He held up the watch.

She came forward eagerly. "Is it—is it that indeed, the watch that the dear grandpethe—?"

He nodded and smiled. "Yes, it has never once stopped since the moment he gave it me in the Vier-Marchi seven years ago. It has had a charmed existence amid many rough doings and accidents. I was always afraid of losing it, always afraid of an accident to it. It has seemed to me that if I could keep it things would go right with me, and things come out right in the end. Superstition, of course, but I lived a long time in Jersey. I feel more a Jerseyman than a Frenchman sometimes."

Although his look seemed to rest but casually on her face, it was evident he was anxious to feel the effect of every word upon her, and he added:

"When the Sieur de Mauprat gave me the watch he said, 'May no time be ill spent that it records for you.'"

"Perhaps he knows his wish was fulfilled," answered Guida.

"You think, then, that I've kept my promise?"

"I am sure he would say so," she replied warmly.

"It isn't the promise I made to him that I mean, but the promise I made to you."

She smiled brightly. "You know what I think of that. I told you long ago." She turned her head away, for a bright colour had come to her cheek. "You have done great things, Prince," she added in a low tone.

He flashed a look of inquiry at her. To his ear there was in her voice a little touch—not of bitterness, but of something, as it were, muffled or reserved. Was she thinking how he had robbed her child of the chance of heritage at Bercy? He did not reply, but, stooping, put the watch again to the child's ear. "There you are, monseigneur!"

"Why do you call him monseigneur?" she asked. "Guilbert has no title to your compliment."

A look half-amused, half-perplexed, crossed over Detricand's face. "Do you think so?" he said musingly. Stooping once more, he said to the child: "Would you like the watch?" and added quickly, "you shall have it when you're grown up."

"Do you really mean it?" asked Guida, delighted; "do you really mean to give him the grandpethe's watch one day?"

"Oh yes, at least that—one day. But I have something more," he added quickly—"something more for you;" and he drew from his pocket a miniature set in rubies and diamonds. "I have brought you this from the Duc de Mauban—and this," he went on, taking a letter from his pocket, and handing it with the gift. "The Duke thought you might care to have it. It is the face of your godmother, the Duchess Guidabaldine."

Guida looked at the miniature earnestly, and then said a little wistfully: "How beautiful a face—but the jewels are much too fine for me! What should one do here with rubies and diamonds? How can I thank the Duke!"

"Not so. He will thank you for accepting it. He begged me to say—as you will find by his letter to you—that if you will but go to him upon a visit with this great man here"—pointing to the child with a smile—"he will count it one of the greatest pleasures of his life. He is too old to come to you, but he begs you to go to him—the Chevalier, and you, and Guilbert here. He is much alone now, and he longs for a little of that friendship which can be given by but few in this world. He counts upon your coming, for I said I thought you would."

"It would seem so strange," she answered, "to go from this cottage of my childhood, to which I have come back in peace at last—from this kitchen, to the chateau of the Duc de Mauban."

"But it was sure to come," he answered. "This kitchen to which I come also to redeem my pledge after seven years, it belongs to one part of your life. But there is another part to fulfil,"—he stooped and passed his hands over the curls of the child, "and for your child here you should do it."

"I do not find your meaning," she said after a moment's deliberation. "I do not know what you would have me understand."

"In some ways you and I would be happier in simple surroundings," he replied gravely, "but it would seem that to play duly our part in the world, we must needs move in wider circles. To my mind this kitchen is the most delightful spot in the world. Here I took a fresh commission of life. I went out, a sort of battered remnant, to a forlorn hope; and now I come back to headquarters once again—not to be praised," he added in an ironical tone, and with a quick gesture of almost boyish shyness—"not to be praised; only to show that from a grain of decency left in a man may grow up some sheaves of honest work and plain duty."

"No, it is much more than that, it is much, much more than that," she broke in.

"No, I am afraid it is not," he answered; "but that is not what I wished to say. I wished to say that for monseigneur here—"

A little flash of anger came into her eyes. "He is no monseigneur, he is Guilbert d'Avranche," she said bitterly. "It is not like you to mock my child, Prince. Oh, I know you mean it playfully," she hurriedly added, "but—but it does not sound right to me."

"For the sake of monseigneur the heir to the duchy of Bercy," he added, laying his hand upon the child's head, "these things your devout friends suggest, you should do, Princess."

Her clear unwavering eye looked steadfastly at him, but her face turned pale.

"Why do you call him monseigneur the heir to the duchy of Bercy?" she said almost coldly, and with a little fear in her look too.

"Because I have come here to tell you the truth, and to place in your hands the record of an act of justice."

Drawing from his pocket a parchment gorgeous with seals, he stooped, and taking the hands of the child, he placed it in them. "Hold it tight, hold it tight, my little friend, for it is your very own," he said to the child with cheerful kindliness. Then stepping back a little, and looking earnestly at Guida, he added with a motion of the hand towards the child:

"You must learn the truth from him."

"Oh, what can you mean—what can you mean?" she exclaimed. Dropping upon her knees, and running an arm round the child, she opened the parchment and read.

"What—what right has he to this?" she cried in a voice of dismay. "A year ago you dispossessed his father from the duchy. Ah, I do not understand it! You—only you are the Duc de Bercy."

Her eyes were shining with a happy excitement and tenderness. No such look had been in them for many a day. Something that had long slept was waking in her, something long voiceless was speaking. This man brought back to her heart a glow she had never thought to feel again, the glow of the wonder of life and of a girlish faith.

"I am only Detricand of Vaufontaine," he answered. "What, did you— could you think that I would dispossess your child? His father was the adopted son of the Duc de Bercy. Nothing could wipe that out, neither law nor nations. You are always Princess Guida, and your child is always Prince Guilbert d'Avranche—and more than that."

His voice became lower, his war-beaten face lighted with that fire and force which had made him during years past a figure in the war records of Europe.

"I unseated Philip d'Avranche," he continued, "because he acquired the duchy through—a misapprehension; because the claims of the House of Vaufontaine were greater. We belonged; he was an alien. He had a right to his adoption, he had no right to his duchy—no real right in the equity of nations. But all the time I never forgot that the wife of Philip d'Avranche and her child had rights infinitely beyond his own. All that he achieved was theirs by every principle of justice. My plain duty was to win for your child that succession belonging to him by all moral right. When Philip d'Avranche was killed, I set to work to do for your child what had been done by another for Philip d'Avranche. I have made him my heir. When he is of age I shall abdicate from the duchy in his favour. This deed, countersigned by the Powers that dispossessed his father, secures to him the duchy when he is old enough to govern."

Guida had listened like one in a dream. A hundred feelings possessed her, and one more than all. She suddenly saw all Detricand's goodness to her stretch out in a long line of devoted friendship, from this day to that far-off hour seven years before, when he had made a vow to her—kept how nobly! Devoted friendship—was it devoted friendship alone, even with herself? In a tumult of emotions she answered him hurriedly. "No, no, no, no! I cannot accept it. This is not justice, this is a gift for which there is no example in the world's history."

"I thought it best," he went on quietly, "to govern Bercy myself during these troubled years. So far its neutrality has been honoured, but who can tell what may come! As a Vaufontaine it is my duty to see that Bercy's interests are duly protected amidst the troubles of Europe."

Guida got to her feet now and stood looking dazedly at the parchment in her hand. The child, feeling himself neglected, ran out into the garden.

There was moisture in Guida's eyes as she presently said: "I had not thought that any man could be so noble—no, not even you."

"You should not doubt yourself so," he answered meaningly. "I am the work of your hands. If I have fought my way back to reputable life again—"

He paused, and took from his pocket a handkerchief. "This was the gage," he said, holding it up. "Do you remember the day I came to return it to you, and carried it off again?"

"It was foolish of you to keep it," she answered softly, "as foolish of you as to think that I shall accept for my child these great honours."

"But suppose the child in after years should blame you?" he answered slowly and with emphasis. "Suppose that Guilbert should say, What right had you, my mother, to refuse what was my due?"

This was the question she had asked herself long, long ago. It smote her heart now. What right had she to reject this gift of Fate to her child?

Scarcely above a whisper she replied: "Of course he might say that, but how, oh, how should we simple folk, he and I, be fitted for these high places—yet? Now that what I desired all these years for him has come, I have not the courage."

"You have friends to help you in all you do," he answered meaningly.

"But friends cannot always be with one," she answered.

"That depends upon the friends. There is one friend of yours who has known you for eighteen years. Eighteen years' growth should make a strong friendship—there was always friendship on his part at least. He can be a still stronger and better friend. He comes now to offer you the remainder of a life for which your own goodness is the guarantee. He comes to offer you a love of which your own soul must be the only judge, for you have eyes that see and a spirit that knows. The Chevalier needs you, and the Duc de Mauban needs you, but Detricand of Vaufontaine needs you a thousand times more."

"Oh, hush—but no, you must not!" she broke in, her face all crimson, her lips trembling.

"But yes, I must," he answered quickly. "You find peace here, but it is the peace of inaction. It dulls the brain, and life winds in upon itself wearily at the last. But out there is light and fire and action and the quick-beating pulse, and the joy of power wisely used, even to the end. You come of a great people, you were born to great things; your child has rights accorded now by every Court of Europe. You must act for him. For your child's sake, for my sake come out into the great field of life with me—as my wife, Guida."

She turned to him frankly, she looked at him steadfastly, the colour in her face came and went, but her eyes glowed with feeling.

"After all that has happened?" she asked in a low tone.

"It could only be because of all that has happened," he answered.

"No, no, you do not understand," she said quickly, a great pain in her voice. "I have suffered so, these many, many years! I shall never be light-hearted again. And I am not fitted for such high estate. Do you not see what you ask of me—to go from this cottage to a palace?"

"I love you too well to ask you to do what you could not. You must trust me," he answered, "you must give your life its chance, you must—"

"But listen to me," she interjected with breaking tones; "I know as surely as I know—as I know the face of my child, that the youth in me is dead. My summer came—and went—long ago. No, no, you do not understand—I would not make you unhappy. I must live only to make my child happy. That love has not been marred."

"And I must be judge of what is for my own happiness. And for yours— if I thought my love would make you unhappy for even one day, I should not offer it. I am your lover, but I am also your friend. Had it not been for you I might have slept in a drunkard's grave in Jersey. Were it not for you, my bones would now be lying in the Vendee. I left my peasants, I denied myself death with them to serve you. The old cause is gone. You and your child are now my only cause—"

"You make it so hard for me," she broke in. "Think of the shadows from the past always in my eyes, always in my heart—you cannot wear the convict's chain without the lagging footstep afterwards."

"Shadows—friend of my soul, how should I dare come to you if there had never been shadows in your life! It is because you—you have suffered, because you know, that I come. Out of your miseries, the convict's lagging step, you say? Think what I was. There was never any wrong in you, but I was sunk in evil depths of folly—"

"I will not have you say so," she interrupted; "you never in your life did a dishonourable thing."

"Then again I say, trust me. For, on the honour of a Vaufontaine, I believe that happiness will be yours as my wife. The boy, you see how he and I—"

"Ah, you are so good to him!"

"You must give me chance and right to serve him. What else have you or I to look forward to? The honours of this world concern us little. The brightest joys are not for us. We have work before us, no rainbow ambitions. But the boy—think for him—-" he paused.

After a little, she held out her hand towards him. "Good-bye," she said softly.

"Good-bye—you say good-bye to me!" he exclaimed in dismay.

"Till—till to-morrow," she answered, and she smiled. The smile had a little touch of the old archness which was hers as a child, yet, too, a little of the sadness belonging to the woman. But her hand-clasp was firm and strong; and her touch thrilled him. Power was there, power with infinite gentleness. And he understood her; which was more than all.

He turned at the door. She was standing very still, the parchment with the great seals yet in her hand. Without speaking, she held it out to him, as though uncertain what to do with it.

As he passed through the doorway he smiled, and said:

"To-morrow—to-morrow!"

# EPILOGUE

St. John's Eve had passed. In the fields at Bonne-Nuit Bay the "Brow-brow! ben-ben!" of the Song of the Cauldron had affrighted the night; riotous horns, shaming the blare of a Witches' Sabbath, had been blown by those who, as old Jean Touzel said, carried little lead under their noses. The meadows had been full of the childlike islanders welcoming in the longest day of the year. Mid-summer Day had also come and gone, but with less noise and clamour, for St. John's Fair had been carried on with an orderly gaiety—as the same Jean Touzel said, like a sheet of music. Even the French singers and dancers from St. Malo had been approved in Norman phrases by the Bailly and the Jurats, for now there was no longer war between England and France, Napoleon was at St. Helena, and the Bourbons were come again to their own.

It had been a great day, and the roads were cloudy with the dust of Mid-summer revellers going to their homes. But though some went many stayed, camping among the booths, since the Fair was for tomorrow and for other to-morrows after. And now, the day's sport being over, the superstitious were making the circle of the rock called William's Horse in Boulay Bay, singing the song of William, who, with the fabled sprig of sacred mistletoe, turned into a rock the kelpie horse carrying him to death.

There was one boat, however, which putting out into the Bay did not bear towards William's Horse, but, catching the easterly breeze, bore away westward towards the point of Plemont. Upon the stern of the boat was painted in bright colours, Hardi Biaou. "We'll be there soon after sunset," said the grizzled helmsman, Jean Touzel, as he glanced from the full sail to the setting sun.

Neither of his fellow-voyagers made reply, and for a time there was silence, save for the swish of the gunwale through the water. But at last Jean said:

"Su' m'n ame, but it is good this, after that!" and he jerked his head back towards the Fair-ground on the hill. "Even you will sleep to-night, Dormy Jamais, and you, my wife of all."

Maitresse Aimable shook her great head slowly on the vast shoulders, and shut her heavy eyelids. "Dame, but I think you are sleeping now—you," Jean went on.

Maitresse Aimable's eyes opened wide, and again she shook her head.

Jean looked a laugh at her through his great brass-rimmed spectacles and added:

"Ba su, then I know. It is because we go to sleep in my hut at Plemont where She live so long. I know, you never sleep there."

Maitresse Aimable shook her head once more, and drew from her pocket a letter.

At sight of it Dormy Jamais crawled quickly over to where the Femme de Ballast sat, and, 'reaching out, he touched it with both hands.

"Princess of all the world—bidemme," he said, and he threw out his arms and laughed.

Two great tears were rolling down Maitresse Aimable's cheeks.

"How to remember she, ma fuifre!" said Jean Touzel. "But go on to the news of her."

Maitresse Aimable spread the letter out and looked at it lovingly. Her voice rose slowly up like a bubble from the bottom of a well, and she spoke.

"Ah man pethe benin, when it come, you are not here, my Jean. I take it to the Greffier to read for me. It is great news, but the way he read so sour I do not like, ba su! I see Maitre Damian the schoolmaster pass my door. I beckon, and he come. I take my letter here, I hold it close to his eyes. 'Read on that for me, Maitre Damian—you,' I say. O my good, when he read it, it sing sweet like a song, pergui! Once, two, three times I make him read it out—he has the voice so soft and round, Maitre Damian there."

"Glad and good!" interrupted Jean. "What is the news, my wife? What is the news of highnesss—he?"

Maitresse Aimable smiled, then she tried to speak, but her voice broke.

"The son—the son—at last he is the Duke of Bercy. E'fin, it is all here. The new King of France, he is there at the palace when the child which it have sleep on my breast, which its mother I have love all the years, kiss her son as the Duke of Bercy."

"Ch'est ben," said Jean, "you can trust the good God in the end."

Dormy Jamais did not speak. His eyes were fastened upon the north, where lay the Paternoster Rocks. The sun had gone down, the dusk was creeping on, and against the dark of the north there was a shimmer of fire—a fire that leapt and quivered about the Paternoster Rocks.

Dormy pointed with his finger. Ghostly lights or miracle of Nature, these fitful flames had come and gone at times these many years, and now again the wonder of the unearthly radiance held their eyes.

"Gatd'en'ale, I don't understand you—you!" said Jean, speaking to the fantastic fires as though they were human.

"There's plenty things we see we can't understand, and there's plenty we understand we can't never see. Ah bah, so it goes!" said Maitresse Aimable, and she put Guida's letter in her bosom.

......................

Upon the hill of Plemont above them, a stone taken from the chimney of the hut where Guida used to live, stood upright beside a little grave. Upon it was carved:

> BIRIBI,
>
> *Fidele ami*
>
> *De quels jours!*

In the words of Maitresse Aimable, "Ah bah, so it goes." FINIS

NOTE: IT is possible that students of English naval history may find in the life of Philip d'Avranche, as set forth in this book, certain resemblances to the singular and long forgotten career of the young Jerseyman, Philip d'Auvergne of the "Arethusa," who in good time became Vice-Admiral of the White and His Serene Highness the Duke of Bouillon.

Because all the relatives and direct descendants of Admiral Prince Philip d'Auvergne are dead, I am the more anxious to state that, apart from one main incident, the story here-before written is not taken from the life of that remarkable man. Yet I will say also that I have drawn upon the eloquence, courage, and ability of Philip d'Auvergne to make the better part of Philip d'Avranche, whose great natural fault, an overleaping ambition, was the same fault that brought the famous Prince Admiral to a piteous death in the end.

In any case, this tale has no claim to be called a historical novel.

# JERSEY WORDS AND PHRASES

*WITH THEIR EQUIVALENTS IN ENGLISH OR FRENCH*

*A bi'tot = a bientot.*

*Achocre = dolt, ass.*

*Ah bah! (Difficult to render in English, but meaning much the same as*
*"Well! well!")*

*Ah be! = eh bien.*

*Alles kedainne = to go quickly, to skedaddle.*

*Bachouar = a fool.*

*Ba su! = bien sur.*

*Bashin = large copper-lined stew-pan.*

*Batd'lagoule = chatterbox.*

*Bedgone = shortgown or deep bodice of print.*

*Beganne = daft fellow.*

*Biaou = beau.*

*Bidemme! = exclamation of astonishment.*

*Bouchi = mouthful.*

*Bilzard = idiot.*

*Chelin = shilling.*

*Ch'est ben = c'est bien.*

*Cotil = slope of a dale.*

*Coum est qu'on etes? }*

*Coum est qu'ou vos portest? } Comment vous portez-vous!*

*Couzain or couzaine = cousin.*

*Crasset = metal oil-lamp of classic shape.*

*Critchett = cricket.*

*Diantre = diable.*

*Dreschiaux = dresser.*

*E'fant = enfant.*

*E'fin = enfin.*

*Eh ben = eh bien.*

*Esmanus = scarecrow.*

*Es-tu gentiment? = are you well?*

*Et ben = and now.*

*Gache-a-penn! = misery me!*

*Gaderabotin! = deuce take it!*

*Garche = lass.*

*Gatd'en'ale! = God be with us!*

*Grandpethe = grandpere.*

*Han = kind of grass for the making of ropes, baskets, etc.*

*Hanap = drinking-cup.*

*Hardi = very.*

*Hus = lower half of a door. (Doors of many old Jersey houses were divided horizontally, for protection against cattle, to let out the smoke, etc.)*

*Je me crais; je to crais; je crais ben! = I believe it; true for you; I well believe it!*

*Ma fe! }*

*Ma fistre! }= ma foi!*

*Ma fuifre! }*

*Mai grand doux! = but goodness gracious!*

*Man doux! = my good, oh dear! (Originally man Dieu!)*

*Man doux d'la vie! = upon my life!*

*Man gui, mon pethe! = mon Dieu, mon pere!*

*Man pethe benin! = my good father!*

*Marchi = marche.*

*Mogue = drinking-cup.*

*Nannin; nannin-gia! = no; no indeed!*

*Ni bouf ni baf } Expression of absolute negation, untranslatable.*

*Ni fiche ni bran }*

*Oui-gia! = yes indeed!*

*Par made = par mon Dieu.*

*Pardi! }*

*Pardingue! }= old forms of par Dieul*

*Pergui! }*

*Pend'loque = ragamuffin.*

*Queminzolle = overcoat.*

*Racllyi = hanging rack from the rafters of a kitchen.*

*Respe d'la compagnie! = with all respect for present company.*

*Shale ben = very well.*

*Simnel = a sort of biscuit, cup-shaped, supposed to represent unleavened*

*bread, specially eaten at Easter.*

*Soupe a la graisse = very thin soup, chiefly made of water, with a few*

*vegetables and some dripping.*

*Su' m'n ame = sur mon ame!*

*Tcheche? = what's that you say?*

*Trejous = toujours.*

*Tres-ba = tres bien.*

*Veille = a wide low settle. (Probably from lit de fouaille.) Also*

*applied to evening gatherings, when, sitting cross-legged on the*

*veille, the neighbours sang, talked, and told stories.*

*Verges = the land measure of Jersey, equal to forty perches. Two and a*

*quarter vergees are equivalent to the English acre.*

*Vier = vieux.*

*Vraic = a kind of sea-weed.*